Peter Hume Brown

John Knox a Biography

Vol. II

Peter Hume Brown

John Knox a Biography
Vol. II

ISBN/EAN: 9783743305236

Manufactured in Europe, USA, Canada, Australia, Japa

Cover: Foto ©Raphael Reischuk / pixelio.de

Manufactured and distributed by brebook publishing software
(www.brebook.com)

Peter Hume Brown

John Knox a Biography

John Knox's House at the Netherbow.
Edinburgh - 1843.

JOHN KNOX

A BIOGRAPHY

BY

P. HUME BROWN

AUTHOR OF 'THE LIFE OF GEORGE BUCHANAN'

IN TWO VOLUMES

VOL. II.

LONDON

ADAM AND CHARLES BLACK

1895

CONTENTS

BOOK IV. (*Continued*).—KNOX IN SCOTLAND— THE RELIGIOUS REVOLUTION

(1559-1560)

CHAPTER I

THE WAR OF THE CONGREGATION—KNOX AT PERTH AND ST. ANDREWS

(1559)

CHAPTER II

THE SECOND RISING—KNOX AS AGENT AND SECRETARY
TO THE CONGREGATION

(1559)

CHAPTER III

THE THIRD RISING OF THE CONGREGATION—KNOX
IN THE BACKGROUND

(1559-1560)

CHAPTER IV

KNOX AND THE RELIGIOUS REVOLUTION

(1560-1561)

CHAPTER V

THE NEW THEOLOGY AND RELIGION

CHAPTER VI

THE BOOK OF DISCIPLINE

BOOK V.—THE SECOND REVOLUTION—THE TRIUMPH OF KNOX

(1560-1572)

CHAPTER I

KNOX AND THE POLITICIANS

(1561-1565)

CHAPTER II

"HISTORIE OF THE REFORMATION IN SCOTLAND"

CHAPTER III

THE SECOND REVOLUTION—KNOX AND MORAY

(1565-1570)

CHAPTER IV

THE CASTLE OF EDINBURGH—KNOX AND KIRKCALDY OF GRANGE

(1570-1571)

CHAPTER V

KNOX IN ST. ANDREWS—BEGINNINGS OF EPISCOPACY

(1571-1572)

CHAPTER VI

KNOX AND THE MASSACRE OF ST. BARTHOLOMEW— LAST DAYS—CONCLUSION

(1572)

APPENDIX A

KNOX IN SCOTLAND
THE RELIGIOUS REVOLUTION

1559-1560

VOL. II

CHAPTER I

IN following the steps of Knox during the next twelve
months we have virtually to relate the history of Scotland. It was more important to the Protestant cause
that the Lord James Stewart and the Earl of Argyle
should have taken it up than Knox: to the former
of these noblemen, as Mary of Lorraine and her
brothers declared, the success of the Protestant cause
was due in greater measure than to any other person
in the country;[1] and had either or both of them
at any period of the struggle gone over to the enemy,
it would have carried greater consequences than if
Knox had never left Geneva. Yet it remains true
that alike by the part he played and his absolute self-
devotion to the issues at stake, Knox remains the
most representative figure of the struggle with which
he is identified.

It was on the 2nd of May 1559,[2] as we have seen,

---

[1] Cf. Forbes, *State Papers*, i. 152, 307, 319. The Regent is
reported as saying that "she marveled of the stiffeness of the lords of
the congregacion, bothe in speciall of my Lord James, who never did
take rest to wyrke in her contrar, though uthers toke summe repose."—
Sadler, *State Papers*, John Wood to Thomas Randolph, 30th November
1559.　　　　　　　　　　　　　　　　[2] *Works*, i. 318 ; v. 21.

that Knox arrived in Edinburgh from Dieppe; and in the midst of the troubles which now beset her, the appearance of such an adversary could not be agreeable to the Regent. She was at Glasgow at the moment of his coming; but she was informed post-haste of such an important event.[1] During his absence on the Continent, as will be remembered, Knox had been subjected to the censure of the Church, and burnt in effigy in the streets of Edinburgh. But this censure had apparently implied civil outlawry, for the third day after he set foot in the country Knox was "blowne loud to the horne" by the Regent's special order.[2] As she was still mistress of Edinburgh, that city could not be a safe place for Knox; and after a stay of two nights, during which he found time to write a hasty note to Mrs. Locke,[3] he passed to Dundee. In Dundee he found the Protestants the masters of the situation, and ready for the boldest measures. At the moment when Knox came among them their feelings were wound to the highest pitch by the Regent's summons of their preachers to appear at Stirling on the 10th of May; and to decide on some course of action a great gathering of Protestants had met in the town. The decision taken was that every man of them should attend their

---

[1] "A Historie of the Estate of Scotland," *Wodrow Miscellany*, i. 57. The author of this History is unknown. In the later editions of his *Life of Knox*, Dr. M'Crie had the use of it in a MS. lent him by Thomas Thomson, editor of the *Acts of the Parliament of Scotland*. It has since been published in the first volume of the *Wodrow Miscellany*. Whoever the author may have been, he writes as a contemporary, or from information supplied by a contemporary, and records many interesting circumstances not to be found elsewhere. What inspires confidence in him is that certain of his facts not recorded by other contemporary Scottish historians are corroborated by the despatches of D'Oysel and others, in Teulet.

[2] *Ibid.* p. 57.   [3] *Works*, vi. 21.

preachers to Perth, and there, in conjunction with their brethren from other parts of the country, make public profession of their faith.[1] Perth was already favourably disposed to the new opinions; and it was moreover a convenient centre for the districts where these opinions were most widely spread.

Throughout their struggle with the Regent the Protestants had been solicitous to give their actions the form of law. Had the multitude now assembled at Perth appeared before the Regent at Stirling, it would have had the semblance of open rebellion, and, to elude this charge and yet not to forgo the object of their meeting, Erskine of Dun was sent forward to lay their demands before the Regent.[2] In view of the forces now arrayed against her she had no course open but to temporise till she was in a position to take stronger measures. By the order of her Council, which was mainly directed by Frenchmen, Erskine was instructed to inform the leaders of the Congregation that the summons of their preachers was postponed,[3] and that there was, therefore, no occasion for their appearing at Stirling. Erskine's letter was variously received by the Protestants, some maintaining that the object of their meeting was attained, and others that the postponement of the summons was a mere artifice. The Regent's policy, however, gained her a temporary advantage. The march on Stirling was stayed, certain of the Congregation dispersed to their homes, and meanwhile she had time to draw together a force on which she could depend.

During the next two months Perth plays the part in the revolution which was subsequently played by

---

[1] *Works*, vi. 22.　　[2] *Ibid.* i. 317; vi. 22; *Wodrow Misc.* i. 57.
[3] *Works*, vi. 22, 23; Buchanan, p. 313.

the town of Leith. Besides being a convenient centre
for the Protestants of Strathearn, Angus, and the
Mearns, Perth was in itself one of the most important
places in the country. It was the only walled town
in Scotland, it had easy communication with the sea,
and its position in the heart of the kingdom brought
a natural advantage to the party that held it.[1] As the
Protestants had little faith in the promises of the Regent,
there was good reason why they should stand by each
other in Perth when trouble seemed still ahead. Thus
at the very outset Knox found work to his hand which
gave full scope to all his enthusiasm and experience.

The Protestants speedily learned that the Regent
had no thought of departing from her late attitude
of hostility. In her understanding with Erskine of
Dun she had publicly cancelled the summons of the
preachers for the 10th of May; yet she proclaimed
them as outlaws when they did not make their appearance. This breach of faith on the Regent's part was
the occasion of the contest that was about to rend
the country for the next twelve months. When
Erskine reported to the Congregation at Perth this
treatment of their preachers, it hardly needed the
eloquence of Knox to hurry them into an act of
defiance. In a series of sermons he had denounced
the idolatries of the Roman Church, and pointed out
the duty of Christian men in regard to them.[2] On
the day following the outlawry of the preachers he
had spoken on the same theme, doubtless with all
the greater fervour in consequence of the news that
had come from Stirling.[3] It was certainly by due

---

[1] Buchanan, p. 315.   [2] *Works*, i. 320.
[3] *Ibid.* p. 319.   It was in the parish church, known as the Kirk
of the Holy Cross of St. John the Baptist, that Knox preached.

forms of law that Knox would have wished to proceed against the Established Church,[1] yet, except
so far as they compromised the cause he had at
heart, the events that followed had his cordial
approval. When the sermon was over, and the
majority of his hearers had left the church, an indis-
creet priest gave the occasion that was needed for a
significant commentary on the preacher's exhortations.
Proceeding to the altar, he prepared, with a curious
fatuity under the circumstances, to celebrate mass ;
and, a forward boy commenting on his action, he
struck him a blow on the ear. It would seem that
the youth in coming to the church must have had
some notion of possible mischief, since he at once
retaliated by throwing a stone, which missed the priest
and broke an image. This was all that was needed
to let loose the feelings of the onlookers. In a
moment the church was in an uproar, and as fast as
their hands could do the work, the late listeners of
Knox made away with every object which they regarded as suggestive of idolatry. Meanwhile, the news
of these doings ran through the town, and the men in
the street took matters into their own hands.[2] In
Perth there had been a long-standing feud between
the citizens and the clergy, and one deed of violence
against the Blackfriars had been done as early as 1543.[3]

---

[1] On the question of the destruction of images Calvin gives this
judgment. "Car Dieu n'a jamais commandé d'abattre les idoles, sinon
à chacun en sa maison et en public à ceux qu'il arme d'autorité."—
Lettres françaises, tome ii. p. 416.

[2] *Works*, i. 322 ; Buchanan, p. 313.

[3] *The Blackfriars of Perth : The Chartulary and Papers of their
House*, edited with Introduction by Robert Milne, D.D., West Kirk,
Perth (Edinburgh, 1893). The deed of violence referred to is thus
described in one of the documents printed by Dr. Milne. "Certain
persons named came to thair [the Blackfriars'] said place, and strack
up thair fore yett, and brak the lokkis and bandis of the samyn, and

Moreover, there was hardly a part of the country which was not more or less familiar with acts of violence against the sacred places of the ancient faith. As we have seen, it had, years before, been necessary to pass Acts of Parliament to prevent spoliation of churches and the destruction of their ornaments ; and in the neighbouring town of Dundee there had been several precedents for these outrages with which the men of Perth must have been perfectly familiar. In almost every country where Protestantism had appeared—in England, in France, in Switzerland, in Holland—the same frenzy of destruction regularly appeared among the lower sections of the populace.[1] In these blind outbursts there was no expression of real religious feeling ; it was simply the instinct of plunder, the natural delight in unlicensed action which in ordinary times is kept in check by the steady pressure of law. It was under such an impulse that the Perth mob now rushed to the work of plunder and destruction. It took them two days to do their business ; but they did it effectually. Of the three places attacked — the monasteries of the Franciscans and Dominicans and the Charterhouse Abbey — only the walls were left standing.[2] Thus had the Beggars' Summons found

sicklyk brak up the durris of the throwgang, on the north syde of the said clowster, and tuke away with thame the lokkis of the said durris and brak up the grater durre, and tuke away out of it chandellaris and glassis, and brak thair kochin durre, and tuke off the fire the kittill with thair mete, and cariet about the toune, and yet withhaldis the kettill and pewdir desheis," etc.—pp. 229, 230.

[1] The following story, told in connection with the first of the Condés, curiously illustrates the spirit of the genuine iconoclast, who did his work not in blind frenzy, but from deliberate conviction. Threatening to shoot a young man engaged in breaking images, he received this answer : "Monseigneur, ayez patience que j'aie abattu cette idole, et puis que je meure, s'il vous plait."—*Bulletin de la Société du Protestantisme français*, tome xiv. p. 130.

[2] *Works*, i. 322, 323 ; vi. 23 ; Leslie, p. 272.

a terrible realisation in one important town in the country. In that manifesto the ministers of the ancient religion had been allowed till the 15th of May to renounce their possessions or abide the consequence. It wanted but four days till the expiry of their promised respite when Perth led the way in putting the threat into execution.

After these doings in Perth the Regent had but two courses open to her. She must either crush Protestantism once and for ever, or cease to govern the country in the interest of France. It was now clear that the Protestants would be satisfied with nothing short of the ruin of the old religion. Compromises might be made, of longer or shorter duration ; but the real issue must sooner or later be faced ; and for the Regent the outrages at Perth had created the best of opportunities. That after such doings she did not carry the country with her is signal proof how widespread was the discontent her government had produced. She had now on her side the whole weight of the clergy, for thenceforward Archbishop Hamilton gave her his steady support even after his brother the Duke had joined the Congregation. At this moment, also, the whole body of the nobility were nominally with her, since as yet the Protestant Lords had not declared themselves for the insurgent party. From the measures she now took it would appear that she realised that the crisis in her affairs had come. She had always her French troops on whom she could count in emergencies ; but she now issued orders to Clydesdale, Stirlingshire, and the Lothians, to provide a force to meet her at Stirling on the 25th of May.[1]

Meanwhile the Protestants at Perth had not been

---

[1] *Wodrow Misc.* i. 58.

idle. After their dealings with the monasteries many of them, apparently thinking that their work in that town was at an end, had gone to their homes; but on the news of the Regent's intentions they had returned to take their stand by their brethren. It was at such a juncture that Knox displayed the plenitude of his powers. He had not been of those who had left the town, as it had been specially laid upon him to instruct the citizens, who as recent converts "war young and rude in Christ";[1] and now in the face of the threatened danger he was called to less apostolic duties. It was the tactic of the Regent all through the coming struggle to create the impression both in Scotland and abroad that the Protestants made religion a cloak for the overthrow of her authority. At this stage of their proceedings such a report at once compromised the cause of the Protestants, and kept the timid from supporting a cause which in their hearts they approved. To counteract the effect of the Regent's representations, three manifestoes, all undoubtedly inspired or written by Knox, were addressed respectively to the Regent herself, to D'Oysel and the French soldiery,[2] and to the whole body of the Scottish nobility.[3] The burden of the first two was virtually to the same effect. The Protestants were the most loyal subjects in the country; but liberty of worship was what they were now bent on maintaining, even at the point of the sword. It is even implied by a dexterous innuendo that the Regent in denying this privilege was acting on her own responsibility, and was not consulting the wishes of their king and queen.

---

[1] *Works*, i. 324.
[2] Some of the French soldiery seem to have been Huguenots.
[3] *Works*, i. 326 *et seq.*

In his appeal to the nobility Knox had two classes to consider—the few who had already declared themselves for the new opinions, and the majority who still adhered to the existing Church. As we shall see, the former class was speedily to take the course to which their new faith of necessity led them, while the latter only waited the issue of events to choose the side which promised greatest advantage to themselves. In a fourth manifesto, addressed to the clergy, the writer made it clear that between them and his fellow-believers there could be now only war to the knife. Charging them with their cruelties in the past, and with being at present the chief abettors of the Regent, he gave them the alternative of changing their lives and ceasing from persecution, or abiding the consequence. "Yea," he concludes, "we shall begyn that same warre whiche God commanded Israell to execut aganis the Cananites, that is, contract of peace shall never be maid till ye desist from your oppin idolatrie and crewell persecution of Godis children."[1] While they thus put before the world their aims and motives, the Protestants took more practical measures to make good their position. They added to the defences of the town, which, as has been said, was the only one in Scotland fortified with walls, and they sent an urgent appeal for help to the Protestants of Ayrshire.[2]

With a force of about 8000 French and Scots, D'Oysel marched on Perth, encamping at Auchterarder by the way.[3] Still the insurgents made no sign of abandoning their position. Though greatly incensed by the late disorders, the Regent must have been well aware that she was not in a position to risk a civil war; and to effect an understanding if possible, she despatched

---

[1] *Works,* i. 336.　　[2] *Ibid.* pp. 325, 335.　　[3] *Ibid.* p. 341.

three lords, Argyle, the Lord James, and Lord Sempill,
to ascertain the demands of the Congregation.   They
were told what they must have known before without
the form of an interview.   The end of all the business
in Perth was not sedition, but simply freedom to worship God according to conscience.   If the Regent
would but leave unmolested such as had embraced
the new faith, they were willing to give up the town
at her discretion.   As Protestants themselves, Argyle
and the Lord James could not gainsay the reasonable-
ness of this offer, and they undertook to give a faithful
report of their interview to the Regent.   But before
they went, Knox in a private meeting with all the
three noblemen gave them a message, which he
besought them to carry to her.   First, they were to
tell her from him, John Knox, that the religion she
professed was "a superstitioun devised be the brane
of man," a fact he was prepared to make good against
any man in Scotland, if freedom of speech were allowed
to him.   Secondly, her present policy was bound to
fail, because she was fighting not against weak man,
but against the eternal will of God.   To make their
message somewhat more tolerable, they were told to
add that the sender was a better friend to her Grace
than the flattering advisers who were urging her on
her present evil course.[1]

To accept the condition proposed by the Congregation would have implied the ignoring of all the late
offences, and encouraged still bolder defiance of her
authority.   The Regent's reply, therefore, was a proclamation in Perth by the Lyon King-of-arms, that

---

[1] *Works*, i. 338, 339.   Knox's message was actually delivered to
the Regent by Lord Sempill, "a man," according to Knox, "sold under
syne, enymye to God and all godlynes."

all men should "avoid the toune under the pane of treasone."[1] But the relative position of the two parties was suddenly changed. The Protestants in Ayrshire had enthusiastically responded to the appeal of their brethren in Perth; and under the Earl of Glencairn and other leaders a body of some 2500 men, by forced marches and in the teeth of all obstacles, had made their way to within six miles of the town.[2] Though the arrival of these reinforcements was unknown in Perth,[3] their coming had a decisive influence on the Regent's measures. At her own request, representative men were sent from Perth to Auchterarder to arrange with D'Oysel the terms of a composition. After some finessing, the proximity of Glencairn, though apparently still unknown to the representatives of the Protestants, forced D'Oysel to concede the original demands which the Regent had refused to entertain. The town was to be surrendered on the double condition that the Protestants should be allowed perfect freedom of worship, and that no French garrison should be quartered on the citizens.[4] These terms being accepted by both parties, the Protestants were to quit Perth with a free bill for all their doings of the preceding weeks.

In the final arrangement of this treaty at Perth all the leading actors in the Scottish Reformation were brought together for the first time. Argyle and the Lord James were there as the representatives of the Regent. Glencairn had also arrived, and with him John Willock, second only to Knox among the reformed preachers. Lords Boyd and Ochiltree,

---

[1] *Works*, i. 340.　　　[2] *Ibid.; Wodrow Misc.* i. 58.
[3] *Works*, i. 342.
[4] *Ibid.* p. 342; vi. 24; *Wodrow Misc.* i. 58; Buchanan, p. 314.

Erskine of Dun, and almost every Scottish gentleman
who had embraced the new opinions, had been brought
to the same place in this crisis of their faith.   Such an
opportunity of a mutual understanding was not to be
lost ; for all knew that the agreement lately made was
a mere temporary compromise forced on both parties
by the exigencies of the moment.   In an interview
with Argyle and the Lord James, Knox and Willock
upbraided them with their desertion of their brethren
in their hour of trial, and called upon them to give
better proof of their faith in the future.   As their
subsequent career showed, both of these nobles were
men with minds of their own, and had doubtless
already decided on the course they meant to follow.
The decision they now took was one that purely selfish
considerations could not have prompted, and which they
thenceforth followed with a consistent fidelity which is
the best proof that higher motives determined them.[1]
Should the Regent, they told the two ministers,
depart one jot from the treaty of Perth, they were
determined to take their stand once for all by the side
of their brethren.[2]   As Knox was absolutely certain
that the Regent would not abide by that compact, this
was all that he could wish in the interests of the
Congregation.   But before they left the town the
Protestants came to a more definite understanding as
to their future conduct.   By the agreement with the
Regent their departure was fixed for the 29th of May,
the day after the conclusion of the treaty.   A few
hours before their going Knox addressed the assembled
Congregation on their present situation and prospects,
warning them that the late arrangement could only be

---

[1] Argyle, as has been said, was subsequently led to leave the party
of Knox for a time.   [2] *Works,* i. 343.

of short duration, and that the success of their cause must eventually depend on their own zeal and constancy.[1] With these adjurations ringing in their ears the Protestants left the town for their respective homes; and the same day their leaders, who still remained behind, took a step which implied all that was soon to follow. As the representatives of the Congregation they signed a bond of mutual defence, pledging themselves "at thair haill poweris to distroy, and away put all thingis that dois dishonour to his name, so that God may be trewlie and puirelie wirschipped."[2] When an important section of the nation had conceived a plan of action that virtually meant a revolution, it only remained to be tried whether their strength was equal to their desires.

The Regent, attended by Châtelherault and D'Oysel, entered Perth on the 29th of May, and immediately gave the occasion for a fresh breach with her Protestant subjects.[3] According to the late agreement she was to quarter no French troops in the town. She obeyed the letter of this condition, but evaded its spirit by quartering Scottish soldiers in the pay of France. By restoring the old religion, also, and by her harsh treatment of all who had Protestant leanings, she gave deep offence to the Lords of the Congregation who still remained in the town. Without signifying their intention these lords suddenly departed,

---

[1] *Works*, i. 343, 344.   [2] *Ibid.* p. 344.

[3] The report of the Regent's repeated breaches of faith reached the Continent. Constable Montmorency, when sending Sir James Melville on his mission to Scotland in 1559, said among other things : "I have also intelligence that the Queen Regent has not kepit all thingis promysed unto them [the Congregation]" (Melville, *Memoirs*, p. 79). Knox expresses great indignation at this craft of the Regent; but we shall find him suggesting a precisely similar subterfuge to the English in favour of his own party. Regarding the Regent's breaches of faith see above, i. 345, *note.*

in a manner which the Regent regarded as an open
act of defiance. When ordered to return under pain
of her displeasure, they refused on the plea that they
could not approve the courses she had now seen fit to
adopt. Travelling in company, Argyle and the Lord
James, who now begin to stand out as the natural
leaders of their party, made for St. Andrews, as the
place which, next to Perth, was their best centre of
action. On their way they issued a summons to the
Protestant gentlemen of Angus and the Mearns to
meet them in that town on the 3rd of June.[1]

By the terms of the late covenant the Protestants
were bound to regard the danger of one of their number
as the danger of all. With Knox in their company,
therefore, the gentlemen who had been summoned
made haste to keep the appointed day at St. Andrews.
In Fife, as will be seen, the new opinions must have
been widely spread, both in the towns and in the
country, and Knox preached by the way at Crail and
Anstruther.[2] But it lay specially near his heart to
bear his testimony in the stronghold where the enemy
should have been most powerful—the archiepiscopal
city of St. Andrews. It was here that he had been
called to be a preacher of the Gospel in circumstances
which had determined the last eleven years of his life ;
and here he had seen Satan complete a triumph that had
seemed to foreclose all hope that the truth should ever
again be heard within the bounds of Scotland. But
there was another reason that quickened his desire to
lift up his voice in a place of such mingled memories.
Long ago, as has been told, when toiling half-dead at
his oar in the galley, he had beheld the cathedral spire
of St. Andrews in the distance, and solemnly assured

[1] *Works*, i. 347.   [2] *Ibid.*

his companions that, unlikely as it seemed, he should one day glorify God in that town. As is proved by other instances, Knox showed a manifest desire to be thought to be in the secrets of Providence. It was not likely, therefore, that he would forgo the present opportunity of making good his claim, though prudence might have suggested a safer means of proceeding.

As at Perth, it is Knox again who is the central figure, and whose words lay the train for the events that follow. St. Andrews, it would appear, was not so wholly given to the new religion as the former city. Reckoning on substantial support, therefore, Archbishop Hamilton, well knowing the result should Knox's voice be heard, came to the town on Saturday (3rd June[1]) with a following of a hundred spears. Arrived in the town, he sent the terrible threat that if Knox dared to preach in his church he should be saluted "with a dosane of culveringis, quherof the most parte should lyght upoun his nose."[2] At this moment, it should be said, the Regent was lying with her forces at Falkland, about twelve miles off. The threat of the Archbishop, therefore, was more than a mere bravado, and the friends of Knox fully realised the fact. When they sought to dissuade him from his intention, however, he put them aside, affirming that God had created the occasion, and that as God's minister he could not neglect it. The next day the Archbishop thought better of the matter of the culverins, and Knox was allowed to go through with his sermon without interruption. His subject was the ejection of the buyers and sellers from the Temple, and its practical application the duty of similar drastic dealings with the churches in their midst. The

---

[1] *Works*, i. 347 *note*.   [2] *Ibid.* p. 348.

effect of the sermon was the same as at Perth, though the work seems to have been done in calmer and more deliberate fashion.[1] By the express wish of the magistrates and the majority of the town every church was stripped of its obnoxious furnishings ; and thenceforward St. Andrews remained one of the most important strongholds of the new religion.

In what followed these events at St. Andrews we have but the repetition of what had lately taken place at Perth. Confident in the strength of her forces, and urged on by the indignant Archbishop, the Regent gave orders for a march from Falkland on St. Andrews. The line of march was to be by way of Cupar, a town which had given unmistakable proof of Protestant leanings. Though they had little over 100 horse, Argyle and the Lord James decided to anticipate the Regent's commanders by occupying Cupar. Arrived in that town, they were speedily joined by detachments from Lothian and Fife, which raised their number to over 3000 men ; and on the morning of the 13th of June they took up their position on Cupar Muir, on the side of the town nearest Falkland. When they heard of the formidable force that blocked the way, D'Oysel and Châtelherault, who led the Regent's army, saw that their intended march had become an impossibility. Their numbers were now inferior to those of the enemy, and many of their

---

[1] Professor Mitchell drew my attention to an error into which certain writers have fallen in connection with this sermon of Knox. There is no evidence to prove that the fabric of the cathedral of St. Andrews was materially injured either on this occasion or in 1560, when the Privy Council passed an order for the purging of the churches. " It is admitted," adds Professor Mitchell, " that the Franciscan and Dominican monasteries were pretty thoroughly demolished in 1559 ; but it is known that the buildings of the Abbey or Priory were spared, and that it was in the Novum Hospitium of the Priory that Knox and his family lodged during their long visit to St. Andrews in 1571-72."

own troops were not to be trusted in the event of an actual engagement. "We do not know our friends from our foes," wrote D'Oysel, "and those who are with us in the morning are against us in the evening."[1] In this state of affairs it was their only course to patch up another arrangement with the Protestants till events should take a better turn. On their side it is evident that the leaders of the Congregation had the utmost reluctance to draw the sword. By the arrangement now made, however, it was proved that their determined front had shown the Regent that she was in presence of a rebellion with which her present resources were unequal to cope.[2] According to the new compromise there was to be a truce for eight days; the Regent's soldiers, lately brought to Fife, were to be removed from that county; and during the period of truce an attempt was to be made to heal the breach between the Regent and her subjects.[3]

Returning to St. Andrews, the Protestant leaders awaited the result of the recent agreement. As was inevitable in the pass to which things had now come, neither party paid much regard to the conditions it imposed. The Protestants proceeded with their purifying of the churches, dealing among others with the Abbey of Lindores;[4] and the Regent sought only to strengthen her hands, and made no further overtures for the pacifying of the troubles. It had, in truth, become clear to both parties that the conflict was only begun, and that it must lead to issues beyond what

[1] Teulet, i. 311.

[2] *Ibid.* (D'Oysel to De Noailles, 14th June), i. 311.

[3] *Works*, i. 353, 354.

[4] *Ibid.* vi. 26. According to Knox, the Regent wished to make it part of the agreement at Cupar that no attack should be made on churches during the eight days' truce; but the Protestant Lords refused to accept this as one of the conditions.

they had dreamt a few weeks before. Simultaneously both looked elsewhere for the strength which they did not find in themselves. The day after the compact of Cupar D'Oysel wrote to the French ambassador in London that only a body of troops from France could restore the authority of his mistress in Scotland.[1] During those days at St. Andrews, also, the Congregation, acting mainly on the suggestion of Knox, made its first appeal to England for assistance against Mary of Lorraine.[2] From the moment the Protestants decided to apply to Elizabeth it will appear that Knox was able to perform services for which his years of exile had specially fitted him. At this point it is sufficient to say that, added to his other labours, these services taxed him far beyond what his strength could now bear. Yet in the thick of his labours at St. Andrews he stole an hour to write a long and interesting letter to Mrs. Locke, in which he recounts all that had happened in Scotland since the day of his arrival, and urges her to hasten the coming of his wife and mother-in-law, and of his Genevan colleague, Goodman.[3]

The truce expired; and things were precisely where they had been at the date of its arrangement. As the experience of the last few weeks had shown them their strength, the Congregation determined to follow up their success. The Protestants of Perth now required the assistance of their more fortunate brethren, as, in defiance of the late treaty, they were now practically denied all freedom of worship. By their mutual pledges each section of the Congregation was bound to assist another in its individual troubles. The order was given by the Lords at St. Andrews, therefore, that on the 24th of June the Protestants should meet

<hr>

[1] Teulet, i. 311.　　　[2] *Works*, ii. 22.　　　[3] *Ibid.* vi. 21-27.

at Perth for the relief of that town ;[1] and on the day appointed they sat down before it in such numbers that those who commanded for the Regent had no choice but unconditional surrender.[2]

Perth, Dundee, and St. Andrews now their own, it seemed as if they were about to sweep the country before them. But before they left Perth they received one more warning of the forces they had let loose, and of the evil report that must go forth concerning the courses on which they were embarked. During the two days that followed the surrender of Perth the Abbey and Palace of the neighbouring village of Scone were burnt to the ground, in spite of the special intervention of Argyle, the Lord James, and Knox himself. On this occasion it was not "the rascaille multitude" who did the work, but those Protestants of Perth and Dundee who had been the mainstay of the Congregation.[3] On the day following the destruction at Scone Knox wrote from Perth to Cecil as follows : " The common bruit, I dowbt not, cariethe unto you the troubles that be laitly heir risen for the controversie in religion. The treucht is that many of the nobilitie, the most part of barrons and gentilmen, with many touns and on[e] cietie, have putt to thare handes to remove Idolatrie and the monuments of the saim. The Reformation is somewhat violent, becaus the adversareis be stubburn ; non that professeth Christ Jesus userpeth any thing against authoritie ; neyther yit intendest [*sic*] to usurpe, onles streangearis be brought

---

[1] *Works*, i. 355.   [2] *Ibid.* i. 358, 359.

[3] *Ibid.* i. 359-362.   For obvious reasons, as compromising their whole enterprise, the leaders of the Congregation were indignant at the havoc wrought at Scone.   "Wharat," says Knox, " no small nomber of us war offended, that patientlie we culd nocht speak till any that war of Dundee and St. Johnestoun."—*Ibid.* p. 361.

in to subern [*sic*] and bring in bondaige the liberteis of this poore contrey.   If any such thing be espied, I am uncertane what shall follow."[1]   The events of the next few weeks were effectually to remove all Knox's uncertainty.

The Protestants had now gone so far that retreat must have involved ruin.   Having heard that the Regent intended to stop their passage southwards at Stirling, Argyle and the Lord James, after a rapid night march, occupied that town, apparently with the approval of the majority of the citizens.   It would seem that they were now assured that the Regent was no longer in a position to meet them ; for quitting Stirling they marched to Edinburgh by way of Linlithgow, where also they had a strong following.[2]

The Regent had prudently not awaited their coming.   Once in the hands of the Protestant Lords she would have been forced to make concessions which would have meant the virtual abdication of her authority.   Attended by D'Oysel and Châtelherault, therefore, she had retreated to Dunbar, leaving Edinburgh at the disposal of the Congregation.[3]   From their doings elsewhere the clergy knew what they had to expect when the Protestants became masters of the town, and they prudently sought to secure the most valuable part of their property.   But the mob was not to be defrauded of the spoils which had fallen to their fellows elsewhere, and before the arrival of the Congregation they had done their work so thoroughly that not even the doors and windows remained in a single church in the town.[4]   In Edinburgh, as was

---

[1] *Works*, vi. 32.

[2] *Ibid.* i. 362 ; Leslie, p. 274.   Both at Stirling and Linlithgow the churches were cleared of all that offended Protestant sensibilities.

[3] *Works*, i. 362.   [4] *Ibid.* p. 363 ; *Wodrow Misc.* i. 61, 62.

afterwards more than once proved, the majority of the respectable citizens were still on the side of the old religion, but the flight of the Regent had shown them that for the present they were the weaker party.

When the Protestants entered the town (29th July) they numbered only 1000 horse and 300 foot.[1] The third day after their arrival, however, they were joined by Glencairn with a force that swelled their numbers to 6000.[2] For the moment, therefore, they were the virtual masters of the country, yet their leaders were keenly alive to the fact that their situation was critical in the highest degree. The conviction was widespread that they were aiming at nothing short of the overthrow of the existing government, and for such a step the country was not yet prepared. From the nature of their forces, also, they could not hold together beyond a few weeks, and their dispersion would imply the restoration of the Regent to the full exercise of her authority. As it happens, we have materials at our disposal which place clearly before us how the crisis was viewed from Edinburgh and Dunbar respectively.

On the day he entered Edinburgh with the Congregation Knox had preached in the church of St. Giles. Immediately after his sermon he sat down to write a letter to Mrs. Locke. "The professors," he wrote, "are in Edinburgh. The Queene is retired into Dumbar. The fine[3] is known unto God. We meane no tumult, no alteratioun of authoritie, but onlie the reformatioun of religioun, and suppressing of idolatrie."[4] In a letter to Sir Henry Percy, written a few days later, we see the same thought uppermost in

---

[1] *Wodrow Misc.* i. 61. [2] *Works*, vi. 35.
[3] End. [4] *Works*, vi. 30.

his mind. " The trubles of this Realme," he says, " ye hear, but the cause to many is not knowen. Persuaid yourself, and assure otheris that we mean neyther sedi- tioun, neyther yit rebellion against any just and lauch- ful authoritie, but onlie the advauncement of Christes religion, and the libertie of this poore Realme."[1] On the same day another leader of the Congregation, Sir William Kirkcaldy of Grange, sent a communication to Percy which is of singular interest for the light it throws on the policy of the Protestants till this period. " Theis salbe to certiffy you I resavit your letter," he writes, " this last of Junii, persavyng thairby the dout and suspitioun ye stand into for the commying for- wardis of the Congregatioun, whome I assure you ye neid not to have in suspitioun; for they meyne nothing bot reformatioun of religion, quhillkis schortly througheout this Realme they will bring to pas; for the Quene and Monsieur Doisell with all the Frenche men for refuge ar retyrit to Dunbar. . . . The manour of thair proceedyngis in Reforma- tioun is this : They pull doune all maner of Freryes, and Abbayes which willyngly resavis not ther refor- matioun. As to paroys churchis they cleyns them of ymages and all other monumentis of ydolatrie, and commandis that no Messis be said in them ; in place therof the Booke sett fourthe be godlye Kyng Edward is red in the same churches. They have never as yet medlit with a pennywurthe of that which pertenis to the kyrk, bot presently they will take ordre throughowt all the partis whare they duell, that all the fruttes of the Abayes and uther churches salbe keipt and bestowet upon the faythfull Ministres unto suche tyme as ane farther ordre be tene. Some

[1] *Works*, vi. 36.

suposes the Quene, seyng no uther remedy, will follow ther desyres, which is ane generall reformatioun throughowt the hole realme to be maid conforme to the pure worde of God, and the Frenche men to be send awaye. Yf hir Grace will so do, they will obey and serve hir and anex the hole revenus of the Abayis to the Crowne : yf hir Grace will not be content with this they are determinet to heare of no agreament."[1]

Of all the Protestant leaders there were none less given to subterfuge or less influenced by selfish considerations than Kirkcaldy and Knox ; and there can hardly be any doubt that in disclaiming any intentions of a political revolution they both spoke in perfect good faith. Yet the enterprise on which they were engaged inevitably involved all that was to follow during the ensuing months. To have granted the demands they now made, Mary of Lorraine must have become a Protestant herself, and set at naught all her traditions as a Guise and a representative of France. But we have the means of knowing how she and D'Oysel understood the late proceedings and present overtures of the Congregation. In a letter to De Noailles written from Dunbar on the last day of June, D'Oysel explains to him the state of affairs in Scotland. The Protestants, he says, are disturbed at the general impression that they are aiming at the overthrow of the Regent's authority. The day before a preacher[2] had mounted the pulpit in Edinburgh with the express purpose of disabusing the minds of the people of this notion. For himself he [D'Oysel] is convinced that religion is only a pretext, and that the real object of the Protestant Lords is the

---

[1] *Works*, vi. 33, 34.

[2] It will be seen below that this preacher was Knox.

setting up of a new authority. There are those on
the watch, however, who will soon discover the truth,[1]
and should it turn out as he expects, there are
important persons in the country who will stand
loyally by the Crown. As for the new religion,
however, he adds that "assuredly all concur in it,
high and low—that is to say, the majority—so that
it is necessary to play another game to divert them
from their purposes."[2]   In certain instructions sent
to France by the Regent herself she speaks to the
same effect as D'Oysel. "The said Protestants," she
says, "caused their doctor, Knox, to preach yesterday
in the said town of Edinburgh. He made it his
chief endeavour to excuse and exculpate the chief
supporters of the religion from aiming at the Crown,
and from entertaining any other motive except the
advancement of the Gospel. There are those near
them who will learn the truth, which will raise up
powerful enemies against them. On the other hand,
if the establishment of the said religion is their only
motive, the greater part of the kingdom will concur
with them."[3]

Every day now told in favour of the Regent.
The forces of the Congregation, which could not
remain in arms beyond fifteen or twenty days,
gradually melted away, and by their third week in
Edinburgh they numbered only about 1500 men.[4]
As there was constant coming and going between

---

[1] Knox complains bitterly of the mischief wrought by these spies in
the camp of the Congregation.

[2] Teulet, i. 318, 319. In this letter D'Oysel says that the Scots
require to be ruled *in virga ferrea.*

[3] Teulet, p. 325. Though both the Regent and D'Oysel assert that
the Protestants were a majority in the country, this is certainly an
exaggeration. Their statement is interesting, however, as showing how
widespread the new opinions were.   [4] *Wodrow Misc.* i. 64.

the two parties, the supporters of the Regent spread reports which further weakened their cause. The story was set afloat both in Scotland and in France that the Lord James, with the consent of the Protestants, was aiming at the Crown for himself, to the exclusion both of the Queen and the Duke.[1] The story was admirably fitted to serve the interests of the Regent, since it kept by her side those whose sympathies with Protestantism were not strong enough to lead them astray from their loyalty, and at the same time secured the equivocal allegiance of the Hamiltons. Meanwhile, however, Knox had been appointed minister of the Tolbooth in Edinburgh,[2] and, as we have seen, did his best to put heart into his hearers, and to counteract the rumours that were undermining the cause. The news of the fatal wound of Henry II. gave a temporary encouragement to the Congregation, which led them to a step of doubtful prudence.[3] On the plea that the Regent had debased the coinage to the hurt of the country, they took possession of the mint, and staid the issue of money till "further ordour mycht be tackin."[4] But this act only gave colour to the suspicion that their real aim was revolution, and still further compromised the success of their cause.

Meanwhile, though she received no great accession

---

[1] Cf. Forbes, *State Papers*, i. 180 (Throgmorton to Cecil, 27th July 1559). Throgmorton doubtless had his information from some French source. But the eagerness with which the Congregation welcomed the accession of the Earl of Arran to their cause is sufficient proof that they never seriously thought of such a scheme. Failing the Earl of Arran, the Congregation might have been driven to put forward the Lord James as the next most likely person.—See *Cal. of State Papers* (Scotland), i. 116, where Crofts actually attributes this scheme to Knox. [2] *Works*, i. 388.

[3] Teulet, i. 326 (D'Oysel to De Noailles, 22nd July).

[4] *Works*, p. 365.

of strength, the Regent had a steady support, which she well knew how to turn to the best account. She could always reckon on that small body of trained soldiers, French and Scots, who formed the garrison of the strongholds which had been in her hands since the peace that followed Pinkie. Moreover, the majority of the nobles still stood by her, and showed some eagerness to save the country from civil war. While at Dunbar, also, she was visited by Lord Erskine, the Governor of Edinburgh Castle, who gave her satisfactory proof that she might depend on his support.[1] Such being the state of the two parties, she had only to bide her time to force the hands of the insurgents. On the day after the arrival of the Congregation in Edinburgh they had sent agents to her with the terms they were then willing to accept. Conferences followed between the leaders on both sides; but they led to nothing, and it became clear to the Protestant Lords that they were only being amused till delay had done its work in breaking up their following.

At length the Regent thought herself strong enough to take a decided step. On the morning of the 23rd of July[2] her forces under Châtelherault and D'Oysel marched on Leith, which they reached early on the morning of the 24th. There had been some understanding between Leith and Edinburgh that they should make a common defence against the Regent's intended attack, and with this object the Protestants in Edinburgh took up their position on the eastern side of the Calton Hill.[3] One shot on the part of Leith was its sole attempt at defence,

---

[1] Teulet, i. 326; *Wodrow Misc.* i. 64.
[2] *Works,* i. 373; Teulet, i. 325-326.
[3] *Works,* i. 374; *Wodrow Misc.* i. 64.

and in a short time the Lords on the Calton Hill saw the town open its gates to the French. Their own action now depended on the line taken by Erskine in the Castle. As they were ignorant of the pledge which Erskine had given to the Regent at Dunbar, they at the last moment sent a final request that he would stand by the faith his conscience approved. His answer was peremptory. If they did not speedily come to terms with the Regent, he would open fire both on them and on the town. Thus driven to bay, the Protestant Lords had no alternative but to make the best of their situation. They sent to D'Oysel and the Duke a list of the conditions they were willing to accept, but with little expectation that they would be seriously entertained. At a meeting on the east slope of the Calton Hill,[1] the Duke and the Earl of Huntly on the one side, and Argyle, the Lord James, and Glencairn on the other, at length came to an understanding. The Congregation was to surrender Holyrood Palace, to give up the coining-irons, and to quit Edinburgh within twenty-four hours. The town was to be left to its own discretion in the matter of religion; no French garrison was to be introduced; the Protestants were to be allowed full liberty of worship, but were to abstain from all violence against the ancient religion : and the arrangement was to hold till the 10th of the following January.[2] Thus the Congregation had gained the point which had been the immediate

---

[1] At what were known as the Quarrel or Quarry Holes, afterwards known as the Upper Quarries.—*Works*, i. 379.

[2] It is worth noting that while Buchanan, Knox, and the writer in the *Wodrow Miscellany* specify as one of the terms of this treaty that no French garrison should be placed in Edinburgh, Leslie and Teulet make no mention of this.

occasion of their rising.   Their preachers were re-
lieved from outlawry, and were allowed to go out
and in among their people and preach at will.   Yet
the victory was only a seeming one.   So long as
the Regent had a permanent body of Frenchmen
at her disposal, she could always in the end prevail
over forces which could not hold together beyond
a few weeks.   On their side, the Regent and her
counsellors had received a warning which they were
not likely to forget; and they were well aware that
the recent compromise was far from meeting the
ends on which the Protestants were now bent.

The very day after the treaty showed the impossibility of a mutual understanding between the two
parties.   On the arrival of the Regent in Edinburgh
she instructed Huntly to see that the terms regarding
religion, as she professed to understand them, should
be at once carried out.   The town, he urged on the
Congregation, was now free to set up whichever of
the two religions it chose.   To settle the point,
therefore, a meeting of the citizens ought to be called
to ascertain the wishes of the majority.   But the
Congregation had not bargained for this.   They knew
that they were in the minority, and that the vote could
go only one way.   The choice, they answered, had
already been made, and there was no need to choose
again.   It was not the Regent's interest to recom-
mence a dangerous contest, and she reluctantly yielded
the point.   During the following months, therefore,
the Protestants continued to meet in the Church of St.
Giles, where John Willock preached with a boldness
and fervour worthy of Knox.[1]

[1] *Works*, i. 389-390; *Wodrow Misc.* i. 65-66.   According to one
of the terms of the Leith agreement, the Congregation was not to be

According to the terms of the late agreement the Congregation left Edinburgh on the 26th of July. As the Regent and he could hardly have abode in the same place, Knox was induced to accompany them. Before their final dispersion, however, a Council was held in Stirling to decide as to their future course of action; and according to their custom they gave effect to their deliberations in a mutual bond. Their fear was that when they were dispersed each would be approached singly by bribes and threats, and that their party would be thus imperceptibly broken up. In this bond, therefore, each took oath that he would receive no overtures from the Regent without the knowledge of his confederates, and that as soon as such overture was received it should immediately be made known to the other signatories. Finally, before parting, they took a step which proves that they were fully aware that the struggle was only begun. They determined to appeal to England, now a Protestant nation, to assist a cause which it was her own special interest to support. In urging this step none was more determined than Knox, and it will be seen that none was more energetic in giving it effect. During the first period of the revolutionary struggle he had all along been in the thick of events. At Perth, St. Andrews, and Edinburgh, he had been at once the hierophant and the protagonist of his party: in the period of the struggle on which we are now about to enter, the part he had to play was yet more important.[1]

molested in their worship; according to another, Edinburgh was to be left at liberty to choose between the two religions. As the Protestants were in possession of St. Giles, it might be urged that to oust them from that church was to "molest" them.

[1] In the Appendix a document will be found, which supplies an interesting commentary on the events recorded in the foregoing chapter.

The document in question is a letter addressed to the Pope by Mary
and the Dauphin, in which they make urgent request for money to
enable them to put down heresy and rebellion in Scotland.   In support
of their claim, they give a vivid picture of the pass to which things had
come in that country—their information being evidently derived from
the Queen-Regent.   The spread of heresy, it is important once more to
notice, they expressly attribute to the ignorance and immorality of the
clergy.   If the evil were to be put right, they add, rebellion must be
crushed by the strong hand, and heresy be met by the importation of
capable religious teachers.   The rising of the Congregation, the in-
effectual meeting of the last Provincial Council, the doings at Perth and
Scone, are successively touched upon—the letter having been written
during the Regent's retreat in Dunbar.   The original is in the collection
of Mr. A. Morrison.—See Appendix B.

CHAPTER II

1559

SINCE the accession of Elizabeth the chief men with
Protestant leanings in Scotland had turned their
thoughts to England. Before the close of 1558
Châtelherault was already in correspondence with
English agents, under a well-grounded suspicion that
should the French king gain his ends in Scotland the
rights of the house of Hamilton would not stand in his
way.[1] The Duke could hardly be called a Protestant,
yet, as his past had shown, he was not likely to stickle
at another change of faith if the interests of his family
might be served. But it was not long before the
genuinely Protestant party in Scotland made direct
efforts to interest England in their quarrel with the
Regent. Early in the spring of 1559 we find Maitland
in communication with Cecil as to the best policy to
be followed by the Congregation. Cecil was not yet
in a position to commit himself to any plan of action
with regard to Scotland; but he showed clearly how
his desires went. "Indeed," he wrote to Maitland,
"I see no such safety as to have the Government in

[1] Keith, i. 364-368, Letter of Sir Henry Percy concerning the
Affairs of Scotland.

the natural born, and the men of war utterly put out." [1]
When the Congregation rose in revolt, he saw that it
must be of vital import to England how the struggle
should end. Should the Protestants prove the stronger,
England would be safe from the ambition of France:
on the other hand, the victory of the Regent would
be a menace to England that threatened her very
existence. [2]

From the letters of Throgmorton, the English
ambassador in Paris during the spring of 1559, we
gather with what concern he regarded the action of
France. When the French king decided to send a
force to the assistance of the Regent, Throgmorton
was convinced that its ulterior destination was the
invasion of England. The death of Henry II. (10th
July 1559) increased the danger of the situation.
During the reign of their son-in-law, Francis II., the
Guises controlled the counsels of France, and directed
all their energies to add England to the crown of
Mary Stewart. In the triumph of the Regent over
the Congregation, therefore, there was an immediate
danger to England to which both Throgmorton and
Cecil were keenly alive, and which they saw could be
averted only by common action with the Protestant
party in Scotland. Yet without some overt act on
the part of France, Elizabeth was in such a position
that she could give no open assistance to the Congre-

---

[1] *National Manuscripts of Scotland*, Part iii. No. xli.

[2] In an instruction sent to France by the Regent, 6th February
1558, we have the following very distinct indication of the intentions of
France towards England : "Estant ledit sieur d'Oysel entré sur le propos
de Barvic, qui est une place forte importante au bien commun des
affaires du Roy et de la Royne d'Ecosse, et laquele estant réduicte en
l'obeissance de Leurs Majestez, ce seroit descouvrir tout cler le Royaume
d'Angleterre, ne se présentant outre ledit Barvich aucune forteresse qui
soit pour arrester une armée jusques à Londres."—Teulet, i. 289.

gation without placing herself in a false position in the eyes of Europe. By the recent treaty of Cambrai peace had been concluded between England and France. To assist a people in revolt against their lawful prince was a bad example for a ruler to set, two-thirds of whose own subjects might be ready on occasion to take arms against herself. By skilful management, indeed, Spain could be played off against France; yet by too vigorous a support of heresy in Scotland it was possible that Spain might be led for once to subordinate policy to religion, and to engage in a crusade worthy of the Catholic king. For these reasons Elizabeth might well hesitate before publicly identifying herself with the cause of Protestantism in Scotland. Yet from the first Cecil had no doubt as to the course which England ought to pursue, and though he was hindered at every step by the indecision of his mistress, he contrived that the Protestant Lords should never lose the hope that England would eventually come forward with the help they needed.

The years he had spent in England marked out Knox as the fittest person to effect an understanding between the Congregation and the English government. He had then made the acquaintance of Cecil and Throgmorton, both of whom had implicit trust in his plain dealing and simplicity of purpose. Of his ability to be of service to England, Throgmorton held strong opinion. "And, sir," he wrote to Cecil, "though that Knox the preacher did heretofore unadvisedly and fondly put his hand to the book;[1] yet, forasmuch as he is now in Scotland, in as great credit as ever man was there with such as may be able to serve the Queen's Majesty's turn; it were

[1] "The Monstruous Blast against the Regiment of Women."

well done not to use him otherwise in mine opinion than may be for the advancement of the Queen's Majesty's service."[1] Though he knew how ill the advice would be taken, Throgmorton dared even to press Knox's claims on Elizabeth. "It may, therefore, please your Majesty to be informed," he tells her, "that (in my poor opinion, saving your Highness' grave judgment) concerning what Knox is able to do in Scotland, which is very much, all this turmoil there being by him stirred as it is; it should stand your Majesty in stead, his former faults were forgotten, and that no means be used to annoy him for the same."[2]

Before he had left Geneva, Knox had warned the Lords of the Congregation of the danger ahead in their controversy with the Regent.[3] Foreseeing that of themselves they could not hold their own against the French power in Scotland, he had on his way home intended to pass through England and confer with Cecil as to the future relation of the two countries. Through Elizabeth's dislike of him, as we have seen, Knox had been forbidden to set foot on English ground; and the revolt broke out in Scotland without any definite understanding with the English government. It was during the breathing-space that followed the arrangement at Cupar that Knox first pressed the necessity of an appeal to England. In an interview with Kirkcaldy of Grange at St. Andrews, he persuaded him to open communication with Sir Henry Percy by way of approaching the English government; and within a few weeks, Cecil, Percy, Knox, and Grange were in active correspondence with a view to some mutual understanding. Knox thus opens his communication

<hr>

[1] Forbes, *State Papers*, i. 119.
[2] *Ibid.* pp. 129, 130.   [3] *Works*, ii. 15.

with Percy, whom it appears he had not previously known : " Richt Honorable, having the oportunitie of this bearer unsuspect, I thought good to requyr of you such freindshipe as that from tym to tym conference and knowledge myght be betuixt us ; I mean not my self and you, but betuixt the faythfull of both the Realmes to the end that inconveniences pretended against both may by Goddis grace and myghty power be avoided. Your faythfull freind Mr. Kyrkcaldye hath reaported to me your gentill behavour and faythfull fidelitie in all thingis laughfull, honest, and godlie."[1]

But there were matters to be discussed which could not be safely trusted to paper. It was Knox's desire, therefore, to meet Cecil at the earliest opportunity, and to consider the terms of a possible agreement. Cecil was as eager as Knox for this meeting ; but he was held back by two considerations. Were it known to the Regent that he had sought an interview with Knox, the most intractable of her subjects, it might lead to a premature breach with France, which it was his chief anxiety to avoid. On the other hand, Elizabeth was so ill-disposed to make any terms with the Scottish insurgents, and so strongly prejudiced against Knox in particular, that if the interview was to be arranged, it must be without the knowledge of Cecil's mistress.

Pending this meeting, letters of the highest importance passed between Cecil and the Protestant Lords. What Cecil wished to be assured of was that the breach between the Regent and the Congregation was beyond healing by mutual concession. Till the very close of the troubles in Scotland, the English government never lost the fear that ancient sympathies

[1] *Works*, vi. 35, 36.

might yet prevail, and that every Scot—Protestant and Catholic alike—might yet take their stand with France against the old enemy of England. In a reply by the Protestant leaders to this doubt of Cecil occurs the following significant passage. This letter, it should be said, is in Knox's hand, and was in all probability composed by him. "Trew it is that as yet we have maid no mention of any change in Authoritie, neyther yet hath any such thing entered our hartes, except that extream necessitie compell us thereto. But perceaving that Fraunce, the Quene Regent heir, together with Preastes and Frenchmen, pretend nothing elles but the suppressing of Christ's evangell, the maintenaunce of idolatrie, the ruyn of us, and the uter subversion of this poor Realme; we ar fully purposed to seak the next remeady to withstand tyrannie, in which mater we hartlie and unfanedlie requyr the faythfull counsall and furtherance att the Quenes and Consalles hands for our assistance. Thus far have we hasarded to mak you participant of our purposes, estate, and request; becaus in the said letters you requyr of the said Mr. Kyrkaldye some farther ground and assurance then his owen wordes and writeing because of the place which you hold and of the personages with whom that matter must be discours; and yet we doubt not but your Wisdom will so prudently and so closelie handell all thingis that the adversaryes have no advantage by discovering of things to all men befor just ripenes of the action so requyr." [1]

Along with the above letter of the Lords, Knox despatched another on his own account to Cecil, in which he once more asks permission to visit England. "By diverse letters," he wrote, "I have required licence

---

[1] *Works,* vi. 42 (19th July 1559).

to have veseted the Northt partes of England ; but as yit I have reseaved no favorable ansuer. The longer, Sir, that it be delayed the less comfort shall the faythfull in those quarteris receave, yea, the weaker shall the Quen's Grace be ; for yf I war not to hir Grace an assured and unfeaned frende, I wold not so instantlie begg such a libertie in seaking wharof I suppose you be persuaded that I greatlie seak not my self. The common estait of thingis heir I dowbt not but ye know. Some thingis I have (as oft I have written), which glaidly I wold communicat with you, but am not mynded to committ the sam to paper and ink. Fynd therfor the meanes that I may speak such a one as ye will creditt in all thingis." [1] It was in this communication to Cecil that Knox enclosed his famous letter to Elizabeth in which he attempts to reconcile her to the principles of the " Monstruous Blast." Only when we understand the circumstances in which it was written do we appreciate the significance of this remarkable letter. The cause which absorbed his life was at stake, and only through Elizabeth could it prosper ; yet he could address her in these singular words : " Forget your birth and all title which thereupon doth hang, and consider deepelie how, for feare of your life, you did decline from God and bow in idolatrie." [2]

It was at length settled that Knox should pay a secret visit to Cecil at Stamford, his country-seat in Lincolnshire. [3] As he was preparing for the journey, however, he received a letter from Sir Henry Percy, requesting a secret interview at Alnwick on the 3rd of August. [4] It was just at this time that the French issued from Dunbar with the intention of attacking

---

[1] *Works*, vi. 45, 46. [2] *Ibid.* p. 50.
[3] *Ibid.* ii. 32. [4] *Ibid.*

Leith and Edinburgh; and the negotiations that
followed delayed Knox's departure till the last day
of July or the beginning of August.[1] As their fully
accredited representative, he bore a list of written
instructions from the Lords which they offered as the
basis of a treaty.[2] On condition that England should
take up the cause of the Congregation, they expressed
a wish for a mutual league against the French and all
other enemies—neither country to make peace or war
without the consent of the other. For themselves they
desired such a league for two reasons—the suppression
of superstition and the setting up of true religion, and
the restoration of their ancient laws and liberties.

As the safest mode of making his journey, Knox,
in company with a brother-minister, Robert Hamilton,
sailed from Pittenweem, on the east coast of Fife, to
Holy Island. Percy, they found, had left the neighbourhood for the time, and they directed themselves
to Sir James Crofts, Governor of Berwick, who had
also been in the secret of the late negotiations.
Proceeding to Berwick at Crofts' request, they remained close within the Castle for two days, apparently awaiting letters from Cecil. In spite of the
pains Knox had taken to keep his journey secret, his
presence in Berwick was known to the Regent, whose
spies were everywhere. But the English government
was not yet prepared to avow its dealings with the
Congregation, regarding whose aims and prospects
they were still uncertain and suspicious.[3] Though
Knox would fain have gone farther into England,
both for the purpose of seeing old friends and of meet-

---

[1] *Works*, ii. 50.

[2] These instructions, dated the 30th of July, are given in Laing's
Knox, vi. 56-58.   [3] *Works*, vi. 62.

ing Cecil, Crofts urged his immediate return to Scotland in the interest of the business on which he had come. Letters having arrived from Cecil addressed to himself and the Protestant leaders, Knox, in company with one Alexander Whitelaw,[1] left Berwick on the 3rd of August for Stirling, then the headquarters of the Congregation.[2] The journey was an adventurous one, as the Regent was aware of his return, and had given orders that he should be seized by the way.[3] On the journey Whitelaw took ill,[4] and Knox, parting company with him, reached Stirling on or before the 6th of August.

The letter of Cecil to the Lords, which Knox brought from Berwick, was not satisfactory.[5] He made various suggestions as to the action they should take if they would bring their enterprise to a successful issue. They need not want money, he told them, if they would but follow the example of Henry VIII., and appropriate the wealth of the Church to a Christian purpose. The letter was full of vague promises of encouragement, but it contained no definite answer to the demands of the Congregation. Two replies to this letter of Cecil, one in the name of the Congregation, and one from Knox, put plainly before him the alternatives between which he must choose. If

---

[1] This Whitelaw was a busy and confidential agent between the Congregation and Elizabeth's ministers. Throgmorton describes him as "a very honest, sober, and godly man, and most truly affectionate to England of any Scottishman I know here."—Forbes, *State Papers*, i. 137.

[2] David Laing points out that Dr. M'Crie was in error in making Knox return by sea.—*Works*, ii. 35 *note*.

[3] *Ibid.* vi. 63.

[4] *Ibid.* ii. 35. Whitelaw, on resuming his journey (from Preston to Edinburgh) in company with Knox's brother William, was chased for three miles. William Knox, it appears, had been mistaken for his brother.　　　　　[5] *Ibid.* vi. 51-55.

England did not come to their help, they could not
of themselves carry on the contest they had begun.
Many of their number would make their peace with
the Regent; France would become supreme in the
country, and Cecil knew whether this would consist
with the interest of England.   On the other hand,
should England decide to support the Congregation,
no time was to be lost in dilatory negotiation.   At
that moment they had 500 men in arms, and money
was pressingly needed to defray the expense of maintaining them.   But such a force was totally inadequate
to the enterprise in which they were engaged.   An
additional force of 1000 foot and 300 horse would be
necessary, and the means to support such a force was
not to be found among the Protestant leaders, who
had already impoverished themselves by their past
efforts.   Things were in a more favourable train,
however, than Cecil's letter had led the Scottish Lords
to expect.   Two days after their reply was written,
Elizabeth granted Sir Ralph Sadler a commission to
effect a secret understanding with the Congregation.[1]
As proof of the sincerity of her intention, Sadler was
entrusted with £3000 to distribute as he should see
fit in the interest of England.   The sum was pitifully
inadequate in the circumstances; but it convinced the
Protestants that Elizabeth found herself constrained
to regard their cause as to a certain extent her
own.

But it was not only as secretary and secret agent
that Knox had served the Congregation during the
last few weeks.   By preaching tours throughout the
country he had done much to spread the Protestant
doctrine, and to strengthen his party for the battle

---

[1] Sadler, *State Papers*, i. 387 *et seq.*

which every one knew to be imminent.[1]   In a letter
to Mrs. Locke (2nd September) he gives the following
account of his labours during July and August: " I
have beene in continuall travell since the day of appointment, and notwithstanding the fevers have vexed me
the space of a month, yitt have I travelled through
the most part of this realme, where (all praise be to
his blessed Majestie) men of all sorte and conditions
embrace the truthe.   Enemeis we have manie, by
reasoun of the Frenchemen who are latelie arrived,[2]
of whom our parteis hope goldin hills [*sic*], and such
support as we be not able to resist.   We doe nothing
but goe about Jericho, blowing with trumpets, as God
giveth strenth, hoping victorie by his power alone.
Christ Jesus is preached even in Edinburgh, and his
blessed sacraments rightlie ministred in all congrega-
tiouns where the ministrie is established ; and they be
these :—Edinburgh, Sanct Andrewes, Dundie, Sanct
Johnstoun, Brechin, Montrose, Stirling, Aire.   And
now, Christ Jesus is begun to be preached upon the
south borders, nixt unto you, in Jedburgh and Kelso,
so that the trumpet soundeth over all, blessed be our
God."[3]

During the following months Knox resided mainly
in St. Andrews, though his labours frequently carried
him elsewhere.   The times were such, indeed, as
strained to the utmost all his energies of mind and

---

[1] Sadler and Crofts in a letter to Cecil (8th September) thus refer
to the efforts of the preachers at this time : " Agayn during this meane
tyme they have had their prechers abrode in the realme, which, by
their preaching and doctrine, have so woonne and allured the people to
their devocion, as he [Sadler] sayeth their power is now double that it
was, in the cause of religion ; and such as yet be not fully persuaded
therto, bere, nevertheles, such hatred to the Frenchmen, as he
thinketh in maner the hole realme favoureth their partie."—Sadler,
State Papers, i. 431.   [2] See below.   [3] *Works*, vi. 78.

body. About the middle of August a French force of 1000 men were landed at Leith,[1] and it was understood that a larger detachment was speedily to follow. As their wives and children came in company with these troops, it was the general conviction that the occupation of the country by Frenchmen could not be far off. So strong was the feeling of the country, that the Regent published a manifesto in justification of her conduct.[2] To Knox apparently was assigned the task of replying to the Regent's apology, and he performed it with his usual vigour. Reviewing her government from the beginning, he showed that it had been inspired by the object of making Scotland the tool of France, that by exorbitant taxation, a debased coinage, and the rapacity of the French soldiery, the Scottish people had all these years been groaning under her tyranny.[3]

According to their agreement, the Protestant Lords met at Stirling on the 10th of September to hold counsel as to their future conduct. At this meeting appeared a personage whose presence marked a new departure in the policy of the Congregation. This was the Earl of Arran, eldest son of the Duke of Châtelherault, and therefore the heir of all the claims of the house of Hamilton. A few months before, his Protestant sympathies had given offence to Henry II., who had sought to lay hands on him to prevent his doing further mischief in propagating heresy.[4] Elizabeth and her ministers had at once seen how useful an instrument Arran might be in working Scottish affairs to their own advantage.[5] Should Arran identify him-

---

[1] *Works*, i. 396. [2] Knox gives this manifesto in full, i. 397-399.
[3] *Works*, i. 400 *et seq.*
[4] Teulet, i. 312 (Henry II. to De Noailles, 21st June 1559).
[5] It was mainly through the agency of Elizabeth that Arran escaped from France, and finally found his way to Scotland.

self with the Congregation, his rank and claims would greatly strengthen their cause. The Protestant leaders, also, were fully aware that the presence of Arran in their midst was in the highest degree opportune. Many who had hitherto stood aloof from them would have their scruples removed when they saw the possible heir to the throne identified with a cause with which they themselves secretly sympathised. In Arran's claims, also, Mary of Lorraine would see a menace to her own daughter, which might constrain her to compromises which otherwise she might not have entertained.

In view of their strained relations with the Regent, despite the late treaty, it was decided by the Lords at Stirling that the Protestants should hold themselves in readiness to take the field at four days' notice.[1] By common consent, also, they passed to Hamilton to come to an understanding with the Duke in the new turn which affairs had taken. Châtelherault had now many reasons to induce him to throw in his lot with the reforming party. His eldest son had narrowly escaped rough handling from the French king, and it was understood that a younger brother of Arran was then actually a prisoner in France.[2] To all appearance the French were now bent on a final subjugation of the country, and, in the event of their success, the Hamiltons would be heavier losers than any other Scottish house.[3] On the other hand, a scheme was taking shape in the minds of the Protestant leaders

---

[1] Sadler, i. 461 (Balnaves to Sadler and Crofts, 23rd September).

[2] Cecil to the Lords of the Congregation, 28th July 1559.—*Works*, vi. 53, 54.

[3] This is specially insisted on by Arran himself in a letter to Cecil (25th September), giving an account of what took place at Stirling and Hamilton. Arran's letter is given in *Illustrations of the Reign of Queen Mary*, pp. 71-73 (Maitland Club, 1837).

which was well fitted to turn the head of a man like
Châtelherault. As it had grown clearer every day
that under French rule the new religion could never
win an assured position in the country, there was no
course left but to find a prince who would meet the
views of Protestants and patriots alike. In Arran it
seemed that both classes found what they wanted to
justify their casting off a queen ruling in the interests
of a foreign power. To concentrate their forces,
therefore, to put before the world what might be
accepted as a plausible pretext for their action, and to
place before themselves a clear issue towards which
they might work with a well-defined purpose, the
Protestant leaders had now fixed on Arran as the most
suitable person to realise their wishes on the throne of
Scotland. But this was only part of a wider scheme
which they had conceived in the interests of Scotland
and Protestantism. It had been in the mind of
Henry VIII. not only to unite his son Edward with
Mary Stewart, but also his daughter Elizabeth with
the Earl of Arran.[1] By this double union he thought
that the two countries would be so interlaced that the
one could not find its interest in breaking away from
the other. In the case of Edward and Mary the plan
had failed miserably ; but it now seemed to the Protestant leaders that the marriage of Arran and Elizabeth lay in the decrees of Providence for the future
wellbeing of the two countries they represented. To
Cecil and other of Elizabeth's advisers such a union
commended itself as the most prudent their Queen could
form in view of the policy she had adopted, and of her

---

[1] Froude, vi. 236. In his thirty-seventh chapter Mr. Froude has
gone into the details regarding the proposed marriage between Arran
and Elizabeth.

position among the great princes of Europe. Meanwhile, at least, the scheme was one which proved of the most practical value for strengthening the confidence of the negotiating parties in each other. In centring their hopes on Arran the Protestant Lords gave to England the surest pledge that they had finally broken with France, and thus removed one of Cecil's strongest fears in supporting them.

Induced by these prospects, Châtelherault now openly identified himself with the Protestant party. While the Lords were at Hamilton, news came that the Regent had begun to fortify Leith;[1] and as this was a distinct breach of the late agreement, they were not slow to remind her of her bad faith. In a letter addressed to her from Hamilton they threatened to take speedy steps to check her if she did not of her own accord put a stop to the work;[2] and to this letter Châtelherault affixed his signature along with the rest, as a definitive intimation to the Regent that he had joined the ranks of her adversaries.

It was now evident to both parties that the recommencement of the struggle could not be long delayed. A few days after the above letter was written a fresh detachment of troops, to the number of 800, arrived from France at Leith.[3] Along with them came the Bishop of Amiens and three doctors of the Sorbonne, whose learning and eloquence, it was hoped, might in some measure counteract the influence of the Protestant preachers. The fortification of Leith, more-

---

[1] Sadler, i. 461; Knox, i. 413.

[2] See this letter in Knox, i. 413, 414. In Teulet (i. 349, 350) there is an interesting letter from De Noailles describing the doings of Châtelherault at this time. De Noailles erroneously assigns the 22nd of September as the date of the letter addressed to the Regent. The real date as given by Knox, who produces the letter itself, was the 19th.

[3] Sadler, i. 464, 470.

over, went on apace, and the Regent meanwhile was
sparing no means to weaken the ranks of her enemies
by promises, bribes, and threats as she found most
convenient. Under these circumstances the Protestant
leaders issued the order that their supporters should
assemble at Stirling on the 15th October, thence to
march on Edinburgh, and bring their forces to bear on
the Regent.[1]

Since the beginning of the revolt the Protestants
had made distinct gains in the country. From the
nobility they had gained the Duke and the Earl of
Arran, while three powerful nobles, Huntly, Morton,
and Erskine, had given indications that they were
moving in the same direction. Maitland of Lethington,
also, who was afterwards to prove such an efficient
ally, had intimated that he was only waiting the opportunity to throw over the Regent, and join the Protestants.[2] Among the people, hatred of the French and
the efforts of the Protestant preachers had materially
increased the numbers of the Congregation. Supported
as they now were by English aid, it might seem that
the Protestants were in a position to impose their will
both on the Regent and the nation at large. In
reality they were not so strong as they seemed.
Owing to a late harvest[3] they had been unable to
assemble in force till the Regent had fortified Leith,
and been reinforced by fresh bands from France. The
men whom they brought into the field were "cuntrie
fellows,"[4] unpractised in war and helpless in presence
of the fortifications raised by skilled engineers round
Leith.   Above all, the want of money paralysed

---

[1] *Works*, i. 417.
[2] Sadler, i. 451 (Sadler and Crofts to Cecil, 16th September).
[3] *Ibid.* i. 431.
[4] Herries, *Hist. of the Reigne of Marie Queen of Scots*, p. 50.

their efforts. In a letter to Sir James Crofts, Knox gives us a glimpse into the affairs of his fellow-workers, which shows how serious he considered the situation to be. At the date when it was written, as will be seen, Knox was still acting as secretary to the Congregation.

"Before I wrote unto yow and unto Mr. Secretary that onles summe supporte were made unto particuler men, and especiallie to those whom I did notifie in writing, that impossible it ware unto them to serve in this action. For albeit that money, by the adversarie partie largelie offered, coulde not corrupt them; yet shulde extreme povertie compell them to remayne at home; for they are so superexpended alreadie that they are not hable to bear oute their trayne, and the same thing I write unto you again, requyering you to signifie the same to suche as tendre the furtheraunce of this cause. If any persuade you that they wool or maye serve without supporte, they doo but deceyve you. If I did not perfetlie understand thair necessitie, I woolde not write so precislie; for I nothing doubte to obteyne of them by the authoritie of God's woord, what lyeth in their power; yea, if they coulde have money uppon their lands, I shulde never solicitt for them; but the knowledge of their povertie and the desier which I have that the cause prosper makith me bolde to speake my judgement. If we lacke those, Sir, whome in my former lettres I expressed, our power will be weaker then men beleve. Fraunce seekith all meanes to make them freends and to diminish our nombre. Ye are not ignorant what povertie on the one parte, and money largelie offred upon the other part, is hable to persuade. Be advertised and advertise you others, as you favour the successe of the cause. I have doon what in me lyeth

that corruption entre not amongst them ; and at my
last departing from them, I verilie beleve that they
were of one mynde to promote the cause enterprised,
but the power of summe is suche as before I expressed." [1]

On the 16th October [2] the Congregation entered
Edinburgh. Two hours before the Regent had left it
for Leith, accompanied by the Archbishops of St.
Andrews and Glasgow, the Abbot of Dunfermline,
and Lord Seton. [3] Her plan of action was precisely
the same as had succeeded so well in the case of the
previous rising. Intrenched in Leith, and with a
garrison of 3000 trained soldiers, she could hold her
own with little difficulty till time should again do its
work. The Congregation were only 8000 strong [4]—
a force, considering the materials of which it was composed, utterly inadequate to a successful attack on her
present stronghold. Money, she knew, was scarcer
than ever with their leaders ; a few weeks would see
their numbers seriously reduced ; and by that time
further reinforcements from France would again enable
her to take the offensive.

The Protestant leaders perfectly understood the
Regent's tactics, and proceeded with the vigour which
the situation demanded. Immediately on their arrival in
Edinburgh they despatched a message requesting her
to desist from fortifying Leith, and to send her foreign
soldiery out of the country. She replied that such a
message would have come better from a prince to his
subjects than from subjects addressing their prince,

---

[1] Knox to Sir James Crofts, 21st September (*Works*, vi. 80). This
letter is signed " John Sinclear," Knox's signature, as we have seen, in
times of danger.

[2] *Works*, i. 437.   [3] *Wodrow Misc.* i. 68.

[4] *Ibid.* A thousand of these were mercenaries.

and that their entire course of conduct more than justified all the precautions she had taken in self-defence.[1] This answer could only have been what the Congregation expected, and they at once took a step which had been in their minds for the last few months. At a meeting held in the Tolbooth on the 21st of October,[2] they went through the form of debating the expediency of deposing Mary of Lorraine from the Regency. As a necessary part of their proceedings they consulted Knox and Willock as the spiritual advisers of the Congregation. From what we have seen of Knox's political teaching there could be little doubt as to how he would answer the question. Both gave their opinion for deposition, Knox adding the safe proviso that if Mary of Lorraine should ever give sure sign of repentance for her past conduct, and should submit to the guidance of the Scottish nobility, she should be reinstated in her office and honours. It was, in truth, in the necessity of their position that the Congregation should sooner or later take the step they now took. Between the demands they made and the policy of Mary of Lorraine there could be no common ground of harmonious action. Moreover, by this definitive rejection of her authority, they at once conciliated the house of Hamilton, and ensured the support of England in their quarrel with France.

Immediately after the Council broke up, it was

---

[1] Knox, i. 440, 441 ; Buchanan, pp. 318, 319. The Regent's reply is very fully given in Buchanan. It is an honourable distinction of Buchanan's History that while he leaves us in no doubt as to what side he approves, he never fails to put the case of the other side in the best light of which it is capable. I have pointed out this elsewhere.—See the *Life of Buchanan*, p. 322.

[2] Knox, i. 441. There is some uncertainty about the precise dates at this point ; but I have followed those of Knox, as he was himself an actor in the events which he records.

proclaimed at the Market Cross that by the " Nobilitie, Baronis, and Broughes convenit to advise upoun the affairis of the commoun - weall," Mary of Lorraine was suspended from the Regency of Scotland.[1]   The Proclamation, which may have been the work of Knox, is drawn up with the skill of a deft and practised hand.   What is remarkable in the document is that the question of religion seems to be deliberately kept in the background.   It is on the plea of the Regent's tyrannical government, of her sacrifice of Scotland to France, that her suspension is based.   The policy of this is evident.   The support of the Protestants in the country the Lords were assured of ; but there was a large number of the people not in sympathy with the new religion who were yet alarmed at the tendency of Mary of Lorraine's government.   It was this section which had to be gained over ; and, as addressed to them, the Proclamation does credit to the astuteness of its author.   By a specious attempt to give the deposition the form of law, the document closes with the hardy affirmation that the step had been taken in the name and authority of their two sovereigns now in France.   All through their proceedings the Congregation had professed to act in the conviction that Mary of Lorraine was not countenanced by their lawful sovereigns.   They must have known that this

---

[1] *Works*, i. 444.   Knox gives the Proclamation in full, but without signatures.   In the MS. of 1566 there is a blank space of half a page, which was evidently intended for the names of those who signed the document.   In a contemporary transcript of a letter sent to the Regent two days after the Proclamation there are ten signatures.   As they are probably the same as those attached to the Proclamation, they are given here : " *Earls*, My Lord Duke's Grace and Earl of Arran, the Earl of Argyle, the Earl of Glencairn ; *Lords*, James of St. Andrews, the Lord Ruthven, the Master of Maxwell ; *Barons*, Tullibardine, the Laird of Dun, the Laird of Pittarrow ; the Provost of Aberdeen for the Burrows."—Knox, i. 451, *note*.

plea had no basis in fact; yet as covering their action with an appearance of law it served its purpose in their appeals to the people.

In the above manifesto the Congregation had sought to justify their action to their own countrymen; but they also desired to explain their motives to the world at large. To this moment we may refer a long address in Latin [1] to the princes of Christendom, in which they recounted the wrongs done to Scotland by France during the minority of Mary Stewart. In this document, as in the other, the question of religion is touched only in the most casual manner. It is the misgovernment of Mary of Lorraine and the tyrannical purpose of France on which they rest the justification of all their action. In the appeal with which they conclude, it is as patriots and not as apostles of a new religion that they speak. "If these representations are just," they conclude, "and come within the duty of a good man, we beseech and conjure all men and princes who bear the name of Christ to show themselves impartial judges of a just cause, to give no faith to the accusations and calumnies of our enemies, but to hold for certain that to this pass we have not been willingly led, but forcibly drawn by the wicked trains, by the insolence and intolerable oppression of the French; that we bring force against no one, and only wish to avert war and keep our common country from pressing danger." Such a document could hardly have satisfied Knox as a statement of the dominant motives which had governed his labours since his return to Scotland. No Scotsman living had better reason to detest France than himself. It was to French interference in Scotland that he owed those years in the galleys

----

[1] This manifesto is given in Teulet (i. 414-428).

which could never pass from his memory. As a lover of his country, also, he must have deeply resented the haughty assumption of France in its dealing with Scotland. But it was neither motives of personal revenge nor motives of patriotism that drove Knox along his present course. Yet there were reasons why the Protestant leaders should give themselves out as patriots rather than apostles. In Scotland hatred of the French was a feeling in which all classes were united. After their own countrymen, England had to be considered in an Apology which was meant for all Christendom. In supporting the Scottish Protestants, as has been said, Elizabeth's main difficulty was that to the world it must seem that she was countenancing the rebellion of subjects against their lawful rulers. But if in her government Mary of Lorraine had been the mere instrument of her brothers the Guises, the conduct of her revolted subjects could not be regarded as mere rebellion. In taking the line of defence they did, therefore, the authors of this manifesto once more gave proof of that worldly wisdom which all along had guided their counsels.

It soon appeared that the Congregation had undertaken a task beyond their strength. The Regent's spies were everywhere, and betrayed their most secret designs. Their mercenaries, not receiving their full pay, could not be depended on, and at any moment might go over to the enemy. In their straits they nobly agreed to coin their silver-plate; but the coining instruments were carried off, and the proposal came to nothing.[1] Their only hope of carrying on the struggle depended on the promised aid from

---

[1] *Works*, i. 453, 454.

England; but of this stay also an untoward accident deprived them. Yielding to the representations of Cecil and others of her advisers, Elizabeth had agreed to send another instalment of £1000 to the Protestant leaders. The transaction was conducted with the utmost secrecy; but Mary of Lorraine was fully aware of the whole proceeding. Acting on her order, the Earl of Bothwell waylaid Cockburn of Ormiston, who was bearing the money from Berwick to Ormiston, wounded him severely, and carried off the whole sum intended for the Congregation.[1] One misfortune now succeeded another, till, with the exception of Arran and the Lord James, the Protestant Lords once more gave up their cause as lost.[2] While some of their best troops were gone in search of Bothwell, a band of the enemy issued from Leith, drove before them the mercenaries of the Congregation, and pursued the fugitives into the streets of Edinburgh.[3] A still more serious defeat on the 5th of November finally convinced them that they were no longer in a position to carry on the struggle.[4]

It was certainly no fault of Knox that things had gone so ill with his party. Daily from the pulpit he and Willock spoke in the ears of crowded congregations. Still carrying on a correspondence with England, he plied every argument which might persuade that country to an open alliance with the Congregation. A piece of information he was able to give Cecil showed that statesman what England might look for should France triumph in Scotland.

---

[1] *Works*, i. 454, 455; Sadler, i. 528, 538, 542, 600; Teulet, i. 379, The sum seized by Bothwell is variously stated. See Teulet's note.
[2] *Works*, i. 464.
[3] *Ibid.* i. 457, 458; Teulet, i. 377 *et seq.*
[4] *Works*, i. 460 *et seq.*; Teulet, i. 377 *et seq.*

In his voyage from Dieppe to Leith, Knox had seen a sceptre meant for the Regent, engraved with the arms of England, France, and Scotland. In reply to an inquiry of Cecil he was also able to tell him that a great seal had lately been sent from France, similarly engraved with the arms of the three countries.[1] As Knox knew, it was only the fear of France that would quicken Elizabeth into active assistance of his party, and these were facts that would carry more weight with her than any arguments as to the justice of his cause.

Never, it would appear, were Knox's labours heavier than now. In addition to his preaching he still performed the duties of secretary to the Lords of the Congregation. His wife, whom he had impatiently awaited since his coming to Scotland, had lately joined him, and to some extent must have lightened his burden. "The rest of my Wife," he wrote, "hath been so unrestfull since her arriving that skarslie could she tell upoun the morrow what she wrote at night."[2] But his own toils and anxieties were evidently beyond what he could long endure. "Mack ye advertisement," he wrote at this time to an English correspondent, "as ye think good, for I cannot write to any, especiall for lack of opportunitie; for in twenty-four hours I have not four free to naturall rest and ease of this wicked carcass."[3] All this while, moreover, he knew that his life was daily sought by the enemy. "Remember my last request for my Mother," he says in the same letter, "and say to Mr. George[4] that I have nead of a good and an

---

[1] *Works*, vi. 86, 88, 89.
[2] *Ibid.* vi. 104.   [3] *Ibid.* p. 88.
[4] His mother-in-law, Mrs. Bowes, and her son George, afterwards Sir George Bowes.

assured horse ; for great watch is laid for my apprehension, and large money promissed till any that shall kyll me."[1]

It was the gloomy prospect of the Congregation, however, that was his main concern. In his desperation he was driven to make a suggestion to his English correspondent, Crofts, which, though perfectly in the spirit of the age, is curiously out of keeping with the whole strain of his character. It is a signal tribute to Knox, indeed, that this passage in his writings strikes us as almost ludicrous in view of his general modes of thought and action. The only hope for the Congregation, he saw, was that England should send a body of troops adequate to a successful siege of Leith, and it was in urging this necessity on Crofts that he suggested the following dubious counsel : " Yf ye fear to offend Fraunce, in hart it is allready att defiaunce with you, and abideth only the opportunitie and advantaige. If you list to craft with thame, the sending of a thousand or mo men to us can breake no league nor point of peace contracted betwix you and Fraunce : For it is free for your subjects to serve in warr any prence or nation for thare wages. And yf ye fear that such excusses shall not prevaile, you may declayr thame rebells to your Realme when ye shalbe assured that thei be in our companye."[2] England was not yet ready to take such an open part against France, and as the best way of meeting Knox's request, Crofts assumed a tone of superior virtue. Crofts, it should be said, was afterwards suspected of playing false to his own country throughout these negotiations with the Congregation.[3] " I have receyved your lettres

---

[1] *Works*, v. 88.   [2] *Ibid.* vi. 90.
[3] Sadler, i. 711 ; Froude, vi. 364, 366, 371.

of the 25," he writes to Knox, "for answer whereunto albeit for myn own part I coulde be well content to satisfie your hole requests with as good will as you seme to desyre it; yet can I not but mervaile that you, being a wise man, woll require of us to such present ayde of men, money, and amunycion, as we cannot minister unto you without an open shew and manifestacion of our selfs to be as open enemyes, where, as you know, by leag and treatie, we be bounde to be frends; prayeng you to consider how we may, without touche of honour and hurte of our commenwealth, being now in good peax and amytie, enter sodenly into open warre and hostylitie."[1] From Knox's reply to this rebuke of Crofts it would appear that he was somewhat ashamed of his suggestion, though even on second thoughts he was not convinced that he had given dishonourable counsel. In making war in Scotland, France was in reality driving at the conquest of England, and had thus practically set aside the treaty of Cambrai. In his reply to Crofts it will be seen that this is the line of defence he takes. "Your reassonable answer to my unreassonable requeaste, ryght Worshipfull, receaved I this 28 of October, and have imparted the contents of the sam to such as partlie induced me befor to write. I was not altogetther ignorant neather what mycht ensew your manifestation in supporting us, nether yet how far did your commission extend in such cases. But considdering (as my slender witt did serve for the tym) whetther was the greatter daunger, the Nobilitie here to be defaitt (or yet frustrat of thare interprise), or ye to abyd the hasard of the future and suspected incommodities, it appeared to

---

[1] *Works*, vi. 91.

me that the former myght justly devour the other.
As tuiching the leage and treatie which now ye
suppose to have with such as· ye term your freinds,
I unfeanedlie wishe that it war so suyr that you should
never have occasion to break any point contracted.
But whether it may stand with wisdom to have such
respect to that which som men do call honour that
in the mean tym I shall see my freind perrishe, both
till his distruction and myn, I reffer to the judgement
of the most honourable. France was under leage and
treaty of peace with England when it did manifestlie
support Scotland to both our displeasure; and yet I
think that thei nether wold have confessed breche
of treaty nor blemyshe of honour." [1]

The defeat of the 5th of November had convinced
the Congregation that the Regent was still too strong
for them. Their position in Edinburgh had become
insupportable. Their soldiers were mutinous; the
majority of the citizens were opposed to them; and
the Castle would show them no favour. Under these
circumstances their leaders determined to vacate Edinburgh that very night. [2] As before, they proceeded to
Stirling to hold counsel as to their future line of action.
They were not in the best of spirits after this second
overthrow of all their hopes; but they had two men
in their ranks who were convinced that the battle was
not lost, and who each in his own way was specially
fitted to make the most of a tottering cause,—Knox

---

[1] Cecil seems to have approved of the snub which Crofts had ad-
ministered to Knox. "Suerly I lyke not Knoxees audacite," he writes
to Crofts, "which also was well tamed in your answer. His writings
do no good here; and therefore I doo rather suppress them, and yet I
meane not but that ye shuld contynue in sending of them."—Sadler, i.
535. As we have seen, Cecil had more than once been made to smart
by Knox's freedom of speech towards himself.

[2] *Works*, i. 465.

and Maitland of Lethington. On the arrival of the Congregation at Stirling, Knox, as at every crisis, was called upon to preach a sermon befitting the occasion. It was at moments like this that Knox showed his essential greatness as an inspirer of men. For himself he was convinced that the cause in which he was engaged might be retarded by the backsliding of men, but that it was in the immutable decree of Heaven that it should triumph at last. The sermon he now preached was long remembered as having renewed the hearts of the faithful at a moment when they seemed ready to faint.[1] After the sermon the Council was held, and resolutions were taken which were to lead to results that fully justified all the confidence of Knox.

As has been said, William Maitland had lately joined the Congregation, and had accompanied them in their flight from Stirling. The very fact that a man of Maitland's insight had taken their side at such a juncture was itself an encouraging proof that their case was not so desperate as it seemed.[2] From his knowledge of the condition of both parties he had strongly protested against the Lords leaving Edinburgh at the time they did.[3] His advice on this occasion had been disregarded; but the Congregation was soon to learn that in Maitland they had secured an ally whose services could hardly be overestimated. To Knox the acquisition of Maitland came as a relief which must have been welcome for more reasons than one. "I hope," he writes to Crofts, "that God hath delivered me from the most part of these civill effares, for now are men of better judgement and greatter

---

[1] Buchanan and the author of the *Historie of the Estate of Scotland*, as well as Knox himself, make special reference to this sermon.

[2] According to Knox, it was at the risk of his life that Maitland remained in the camp of the Regent.—i. 463-464.   [3] *Ibid.*

experience occupied in these maters. Young Ledington, Secreatarie, is delivered from the fearfull thraldom
of the Frenchmen, and is now with us in Edinburgh,
who, I trust, shall releaf me of the presupposed journey." [1] At the Council which was held at Stirling, it
was this journey of Maitland that was the main subject
of consideration. As there was no thought but to
continue the struggle, it was more imperative than
ever that powerful and speedy assistance should be
obtained from England. To compass this end it was
decided that Maitland should proceed to the English
Court with such instructions as seemed likely to lead
to a mutual understanding. Meanwhile, the Lords
and gentlemen of the Congregation, retiring to their
respective localities, were to use their best endeavour
for the common cause. On the 16th of December
they were to reassemble at Stirling, and consider their
further plans of action.[2]

[1] *Works*, vi. 94.

[2] It is probably to this period that we must assign an interesting
document, referred to by Tytler (*Hist. of Scot.* vi. 80, *note*). It is
entitled "The Apologie off our Departure," and is a reply on the part
of the Protestants to the charge of cowardice in fleeing from their
enemies. As neither names nor dates occur in it, it is impossible to fix
the precise circumstances under which it was written. Tytler thought
it was the production of Knox, in justification of his flight from Scotland
in 1556. But the original is not in Knox's handwriting, nor does its
style remotely suggest that of Knox. Laing thought it must be the
work of Maitland or Erskine of Dun. Maitland's it can hardly be ; but
the writer's manner does resemble that of Erskine in the writings of his
we possess. The document is printed by Laing.—Knox, *Works*, vi.
683 *et seq.*

CHAPTER III

THE THIRD RISING OF THE CONGREGATION—KNOX
IN THE BACKGROUND

1559-1560

DURING the third and last stage of the revolt against
Mary of Lorraine, Knox plays a less prominent part
than in the previous two. His work as secretary and
agent for the Congregation had been taken in hand by
Lethington, and for the most part his duties were confined to preaching and exhortation. Even as a preacher
he had not the same opportunities for such dramatic
appearances as had occurred at Perth, St. Andrews,
and Edinburgh. But there was another reason why
during this closing struggle Knox should fall into the
background. Thenceforth, till the treaty of Leith
(July 1560), it is no longer religion that is put forward
as the plea for revolt. In all the manifestoes of the
insurgents during the next six months the threatened
French conquest is the rallying cry with which they
seek to rouse the country. The cry for a Reformed
religion had failed to bring the bulk of the nobility to
their side; and to commend their cause to Elizabeth
they must place themselves before the world as a
people oppressed by foreign laws and menaced by a
foreign power. Such a representation of the cause to
which he was giving his life could not meet the

approval of Knox. To keep back the fact that the renewal of religion was the main object of the Congregation was to invite the judgment of Heaven on their enterprise. Knox, therefore, could no longer be what he had been, in the developments the struggle had now taken. He was himself perfectly aware that things had changed between himself and the leaders of the Congregation. "I am judged amongis ourselves too extream," he writes, "and be reason therof I have extracted myself from all public assemblies 'to my privat study."[1]

As has been said, the Lords of the Congregation, on leaving Stirling, broke up into two companies. Châtelherault, Argyle, and Glencairn, the Lords Boyd and Ochiltree, proceeded to Glasgow; Arran, the Lord James, the Lords Rothes and Ruthven, to St. Andrews. In these two towns it was judged that they could most effectually consolidate the discontented elements of the people. By the arrangement of the Protestant leaders Knox made his headquarters at St. Andrews, and was charged with the duty of representing the Protestants throughout Fife.[2] Till the following spring, therefore, Knox's activity lay mainly in St. Andrews; though, as we find him again expressing his great need for a good horse, he must have been going and coming, at least in the immediate neighbourhood.[3]

About the middle of December a message came from Maitland desiring further instructions from the Congregation regarding his mission to England.[4] As

---

[1] *Works*, vi. 105 (Knox to Gregory Raylton, 29th January 1560).
[2] *Ibid.* ii. 40.
[3] *Ibid.* vi. 107 (Knox to Gregory Raylton, 29th January 1560).
[4] *Ibid.* ii. 4. The message from Maitland was brought by Robert Melville, who had accompanied him to England.

had been previously agreed, the Lords from St. Andrews and Glasgow met at Stirling to consider Maitland's report. Their meeting was unexpectedly disturbed. While they had been laying their plans the Regent had not been idle. The day after they had left Edinburgh she had entered it, and was now doing her utmost by threats and promises to win the Castle.[1] About the same date that Maitland went to England she despatched an agent to counteract his mission.[2] In the beginning of December fresh reinforcements from France landed in Leith,[3] and a still stronger force was immediately to follow. Since the beginning of the troubles her prospects had never been brighter; and when the news reached her that the Lords were met at Stirling, her Council resolved on a decided step. On Christmas Eve a body of troops stole from Edinburgh with the intention of surprising the assembly at Stirling; and next day these were followed by another detachment, commanded by D'Oysel in person.[4] Against such a force, amounting to 2500 men,[5] the Lords were not in a position to make head, and before the arrival of the enemy they precipitately left the town.[6]

This new enterprise of the French filled the Congregation with the utmost alarm. Knox, who had been one of those present at Stirling, writes as follows

---

[1] *Wodrow Misc.* i. 73, 74.

[2] Stevenson, *Illustrations of the Reign of Queen Mary*, p. 78. (The Lord James to Sadler and Crofts, 17th November 1559.) The Regent's agent was De Rubay, who filled the office of Chancellor of the kingdom.

[3] *Wodrow Misc.* i. 74.

[4] Teulet, i. 404 (D'Oysel to De Noailles).

[5] This is the number given by the writer of the "Historie" in *Wodrow Misc.* i. 75. D'Oysel, however, in the letter above referred to, speaks of thirteen ensigns, which would make the number about 1500.

[6] *Wodrow Misc.* i. 75.

from St. Andrews the day after the new dispersion: "The common bruite is that the French have in hand som haisty and som great enterprise; and the rumour lackest not appearance, for thei have shipped much ordinaunce, and ar not verrey sollist to re-enforte the ruptures and daly decayes of Leyth. It is feared that either thei shall tack Styrviling or Sanctandrois; and, therfor, I was send by the Lordis from Styrviling in diligence to advertiss that thare earnest desyr is that your shippes with possible expedition schew them-selves upon these coastes."[1]

D'Oysel's object soon became apparent. After a few days' delay by reason of the weather, he despatched his troops across Stirling Bridge through Fife, and himself passed over from Leith with between three and four hundred men.[2] By throwing such a force into Fife D'Oysel could only be meaning to drive the Protestants from St. Andrews as they had already been driven from Edinburgh and Stirling. Divining his purpose, the Protestant Lords and gentlemen in Fife debated every inch of the ground. For the space of a month there was almost daily skirmishing, in which neither party had a decisive superiority; but which, as it appeared, could only end in one way. Arran, the Lord James, and Kirkcaldy of Grange, fought in a manner that won Knox's admiration, though he trembled for the consequences should they come to misfortune. "The said Erle and Lord James," he says, "for twentie and ane dayis thei lay in thair clothes; thair buttis never come of; thei had skarmissing almost everie day; yea, some dayis, from morne to evin."[3] With the

---

[1] *Works*, vi. 102 (Knox to Crofts, 26th December).
[2] Teulet, i. 404, 405.   [3] *Works*, ii. 9.

handful of men at their disposal, however, they could not long make head against such odds, and D'Oysel steadily forced his way towards St. Andrews. Never had the cause of the Congregation been so desperate. To fill up their dismay, another band of French soldiery to the number of 900 had landed in Leith during the first days of January.[1] The Regent was triumphant, and in the hearing of those who reported her words to Knox, exclaimed, "Whair is now Johne Knox his God? My God is now stronger than his, yea even in Fyff."[2]

Knox fully realised the extremity to which his party was reduced. Writing to Mrs. Locke on the last day of December he tells her that "one day of trubles since my last arrivall in Scotland hath more peirced my heart than all the torments of the galeyes did the space of 19 moneths; for that torment, for the most part, did tuiche the bodie, but this pearces the soule and inward affectiouns."[3] Yet he never doubted that sooner or later the true evangel must triumph in Scotland. In the midst of the French invasion of Fife he appeared before the Protestant leaders at Cupar and preached a sermon, which put fresh heart into his hearers. As usual he produced a Scripture parallel for the case in which they now found themselves. They were now, he told them, like the disciples on the Sea of Galilee when the night fell and the storm broke, and their Master was absent on the mountain. The fourth watch was not yet come; but it was at hand, and their deliverer would appear

---

[1] Under De Martigues. According to the *Diurnal of Occurrents* the landing took place on the 11th January. This detachment, as we shall see, was only part of a larger force which had been sent from France. —Forbes, i. 307.

[2] *Works*, ii. 8.

[3] *Ibid.* vi. 104.

upon the waters.[1]   But while he thus spoke encouragement, he did not spare rebuke of those through whose shortcomings their cause was weakened.   On this occasion the Earl of Arran was the chief mark at which he aimed.   In a comparison between the Earl and Jehoshaphat he told him that he did not appear to advantage.   While Jehoshaphat went in and out among his soldiers and people, and cheered them by his words and presence, Arran " keipit himself more close and solitary than many men wald halfe wisshed." [2] We cannot wonder that Arran winced under this plain speaking, and gave the preacher to understand that his advice was unwelcome.

Deliverance was nearer than Knox probably expected.   The French in their progress along the coast on their way to St. Andrews had crossed the river Leven, when (23rd January) a fleet of armed vessels was seen to enter the Firth of Forth.[3]   For the last few weeks the Marquis D'Elbœuf had been expected in Scotland with a force that was effectually to crush all the enemies of France.   It was D'Oysel's first thought that D'Elbœuf had come at last to relieve the Regent and himself from all their anxieties.   In this belief he pursued his march as far as the mouth of the Firth.   Here he speedily learned his mistake.   Before his very eyes the strangers seized two ships on the way from Leith with provisions for his own camp.[4] The strange vessels were, in truth, the advanced squadron of a fleet which Elizabeth had sent with the express purpose of blocking the Firth against the

---

[1]   *Works*, vi. 8.   [2] *Ibid.* p. 9.

[3]   *Ibid.* p. 13 ; Sadler, i. 698.   (Arran and the Lord James to Sadler and Crofts, 26th January.)

[4]   *Diurnal of Occurrents*, p. 55.

landing of fresh troops at Leith.[1]   With all expedition
D'Oysel retreated towards Stirling, beset at every step
by the enemy, cut off from all supplies, and marching
with difficulty over roads which a month's storm had
rendered almost impassable.   Not till he reached
Linlithgow did he consider himself safe from his
pursuers, goaded to fury by the rapacity of his soldiers
during the late expedition.[2]

As appears from Knox's own account, the English
fleet had not appeared a day too soon for the safety of
St. Andrews.   From a letter to Mrs. Locke, written
about a fortnight after the retreat of the French, we
learn with what dismay their approach had been
regarded.   "I remained all the time in Sanct
Andrewes," he writes, "with sorrowfull heart; and
yitt as God did minister his Spirit, comforting the
afflicted; who, albeit they quaiked for a time, yitt doe
now praise God, who suddanlie diverted frome them
that terrible plague devised for them by the ungodlie.
The Frenche men approached within six miles, and
yitt at a sight of certain of your ships they retired
more in one day than they advanced in ten."[3]

Meanwhile, the mission of Maitland to the English
Court had borne fruit.   In the beginning of January
the Duke of Norfolk came to the north of England
with instructions to open negotiations with the Protestant Lords.[4]   The proposal for a meeting was first
conveyed to Châtelherault and the Lords at Glasgow,
who fixed on Carlisle as the place most convenient for

<hr>

[1] Keith, i. 408. (Instructions given by the Queen's Majesty to
William Winter, Esq., Master of the Ordnance of her Majesty's
Admiralty, sent at this present to the seas with fourteen armed ships to
sail to Scotland.)
   [2] *Works*, ii. 13, 14; *Wodrow Misc.* i. 77, 78; Sadler, i. 698, 699.
   [3] *Works*, vi. 108.
   [4] *Ibid.* ii. 39; Sadler, i. 669, 670.

themselves, and sent a message to the Lord James to that effect. As has been said, it had been assigned to Knox to conduct the correspondence of the Protestants in Fife. This message, it appears, was by no means to his mind, and he addressed a letter to Châtelherault and the other lords in which he stated very frankly his opinion both of this proposal and of their conduct during the last few weeks. When their brethren in Fife had been in such extremity, they had made no strenuous effort to relieve their distress. When the enemy in their late retreat had lain near Stirling in comparatively small numbers, they let slip the opportunity of taking them at a disadvantage. The English fleet had now been in the Firth fifteen days, yet the Duke and his friends had paid them no more attention than if they had been their mortal enemies. As for the proposal that the Lord James should proceed to Carlisle by way of Glasgow, it was too absurd to entertain. At that moment he could not get six honest men in Fife to accompany him. Altogether, the conduct of the Duke and his friends had been so half-hearted that if they did not look to it, the ruin of their cause could not be far off.[1]

Knox carried his point; and about the middle of February the Lord James, accompanied by Lord Ruthven, the Master of Lindsay, Henry Balnaves, and the laird of Pittarro sailed from Pittenweem to Berwick-on-Tweed.[2] The agreement was concluded on the 27th, and was simply a bond of mutual defence

---

[1] *Works*, ii. 40-43. Knox's suspicions of the Duke were but too well-grounded. On the 25th of January he wrote a cringing letter to Francis II. asking pardon for his past doings, and promising fidelity for the future. The Duke afterwards denied having written this letter.— Teulet, i. 407, 566, 567.

[2] *Wodrow Misc.* i. 79; Knox, ii. 45.

against the French. On the part of the Scots the preamble stated that their sole reason for seeking the compact was their fear of France, and their desire for the friendship of England. Its immediate implication was that an English force should at once enter Scotland, and assist in driving the French out of Leith. Should the French ever invade England, the Scots bound themselves to lend similar assistance to Elizabeth. As has been more than once said, it was the fear of Elizabeth's advisers that the Congregation might one day make friends with their old allies of France and turn upon England. It was a point gained, therefore, when the Scots agreed to send hostages to England to remain till a year after the dissolution of the marriage of the Scottish queen and Francis II. On the part of the Scots the arrangement concluded with an affirmation of their allegiance to their natural sovereigns, in so far as they should rule in accordance with the ancient laws and liberties of Scotland.[1]

The news of the coming English army again threw Scotland into a ferment. As now appeared, fortune was no longer on the side of the Regent. Her health had long been precarious, and during the preceding autumn the rumour went more than once that she was dead. The great expedition of her brother, the Marquis D'Elbœuf, had come to nothing—his main fleet having been driven back by storms, and damaged so severely that it could not again put to sea. Nor was the French government in a position to spare any of its resources for the affairs of Scotland. The

---

[1] In a draft of the agreement among Cecil's papers, there are some words bearing on religion, which do not appear in the versions given by Knox and in Rymer's *Fœdera.*—Froude, vi. 327.

Protestants at home were showing such a menacing face that civil war might be looked for any day.[1] The Regent could thus look for no immediate assistance from France, and her only course in view of the coming English army was to entrench herself in Leith till her affairs should take a more promising turn. Before the English appeared, however, her Council resolved to strike one more blow at the Congregation. On the 7th of March a body of 2000 foot and 300 horse issued from Leith, and after encamping the first night at Linlithgow, marched the next day upon Glasgow. The Duke and the other lords made a rapid flight to Hamilton, and left the town defenceless. After working their will on Glasgow, the French returned with all speed to Linlithgow, closely followed by Arran with a troop of horse. In Linlithgow they remained above a week, laying hands on everything that might be serviceable in the siege which was before them; and on the 29th retired within the fortifications of Leith. As the English had now crossed the Border, the Regent at her special request was received into the Castle of Edinburgh with a small company, among whom were Archbishop Hamilton and the Bishops of Dunkeld and Dunblane.[2]

On their side the Protestant leaders had been doing their best to rouse the country to united action against the French. By their own admission their

[1] The Congregation were in close communication with their brother Protestants in France. Thus on the 19th of January, several weeks, therefore, before the conspiracy of Amboise, Arran and the Lord James wrote as follows to Sadler and Crofts : " We are assured by the ministers of France that the whole congregacions are secretly resolved to take the fields uppon a daye, alreadie appoynted in all parts, with assistance of a prince of the Courte, and of the bloode royall."—Sadler. i. 691.

[2] *Wodrow Misc.* i. 80, 81 ; *Diurnal of Occurrents.* pp. 56, 57.

appeals had been but partially successful. The Lords of the West had proclaimed a gathering at Glasgow on the 26th of March; but except their own immediate followers no one else appeared.[1] On the following day they made a last appeal to all patriotic Scots to meet at Prestonpans and unite with their English allies against the common enemy. In this proclamation there is no mention whatever of religion. Love of country, revenge for past injuries, the threat of greater oppression to come — these are the sole motives which are urged for the taking up of arms against the representative of their sovereign.

On the 4th of April the English and Scottish forces met at Prestonpans, the latter 10,000, the former 9000 strong. The sight was certainly a strange one—Scot and Englishman joined in common enmity and in arms side by side against France. So strange, indeed, did the alliance seem that men could hardly believe that it would come to good. It was not yet thirteen years since the battle of Pinkie and the misery that followed it, and ever since Pinkie the immemorial strife between Scot and Englishman had never ceased on the Border counties. It was difficult to realise that the hate of centuries could thus be so suddenly transformed into good fellowship by common interests and common aspirations. In this strangeness

---

1 "Copie of the Congregacion Lettre to the Lords of Scotland" (Sadler, i. 713, 714). It is curious to note how the Reformers of the sixteenth century complain of the unreasoning conservatism of the people. Thus, the Lords of the Congregation write to Crofts (6th August 1559): "Ye are not ignorant, sir, how difficil it is to persuade a multitude to the revolt of an Authoritie established." Buchanan, in his *De Jure Regni*, has the following passage to the same purport: "Reliqua est imperita multitudo, quae omnia nova miratur, plurima reprehendit, neque quicquam rectum putat, nisi quod ipsa aut facit, aut fieri videt. *Quantum enim a consuetudine majorum receditur, tantum a justo et aequo recedi putat.*"

of the situation, indeed, we must find the explanation of a fact that naturally surprises us. Alike from the testimony of the Scots, the English, and the French themselves, we gather that there was a general impression in Scotland that France was aiming at the conquest of the country. Why then, we ask, did not Scotland rise as it did at Pinkie and concentrate its forces on the invader? The only adequate explanation is that between their new friends and new enemies a large body of the nation could not make up their minds to act with decision. They could hardly persuade themselves that the English, though now apparently their best friends, had not some ulterior motive which for the time it was their interest to conceal. Suppose the French driven from the country, had they any assurance that England would not take their place? We have seen that the English government in its negotiations with the Protestant leaders had always before it the probability of a settlement between the Regent and the Congregation. On their side, we shall see that the Congregation had equal distrust of the English, and felt a lively alarm lest England should make its own peace with France and take no account of themselves. Between distrust of England and hatred of France Scotland was in a state of indecision which made impossible the unanimous action of its people.

Before they marched on Leith the Lords of the Congregation made one last appeal to the Regent to comply with their demands. In a letter addressed to her from Dalkeith on the 4th of April, they laid before her the grounds of their revolt, and the reasons which had induced them to call in the assistance of England. In this document, also, there is no reference to religion.   All they now ask of her is that she will dismiss her French soldiers, and govern the country in accordance with its ancient laws and by the advice of native counsellors.   Because she had hitherto refused to comply with these demands, they had been forced to seek help from England in driving foreigners from the country.   While they had taken this step, however, they would never cast off their allegiance to their natural sovereigns so long as they did not trample on the rights of their subjects.[1]   It could have been in no hope that the Regent would give way at the last hour that the Lords wrote this letter.   As a justification at once of their own action and of the interference of England, however, the letter was a form which it was politic not to have passed over.

On the 6th of April the two armies sat down before Leith " with such quiett and peaceable enterteinment betwixt English and Scotts that it was a wonder."[2]   On the day of their arrival a protracted skirmish took place before the walls, which ended in the French being driven back into the town with considerable loss.   Lord Grey, the English commander, soon found that he had no easy task before him. There were 4000 trained soldiers in Leith, and the wall which had just been built was a mile long.[3] Instead of 8000 men, the largest number[4] that Grey at any time commanded, 20,000 would not have been more than sufficient for the successful siege of a town

---

[1] Buchanan, pp. 322, 323.   On 24th March Elizabeth had published a proclamation explaining her motives for intervening in the affairs of Scotland.—Haynes, i. 268.   Cf. also Teulet, i. 436.

[2] *Wodrow Misc.* i. 83.

[3] *Works*, ii. 61.

[4] This is Knox's statement (*ibid*).   On 28th May the whole army, English and Scots, before Leith, was reported to be 12,466.—Haynes, i. 348.

so fortified and manned.[1] Even the forces at his disposal could not be depended on for the steady work of a protracted siege. His Scottish allies, who could not keep the field longer than twenty days at a time, contributed little to his effective strength. As they wearied of their labours, also, Grey's own troops fell off, till by the end of May there were not above 5000 before Leith.[2] Two severe checks in succession also showed that in discipline and organisation the English were inferior to the French. On the 14th of April the besieged made a sally from the town, broke through the enemies' trenches, and slew above 200 men.[3] On the 7th of May a combined assault on the town was repulsed with deadly effect, the allies leaving 800 dead and wounded in the trenches.

Since the beginning of their revolt the Lords of the Congregation had spared no labour to gain the support of England. Now that English soldiers were fighting by their side, however, their anxieties were far from being at an end. Two fears were before them from the very outset of the siege. The English might conclude a peace with France, and leave them to fight it out themselves with the Regent. On the very day of the encampment before Leith an incident happened that was fitted to raise their suspicions. At the request of the Regent, Lord Grey had sent Sir James Crofts and Sir George Howard to hold an interview with her in the Castle of Edinburgh.[4] The interview apparently led to nothing; but, as it proved, Crofts was in reality their secret enemy, and was doing all he could to injure them with the English. Their other fear was

---

[1] Cal. of State Papers (Scotland), 14th April (Maitland to Killigrew).   [2] Haynes, i. 346.
[3] *Wodrow Misc.* i. 83.   [4] *Ibid.* i. 82.

that in the prolonged uncertainty of their hopes their
party could not long resist the disintegrating forces
which, within and without, were daily working against
them.   A personage who appeared in the English
camp at the beginning of the siege gave good grounds
for their uneasiness.[1]   This was Jean de Monluc,
Bishop of Valence, who had been sent by the French
government to do all in his power to prevent Elizabeth
from giving help to the Scots.   It also lay in his mission to effect, if possible, a reconciliation between the
Regent and the Protestant Lords.[2]   Monluc had been
chosen for these ends because he had special qualifica-
tions for bringing them about.   He was a veteran
diplomatist ;[3] had been long associated with the affairs
of Scotland,[4] and, above all, was favourably disposed
to the new religion.[5]   On his arrival in the camp he
came and went between the Regent and the Protestant
leaders, apparently with the intention of effecting a
mutual understanding.[6]   In the position in which both
parties now stood such an understanding was further
off than ever.   What the Congregation feared was that
Monluc's coming and going between them and the
Castle might breed suspicion and distrust in their ranks
and break up their party before they were aware.   At
this moment there were two powerful nobles whose
adhesion they were specially anxious to secure—the
Earl of Huntly and the Earl of Morton.   These
nobles had long hesitated between the Regent and
the Congregation, and since the appearance of the
English had been sorely put to it to determine which

---

[1] Haynes, i. 279.   [2] *Ibid.* i. 274.
[3] Brantôme describes Monluc as " fin, délié, rinquant, rompu et
corrompu, autant pour son sçavoir que pour sa pratique."
[4] As early as 1546.—*Maitland Misc.* i. 40, 215.
[5] Teulet, i. 429, *note.*   [6] Buchanan, p. 323.

was likely to prove the winning side.[1]   On the whole, however, they had lately shown a disposition to take the side of the Protestant Lords against the Regent. To consolidate their ranks, therefore, and probably to bring Morton and Huntly to a point, the Lords of the Congregation took what was their invariable step,— on the 26th of April they drew up a bond of mutual action and defence against all who resisted their " godly enterpryses."

It is possible that this bond was drafted by Knox. who was then preaching in Edinburgh.[2]   If so, it could only have been wrung from him by the exigencies of the moment when it was produced. In this document the reformation of religion has a place ; but the terms in which it is put forward are so vague that a good Catholic could have no difficulty in subscribing them. The signatories bind themselves to " sett fordwart the Reformatioun of Religioun according to Goddes word, and procure be all meanis possibell that the treuth of Goddes word may haif free passage within this Realme, with ane administratioun of the sacramentis, and all thingis depending upoun the said word."[3]   In the contrast between these vague phrases and the unflinching precision of previous manifestoes, we have one more curious illustration of the friction of circumstance on the original idea.   The signatories further took oath to " effectuallie concur and joyne togidaer, taiking anefald plane pairt for expulsioun of the said strangeris, oppressouris of oure libertie furth of this Realme, and recovery of oure ancient fredomis and liberties."   The origin of the bond, however, is

---

[1] Cf. Haynes, i. 315-317.

[2] *Works*, ii. 68.—Hay Fleming, *Records of Kirk Session of St. Andrews* (Scot. Hist. Soc.) ; Records of Town Council of Edinburgh.

[3] *Works*, ii. 61.

doubtless to be found in the statement that "never one of us sall half pryvey intelligence be writting, message, or communicatioun with ony of oure saidis ennemies or adversaries in this cause, bot be the advise of the rest (at least of fyve) of the Counsale." Since the deposition of the Regent the Protestant Lords had always given themselves out as the provisional executive of the country, and in the present bond they do not forget to state that all Scotsmen who oppose their commands will be held as enemies of the State. The immediate object of the bond was certainly gained. Huntly and Morton both signed it, and their example brought others who were wavering to a similar decision.[1]

All the parties engaged in the siege of Leith were eager for a peace if it could be had on anything like tolerable terms. The Guises, occupied with the troubles that had followed the conspiracy of Amboise, needed every soldier they had, and could send no help to their sister in Scotland. Elizabeth had always been half-hearted in her support of the Congregation, and the expenditure of men and money before Leith made her less satisfied than ever that she had done right in interfering between subjects and their prince. The Protestant Lords equally desired some settlement, though their fears increased every day that any settlement proposed would not meet their demands.

The eagerness of all parties for the conclusion of hostilities was quickened by the death of the Regent in the Castle of Edinburgh at midnight on the 10th of June. Judged by the consequences of her rule, Mary of Lorraine must be regarded as one of the most important figures in the history of Scotland. More than

---

[1] *Works*, ii. 62, 63.

any other person, it will have appeared, she is responsible for the revolution that ended in the overthrow of the ancient Church, and for all the misfortunes that pursued her daughter till the last hour at Fotheringay. From the death of her husband, James V., she had pursued a policy which at different times placed her in opposition to every interest of the country which she governed. Catholic writers have given her their blessing ; but this can only be because she professed the Catholic religion, and was the opponent of Knox and the Reformation. In the interest of the house of Guise she had favoured Protestantism at the expense of the old religion till it grew to be a power in the country too strong for her to put under, when it was her policy to check it in turn. By surrounding herself with French counsellors she alienated the native nobility in such degree that, when the hour of her trial came, she could not depend upon their loyalty. In the interests of her own family she even forgot her own daughter, and bequeathed to her a legacy of troubles under which she herself had sunk, and with which Mary Stewart was the last person in the world successfully to cope. With her natural firmness, tact, and self-command we can see how different a turn events might have taken had she governed the country in her daughter's interests, and not in the interests of the family of Guise. Had she been content to remain a private person she might have maintained a balance of interests in the country which might have ensured the continuance of the old order. Had she allowed Arran to remain in the Regency she would have had the house of Hamilton at her back, and Protestantism could not have grown into the power it did throughout the country. In other countries the new religion had

been crushed by the ecclesiastical and secular powers ;
and united action in Scotland might have effected
a similar result. The Hamiltons could not have
become a real menace to her daughter, since the feeling of the country would never have permitted their
usurpation of the royal authority.   As it was, her
government brought about results which, at the
moment she assumed power, would have seemed in-
credible to the most far-seeing observer.   Within the
five years she ruled the country she converted the
national predilection for France into fear and hatred,
and the national detestation of England into forbearance and kindly feeling.   In truth, at her death the
representatives of every interest in the country had
reason to say, with Knox, that she was "unhappy . . .
to Scotland fra the fyrst day sche enterit into it unto
the day she fynischeit hir unhappy lyfe."[1]   To Knox
she was the incarnation of every principle for which
the kingdom of Antichrist existed on earth, and in
her death he saw the divine punishment of her wilful
closing of her eyes to the truth.   For her misfortunes
and long suffering from a painful disease he has no
words of relenting.   He records with triumph how, in
her last hours, she consented to receive Willock and
listen to his ministrations, and how she professed the
Protestant doctrine of salvation through the death of
Christ.[2]   Yet he does not express even a hope that
her admission might stand her in stead where she had
gone.   Like St. Columba, St. Bernard, and other
religious leaders of the same type, Knox is absolutely
incapable of pity or sympathy in the case of such as he
thought to be wilful enemies of the truth.   If religion
were the absolute thing they believed it to be, beyond

[1] *Works*, ii. 71.   [2] *Ibid.*

ST. GILES' CHURCH, EDINBURGH, FROM THE NORTH-WEST, BEFORE 1827

a doubt their very relentlessness was the highest form of piety. To show relentings towards the enemies of God was to trifle with the eternal salvation of their fellowmen.

During the late months Knox had only had to stand by and watch the results which he had been one of the chief agents in bringing about. Since England had been led to interfere in the affairs of Scotland, the latter country had been fairly swept into the mid-stream of European politics. All the great powers—Spain, France, and England—had their respective interests at stake in the issues between the Congregation and their sovereigns. During the siege of Leith, Knox was probably in Edinburgh engaged in his ordinary labours of preaching and exhorting his hearers to soundness of faith and united action.[1] Directly, he took no part in the settlement which brought the long struggle to a close, yet he had the satisfaction of seeing his party triumph even beyond his hopes. That the Congregation triumphed so completely he could with the fullest justice largely ascribe to his own indefatigable exertions of the preceding year.

On the 16th of June, six days after the death of the Regent, commissioners from England and France arrived in Scotland with powers to effect an understanding between the three contending parties. England was represented by Cecil and Dr. Wotton, Dean of Canterbury and York; France by the Bishop of Valence and Charles de la Rochefoucauld, Sieur de Randan. There were numberless difficulties in the way of an agreement, and the proceedings were more than once in danger of being broken off. Cecil was hampered by Elizabeth, whose uncertain humour

---

[1] *Works*, ii. 68.

almost drove him to despair;[1] and it was the absolute
condition on which the French commissioners agreed
to open the proceedings, that the treaty under consideration should be understood to be between England
and France.　The Congregation were subjects with
whom their sovereign would in nowise agree to treat
on equal terms.　Any settlement made with them must
be understood to be made solely at the intercession
of the Queen of England.[2]　The Lords of the Congregation, thus excluded from a direct part in the
negotiations, were in terror lest their interests should
be betrayed by the English commissioners.　In reality
they had little ground for alarm, as every concession
made in their favour was an advantage for England
over France.　Cecil and Wotton were fully aware of
this, and pressed Monluc and De Randan to the
utmost point they could go without endangering their
own separate treaty with France.　Out of the sixteen
days spent in the conference, three-fourths of the time
was devoted to the affairs of Scotland.[3]

The treaty was signed at Edinburgh on the 6th of
July.　While its conditions were in the last degree
humiliating to France,[4] England gained every point she
could reasonably have looked for when she interfered
in the affairs of Scotland.[5]　Francis and Mary were to
give up using the arms of England; and the French
troops in Scotland, which had been a standing menace
to England, were to be removed from the country.
The concessions made to the Congregation made them

---

[1] Forbes, i. 660, 661 (Cecil to Throgmorton, 22nd May).

[2] Keith, i. 294.　Keith translates the text of the Treaty from the
original Latin given by Rymer.

[3] Haynes, i. 336 (Cecil to Elizabeth).

[4] Francis II., writing to the Bishop of Limoges, speaks of the conditions as "*dures et intolérables.*"—Teulet, i. 606.

[5] Cf. Froude, vi. 399.

practically the masters of the country. A general amnesty was granted; the fortifications of Leith were to be demolished; the French troops were to be sent home;[1] and no Frenchman was thenceforth to hold any important office. During the absence of Mary the country was to be governed by a Council of twelve, of whom seven were to be chosen by the Queen and five by the Estates. A Parliament was to be summoned for the 10th of July, and all its acts were to be held as valid as if it had been summoned by the King and Queen.[2] With the burning question of religion the commissioners refused to deal; yet they must have known that the Scottish nobility, with the powers now granted to them, would not be slow to settle the question for themselves.[3]

Thus by the Treaty of Edinburgh the Congregation had gained every point for which they had originally taken up arms. In the beginning of the struggle they had put forward religion as the sole ground of their revolt against the Regent; but they discovered that Protestantism was not so great a force in the country as they had supposed. Moreover, they found that if they were to justify their proceedings to the world, and above all to gain the support of England, they must plead another cause for open rebellion. Nevertheless the fact remains that it was out of religion that the struggle arose, and that it was the zeal and policy of Knox and the Lords of the Congregation which were mainly instrumental in carrying it to a successful issue.

---

[1] With the exception of the garrisons of Dunbar and Inchkeith.

[2] Keith, i. 300. The Parliament was to be adjourned from the 10th July till the 1st August.

[3] Elizabeth, with her notions on Church government, could not be expected to approve the setting up of the Calvinistic order in Scotland.

CHAPTER IV

ON the 15th of July the French forces sailed from Leith, and on the same day those of England began their march towards the border.[1] Four days later the Congregation held a solemn thanksgiving in the Church of St. Giles, in which the leading part was assigned to Knox. In view of the great events in the near future the preachers had assembled in full force, and were eagerly pressing on the Protestant Lords the necessity of an immediate religious settlement. As in all his pulpit deliverances, Knox seized the opportunity of pointing out the course which, as a nation of true worshippers, they were bound to follow. The security of the late victory, he knew, depended on the continued friendship of England, and, saving always the purity of religion, that friendship must be maintained at all costs. The sermon he preached has not been recorded, but his prayer of thanksgiving at its close suggested the future programme of the Protestant party. One sentence from this prayer illustrates his manner of combining devotion and practical politics. "And seing that nathing is mair odiouse in thy presence, O Lord, than is ungratitud and violatioun

[1] *Diurnal of Occurrents*, pp. 60, 61.

of ane aith and convenant maid in thy name; and seing that thou hes maid our confederatis of Ingland the instrumentis by quhom we are now sett at this libertie, to quhom we in thy name have promeisit mutuall fayth agane; lett us never fall to that unkyndnes, O Lord, that ather we declair oure selfis unthankfull unto thame, or prophanaris of thy holy name."[1]

In response to the urgency of the preachers one step was immediately taken in furtherance of the new religion. By a committee composed of Commissioners of Burghs, and of certain of the barons and nobility, the leading Protestant ministers were assigned special spheres of labour in different parts of the country. Doubtless in view of the services which he was the fittest man to render, Knox was restored to his former charge in the Church of St. Giles.[2] At no previous period of his career, indeed, was Knox called to mightier efforts than during the first part of his ministry in Edinburgh. In accordance with the Treaty of Edinburgh, Parliament met on the 1st of August, though its members were not in full attendance till the 8th of that month.[3] During its early meetings Knox preached to crowded audiences on the prophecy of Haggai regarding the rebuilding of the temple. "The doctrin," he tells us, "was proper for the tyme; in applicatioun quhairof he was so speciall and so vehement, that sum (having greater respect to the warld than to Goddis glory), feilling thair selffis prickit, said in mockage, 'We mon now forget our selffis, and beir the barrow to buyld the housses of God.'"[4]

[1] *Works*, ii. 84-86.　　　　　　[2] *Ibid.* p. 87.
[3] *Diurnal of Occurrents*, p. 61.
[4] *Works*, ii. 88, 89. Calderwood, doubtless with justice, ascribes the flout to Maitland.—*Hist. of the Kirk of Scotland*, ii. 12.

The efforts of Knox and his fellow - preachers, however, were not in vain, as the question of religion took precedence of all others in the new Parliament. Among the first days of its meeting there was laid before it a " Supplicatioun," signed by barons, gentlemen, burgesses, and others, in which the Estates were called upon to deal summarily with the old religion and its representatives.   On the ground of false doctrine, dishonoured sacraments, the impiety of the papal claims, the clergy are to be " decernit unworthy of honour, authoritie, charge, or cure within the Kyrk of God, and sa from hencefurth never to joy vote in Parliament."[1]   From the constitution of the new Parliament there could be little doubt as to how its vote would go.   As was to be expected from the special circumstances in which it met, its numbers were far beyond the average attendance on ordinary occasions.[2]   The nobles had not appeared in such force for many a day.[3]   An unusual element, also, was the numerous body of smaller barons or lairds, whom their zeal for the reformed religion had induced to quit their homes, and be at the charges of a few weeks in the capital.   So strange was the appearance of these lairds in the assembly that a discussion actually arose as to their right to sit as national representatives,[4] and it had to be pointed out to the house that their right went so far back as the reign of James I.[5]   A

---

[1] *Works*, ii. 92.

[2] In the instructions given to the Lord St. John, who was sent by the Estates to Mary, it is stated that there were present " the Duke and thirteen earls, the Archbishop of St. Andrews and five bishops, nineteen lords, twenty ecclesiastics, as well abbots as priors, the commissioners of twenty-two burghs, a hundred and ten barons, and many others."—Teulet, i. 614.

[3] Randolph to Cecil, 15th August 1560.

[4] *Ibid.* 19th August 1560.   [5] In 1427.

more formidable objection was raised as to the legality of the present meeting of the Estates. Could a Parliament be called a legal assembly, for which the sovereign had issued no writs, and at which she neither was present in her own person nor was represented by any commissioner? This was a natural objection to be raised by the minority, who looked with dread to the impending legislation; but the objection was a legal quibble, by which a revolutionary assembly was not likely to be turned aside from its deliberate purpose. In accordance with the Treaty of Edinburgh a Parliament had duly met on the 1st of August. The treaty had been signed on the 6th of July, and since that date there had been time for a royal commissioner to arrive in Scotland.[1] But by the very fixing of the meeting of the Estates at so early a date it had been implied that no commissioner was needed to constitute the meeting a legal assembly. It may be regarded, therefore, as a curious proof of their regard for forms of law that the overwhelming Protestant majority gave a full week to the discussion of this trivial objection of their opponents.

These preliminaries over, the Estates proceeded to consider the petition regarding religion. It was decided that the representatives of the new faith should

---

[1] There has been much discussion as to the legality of this meeting of the Scottish Estates; but, as we have seen, the question is set at rest by certain letters of Francis II. himself (Teulet, i. 606, 607; De Ruble, *La Jeunesse de Marie Stuart*, pp. 312, 313). From these letters it distinctly appears that Francis regarded the Treaty of Edinburgh as perfectly valid, though he felt keenly its hard conditions. But if the Treaty of Edinburgh was valid, its terms necessarily imply the legality of the Parliament of August. We shall see that at a later date Francis raised another objection to that legality. The details of the various negotiations that led up to the Treaty of Edinburgh are fully discussed by Dr. Ernst Bekker in his *Beiträge zur englischen Geschichte im Zeitalter Elizabeths* (Giessen, 1887).

draw up a statement of their own doctrines, which might enlighten Parliament in its dealings with all matters of ecclesiastical policy. The task was one of easy execution for Knox and his colleagues. The mysteries of their faith were the subjects of their daily talk and meditation, and the drafting of creeds was a familiar occupation of the Protestant theologians of the sixteenth century. Only a year before, one other confession had been added to the already abounding symbols of Protestantism. In May 1559 the Huguenot ministers had met in Paris, and in the space of three days had embodied their creed and discipline in a series of eighty articles.[1] In four days the Scottish ministers completed their task, in which, as we may believe, Knox had a principal part.[2] In accordance with the rules of Parliamentary business, the new Confession came first before the Lords of the Articles, who, after hearing the opinion of Knox and Willock on the one side, and of certain bishops on the other, transmitted it to the assembled Estates.[3] There it might have been expected that the supporters of the old order would have made a stand worthy of their cause and the greatness of the occasion. The adoption of the new creed meant the setting up of another religion and the overthrow of a Church which for centuries had been an organic part of the national life, yet in this crisis of its fate not one champion was forthcoming to grace its fall with a protest, which, though unavailing, would have reminded men of the

---

[1] Théodore de Bèze, *Histoire Ecclésiastique des Églises Réformées au Royaume de France*, i. 109-121 (Lille, 1841).

[2] The ministers charged to prepare the Book of Discipline were Knox, Wynram, Spottiswoode, Willock, Douglas, and Row (*Works*, ii. 128). It is probable that the same persons drafted the Confession of Faith.   [3] Randolph to Cecil, 15th August.

heinousness of the act to which they were about to lay their hands.[1] Article by article the Confession was read before the House, and the vote successively taken.[2] As it was expected that certain of the churchmen might raise difficulties regarding the doctrines of the Confession, preachers were present throughout the proceedings to meet the arguments of their opponents. But the presence of the preachers was hardly necessary. The Bishops of St. Andrews, Dunkeld, and Dunblane raised a protesting voice, but with so little heart in what they said that they seemed to give away the cause of which they were the natural defenders. Amid enthusiasm, which in the case of many of those present was beyond question the legitimate joy at the triumph of a good cause, the Confession was ratified and approved by an overwhelming majority of the Estates. In the minority only five lay peers and three bishops are mentioned as having lodged their dissent.[3] " I never heard," wrote Randolph to Cecil; "I never

[1] In a letter to Bishop Keith, Father Innes has the following sentence regarding the conduct of the Catholic bishops on this occasion. "As for most of the other Bishops, what could be expected from men that, by anything that yet appear'd, made not so much as a protestatioun for their religion and calling in the pretended Parliament of 1560?"—Quoted by Joseph Robertson, *Stat. Scot. Eccles.* i. xii. *note.*

[2] The reading and the voting took place on different days.—*Works*, ii. 121.

[3] Knox specially names the Earl of Atholl, and the Lords Somerville and Borthwick (ii. 121); and Randolph, the Earls of Cassillis and Caithness, the Archbishop of St. Andrews, and the Bishops of Dunkeld and Dunblane (Randolph to Cecil, 19th August 1560). In the *Hamilton Papers* (ii. 748) there is an interesting statement regarding the relative strength of parties in 1560. It is in the form of a list of the most influential persons, (1) who favoured the Congregation, (2) who stood neutral, and (3) who were faithful to the Crown. In another list the various districts of the country are similarly assorted according to their religious and political sympathies. In several points, however, these lists conflict with what we know from trustworthy authorities.

heard matters of so great import, neither sooner despatched nor with better will agreed to."[1]

But the passing of the new Confession was only preliminary to the real work of revolution. A week later the fabric of the Church itself was the matter in question. Three Acts, all passed in one day, did the work of destruction as completely as such work could be done by mere legislation. By the first of these Acts the jurisdiction of the Pope was abolished; by the second, all doctrine and practice contrary to the new creed was condemned; and by the third, the celebration of mass was forbidden within the bounds of Scotland. The penalties attached to the contra-vention of these Acts gave portentous proof that the legislators were in all earnest in their work. To say or hear mass was for the first offence to incur con-fiscation; for the second, exile; for the third, death.[2]

The work of Knox's life seemed thus to be accom-plished, but none knew better than he the uncertain foundation on which it rested. The future of the reformed religion was, for good or ill, inextricably bound up with the Councils of England and France. So long as the Scottish Queen was under the dominion of the family of Guise, hostility secret or open was always to be reckoned with on the part of the latter country. With France, therefore, Knox was in constant communication. Through persons connected with the French Court, and through the ministers of the Huguenot churches, he received regular informa-tion regarding affairs in France, which he duly com-municated to the Protestant Lords. It was through Knox that they first learned the death of Henry II.,

[1] Randolph to Cecil, 19th August 1560.
[2] *Act. Parl. Scot.* vol. ii. 24th August 1560.

and, as we shall presently see, it was through Knox that they were first made aware of a still more important event.[1]

With France in the meantime the Scottish Estates had one piece of business to transact which could only lead to renewed misunderstanding and recrimination. By a clause in the Treaty of Edinburgh "some persons of quality "[2] were to be despatched to France for the ratification of whatever Acts might be passed in the Scottish Parliament. In their dealings with this clause the Protestant leaders showed either how little importance they attached to it or how little they expected from obeying it. On the 24th of August the Parliament designated Sir James Sandilands, Lord St. John, as the person to submit its doings to Mary and Francis;[3] yet he did not set out on his journey till the 23rd of September.[4] Whatever representatives might have been sent, it is difficult to think that the two sovereigns could have set their hand to the revolutionary measures of this Parliament. But by sending only the Lord St. John the Scottish Estates both touched the pride of their sovereigns, and gave them an excuse for refusing to ratify the measures submitted to them.[5] After being kept hanging about the French Court for more than two months, St. John

---

[1] *Works*, ii. 137, 138.　　　　[2] Keith, i. 306.

[3] *Act. Parl. Scot.*

[4] *Diurnal of Occurrents*, p. 62.

[5] From the instructions given to Sandilands it would appear that the Estates had the intention of sending certain nobles as deputies at a later date (Teulet, *Instructions données à Monsieur de Saint-Jehan par les Trois Estats du royaume d'Escoce*, i. 615). There was, indeed, excellent reason for not sending deputies of high rank to France. There was not a Catholic or Protestant noble in Scotland whose conduct during the preceding two years had given satisfaction to Francis and Mary. According to Buchanan, St. John was chosen because he had stood aloof during the late months.

returned, as had been fully expected, with his object unaccomplished. "But that," says Knox, "we litill regarded, or yit do regarde; for all that we did was rather to schaw our debtfull obedience, than to bege of thame any strenth to our Religioun, whiche from God hes full powar, and neideth nott the suffrage of man, but in so far as man hath neid to beleve it, yf that ever he shall have participatioun of the lyfe everlasting."[1]

Very different from this cool attitude towards France were the eager approaches made to England. As has already been mentioned, the marriage of Elizabeth and the Earl of Arran had been mooted in the autumn of the preceding year. To Cecil and Throgmorton,[2] as well as to the Lords of the Congregation, it had seemed that this union was in the best interest of both countries. So pressing did the Estates consider the matter, that at an early meeting they appointed an embassy to carry their desires to the English Court. The alliance, it would seem, not only commended itself to the Protestant leaders and the family of the Hamiltons, but also to the most influential of the Catholic clergy. The order for the commission was signed by the Archbishop of St. Andrews, who might see his own family interests served in the union; but it was also signed by other churchmen, and notably by the bishops of Dunkeld and Dunblane.[3] As a check to future encroachments of France, indeed, it may have seemed to these bishops that the alliance was one which a patriotic Scotsman could cordially approve. Into this project, however, no one threw himself more heartily than

---

[1] *Works*, ii. 126.
[2] Throgmorton openly advocated the marriage, and Cecil secretly approved it.—Cf. Froude, chap. xxxix.   [3] Keith, ii. 7-8.

Knox. He had maintained from the beginning that England and Scotland must stand side by side if the truth was to prevail in either of the two countries; and in the proposed marriage he saw the surest pledge that things would turn out as he prayed. Of Arran, moreover, he had formed hopes which were not to be realised. At this time, he writes, the Earl "was in no small estimatioun with us";[1] and, as several circumstances prove, Knox was his closest counsellor both in spiritual and temporal matters. But though the Estates did all in their power to effect the desired union, the result did not meet their wishes. The Commission, consisting of the Earls of Morton and Glencairn, and Maitland of Lethington, accompanied by a train of fifty-four horsemen, set out on the 11th and 12th of October,[2] and were graciously received at the English Court. They did not return till the 3rd of January in the following year;[3] but the result of their mission was not long in being divined. Elizabeth expressed her gratitude for the good will of the Scottish Estates, heartily echoed their desires for the continued friendship of the two countries, but did not find herself "presently disposed to marry."[4]

During the closing months of 1560, Knox bore his full burden of all that was doing in politics and religion. One of the duties laid on the ministers by the late Parliament was "to draw in a volume the Polecy and Disciplyn of the Kirk, as weill as thei had done the Doctrin."[5] The task was one of far greater

---

[1] *Works*, ii. 130.

[2] *Diurnal of Occurrents*, pp. 62, 63. [3] *Ibid.* p. 63.

[4] Keith, ii. 9-11, where Elizabeth's reply to the Scottish Estates is given in full.

[5] *Works*, ii. 128. As we shall see, the same commission had been given at an earlier date.—*Ibid.* ii. 182.

difficulty than the drawing up of a Confession of Faith. To draft an adequate scheme of church government, as it was conceived in the sixteenth century, was in itself a formidable undertaking. But, as the reception of the book proved, there were other difficulties inherent in the task, which demanded all the boldness and tact that lay in Knox and his brother ministers. As the document was to be submitted to the next meeting of the Estates, therefore, it doubtless engrossed the thoughts of Knox and his friends in the interval. Another task had been assigned exclusively to Knox :[1] this was to produce a narrative of the doings of the Congregation from which the world might judge what had been the real character of all their endeavours. In his *History of the Reformation in Scotland*, into which his narrative eventually grew, Knox justified the choice of his fellow-confessors by a work which is the literary monument of the revolution which it commemorates. Begun in the autumn of the previous year,[2] it was now one of the labours of Knox's life to see that it was accomplished in a manner worthy of its theme.

During the period of which we are speaking public cares and private sorrow brought a full reaction to Knox after the triumph of the Parliament of August. The refusal of Elizabeth to consider the Arran marriage woke both fear and indignation in the Protestant party in Scotland.[3] England, they found, had gained all she wished by the Treaty of Edinburgh, and, considering the costs of her late interference in Scottish affairs, was not likely to renew them in the event of fresh efforts on the part of France. In their refusal to ratify the

---

[1] Randolph to Cecil, 23rd September 1560.
[2] *Works*, vi. 87.　　　　[3] Randolph to Cecil, *passim*.

late treaty, Francis and Mary showed that they were only waiting their opportunity to recover their lost ground in Scotland ; and their friends were busy sowing disunion among the Scottish nobles, certain of whom were giving serious alarm by their evident leaning to France. Lord Ruthven was only half-hearted in the cause of the new religion, and the great Earl of Huntly was kept in check only by a coalition of powerful barons specially formed against himself.[1] The rumour went also that the following spring would see a French army in Scotland which would finally crush the national independence. "The certane knowledge of all these thingis," writes Knox, "come to our caris, whairat many were effrayed. The principall conforte," he adds, "remaned with the preachouris";[2] and among these preachers, as we know from the letters of Randolph, none was more fervent than Knox himself.

To Knox's public anxieties was now added a private loss which in his advanced years was the heaviest that could have befallen him. His wife, Marjorie Bowes, died leaving him with two young children, with only his mother-in-law to fill her place. Since her return to Scotland we have seen that she had been an invaluable helpmate in all his labours. From the terms in which he always refers to her we gather that their union had been one of cordial respect and affection. Their mutual regard must have lain in that attraction of opposite types which is the most solid basis of permanent understanding in all family relations. The charm and sweetness of her character, to which the austere Calvin himself bears testimony,[3] was pre-

---

[1] Randolph to Cecil, 7th and 23rd September.
[2] *Works*, ii. 132.
[3] Calvin speaks of her as *suavissima*. In a letter to Knox he also

cisely the force which would insensibly sway the stormy
temper and imperious will of her husband.   Knox has
but one brief reference to his bereavement ; but we
may believe that the passing of that gentle presence
from his home made his step the heavier during the
years that were still before him.

An event of the first importance, not only for
Scotland but for Christendom, roused Knox in the
depths of his private sorrow.   On the 5th of December Francis II., the husband of Mary Stewart, died
suddenly at Orleans.   Through his correspondents
in France, Knox was the first to hear the welcome
news, and made haste to communicate it to the Protestant chiefs.   Proceeding to the Kirk of Field to
the residence of the Duke of Châtelherault, he found
him closeted with the Lord James, both being as yet
ignorant of the momentous intelligence.   Each in his
own way, these three individuals were the most important persons then within the bounds of Scotland ;
and on their action depended, in great measure, many
of the issues opened up by the death of the French
King.   As was to be expected from their different
characters and interests, they did not see eye to eye on
the questions they discussed.   According to Knox they
reasoned "in diverse purposes ; and he upoun the
one hand conforting thame, and thei upoun the other
parte conforting him (for he was in no small heaviness
be reassone of the late death of his dear bedfellow,
Marjorie Bowes.")[1]

From his knowledge of affairs in France, Knox
was fully aware of the deliverance that had been

writes : "Uxorem nactus eras cui non reperiuntur passim similes."
Both of the letters in which these expressions occur are given by Laing
in the sixth volume of Knox's *Works*, pp. 123, etc.

[1] *Works*, ii. 138.

wrought by the death of the French King. The
Guises, he knew, must now cease to control the
counsels of France. Whatever policy Mary should
mark out for herself, therefore, she would no longer
have behind her the armies of France directed by that
family. Nevertheless, it was of the first importance
that the young Queen should be won over to the cause
that had triumphed in the Treaty of Edinburgh and in
the late Parliament. As a means to this end, Knox
entered into a scheme which, in the light of subsequent
events, is an odd enough passage in his history. On
the Earl of Arran, as has been said, Knox had come
to centre the hopes of the Protestant party. He had
looked to the Earl's marriage with Elizabeth as the
salvation of all the interests he had at heart. That
prospect having miscarried, it now seemed to him that
a union between Arran and Mary might lead to equally
favourable issues. At this time, as Knox is careful to
inform us in speaking of Mary, men suspected not her
nature ;[1] and he probably thought that a girl of eighteen
would offer no formidable obstacle to fitting counsellors.
Arran himself was apparently better pleased with the
prospect of this union than the other, and lost no time
in taking steps to bring it to a point. Before the
French King was a month dead, he secretly despatched
to Mary a letter and a ring with overtures she could
not misunderstand. The whole scheme, as it appears,
did not commend itself to the other Protestant leaders,
since Knox alone was privy to it.[2] But Mary had
conceived a future far different from that which Knox
had imagined for her. By the date when Arran's
message reached her, it was already a possibility in
European politics that she should sit on a prouder

[1] *Works*, ii. 142.   [2] Randolph to Cecil, 3rd January 1561.

throne than that from which she had been forced to descend.[1] Mary, therefore, could have no hesitation regarding the proposals of Arran, and her reply was such that "he maid no further persuyte in that mater."[2] As the Earl's confidant in this second miscarriage of his matrimonial enterprises, Knox further puts it on record that "he bare it heavelie in harte, and more heavelie than many wold have wissed."[3]

Mary's decisive rejection of Arran must have warned Knox that she had definite notions of her own regarding her future. Should she choose to identify herself with the Catholic party in Scotland, her return would be an ominous contingency with which the Protestants would do well to reckon. The old religion had still a numerous and powerful following to which the presence of the Queen would communicate fresh strength and spirit. Another far-sighted observer besides Knox was satisfied that the death of Francis was not so complete a deliverance as their party imagined. In the councils of the Protestant leaders Maitland reminded them that their present position was far from being assured, and that the dangers they had so lately left behind might any day again stare them in the face.[4] From the pulpit Knox spoke to the same effect, and strove to rouse his hearers from their false security.[5] Knox, indeed, had even less reason than Maitland to be satisfied with the existing outlook. In the Parliament of August the triumph of the Reformed faith had been more seeming than real. The Confession embodying the new creed had been

---

[1] Immediately after the death of Francis, the marriage of Mary and Don Carlos, the son of Philip II., was a possibility that exercised all the leading personages in Europe.

[2] *Works*, ii. 137.   [3] *Ibid.*

[4] Randolph to Cecil, 6th February 1561.   [5] *Ibid.*

enthusiastically adopted; but the new church had not been legally organised, nor had such provision been made for its ministers as would ensure its permanent existence as a living spiritual body in the country. To effect this end the ministers had been charged to draft the Book of Discipline, in which they were to suggest "a good and godly policy" to be submitted to the next meeting of the Estates. That meeting was now fast approaching; but Knox had good reason to fear the reception the Book would meet from many who were ostensibly members of his own communion. It had already been privately examined by many of the nobles, who were naturally interested in a document which bore equally on their spiritual and temporal well-being. As expressed in private, their opinions had been various and conflicting. "Some approved it," says Knox, "and willed the samyn have bene sett furth be a law. Otheris, perceaving thair carnall libertie and worldlie commoditie somewhat to be impaired thairby grudged, insomuche that the name of the Book of Discipline became odious unto thame. Everie thing that re-pugned to their corrupt affectionis was termed in thair mockage, 'devote imaginationis.'"[1] When such was the opinion of the Book among persons in authority, Knox and his fellow-ministers could not but look forward with anxiety to an assembly in which such important issues were to be determined.

The new Convention met in Edinburgh on the 15th January 1561. There is no complete record of its proceedings; but in the eyes of contemporaries as well as of posterity its most important business was its dealings with the Book of Discipline.[2] Before this assembly the Book "was perused newlie oure agane, for some

---

[1] *Works*, ii. 128.   [2] Cf. *Diurnal of Occurrents*, p. 63.

pretended ignorance be reassone thei had not heard it."[1] As at the Parliament of the preceding August there was again a crowded attendance of the nobility,[2] certain of whom looked with little favour either on the doctrine or the scheme of Church policy recommended for their adoption. The discussion on the Book was long and vehement,[3] and in the end no collective decision was reached. In witness of their own conviction, however, a large number of the nobles and barons subscribed the document as being "goode and conforme to Goddis word in all poyntis."[4] One condition only they attached to their subscription. The clergy of the old Church, who had embraced the new religion, were to retain their benefices provided they maintained Protestant ministers in their respective districts.[5] With this unsatisfactory conclusion to all his aspirations, Knox had in the meantime to be content. From the pulpit he thundered at the rapacity and shortsightedness of hollow professors; but even after his varied experience of life he was still to learn new lessons of the inability of the mass of men to rise to the height of a great cause.

With greater satisfaction than in recording the fate of the Book of Discipline, Knox relates another incident of the same Convention. By order of the Protestant Lords, representatives of the ancient Church appeared to defend its discredited doctrine and practice. Of the champions put forward the names of only two are recorded: Alexander Anderson, Principal of King's College, Aberdeen, and John Leslie, subsequently Bishop of Ross.[6] On the other side, Willock, Good-

---

[1] *Works*, ii. 138.
[2] *Ibid.* p. 129.
[3] *Diurnal of Occurrents*, p. 63.
[4] *Works*, ii. 129, 130.
[5] *Ibid.*
[6] *Ibid.* pp. 138, 139; Leslie, p. 293.

man, and Knox stood forth as the challengers. The
conditions of the discussion show how far things had
gone since Knox's arrival in Scotland in the summer
of 1559. It was now the representatives of the old
religion who were put upon their defence. With the
new creed they were told they had nothing to do: of
its absolute truth, as tested by the line and rule of
Scripture, their judges were convinced beyond the
questionings of men.[1] By Knox's account the overthrow of the champions of Rome was complete.
Anderson having been disposed of, Leslie was ordered
to his rescue, but with no better fortune. By an un-
lucky reply, he fastened on himself a nickname by
which he continued to be known among his opponents.[2]
But the interesting fact regarding this discussion is that
it should have taken place at all. By the acts of the
last Parliament the severest penalties had been pronounced against all who in public or private took any
part in the worship of Rome. Yet six months after
these acts became law the doctrines of that Church
were formally debated in the very assembly that had
passed them. In accordance with their own enactments the Protestant Lords should have taken summary
proceedings against Anderson and Leslie; yet all they
now did was to place them under ward in Edinburgh,
and to debar them from preaching in all time coming.[3]

In spite of every discouragement, Knox and those
who stood by his side toiled at their task of regenerat-
ing the nation. "The Communion was ministered here

---

[1] *Works,* ii. 139.

[2] *Ibid.* p. 141. Leslie, as may be imagined, gives a very different
account of the discussion; but the story about the nickname shows that
Knox's report is not very far from the truth.

[3] Leslie, p. 293. As we shall see, Leslie could not have been kept
very long in ward. On the 14th of April he left Scotland for France on
an important mission.

on Sunday last," wrote Randolph to Cecil on the 5th of March, " I assure your honour with great decency and very good order. There were none admitted but such as made open protestation of their belief, examined and admitted by the ministers and deacons to the number of xiii. and odd."[1] On the Sunday following the one referred to by Randolph, another solemnity took place in St. Giles's, which showed the determination of the ministers to take possession of the country. Before the meeting of the Estates in the preceding year, five leading preachers had been chosen to exercise superintendence over the religious condition of special districts. It would seem, however, that the nomination had remained a dead letter.[2] At all events, on Sunday the 9th of March 1561, Knox officiated at the setting apart of one of their number, John Spottiswoode, father of the well-known Archbishop of St. Andrews ; and in other towns the same ceremony was performed in the case of the different nominees.[3]

Meanwhile, the future turn of affairs in Scotland grew every day more uncertain. From Knox's History we learn in what vague apprehension he lived during the months immediately preceding the Queen's return. On the 18th of February deputies had come from Mary with instructions to the Estates.[4] The chief point in their message made it clear to Knox and his party that Mary had plans which, sooner or later, must conflict with their own. She urged the Estates to give proof of their loyalty by renewing that ancient league

---

[1] Randolph to Cecil, 5th March 1561.

[2] At a meeting of the Reformed Church on the 20th December 1560, there was a nomination of ministers and commissioners.—Peterkin, *The Booke of the Universall Kirk of Scotland*, pp. 1-3.

[3] *Works*, ii. 141 *et seq.* Randolph to Cecil, 5th March 1561.

[4] *Diurnal of Occurrents*, p. 64.

with France which had been the source of such good
to both countries in the past.[1] Besides this ominous
message, the deputies bore about three hundred letters
to various persons in the country, which could not but
work mischief to the existing settlement. A few
weeks after Mary's deputies, an ambassador arrived
from Catharine de' Medici with recommendations to
the same purport—pressing on the Estates the renewal of old friendship.[2] Thus far, at least, Mary and
Catharine, now at the head of affairs in France, were
at one—that English influence should not direct the
counsels of Scotland. Catharine might not be willing
to sacrifice so much as the Guises to effect this end ;
but to a certain point, Mary could reckon on her
mother-in-law's support in making her mistress in her
own kingdom. "Whenever she [Mary] comes," wrote
Randolph, "I believe here will be a mad world ;"[3]
and his opinion was shared by observers of every shade
of opinion.

The certainty that Mary was on their side gave
fresh heart to the supporters of the old order. At
Stirling the bishops met in council to consider what
steps it became them to adopt in the promising turn
which affairs were now taking.[4] In concert with them
were now bound to common action the Earls Huntly,
Atholl, Crawford, Marischal, Sutherland, and Caithness.[5]
In the same ranks was now found the Earl of Bothwell,
who had lately come from France " to work also what
mischief he can, or at least so far as his credit will extend."[6] So threatening a front did the Catholic party

---

[1] Labanoff, i. 80 *et seq.*
[2] *Ibid.* i. 86.
[3] Randolph to Cecil, 26th February.
[4] *Works*, ii. 156.   [5] Leslie, p. 294.
[6] Randolph to Cecil, 26th February.

now present that they were credited with the intention
of seizing the capital before the meeting of Estates appointed for May.[1]   The situation was, in truth, more
serious than Knox and his friends imagined.   We now
know, what was unknown to them, that the Earls
above named had sent proposals to Mary, which, if
carried to a successful issue, might have changed the
destinies of Scotland.   On the 14th of April, John
Leslie, the unhappy disputant of whom we have just
heard, presented himself before Mary with the suggestion from these lords that she should land at some
northern part of Scotland, where they would meet her
with 20,000 men.   For reasons which were doubtless
well weighed, Mary rejected the suggestion, expressing
at the same time her satisfaction with the loyalty of
those who made it.[2]

At this time also, Knox had to regret the absence
of the strongest man on the Protestant side—the Lord
James Stewart.   By the order of the late Convention
he had been sent to Mary with the object of disposing
her in favour of those he represented.   He bore no
special commission ;[3] but from his own correspondence
we know the tenor of his message.[4]   It was expedient,
both in her own interest and that of her kingdom, that
she should return to Scotland at the earliest opportunity.   Further, if she was to govern her country in
peace she must be guided by two counsels.   She must
leave religion as she found it, and she must take as her
advisers the nobles who were then at the head of

---

[1] *Works*, ii. 156.
[2] Leslie, *De Rebus Gestis Scotorum.*
[3] Labanoff (Mary to Throgmorton, 22nd April 1561), ii. 94.
[4] James Stewart to Mary, 10th June 1561.   This interesting and
important letter was first published by M. Philippson.—*Histoire du
Règne de Marie Stuart*, iii. Appendix A.

affairs.[1]   Mary had seen the agent of the Catholic
nobility only the day before, and had been warned by
him against anything the Lord James might say.   But
Mary or her advisers saw that in her own interests the
course recommended by her brother was the only one
it was prudent to follow.   Doubtless, each saw that in
reality there was the width of heaven between their
views as to the future of their country.   Meanwhile,
however, they parted with the mutual conviction that
for the time they must walk the same path together.
On Mary's return to Scotland we shall find that for
a season she actually followed the counsels of her
brother.[2]

[1] *Ibid.*; Leslie, p. 577.

[2] As far as this point in his career, two charges are brought against
the Lord James Stewart.   The one is, that in all his action during the
Revolution he was secretly aiming at the throne.   As has been said, it
was natural that this report should be spread by Mary of Lorraine.   Of
its inherent probability the reader may judge from the account of
Scottish affairs given in the text.   The second charge is, that in his
mission to France, he acted dishonourably by his sister.   The truth is
that, if such terms are to be used, it is to the conduct of Mary rather
than to that of her brother that they are applicable.   Throughout his whole
mission, he never concealed from Mary that he was a convinced Protestant, that he preferred the English to the French alliance, and that, if
she returned to Scotland, she must be guided by Protestant counsellors
and leave religion as she found it.   The proof of this is found (1) in his
own letter to Mary already referred to; (2) in a letter of Throgmorton to
Elizabeth (31st May 1561); and lastly, in the account of his mission
given by Leslie, who had anticipated him in his visit to Mary in France
(*De Reb. Gest. Scot.* p. 577).   Both going and coming, also, the Lord
James publicly visited the French Court, as well as the English
ambassador, Throgmorton, in Paris.   On the strength of a passage in
a letter of Throgmorton to Elizabeth (29th April), it has been said that
his second visit to that ambassador was made unknown to Mary.   So
far was this from being the case that he himself tells Mary that he had
paid the visit (Philippson, iii. 438).   On the other hand, the conduct of
Mary was characterised by no such frank admission of her real intentions; though *dishonour* is too strong a term for what was a diplomatic
necessity.   M. Philippson, who does his best to put Mary in a good light,
thus describes her action on the occasion of which we are speaking : "La
jeune veuve reçut son frère avec les démonstrations d'une vive affection.

Towards the end of May Knox found an opportunity of emphasising the case in which the Protestants
now stood. In the closing days of that month the
Convention of the Estates and the Assembly of the
Reformed Church[1] met simultaneously in Edinburgh.
The crowded attendance of the different sections of
the Estates showed that they were awake to the crisis
through which they were passing. Numerous bands
of the supporters of the old order had flocked to the
town, and carried it like men confident that their hour
of triumph was at hand. Only by the prudent conduct
of the Protestants, Knox tells us, was an actual trial of
strength prevented.[2]

Certain important matters had for some time been
waiting the decision of the Estates. The ambassador
of Catharine de' Medici had been in Scotland since
the 11th of March, and had not yet received an answer.
The answer now given proved that the men who had
carried through the late revolution were as resolute as
ever to see the end of their work. De Noailles was
told that they had no intention of making any league
with France which would compromise their relations
with England. As for their dealing with the clergy
and the property of the Church, they had taken these
steps with due deliberation, and were fully resolved to
abide by them.[3]

En effet ses conseillers français, l'évêque D'Amiens, MM. D'Oysel, De
Martigues et De la Brosse, qui tous connaissaient parfaitement l'Écosse
pour y avoir séjourné et travaillé, lui donnaient l'avis unanime de ne
pas exaspérer le parti protestant, de beaucoup le plus influent pour le
moment, mais de le flatter jusqu'au jour où elle serait assez forte pour
prendre l'offensive," i. 293.
  [1] This is known as the Second General Assembly.—*The Booke of
the Universall Kirk*, p. 5.   [2] *Works*, ii. 161.
  [3] *Works*, ii. 166, 167. In condensing the replies given to De
Noailles, Knox has doubtless accentuated their point ; but their purport
could not have been materially different from what he reports.

Besides the affair of the French ambassador, the Estates had also before them certain demands on the part of the ministers, in which the hand of Knox is unmistakably present. Assembling in the Tolbooth, the representatives of the Reformed Church drew up seven articles to be laid before the Estates. The burden of these articles was, that free course should be given to the preaching of the Gospel; that fitting provision should be made for the maintenance of its ministers; that the mass should be abolished, and those who took any part in its celebration punished according to the late Acts of Parliament. The articles were accompanied by a "Supplicatioun," which is almost certainly the work of Knox. The danger that now threatened the Protestant cause had roused all his energies, and in this utterance he even surpasses himself in the vigour of his denunciation and the audacity of his appeals. One sentence gives the point of the whole address. " Honestie cravis and con-science movis us to mak the verray secreittis of oure hertis patent to youre Honouris in that behalf, quhilk is this, ' That befoir that ever thai tyrantis and dumb doggis impyre abufe us, and abufe suche as God hes subjected unto us, that we Barronis and Gentilmen professing Christ Jesus within this Realme ar fullie determined to hasard lyffe and quhatsoever we haif received of our God in temporall thingis.'" [1] The manner in which the Lords of the Articles received these petitions proved that there had been no cooling of their zeal. They ratified all the seven articles; and one of them they put into immediate and vigorous execution. The Earl of Arran, accompanied by Argyle and Glencairn, set out for the west on an iconoclastic

[1] *Works,* ii. 162, 163.

tour, in which they burnt a large part of the Abbey of
Paisley, and wrecked those of Failford, Kilwinning, and
Crossraguel.   On a similar expedition, Maitland and
the Lord James, who had just returned from France,
"maid sick reformatioun as nathing contentit the Erle
of Huntlie."[1]

While Knox was thus exercised regarding the
general prospects of his religion, his special function
as minister in Edinburgh brought him vexations which
were sufficient of themselves to disturb his peace of
mind.   In Edinburgh the mass of the inhabitants
were not in sympathy with the late changes in religion.
The new code of discipline so rigidly enforced by the
new spiritual guides could not but be irksome to men
who had been brought up under the easy rule of the
ancient Church.   More than once the ministers were
made to see that their yoke was borne with impatience.
One of the laws passed at the instance of the preachers
was that adulterers should be "carted" through the
town, and afterwards banished.   In November 1560,
a flagrant breach of this law necessitated the infliction
of its penalty ; but while the delinquent was being led
through the streets, a mob rushed to his rescue, broke
up the cart in which he was being led, and carried him
off in triumph.[2]

In July 1561 a still more formidable riot showed
the mind of the populace.   In 1555, under the Regency

---

[1] *Works*, ii. 167, 168.   In a letter to Cecil, Maitland thus refers to
the expedition in which he had been engaged with the Lord James.
" I have been these forty days in the North of Scotland with my Lord
James, where we have not been altogether unoccupied, but so far forth
as occasion would serve, advancing the religion and the common cause."
When a man like Maitland could write thus, it is clear proof that the
iconoclasts of the sixteenth century were not necessarily the fanatics
they are sometimes called.   These words of Maitland might pass for
Knox's own.—Keith, iii.   [2] *Works*, ii. 155.

of Mary of Lorraine, an Act of Parliament had been passed forbidding the games of Robin Hood, as leading to undue licence and disorder. But the people could not be restrained from some attempts at their ancient pastime. For his share in such an attempt in May of 1561 a certain John Gillon was imprisoned, tried, and condemned to death. There must have been few important events in the life of the town with which, directly or indirectly, Knox had not something to do, and in the present affair he played his own part. As one whose word must go far in such a case, Knox was waited on by a deputation of craftsmen, and besought to use his influence to have the execution of Gillon delayed. Knox, it would appear, had more than once been induced to interfere in behalf of breakers of the law; but on this occasion he was not to be moved. If the execution was not stayed, he was told, " bayth he and the Baillies suld repent it." This was not a remark likely to move Knox from a resolution, and he proudly replied that " he wald not hurt his conscience for ony feir of man." Knox and the magistrates being alike obdurate, the mob took the matter into their own hands and, forcing their way into the Tolbooth, carried off Gillon and several other prisoners who were awaiting their punishment.[1]

Thus, with an uncertain hold on the mass of the people, with a powerful body among the nobles and with the hierarchy of the ancient Church arrayed against them, the Protestants had good grounds for alarm as to what the next few months might bring forth. The one matter that now engrossed all men's minds was the imminent return of Mary to her native country. The Protestant leaders were themselves divided in

---

[1] *Works*, ii. 157-160 ; *Diurnal of Occurrents*, pp. 65, 66.

opinion regarding the probable effects of the Queen's presence.[1] Maitland was, on the whole, disposed to think that it was better she should remain where she was. " I assure you," he wrote to Cecil, "this whole realm is in a miserable case. If the Queen, our Sovereign, come shortly home, the dangers be evident and many; and yet if she shall not come, it is not without great peril."[2] On the other hand, it was the opinion of the Lord James that Mary's return was a pressing necessity in the interests of the public peace.[3] He well knew that, left to herself, she would with all speed undo the whole work of the Congregation during the past twelve months. This was proved by the fact that in spite of all Elizabeth's representations she had steadfastly refused to ratify the Treaty of Edinburgh. But the Protestants were now the strongest party in

[1] Randolph wrote to Cecil (9th August) that "some of them care not tho' they never saw her face."—Robertson, *History of Scotland*, iii. 287 (1812).

[2] Maitland had personal grounds for not desiring Mary's return. As having deliberately deserted her mother, Mary of Lorraine, at a critical juncture, he had special reasons for dreading Mary's vengeance. His letters during the months previous to her return clearly show his apprehension.

[3] The evidence regarding the attitude of the Protestant party on the question of Mary's return is somewhat conflicting. With reference to the Lord James, a letter of Throgmorton to Cecil (26th July) quoted by Tytler, would seem to indicate that he had changed his mind as to the desirability of Mary's return. Camden also (*Annales Rerum Anglicarum*, pp. 67, 111, edit. 1615) states that the Lord James on his return from France advised Elizabeth to have Mary seized in the course of her voyage home. Against the testimony of Camden, who gives no authority for his statement, we must put the fact that in his interview with Throgmorton in Paris after he left Mary, her brother strongly counselled her return (Throgmorton to Cecil, 26th July). Further, as late as the 6th of August, only eight days before Mary sailed, he wrote to Elizabeth recommending that she should publicly recognise the Scottish Queen as her successor, and thus heal the breach between them (Lord James Stewart to Queen Elizabeth, 6th Aug. 1561 ; Froude, vi. 502). Such advice was surely inconsistent with any traitorous intention on the part of the man who gave it.

the country, and in spite of herself Mary would be driven to act according to their interests. Willing or unwilling, should Mary thus identify herself with the Congregation, it must strengthen the position of her brother and those who acted in concert with him.

Between Mary and Knox there was already war before they had seen each other's face. It had come to Knox's ears that Mary had urged certain learned men in different countries to prepare a reply to his " Monstruous Blast," and, further, that she had sought "to inflame the heart" of the Queen of England against himself. The subject was a delicate one on which to approach Elizabeth ; but he had an argument at hand which he used with some dexterity. The Scottish Queen, he told Elizabeth, could not be so eager against the book from any fear of harm to herself or the English nation. There must be another reason for Mary's anxiety regarding its evil tendency. Knox does not specify what this reason might be ; but Elizabeth could not have misread the hint. Among her adversaries in Scotland Mary knew that she would have none more formidable than Knox. If Elizabeth could be persuaded to have him removed or silenced, this would be an advantage for Mary on which she might well congratulate herself. But the removal of Knox would be a blow to English interests in Scotland which, with all her dislike to Knox, Elizabeth would think twice before she inflicted. It was this dilemma that Knox placed before Elizabeth, and he knew enough of her to be persuaded that she would not hesitate in the choice of alternatives.[1]

Thus, even before she set foot in Scotland, Knox was left in no doubt as to how Mary regarded him.

[1] *Works*, vi. 126, 127.

Yet he could hardly have realised that in this girl of
nineteen he was to find one who by instinct and
upbringing was the incarnate antithesis of all that he
thought and felt most deeply regarding God and man ;
to whom that work of reformation, which for him was
the victory of God's will on earth, was the work of
rebels and heretics, with whom as an anointed sovereign
and a daughter of the Church she was bound to keep
no terms.　In what this work of Knox essentially consisted, it is now time to consider.

CHAPTER V

As we are now aware, a nation stamps the religion it embraces with its own specific character and tendency. The Catholicism of Spain is in spirit as essentially different from the Catholicism of France as the religion of Calvin from that of Luther or the Church of England. Out of the many developments of Protestantism during the sixteenth century Scotland made deliberate choice of the system of Calvin as its national religion. It was once thought a sufficient explanation of this choice that John Knox, the strongest spirit among the Scottish Reformers, had lived in Geneva, and, having imbibed the doctrines of Calvinism, transplanted them to his native country. We now see that the causes of revolutions lie deeper than such an explanation even suggests.

By the middle of the sixteenth century Scotland had come to a full consciousness of itself:[1] a sufficient body of educated men now existed to create a national character with collective aims and aspirations. In the breaking up of mediævalism and the beginnings of the new era, Scotland, like other countries, had to choose

---

[1] According to Michelet, France attained this self-consciousness in her contact with the Italy of the Renaissance towards the end of the fifteenth and the beginning of the sixteenth century. In the case of Scotland this stage was reached in the conflict of the old and the new religions towards the middle of the sixteenth.

the path along which her development should lie.   As we have seen, in politics she rejected the alliance of France, and threw in her lot with England.   On the other hand, in religion she followed from the beginning such different courses from England that it was apparent to every observer that on this subject the peoples north and south of the Tweed could never reach a common understanding.[1]   In this decisive choice of a national ideal we can see only the action of moral and intellectual affinities which were the outcome of the special history of the Scottish people.   In this fact, indeed, lies the essential distinction between the pre - Reformation and post - Reformation Church of Scotland.   Of the Columban or the Roman religion it cannot be said that it was national in the sense that it grew out of the heart and mind of the people.   Imported into the country when the nation was incapable of conscious choice, the Roman faith remained to the end a mere superstructure imposed from without, with no special traits to mark it off from the other churches of Christendom.   Had the ancient Church conquered in the religious struggle of the sixteenth century, she must have risen to a new life as distinctive as that of the Church that triumphed.   As it was, she proved unable to survive the convulsion out of which the Scottish character and genius came forth with those peculiar features which have since become plain to all the world.

That Scotland chose Calvinism as its national

---

[1] "I have talked of late with them all," writes Randolph to Cecil, "to search their opinions how a uniformity in religion might be had in both the Realms. They seem willing that so it were ; many commodities are alleged that might ensue herof. Howbeit I find them so severe in that they profess, and so loth to remit anything of that they have received that I see little hope hereof."—Randolph to Cecil, 24th August 1560.

faith, therefore, was due to far deeper causes than the idiosyncrasies or the personal history of Knox. Between Calvinism and the Scottish genius as it now defined itself, there was a natural affinity which the subsequent religious history of Scotland has sufficiently demonstrated. Knox and his brother-ministers—the barons, gentry, and citizens who responded to their teaching—only expressed what we now see to have been the essential tendencies of the national thought and feeling. In choosing Calvinism in preference to any other form of Protestantism Scotland showed what religion it instinctively took to its heart; but it is in the peculiar character it gave to Calvinism, in the temper with which it embraced it, that we see the religious instincts of the Scottish people in their fullest working. It will presently appear how much the Scottish Reformers owed to Calvin ; but it will no less appear that, in borrowing as they did, they added, and rejected, and modified in a degree and fashion that gives to their work a character entirely its own.

Equally as a theology and a religion Scotland adopted the new faith with a fervour which could have come only of natural propensities finding their scope and gratification. In the theology of the Calvinistic system the Scottish intellect found scope for that abstract dialectic which has always been its natural function. The history of Scottish thought since the Reformation leaves us in no doubt that the intellectual side of Calvinism had a natural attraction for Scotsmen beyond that of any other theological system. It is in abstract thinking in the domain of theology and philosophy that Scotsmen have expended their main intellectual endeavour during the last three centuries ; and in this abiding mental habit we have the best proof that Calvinistic theology did not find a home in Scotland through any mere fortuitous conjunction of circumstance. On the side of dogma the Scottish reformation was the assimilation of beliefs and of methods of thought which met the highest needs of the national mind.[1]

It was the dominating thought of Knox and his associates that "the reverent face of the primitive and apostolick churche should be reduced agane to the eyes and knowledge of men." Yet in much of the creed they adopted, in many of the reasonings with which they supported it, they were as essentially mediæval as the Church of Rome itself. They rejected certain dogmas of Rome, and put forth others of their own; but they still moved in the same order of ideas and applied precisely the same intellectual methods as did the scholastic theologians of the Middle Age. In Knox's handling of Scripture, as has been more than once said, we have precisely the same methods as those of the schoolmen in their interminable commentaries on Aristotle. By the ingenious combination of texts, divorced from their natural and historical meaning, he arrived at a system of dogma which to a large extent would have been unrecognisable by any writer either in the Old or in the New Testament. In the metaphysical theology of *Paradise Lost* and the *Divine Comedy* we have a signal illustration of this essential identity of the Protestant and mediæval theology. Widely as they differed in particular beliefs, Milton, the poet of Puritanism, and Dante, the poet of the mediæval Church and Empire, were sundered by no

---

[1] It is worth noting that in the subsequent centuries Geneva was not so faithful to Calvin as Scotland to Knox and his brother-reformers. In Geneva, Calvinism was imposed on the citizens largely through the influence of Calvin and the foreigners whom he was the means of introducing into the town. In Scotland Calvinism was an organic development.

gulf in their modes of thought and feeling on the subjects that had the profoundest interest for both.[1]

In his mental attitude no less than his modes of thought, Knox was in reality in the same plane as his old master, the schoolman John Major. When Knox had extracted his theological system from the Bible, and held it in his hand embodied in an elaborate confession of faith, his labour as a thinking agent was at an end. To add to this compendium or take from it was alike an impiety which deserved due penalties in this world, and would certainly ensure them in the next.[2] By these paper-popes, as confessions were sarcastically called, the Protestants were thus as rigidly bound to the same mental attitude as the schoolman who had to regulate his thinking by the decisions of popes and councils.

But if Knox was as fast bound by authority and metaphysics as any scholastic theologian, there was a force behind his thinking of which the typical school-man knew nothing. Along with the theology of Calvin, the Scottish reformers adopted the religion which that theology necessarily implied. But this religion incul-cated a view of life and an ordering of conduct which the Roman Church had long since abandoned as an impos-sible ideal outside the cloister. In the view of primitive Christianity there was but one thing of essential import-ance to men both as regards this world and the next —the relation in which they stood to God and His Son. All other interests were but so many distractions that diverted men's minds from the master concern. But as

---

[1] Compare, for example, Beatrice's discourse in *Paradiso*, Canto VII. with *Paradise Lost*, Book iii. lines 80 *et seq.*

[2] In the exordium to the Confession of Faith, its authors invite criticism ; but in such terms that the concession is merely a form of speech.

the Christian Church grew, it had to make terms with
the world. The essentially Christian view of life was
relegated to monasteries, and ordinary men and women
were permitted to blend secular interests with their
religion to an extent that grew with the greatness of
the Church and its successive heads. By the sixteenth
century it may be said that as regards rule of life the
Church of Rome had departed as far from the Church
of Jerusalem as any institution can possibly depart
from its original ideal. Between Leo X. the head of
Christendom, and St. James, the head of the Church at
Jerusalem, the distance is so great that all the intervening centuries are needed to satisfy us of the historic
relation of the one to the other.

It was this contrast between the Church of the
Apostles and that in which they had been brought up
that explains at once Knox's prophetic zeal and the
success of his mission. The dogmas he accepted no
more than the dogmas of Rome really expressed the
mind of the primitive Church. By mere abstractions,
moreover, the hearts of the majority of his hearers
could not have been quickened into revolt against the
traditions of centuries. On the other hand, the contrast between the religion of the apostles and the
religion of Rome appealed to elementary instincts
which breed the inevitable conviction of enthusiasts
and reformers. The simplest of Knox's hearers could
understand that in the Church of Rome, as they saw it,
with its gorgeous furnishings and worldly officials,
there was little resemblance to the original Christian
Society.

As the Calvinistic theology appealed to the argu-
mentative and speculative turn of the Scottish genius,
so the Calvinistic religion with its rigid definition of

human interests and activities commended itself as the true ideal of the Christian life on earth. By the physical character of their country, by their very struggle to wring from it the common necessaries of life, the Scottish people, when they deliberately chose a religion for themselves, naturally chose one whose worship and whose code of duty were in harmony with the hard realities and the limited scope of their daily life. To an Italian ecclesiastic, nursed in luxury and half a pagan at heart, the Galilean scheme of life was as impossible as the pastoral life he described in his neo-Latin verse. To men with the upbringing and instincts of Knox, on the other hand, the life of the first Christians was no impossible ideal which it was irrational to seek after at the stage to which the world had now come.

In this sense that they had recovered the lost ideal of their religion the Scottish Reformers found the motive power by which they were enabled to renew the spiritual life of their countrymen. The very austerity of the new Gospel was the convincing argument of its truth for a people to whom the pride of life and the contradictions of existence were equally unknown. The Catholic Church itself had never been without a succession of great teachers who viewed with horror the gulf that separated the religion of their contemporaries from that of the first Teacher. St. Bernard's view of the Christian life was as narrow and absolute as that of Knox or Calvin: of the vanity of gorgeous temples and mere accessories to worship Knox himself did not speak with more emphatic contempt.[1] If Savonarola could have realised his aims, he

---

[1] Cf. Cotter Morison, *The Life and Times of St. Bernard*, pp. 147 *et seq.* As an interesting comment on the attitude of St. Bernard

would have bound the society of Florence to as simple a scheme of living as the Scottish Reformers succeeded in imposing in Edinburgh. But what was practical in Scotland and Geneva was in Italy a chimerical enterprise which could only issue in the melodrama in which Savonarola was the central figure. To reproduce primitive Christianity in the Italy of Lorenzo de' Medici and Cardinal Bembo,[1] would have been to reverse the miracle of changing water into wine. Nevertheless, it remains true that in religion as distinct from theology there had always been in the Church of Rome, and these among the noblest of her servants, men who ardently desired a return to the simple ideals of the original gospel. With Knox and Calvin these men were perfectly at one in setting down as blind folly every interest of life that did not directly bear on the one concern of working out their salvation with fear and trembling.

It has been constantly affirmed that Knox and his brother Reformers went to the Old Testament rather than the New for the spirit and burden of their teaching. The resemblance between Knox and the ancient Hebrew prophet is sufficiently obvious; but Knox himself would have vehemently denied that there was any essential difference between the spirit of the two volumes. On two articles of belief, he would have maintained that he was borne out by Christ and St. Paul not less than by Isaiah and Jeremiah. It is the root of the Galilean as of the Pauline Gospel that there

to "the pride of life," Morison quotes the following sentence from Ruskin (*Stones of Venice*, ii. 103): "I never met with a Christian whose heart was thoroughly set upon the world to come, and, so far as human judgment could pronounce, perfect and right before God, who cared about art at all."

[1] Bembo dissuaded Cardinal Sadoleto from reading the epistles of St. Paul on the ground that they would corrupt his style.

is a gulf fixed both for this world and the next between saved and unsaved. But it was this conviction that was the motive-force of all Knox's speech and action, and that explains his absolute attitude in all his dealings with his fellows. In giving effect to this conviction he had no need to confine himself to the Old Testament for unsparing denunciation of all whom he deemed the enemies of God. Luther used language towards his opponents as violent as that of Knox, and he justi-fied himself by quoting the example of Christ in his rebukes to the Scribes and Pharisees.[1] On another article of faith, we have seen, the teaching of Knox was as true to the New Testament as to the Old. With Jesus and St. Paul he taught that it was frivolous distraction to occupy the mind with matters which, however innocent in themselves, are in their essence only mundane and temporary.

In the document we are about to examine, there-fore, there is a veritable reproduction of that view of human life and destiny which was announced equally by Christ and the Prophets. So far was the attempt from being novel, that zealous spirits throughout all the centuries of mediæval Christianity had never lost sight of it ; and had in their turn striven to restore it. In Scotland, by a peculiar combination of persons, and times, and circumstances, it was found possible, after fifteen centuries, to codify and give effect to this ideal of a divine republic. In a measure far beyond the people who originally conceived it Scotland adopted this ideal and wrought it into the national life.

---

[1] For Knox, as for Calvin and Luther, it should be remembered, Jesus was not the emasculated figure of certain types of Christianity, but as much "a son of thunder" as any of the ancient prophets.

CHAPTER VI

THE new theology and religion were embodied in the
Confession of Faith and the Book of Discipline—both
drawn up, as we have seen, at the express command
of the Estates that met in August 1560. As these
two documents may be regarded as in some sort the
definitive record of all Knox's labours, they can hardly
be passed over in a detailed account of his life and
work. Had Knox never returned from Geneva, the
Confession of Faith and the Book of Discipline would
doubtless have made their appearance at the time and
under the circumstances they did; yet it is beyond
question that, more than any other single person, he
left his individual stamp on both of these documents.

Of the Confession it is unnecessary to speak at
length. To all intents and purposes it is a mere
compendium of Calvinistic theology in the fully de-
veloped form it had assumed in Calvin's later days.
Like every Church that had broken from Rome, the
Scottish Protestants had taken the earliest opportunity
of defining their position in a symbol of their faith.
Such symbols rose out of the necessity in which the
Reformers found themselves. They at once con-
solidated the faithful, excluded unbelievers, and were
a manifesto to the world, in which calumnies were

answered, and the truth declared to all who were prepared to receive it. The adversaries of Reform added that each Confession was but another paper-pope, to the letter of which each sectary gave and exacted more unquestioning submission than any Catholic to the decrees of councils and popes. Though completed in the short space of four days, the Scottish Confession of 1560 has always been regarded as an admirable summary of the faith it embodies. Till the Westminster Confession of 1647 was accepted as the common standard of English and Scottish Presbyterianism, it remained the foundation of the Church of Scotland; and even after that date, it was still this Confession of Knox and his colleagues to which the Church looked as the purest expression of its mind and heart.[1]

But the Book of Discipline was far more distinctively the product of the Scottish Reformation. The conditions out of which it sprang were peculiar to Scotland among the countries which embraced Reform. Among the various states of Germany which left Rome for Luther we have no parallel to the position of the Reformers in Scotland. As a member of the Empire, no German state formed an individual nation like Scotland with the right to

[1] According to Edward Irving, this first Confession of Scottish Reform "was the banner of the Church in all her wrestlings and conflicts; the Westminster Confession, but as the camp colours which she hath used during her days of peace—the one for battle, the other for fair appearance and good order" (*Collected Writings*, i. 602, Lond. 1864). It is interesting to compare the respective chapters on the power of the Civil Magistrate in the first Scottish Confession and in that of Calvin (1537). In the latter the rights of the Church are much more emphatically pressed. The difference of statement was due to the fact that the Scottish Reformers were working in harmony with the leading nobles, while Calvin had not yet attained his mastery in civil affairs.

follow its own destinies wherever they might lead. The church orders devised by the different Protestant States have many points in common with the Book of Discipline ; but those who drafted them had no call and had no power to frame a scheme which implied an independent national life in the people for which it was prepared. In Geneva Calvin wrought under circumstances widely different from those in which Knox did his kindred work. While Calvin had to legislate for a town of some 12,000 inhabitants and a few adjoining villages, Knox and his colleagues had to adjust the new Church to the needs of a Kingdom. In the intricate relations of ministers and magistracy Geneva had a further peculiarity to which there was no close analogy in Scotland. Only after a struggle of fourteen years did Calvin attain the power which the Scottish Reformed Church possessed from the beginning—that of refusing the sacraments to unworthy members. In England a document with the character, aim, and scope of the Book of Discipline had never been a possibility at any period of the religious revolution. On his breach with Rome Henry VIII. dictated the creed and church order which the nation was to adopt. The *Reformatio Legum Ecclesiasticarum*, prepared by Cranmer and others in the reign of Edward VI., is the English analogue to the Book of Discipline ; but it bears on its face the difference of its character and origin. The English document is much the lengthier of the two ; but its authors had no such comprehensive ends before them as constitute the interest of the Scottish Book. One essential difference between the two documents, however, reveals the gulf that separated the English from the Scottish Reformers. While the authors of the Book of Discipline merely invoke the State to give validity to a work which has already the sanction of Heaven, the English book is delivered to the nation as the simple fiat of the royal will.[1] In the religious settlement under Elizabeth the clergy had as little influence as under that of Henry VIII.; and this fact alone was sufficient to preclude a common religious basis between England and Scotland. A year before the Scottish Confession and Book of Discipline appeared, the Protestants of France drew up their creed and church order. But they did so under circumstances far different from those of their fellow-believers in Scotland. While the Scottish Protestants were the virtual masters of the situation, the Huguenots, in the words of one of their own historians, had "no protection but Heaven, and no asylum but caves and deserts."[2]

Produced under special circumstances, therefore, the Book of Discipline has a character and scope that distinguish it from every contemporary document of the same kind. On the 29th April 1560, the ministers had received instructions from the Protestant Lords to draw up a scheme for the reformation of religion,[3] and the injunction was renewed by the Parliament of the following August. By the 25th of that month the Book seems to have been completed,[4] though during the following months it may have undergone con-

---

[1] Quapropter omnes homines ad quos imperium nostrum ulla ratione pertinet Christianam religionem suscipere et profiteri volumus et jubemus.—*Reformatio Legum Ecclesiasticarum*, p. 1 (Lond. 1640).

[2] I. D'Huisseau, *La Discipline des Églises Reformées*, p. 6 (Charenton, 1667). [3] *Works*, ii. 183, 184.

[4] "Their booke of comen reformation is nowe in translatynge into Latyne, and shalbe sent unto Calvine, Viret, Beza, in Geneva, to Mr. Martyr, Bullinger, and others in Zurich."—Randolph to Cecil, 25th August 1560.

siderable modification. Yet even as we now have it, the Book bears traces of haste, and of its various authorship. Terms are introduced before they are defined ; there is much needless repetition ; and subjects are separated which logically fall under identical heads. But these defects of composition do not touch the unity and main drift of the Book, which is emphatically an organic whole—the product at once of clearly defined aims and of enthusiastic feeling.

As the preface to the Book bears, it was composed at the express command of the Great Council of Scotland.[1] Its authors also address the Lords in a tone of due respect and humility. But while they thus profess to wait on the sanction of the state for their work, we cannot misunderstand their real feeling as to the relation of Church and State. We have seen what importance Knox attached to Mary's ratification of the religious changes made by the Estates in 1560. Religion, he says, " neideth nott the suffrage of man, but in so far as man hath neid to beleve it."[2] In the epilogue to the Book its authors finish in a strain which proves how far they were from regarding themselves as suppliants waiting on the will of nobles and princes. " Yf obedientlie," they say, " ye hear God now calling, we doubt not but he shall hear you in your greatest necessitie. But yf, following youre awin corrupt judgmentis, ye contempt [*sic*] his voice and vocatioun, we ar assured that your formare iniquitie and present ingratitude, shall togither crave just punishment frome God, who can not long delay to execute his most just judgmentis, when after many offenses and long blyndness, grace and mercy offered is contemptuouslie refused."[3]

<hr>

[1] *Works*, ii. 183, 184.

[2] *Ibid.* p. 126.   [3] *Ibid.* pp. 256, 257.

As will presently be seen, the authors of the Book of Discipline drew freely on the church orders of the different Protestant churches.[1] To two of these churches, however, they owed so special a debt that it deserves to be emphasised. It is impossible to read the *Ordonnances* of the Church of Geneva between 1537 and 1554 without the conviction that they form the main source from which the Scottish Reformers took their model and inspiration.[2] After Geneva, the formulary of the German Church, founded in London in 1550, undoubtedly contributed most materially to the Scottish book. With the chief minister of that Church, the Polish nobleman, John à Lasco, Knox must have been acquainted during his five years' sojourn in England. On the death of Edward VI., à Lasco, with the other foreign Protestants settled in England, had to seek a new asylum on the Continent. Like Knox, also, he had for a time made his stay in Frankfort-on-the-Main ; and it was there that in 1555 he drew up the elaborate formulary of the Church to which he ministered.[3] In all probability the work of à Lasco fell into Knox's hands during his residence in Geneva ; and its general drift and character must have met his ardent approval. Thoroughly Calvinistic in spirit, à Lasco's book enters

---

[1] Cf. *passim* vol. ii. of " Die evangelischen Kirchenordnungen des sechszehnten Jahrhunderts—Urkunden und Regesten zur Geschichte des Rechts und der Verfassung der evangelischen Kirche in Deutschland, herausgegeben von Dr. Aemilius Ludwig Richter (1846)."

[2] These *Ordonnances* are all given in vol. x. part i. of Calvin's Works in the *Corpus Reformatorum*.

[3] " Forma ac ratio tota ecclesiastici Ministerii, in peregrinorum, potissimum vero Germanorum Ecclesia : instituta Londini in Anglia, per Pientissimum Principem Angliae etc. Regem Eduardum, ejus nomini sextū ; Anno post Christum natum 1550. Addito ad calcem libelli Privilegio suae Majestatis.—Autore Joanne à Lasco Poloniae Barone."— It is printed in the edition of à Lasco's Works published at Amsterdam in 1866.

into details of church order and government, which have no place in the Genevan ordinances—for the simple reason that there was no need to consider them. In what follows it may be sufficient to indicate casually the extent to which Calvin and à Lasco contributed to the framework of the Scottish book.

The Book of Discipline fills seventy-five large octavo pages—the various matters of which it treats being classed under nine heads. The opening sentence unflinchingly announces the revolutionary character of its proposals. All doctrine contrary to the evangel must be suppressed as " damnabill to manis salvatioun." In spite of the modest disclaimer in their Confession of Faith, this was, in truth, but to say in other words that the new Book was to be unconditionally received by every Scotsman at the peril of soul and substance. In keeping with this significant announcement the authors logically give the first place to a statement of what they considered the true doctrine to be. The true doctrine, they say, is what is contained in the Old and New Testaments ; and the false, what is contrary to either of them. The test of all true doctrine being thus laid down, the Sacraments are next considered as being essential concomitants of an evangelical Church. In the opinion of all the Protestant Reformers, Luther as well as Calvin, the corruption of the Church of Rome was in nothing more heinous than in its teaching and practice with regard to the sacraments. As in every Protestant Order, therefore, this head is treated with special fulness and precision. It is taken for granted that only two sacraments, Baptism and the Lord's Supper, have any warrant in Scripture. In the administration of each there were special evils to be avoided, which had been notoriously illustrated in the practice of Rome. Baptism had come to be regarded as a magical rite indispensable to salvation. To preclude this delusion, children were to be baptized in church, and after a discourse explaining the nature of the ordinance. In the case of the Lord's Supper there were two attendant evils which it was the duty of the Church to avert by all the means in its power: the one was the "superstitioun of tymes," and the other the danger to true religion of unworthy communicants. To obviate the first the ordinance was to be celebrated only four times a year,[1] feast-days of the Roman Church being specially avoided. As to the right of the Church to exclude from the table, the authors of the Book take it for granted; and the subsequent history of Scottish Presbyterianism proves how vigorously they used it. Following these positive ordinances on doctrine and the sacraments, comes a negative head on Idolatry. Truth and falsehood, it is argued, cannot co-exist; and if the new Church is to have its foundation sure, every home of the ancient superstition must be cleared from their midst.

The spiritual foundation of the Church being thus laid, the remaining six heads propound the means whereby it shall best take body and substance. To

---

[1] It is interesting to note Calvin's earlier opinions regarding the fitting times for celebrating the Lord's Supper. In 1536 he wrote "Qu'il serait bien à désirer que la Cène de Jésus Christ se distribuât au moins tous les dimanches, car elle a été instituée pour que nous y soyons faits participants du corps et du sang de Jésus, de sa mort, de sa vie, de son esprit et de tous ses biens. Mais ce fréquent usage de la Cène, reçu dans l'ancienne Eglise, a été aboli par l'abomination des messes, où il a été établi qu'un seul communierait pour tous." And he proposes that the sacrament should be celebrated once a month in each of the three Genevan churches.—Albert Rilliet, Théophile Dufour, *Le Catéchisme français de Calvin*, pp. xxiii.-xxiv. (Geneva, 1878). In the *Book of Common Order* (1564), it is stated that the Lord's Supper "commonly is used once a month."—Knox, *Works*, vi. 324.

this end an efficient ministry is the first and indispensable condition. The fourth head, therefore, deals with the " election, examination, and admission " of ministers. While in Geneva the right of election lay with the ministers,[1] in the Book of Discipline, as in à Lasco's order,[2] it is emphatically stated that this right lay with the congregation. In another important circumstance election in Scotland differed both from the rule of Calvin and à Lasco. In the ordinances of Geneva and of à Lasco it is expressly stated that the election of the minister must be supplemented by an oath to the magistrate,—in Geneva to the Council, in England to the king.[3] It indicates the high ground taken by the Scottish Reformers that no such oath is even suggested in the Book of Discipline. For the rules regarding the "examination" of those nominated by the congregation, à Lasco and not Calvin supplied the model.[4] In the ceremony of " admission " we have another divergence from the practice of other Churches which marks the independent action of the Scottish Reformers. " Other ceremonie," they say, " then the publict approbatioun of the peple and declaratioun of the cheiff minister that the persone thair presented is appoynted to serve that Kirk, we can nott approve ; for albeit the Apostillis used the impositioun of handis, yet seing the mirakle is ceassed, the using of the ceremonie we juge is nott necessarie."[5]

---

[1] Calvin, *Opera*, vol. x. part i. p. 17.

[2] À Lasco, *Opera*, ii. 65-67.

[3] Calvin, *Opera*, vol. x. part i. p. 18 ; à Lasco, *Opera*, ii. 65-67.

[4] À Lasco, *Opera*, ii. 69 *et seq.*

[5] *Works*, ii. 193. À Lasco approved the laying on of hands.—*Opera*, ii. 72. Though the Scottish Reformers took so much from à Lasco, in this matter they followed Calvin.—Calvin, *Opera*, vol. x. part i. p. 18.

It was one thing to lay down these high standards for an efficient ministry ; but where were the persons of the requisite gifts and graces to be found ?   " We are not ignorant," they say, " that the raritie of godlie and learned men sall seme to some a just reassone quhy that so strait and scharpe examinatioun suld not be takin universallie." [1]   To remedy this defect a recommendation is given which reveals the vast function they claimed for the Church. Your Honours, the Lords are told, " with consent of the Kirk, are bound by your authoritie to compell suche men as have giftis and graces able to edifie the Kirk of God, that thai bestow thame quhair greittest necessitie salbe knawin ; for no man may be permitit to leve idill, or as thame self list, but must be appointed to travell quhair your Wisdomes and the Kirk sall think expedient." [2]

Meanwhile, to supply the lack of ministers a class of men was created whose duties were defined with careful precision. These were to be known as *Readers*, and their chief function was to read the Common Prayers [3] and Scriptures in such churches as were not supplied with ministers. [4] Not till they were admitted to the ministry, however, were these readers either to preach or to administer the sacraments. Like their prototypes, the *docteurs* in Geneva, the readers might also be entrusted with the duty of instructing the young in the elements of religion. Subsequently these readers gave frequent trouble by usurping the functions of ministers ; but it is evident that as a class

[1] *Works*, ii. 194.   [2] *Ibid.* p. 195.
[3] See above, i. 327, note 1.
[4] The idea of these *readers* was doubtless taken from the *docteurs* in Geneva. In the primitive Christian Church the *anagnostes* or *lector* performed duties analogous to those assigned to the *readers*.

they were well fitted to do excellent service to the new Church.[1]

Under the fifth head the authors had to deal with a subject which engaged neither Calvin nor à Lasco,—an adequate provision for all who had claims on the Church. Though afterwards so miserably deceived, they take for granted that the entire inheritance of the ancient Church is to be at their disposal. As far as was practicable, every separate congregation was to be self-supporting. With regard to the ministers provision was to be made "not onlie for thair awin sustentatioun during thair lyiffes, but also for thair wiffis and childrene eftir thame."[2] Readers were to be remunerated at a rate proportioned to the inferiority of their office. To each Church, also, is assigned the support of the poor within its own bounds ; and in this connection we have another proof of the extended sphere of action assumed by the Church of the Reformation. A sentence like the following suggests the Statute-book rather than a document expressly dealing with ecclesiastical order : " All must not be suffered to beg that gladlie so wald do ; neather yit most beggaris remane whare thei chuse ; but the stout and strong beggar must be compelled to wirk, and everie persoun that may nocht wirk, must be compelled to repair to the place whare he or scho was born (unles of long continuance thai have remaned in one place), and thair reassonable provisioun must be maid for thair sustentatioun, as the Churche shall appoint."[3]

Besides the ministers, the readers, and the poor,

---

[1] In the Second Book of Discipline it is affirmed that the office of reader " is no ordinary office within the Kirk of God."

[2] *Works*, ii. 197.   [3] *Ibid.* p. 201.

there was still another class for whom the Church must make temporary provision. The great problem before Knox and his associates was to meet the spiritual needs of the people with the inadequate means at their disposal. Ministers in sufficient numbers were not forthcoming ; and the readers, being privileged neither to preach nor to administer the sacraments, could not satisfactorily supply their place. In their strait the authors of the Book of Discipline took a suggestion, not from Geneva,[1] but from the Protestant Churches of Germany, and from that of the Foreigners in London. In Germany an important function had been assigned to a class of persons known as *Superattendenten* or *Superinten-denten*,[2] and the name and function had been adopted by the Church under the charge of à Lasco. In adopting this office the Scottish Reformers assigned it a character and function suitable at once to their own views and their special circumstances. Both in Germany and by the Church in London the superintendent is recognised as a permanent official with a definite charge over the affairs of the churches within a district assigned to him. In Scotland the office was

---

[1] The circumstances of the Church in Geneva did not necessitate superintendents. The nearest approach to the office was that of the *visitors*, regarding whom we have the following direction in an ordinance of 1546. " Premierement, affin de conserver bonne union de doctrine en tout le corps de lesglise de Geneve, cest a dire tant en la ville aux parroiches dependantes de la seigneurie, Que le magistrat elise deux des seigneurs de leur conseil et semblablement les ministres en elisent deux de leur congregation qui ayent la charge daller une foys lan visiter chascune parroiche pour senquerir si le ministre du lieu auroit point mys en avant quelque doctrine nouvelle et repugnante a la purite de levangile."—Calvin, *Opera*, vol. x. part i. pp. 43, 44.

[2] They were appointed by the civil magistrate, and their duties mainly consisted in supervision of the ordinary ministers.—Cf. Richter, *Die Evangelischen Kirchenordnungen des sechszehnten Jahrhunderts*, vol. ii. (*passim*).

to be merely temporary, as the reason for its existence would be removed as soon as ministers were forthcoming to meet the wants of the people. In the following sentences we have both the grounds for the appointment of superintendents, and a clear definition of their duties : " We considder that yf the Ministeris whome God hath endewed with his [singular] graces amangis us, should be appointed to severall and certane placis, thair to mak thair continuall residence, that then the greatest part off this Realme should be destitute of all doctrine ; whiche should not onlie be occasioun of greate murmure, but also should be dangerus to the salvatioun of manye. And thairfore we have thocht it a thing most expedient for this tyme that frome the whole nomber of godlie and learned [men] now presentlic in this Realme, be selected twelf or ten (for in sa mony Provincis have we divideit the hoill), to whome charge and commandiment shalbe given to plant and erect churches to set ordour and appoint ministeris (as the former Ordour prescribeth) to the contreis that sall be appointed to thair cayre whaire none ar now." [1]

---

[1] *Works*, ii. 202. It was in connection with the office of superintendents that the authors of the Book of Discipline drew most largely on the work of à Lasco. In Knox (ii. 144 *et seq.*) we have " The Forme and Ordour of the Electioun of the Superintendents, quhilk they serve also in Electioun of all uther ministers." By printing passages in parallel columns Dr. Mitchell has shown that in many parts the Scottish form is virtually a translation from that of à Lasco."—*The Wedderburns and their Work*, pp. 83 *et seq.* (Blackwood and Sons, 1867). Nevertheless, as stated in the text, the Superintendent of the Book of Discipline differs from the same official in the Church of the Foreigners both in the special function assigned to him, and in the temporary character of his office. It was formerly maintained by certain writers that superintendents were only bishops under another name. From the account of the superintendents in the text it will be seen that the authors of the Book of Discipline specially aimed at preventing such a misunderstanding. This is now recognised by historians of all shades of religious opinion.

Still under the head of the distribution of the Church's revenues, the subject of education is next considered. For no part of the Book of Discipline have its authors received greater credit than for their projected system of national education. Here, as elsewhere, they owed many hints to other Churches; yet no section of their work is at once so admirable and so original in conception. Luther, Melanchthon, and Calvin, were as eager in the cause of education as any Scottish Reformer; but their position never called them to contemplate a system of public instruction which should be co-extensive with the wants of a nation. In the *Liber Visitatorius* (1528) drawn up by Melanchthon, and approved by Luther, due place is assigned to education among other matters to be looked to by a well-organised Church; but from the limited scope of Melanchthon's suggestions the Scottish Reformers could have learned little or nothing for their special purpose.[1] In Geneva the efforts of the ministers had been confined to the establishment of a great institution which, like the mediæval university, should be at once an elementary school, a secondary school, and a university.[2] In Cranmer's *Reformatio* a section is devoted to education; but its authors had no thought of a system of public instruction which should embrace all ranks of the people. To create such a system was precisely the task to which the authors of the Book of Discipline addressed themselves. Taken in detail,

---

[1] In the *Liber Visitatorius*, Melanchthon merely lays down the subjects to be studied in the three grades into which he divides his educational curriculum.—*Opera*, vol. xxvi. pp. 90 *et seq.* (Bretschneider).

[2] The *Ordonnances* of the Genevan Academy are given in Calvin's *Opera*, vol. x. part i. pp. 65 *et seq.* In my *Life of Buchanan* (chap. xv.) and in my edition of his *Vernacular Writings* (Scottish Text Society) I have spoken at length on the relation of Geneva to Scottish education.

there was no part of their scheme which was strictly original. Where their merit lies was in the thoroughness, the comprehensiveness, the vigorous purpose with which they conceived the idea of national instruction as an organised whole. From no foreign source does it appear that they could have borrowed a model that would have met the objects they had in view.

The scheme proposed was a graduated system of elementary schools, secondary schools, and universities. The ancient Church had endeavoured with imperfect success to establish schools in connection with every parish church.[1] On this arrangement the authors of the Book insisted as indispensable to the well-being of Church and State. Each church was to be at charges for its own teacher, and for the instruction of the poorer children of the parish. The subjects to be taught in these primary schools were Grammar, Latin, and the Catechism in English [2]—four years being the maximum length of attendance. Attendance was compulsory both for rich and poor; for this, it is said, "must be cairfullie provideit that no fader, of what estait or condition that ever he be, use his children at his awin

---

[1] This may be inferred from the accounts preserved regarding education in Scotland prior to the Reformation. See Grant, *Burgh Schools of Scotland*, Part I. In preparing the section on Education in the Book of Discipline, its author may have had before him the *Consultatio* of Hermann, Archbishop of Cologne, published in 1543, and translated into English in 1548. Among other reforms in his diocese, Hermann proposes to establish a Latin school in every town, large and small, and one great theological school at Bonn. In one or two passages the phraseology of the Book of Discipline closely approaches that of Hermann. In Hermann, however, there is nothing to suggest the comprehensive treatment of national education, which is the distinguishing characteristic of the Scottish Book.

[2] This "Catechism" was embodied in the Book of Common Order, or Order of Geneva, which had been compiled for the use of the English Congregation in Geneva.

fantasie, especiallie in thair youth-heade; but all must be compelled to bring up thair children in learnyng and virtue."

By regular visitation and examination the aptest pupils in the elementary schools were to be selected and compelled to proceed to the secondary schools, which, after the model of the cathedral schools of the Middle Age, were to be established in "everie notable toun, and especiallie in the toun of the Superintendent."[1] The secondary school was to be of the nature of a college with provision both for the board and education of the scholars.[2]   Here, also, attendance was compulsory, poor scholars being supported at the public expense.   The subjects taught in the colleges were Latin, Greek, Logic, and Rhetoric.   At the close of this second course, scholars were again to be tested, and the most promising sent to the university, there to be prepared for the church, law, or medicine.

In proportion to its population Scotland was perhaps better supplied with universities than any other country in Europe; yet none of the three, St. Andrews, Glasgow, or Aberdeen—was in anything like a desirable state of efficiency.   This was not only due to the fact that the endowments of all three were inadequate to their ends.   Even more than from want of funds they had suffered from defective organisation and the absence of central supervision.   In St. Andrews the three colleges, which composed the university, had no common understanding, and by their overlapping functions produced needless rivalry and unnecessary expense.   By the proposals of the Book of Discipline this state of affairs would have been set right once and

---

[1] *Works*, ii. 210.   [2] *Ibid.*

for all. The scope and function of each college was
clearly defined, and all were to be brought into organic
connection with the elementary and secondary schools.
At Glasgow and Aberdeen there were to be two
colleges, and at St. Andrews, as the most important,
there were to be three.[1] With regard to these colleges,
the arrangements proposed for St. Andrews may be
taken as the model. Before the student could enter
the university he had to produce testimonials as to
his character and attainments from the minister and
teacher of the town whence he came. These being
satisfactory, he had to undergo an examination prescribed by the university itself. In the first college
there were to be four courses—Dialectics, Mathematics,
Physics, and Medicine, of which the first three were
compulsory for all, and occupied three years. At the
close of this term the student might graduate in
philosophy if he passed the prescribed "tryell and
examinatioun." This stage of his studies over, he
had to choose between law, medicine, and theology.
If his choice were medicine, he remained in the first
college, and, after a curriculum of two years, was in a
position to take his diploma as a practitioner of physic.
Should he choose theology or law, he must proceed
to the second college, where courses were provided in
moral philosophy and civil law. After a year's course
in philosophy he had next to decide between the law
and the Church. If he chose the former, he remained
in the second college, and after four years he might
pass to the doctorate of laws. Choosing the Church,
he entered the third college, which was exclusively
devoted to the study of theology. Here a five years'
course in Greek, Hebrew, and Divinity, qualified him

---

[1] In every college there were to be twenty-four bursars.

to proceed to graduation in theology,[1] and, thereafter,
to be eligible as a minister of the church. By the
age of twenty-four it was definitively prescribed
that "the learnar most be removed to serve the
Churche or Commoun-wealth."[2]

From this account of the educational system proposed by Knox and his colleagues it will appear that
it was planned on lines already laid down by the
ancient Church. The universities already existed, the
cathedral schools suggested the colleges in the headquarters of the superintendents, and the idea of parish
schools was not the birth of the Scottish Reformation.
From the Church of Rome, also, the authors of the
Book of Discipline directly derived the notion that
from base to summit education must be controlled and
directed by the Church. Scholars, teachers, and
subjects taught, must alike be regulated by the
standards of the Church's faith, and in the interest of
the Church's welfare.[3] Under the system projected
by the Scottish Reformers it may be safely said that
freedom of thought would have been less possible
than in any mediæval university. The regret has
often been expressed that this system was never
carried out, as it was conceived by its authors. Yet
it may be fairly questioned if Scotland would have

---

[1] In the mediæval universities the doctorate in theology could not
be taken before the age of thirty-five.

[2] Students in advanced life were the greatest source of trouble in
the mediæval universities. Cf. Bass Mullinger, *The University of Cambridge*, p. 131.

[3] In the year of his death Knox wrote as follows: "Above all
things preserve the Kirk from the bondage of the Universities.
Persuade them to rule themselves peaceably, and order their schools
in Christ; but subject never the pulpit to their Judgment, neither yet
exempt them from your Jurisdiction" (*Works*, vi. 619). As will afterwards be seen, there was an immediate special cause for this utterance
of Knox.

thriven the better by imprisonment in an iron frame-work, the very excellence of whose structure would have preserved it from all modification from within and without. But such criticism is an injustice to the men who conceived an ideal in advance of anything that Christian Europe could yet show. It must not be forgotten that they have the supreme merit of conceiving education, not as the privilege of a class, but as a common need and right of all. The mediæval Church was very far from neglecting the general interests of education ; but the idea of public in-struction, equally within the reach of every section of society, was incompatible with the civil and religious principles on which mediævalism was based.

As we have seen, it was declared to be the Church's duty to make provision for the superintendents, masters, readers, parish-school teachers, and the poor. But in the ruin of the old Church the question rose where the revenue was to be found to meet these responsibilities. Under the sixth head, this question is treated with a candour of statement and precision of detail which could not be welcome to many of the Lords to whose approval the Book was submitted. It was this special section, indeed, that determined the fate of the Book, and suggested the sarcastic description of its whole contents as "devote imaginationis." The authors of the Book in the first place made un-hesitating claim to the inheritance of the Church they had displaced. But a double difficulty lay in the way of their giving effect to this claim. Was it just that the old clergy should be deprived of the means of subsistence, even though they were the ministers of Satan and not of the truth?[1] This difficulty, it

---

[1] Knox had consulted Calvin regarding this question. In Calvin's

would seem, was purposely left for the Great Council to settle, and the authors make no suggestion as to the best method of solving it. But it was another difficulty that was the rock ahead in every plan for the satisfactory settlement of the Reformed Church. For many years before the revolution of 1560 ecclesiastical property had been passing into the hands of the nobles, barons, and gentry. From the Book of Discipline itself we learn that the possessions which had changed hands must have amounted to a considerable proportion of the entire revenue of the Church. In most cases, also, the exchange had been effected under forms of law which rendered it difficult for the Church to recover its own.[1] In the unsettlement which preceded the Reformation, the beneficed clergy had increasing difficulty in drawing the revenues of their charges ; and under these circumstances, and with the consent of the Pope himself,[2] they made over the Church's claims to powerful laymen, who assured them at least a moiety of their income.

But if the new Church was to discharge its duty to the nation, these laymen must be prepared to meet its just claims. It was largely through their influence that true religion had at length triumphed over its adversaries, and on them, therefore, it specially lay that the Reformed Church should present such a face as would prove to the world the divinity of its origin. Under the head of which we are speaking it is this urgent

---

reply, printed by Laing (Knox, *Works*, vi. 94 *et seq.*), occurs the following sentence: "For, although those who give none of their labour to the church have no right to claim their maintenance, yet, since they have ensnared themselves through ignorance and error, and have spent part of their life in idleness, it were hard that they should be totally deprived of it " (p. 97).

[1] *Works*, ii. 223.

[2] Cook, *Hist. of the Reformation in Scotland*, ii. 331.

appeal to the nobility that is the main concern of the authors. We may have doubts in assigning certain portions of the Book to their respective writers; but in the following passage we seem to have the unmistakable accents of Knox : " And thairfore provisioun must be maid how and of whome suche soumes must be lifted. But befoir we enter this heid we must crave of your Honouris in the name of the eternall God and of his Sone Christ Jesus, that ye have respect to your pure brethren, the lauboraris and manuraris of the ground ; who by these creuell beastis the Papistis have bene so oppressit that thair life to thame have [*sic*] bene dolourus and bitter. Yf ye will have God author and approver of youre reformatioun, ye must nott follow thair futesteppis ; but ye must have compassioun upoun your brethren, appointing thame to pay so reasonabill teyndis that thei may feill sum benefit of Christ Jesus, now precheit unto thame. With the greaf of our heartis we heare that sum Gentilmen are now als creuell over thair tennentis as ever war the Papistis, requiring of thame whatsoever before thay payit to the Churche ; so that the Papisticale tirranye shall onlie be changeit in the tirranye of the lord or of the laird. We dar not flatter your Honouris, neathir yit is it proffitabill for you that so we do : if you permit suche creualtie to be used, neather shall ye, who by your authoritie aucht to ganestand suche oppressioun, neather thei that use the same, escheip Goddis hevy and feirfull judgementis." [1]

The ruin of the ancient Church in Scotland, as elsewhere, had been largely due to a slackening of penitential discipline, which gradually sapped alike the faith and the morals of its adherents. In the words of the

[1] *Works*, ii. 221, 222.

Book of Discipline, it had come to pass that "neather was virtu richtlie praysit, neathir vice seveirlie punisched."[1] If the new Church was to be worthy of its calling, therefore, primitive piety not less than primitive doctrine must be maintained in its midst; and it is with this weighty matter that the authors deal in their seventh head. What law is to the commonwealth, they say, discipline is to the Church : with the right of discipline is bound up the very existence of the Church as a corporate body. For this right Calvin had struggled in Geneva, and only after many years had attained his end. In that town, as we have seen, Knox had found the ideal of what a religious society on earth should be ; and Geneva was doubtless the model which he would have wished Scotland to follow. In the seventh head of the Book of Discipline, however, it was à Lasco rather than Calvin whom its authors had before them. Even during its brief existence, the Church of the Foreigners in London had been taught the necessity of stringent discipline, and in à Lasco's book the conditions of Church communion and the methods of dealing with recalcitrant members are treated with special care and minuteness.[2]

It is this section of the Book of Discipline beyond every other that expresses the essential character and tendency of the Reformed Church of Scotland. It contains nothing, indeed, which had not been explicitly taught by the Church of Rome. The scheme of life it implies, the conditions of church membership it dictates, were identical with what the Church of Rome at least nominally approved. The offences visited, and the methods of visiting them, were no inventions of the Scottish Reformers. In fashioning his religious republic

---

[1] *Works*, ii. 227.　　　[2] À Lasco, *Opera*, ii. 170 *et seq.*

in Geneva Calvin only revived laws which the ancient Church itself had prescribed for the pious going of the citizens. In their views of the end and scope of discipline the Scottish Reformers were thus in no respect original.[1] Where their originality lay was in their unflinching application of terms which the Church of Rome had adjusted to "the average sensual man." Many of the suggestions of Knox and his colleagues never took practical shape ; but their injunctions on the subject of discipline determined the character of the Church which they founded. Within that Church itself its members were formed after the type involved in its inexorable laws of life and conduct. To the world outside, also, it presented a collective character not less distinctly marked. The conditions of its communion constituted it an *imperium in imperio*, a distinct organism within the larger organism in the State. A passage like the following implied the whole subsequent struggle which, for above a century, set Church against State in the religious development of Scotland. Literally taken, the passage could only mean that to all intents and purposes, excommunication was virtual outlawry. "After whiche sentence," the passage runs, "may no persoun (his wife and familie onlie excepted) have ony kynde of conversatioun with him, be it in citing and drinking, buying or selling, yea, in saluting or talking with him ; except that it be at the commandiment or

---

[1] They thus distinguish between the respective spheres of Church and State : " Blasphemye, adulterie, murthour, perjurie, and uthir crymes capitall, worthie of death, aucht not properlie to fall under censure of the Churche ; becaus all suche oppin trangressouris of Goddis lawis aucht to be tackin away be the civill swearde. But drunkynnes, excesse (be it in apparell, or be it in eating or drinking), fornicatioun, oppressioun of the poore by exactionis, deceaving of thame in buying or selling be wrang met or measure, wantoun wordis and licentious leving tending to sklander, do propirlie appertene to the Churche of God, to punnische the same as Goddis word commandeth."—*Works*, ii. 227.

licence of the Ministerie for his conversioun ; that he by suche meanis confoundit, seing him self abhorit of the faythfull and godlie, may have occasioun to repent and be so savit. The sentence of his Excommunicatioun must be publischeit universalie throwhout the Realme, least that any man sould pretend ignorance." [1]

The eighth head bears evident traces of hasty composition, and is, moreover, logically out of place in the general plan of the Book. Its subject is the manner of electing elders and deacons, and the function that should pertain to each. Both offices Knox had seen in full working in Geneva; but to the elders the Scottish Reformers assign an authority and importance which is another proof of the independent character of their work. Chosen by the congregation,[2] the elders were to be the spiritual censors of people and minister alike. But it is in the relation of the elders to the minister that we note the special stamp of the Scottish Reformation. Everywhere in the Book of Discipline we see that its authors are inspired with a pious horror of the evils they had seen in the fallen Church. In drawing up this section they had before them the scandals that had arisen from the irresponsibility of the old clergy ;

---

[1] *Works*, ii. 230. Compare the following passage from the *Consultatio* of Hermann of Cologne (p. cii.) " Et si Magistratus civilis concedat excommunicato usum politici status, et consuetudinis civium, excommunicatio Ecclesiae civilem communionem impedire non debet ; Licetque veris et obedientibus Ecclesiae membris hujusmodi hominis uti consuetudine in rebus civilibus, et in administratione Rei pub. in publicis judiciis, in emendo et vendendo, et similibus negociis civilis societatis et necessitatis hujus vitae. In aliis autem non necessariis rebus vitanda est membris Christi talium consuetudo, ne se peccatis alienis contaminent. Imo sic se gerere erga hujusmodi debent, ut et ipsi et alii intelligant eos graviter dolere et tristari, propter ipsorum flagitia et scandala, quae Ecclesiae Dei obiiciunt."

[2] In Geneva the *Conseil Étroit* nominated the elders, who were then approved by the ministers.—Calvin. *Opera*, vol. x. part i. pp. 22, 23.

but in their zeal to avoid this evil they went to an opposite extreme which could only have led to disasters of another kind. By the powers they proposed to confer on elders, they gave signal proof of their sincerity of purpose ; yet, exercised to the full, these powers must inevitably have crippled the ministry of the Church. "Yea," they write, "the Seniouris aught to take heyde to the life, manneris, deligence, and studye of thair Ministeris. Yf he be worthie of admonitioun, thei must admonische him ; of correctioun, thei must correct him : And yf he be worthy of depositioun, thay with consent of the Churche and Superintendent, may depose him, so that his cryme so deserve. Yf a Minister be licht in conversatioun, by his Elderis and Seniouris he aught to be admonisched. Yf he be negligent in studie, or one that vaketh not upoun his charge and flocke, or one that proponeth not frutefull doctrine, he deservith scharpear admonitioun and correctioun."[1]

The ninth and last head deals at some length with the "polecie of the churche"—policy being defined as "ane exercise of the Churche in suche thingis as may bring the rude and ignorant to knawledge, or ellis inflambe the learned to greater fervencie, or to reteane the Churche in gude ordour."[2] Consistently with this definition, this section is mainly occupied with a plan of religious instruction, which should meet the wants of every rank of the people. Better fortune attended this plan than the proposed scheme of national education. Through the means suggested under this head Scotland became the nation of theologians with which the world is familiar. In "greit Tounis" there was to be a sermon or "Commoun Prayeris" daily "with

<hr>

[1] *Works*, ii. 235.　　　　[2] *Ibid.* ii. 237.

some exercise of reiding the Scripturis;" and in each "notable Toun" there was to be sermon and prayers on one day of the week besides Sunday. In every church there was to be a Bible "in Inglesche," which was to be read systematically to the congregation from beginning to end. Each head of a household was to be responsible for the religious knowledge both of his children and his servants. "And gif thay stuburnlie continew, and suffer thair children and servandis to continew in wilfull ignorance, the discipline of the Churche must proceid against them unto excommunicatioun; and then must the mater be referred to the Civill Magistrat."[1]

From à Lasco, an institution was borrowed which was singularly fitted to keep alive theological interests, and, within certain limits, to foster the best talent in the country.[2] In every place, where men of fitting gifts were found, there was to be a weekly meeting for the discussion of such passages in Scripture as might tend to mutual edification. At these weekly "prophesyings," as they are termed, all were to be present to whom any talent had been committed for the spiritual profit of their fellows. "And yf any be found disobedient," is the solemn threat, "and not willing to communicat the giftis and spirituall graces of God with thair brethren, after sufficient admonitioun, discipline must procead against thame; provided that the Civile Magistrate concur with the judgement and electioun of the Churche. For no man may be permitted to leave [live] as best pleasseth him within the Churche of God; but everie man must be constrayned by fraternall admonitioun and correctioun to bestow his laubouris when

---

[1] *Works*, ii. 241.
[2] À Lasco, *Opera*, ii. 101 *et seq.*

of the Churche thei ar required to the edificatioun of otheris." [1]

As has been said, the system of national education proposed in the Book of Discipline was realised only in the most imperfect fashion. On the other hand, its system of religious instruction was carried into effect with results that would alone stamp the first Book of Discipline as the most important document in Scottish history. Through the various means of edification provided for him, every Scotsman was subjected to a moral and intellectual discipline such as no other country succeeded in giving to its people. To this discipline, far more than to the parish schools, has been due that

> Stately speech ;
> Such as grave Livers do in Scotland use,
> Religious men, who give to God and man their dues.[2]

The Book of Discipline expresses the ideal which its authors conceived of a society, existing on earth, but whose main concern is heaven. Yet this ultimate reference to another sphere of being never affected their practical wisdom. As it happened, many of their best suggestions never bore fruit ; but their proposals as a whole cast the mould in which the Scottish character and intellect were formed for more than two centuries. From the above analysis of the Book it will have appeared that the modern phrase " Christian socialism " would be no inapt description of the scheme

---

[1] *Works*, ii. 245.

[2] Wordsworth, *Resolution and Independence*. Speaking of the Scottish peasantry, Scott, who knew them so well, has the following passage in his Introduction to *The Antiquary :* "The antique force and simplicity of their language, often tinctured with the Oriental eloquence of Scripture, in the mouths of those of an elevated understanding, give pathos to their grief and dignity to their resentment."

it embodies. In all its proposals the individual is merged in the society with a completeness that would meet the approval of the most absolute socialist of the present day. By the combined authority of Church and State he was to be sent to school and university till the special talent was discovered by which he could best serve the community. His career thus marked out for him, his subsequent conduct and opinions must be shaped in accordance with the creed and discipline of the Church. Those who fell out of the race were to be forcibly reminded that they were not their own masters. The unable were to be the care of their respective parishes, and the able-bodied, but idle, should be compelled to put their hands to such work as was provided for them. Community of goods is not proposed, but for this there was an excellent reason. As one of the tenets of the Anabaptists, it had been discredited in the deplorable history of that sect in Germany and elsewhere. Moreover, if the ecclesiastical system of the Book of Discipline had been fully realised, such regulation of property would hardly have been necessary. In the parish as the unit of society it would have been the function of the Church to see that there was no excessive luxury on the one hand and no absolute need on the other.[1] Ministers, elders, and deacons, if they did their duty, would constitute an authority which would enforce the principle of Christian charity. Alike as regards property and life, therefore, the scheme of the Scottish Reformers was practically a form of socialism such as seems implied in the very essence of the Christian teaching.

[1] In the "Order of Excommunication," issued in 1569, " superfluitie or ryotousnes in cheir or rayment " are expressly specified as deserving of " admonitioun."—*Works*, vi. 453, 454.

The most delicate task of the authors of the Book of Discipline was to distinguish the respective functions of Church and State. In the early Middle Age these functions had been so confounded that a clear line of separation between them was impossible. In the development of the different countries, however, the sphere of the State had become more clearly defined, with the result that the jurisdiction of the Church was driven within ever-narrowing limits. With the experience of the Middle Age behind them, the Protestant Reformers were fully aware of the evil consequences to religion of any antagonism between the Church and the State. Both in his writings and his practice Calvin had sought to mark the precise sphere of both.[1] In the Book of Discipline its authors had distinctly before them the necessity of a clear line of demarcation; but we now see that they attempted a problem which the growth of opinion alone could solve. As implied in their scheme, the functions of Church and State overlapped in a manner that made friction inevitable. The State was to give effect to all their proposals, but only in the mode and degree which they dictated. The State was to allocate the superintendent,[2] and was to punish all such persons as the Church should see fit to surrender to its judgment. On the other hand, the Church reserved a freedom of action with regard to affairs of State which might easily render Government impossible. Time was to show that in Protestantism there was a principle of development of which Knox to the last had never a suspicion. Out of the conflict of opinion,

---

[1] *Institutio Christianae Religionis*, caput xx.

[2] *Works*, ii. 208 ; and cf. *Booke of the Universall Kirk*, p. 13. The State on some occasions even appointed the Moderator of the General Assembly.—*Ibid.* p. 17.

provoked by the schism from Rome, grew that secular spirit, which, as the antithesis of mediævalism, is in direct hostility to any pretence of the Church to speak on equal terms to the State.[1]

[1] It is worth noting that the First Book of Discipline was subsequently adopted by the Puritan, Cartwright, as the manifesto of his party.—Prothero, *Select Statutes and other Constitutional Documents illustrative of the reigns of Elizabeth and James I.* (1894), pp. lv., 247, 248.

BOOK V

THE SECOND REVOLUTION—THE TRIUMPH OF KNOX

1560-1572

CHAPTER I

1561-1565

MARY landed at Leith on the 20th of August 1561;
and with the moment of her arrival begins a new
period in the life of Knox and in the history of
Scotland.   It was not long before Knox saw that the
Queen's return was the most untoward event that could
have happened to the new Church.   During the next
four years wounded self-love and pious apprehensions
kept him in a chronic disquiet, which often drew from
him the wish that the weary fight were over.   Within
a fortnight after Mary's return he writes as follows to
his old friend and confidant Mrs. Locke: "I have
finished in open preaching the Gospell of Sanct Johne,
saving onlie one chapter.   Oft have I craved the
misereis of my dayes to end with the same; for now,
sister, I seeke for rest."[1]

The special form of the new danger was doubly
galling to one who, like Knox, was incapable of even
seeming to palter with his heart's deepest convictions.
We have seen that for some months before the Treaty of
Edinburgh, the Lords of the Congregation had allowed
religion to drop into the background, and, to a certain
extent, neglected the counsels of Knox.   The necessity

[1] *Works*, vi. 130.

of winning England in their conflict with France had
driven them into a policy which had at least resulted
in the victory of July 1560.   Knox had viewed this
policy with deep displeasure, and had not spared the
most powerful of those who had carried it through.
He was now to see a line of conduct followed which
in his opinion could only call down the judgment of
Heaven on their country.   " Who wold have thought,"
he bitterly exclaims, " that when Joseph reulled Egypt
that his brethren should have travailled for vittallis,
and have returned with empty seckis unto thair
families ? " [1]

Mary had not been many days in the country before
the policy of the next few years defined itself with
perfect clearness.   From the position of all parties
interested in the future of Scotland, this policy was
of necessity a temporary compromise.   For Spain,
France, and England, it was still of high moment
what paths Scotland should follow under the immediate
government of Mary.   As an exemplary Catholic, it
was the devout desire of Philip II. that the country
should be restored to the true fold.   Unfortunately,
this happy consummation could be effected only through
France ; and France in full control of Scotland would
have implied the conquest of England and the ascendency of the French monarchy in the counsels of Europe.
To help France in such an enterprise was a reach of
devotion beyond even the faith of Philip, and he was
content to stand by and fashion his diplomacy according
to the course of events.   Of herself France at this
moment was powerless to interfere decisively in the
affairs of any foreign country.   By the death of
Francis II. the Guises had lost their preponderating

---

[1] *Works,* ii. 310.

influence; and Catharine de' Medici, who governed the new king, thought only of preventing their return to power. The Huguenots, moreover, had now become a force which threatened to dismember France as a nation. Thus France also could confine herself only to diplomacy in her relations with Scotland. By the Treaty of Edinburgh England had obtained all that she had sought in meddling with Scottish affairs. That Treaty, indeed, had never received the formal sanction of Mary; but by skilful conduct this sanction might be gained without recourse to the strong hand. As things now stood, Elizabeth was not in a position to browbeat the Scottish Queen. At home the divided faith of her subjects was a chronic source of weakness; and her enemies abroad were on the watch for every false step which might present an opening for her ruin. During the first years of Mary's reign, therefore, the attitude of the three great powers to Scotland was simply a watchful jealousy, lest one should overreach the other in attaching her to its own special interests.

Within her own borders the Government of Scotland adjusted itself in a similar spirit of jealous compromise. In the circumstances in which she found herself Mary had hardly a choice of alternatives as to her immediate policy. As we have seen, she could count on no effective support from France, and, at the date of her arrival, the Protestant party, through the fervour of its convictions and the ability of its leaders, was the prevailing power in the country. From the first, therefore, Maitland and the Lord James were her chief counsellors, and to them is due the policy of the country during the early years of her reign. On the other hand, the Protestant leaders were in as precarious a position as Mary

herself. The course of events since the meeting of
the Estates in August 1560 had shown that the
triumph of Protestantism was by no means assured.
The majority of the nobles and the majority of the
people were still Catholic. But it was to the party
of the old Church that Mary by all her instincts was
naturally drawn, and her very presence served to
consolidate its strength and to define its aims. By
the consenting testimony of the time, the return of
their Queen, with all the glamour of youth, beauty,
and an interesting personal history, went to the heart
of the Scottish people. Skilfully used, the charm of
her youth, her sex, her grace and accomplishments,
should eventually have assured her the general support
of the country. Fortunately for the future of Protestantism, Mary possessed little of the steady prudence
and personal dignity of her mother.[1] Yet, such as she
was, her personal qualities materially increased the
difficulties of the Protestant leaders. Devoid of the
higher qualities of mind and character, she was clever,
self-willed, and ambitious. With such a character
and schooled by her already varied experience, Mary,
in spite of her youth, was no passive instrument in
the hands of her advisers. Through the weakness of
their respective positions, therefore, Mary on the one
hand and the Protestant Lords on the other, were
driven to mutual concessions, which in their hearts
they were equally bound to disapprove.

Mary's desire would have been to bring back the
old religion, and with the aid of France to place
herself on the throne of England ; but, as things now

---

[1] By her lack of these qualities as well as by her adventures with
the other sex, Mary reminds us of her grandmother, Margaret Tudor,
the sister of Henry VIII.

went, such a plan could be only a dream of the future. Left to themselves, Maitland and the Lord James would have maintained the late religious settlement at once out of policy and honest conviction. In the interest of both countries they desired their speedy union. As England had definitively broken with Rome, it was in the nature of things that Scotland should show the same front. Thus, what Mary desired mainly for personal reasons, Maitland and the Lord James desired for the well-being of the two countries ; and it was this common object that supplied the basis of mutual understanding and a common policy. Mary gave herself to the Protestant leaders on the condition that they secured to her the English throne ; they, on their part, made compromises in religion and politics, which, during the next four years, it was the burden of Knox to denounce as an ill-omened compact between God and Antichrist. Even in the point of worldly wisdom, events were to prove that Knox had seen deeper into the possibilities of things than the politicians themselves.

Within a week after Mary's return Knox found himself in sharp opposition to those in whom he had hitherto placed his chief hope for the future. On Sunday the 24th of August mass was celebrated in Holyrood Chapel with the consent of the Lord James, " the man whom all the godlye did most reverence." [1] The Protestant politicians knew as well as Knox that, as men then thought and felt, the two religions could not coexist without social convulsion. Conscious of their own weakness, however, and fearful of another civil war, they thought by this temporary compromise at once most surely and most speedily to attain their

[1] *Works*, ii. 271.

end.   On the following day the Council, though
mainly composed of Protestants, gave further proof
of its weakness.   They passed an act to the effect that
in religion things were to remain as the Queen had
found them.[1]

For Knox the whole labour of the last two years
had for its end the destruction of the old religion and
the setting up of the new.   In 1560 the victory had
seemed to be in their hands, and the Parliament of
that year had vigorously entered on the right way.
What Knox would now have wished was the com-
pletion, with or without the consent of the Queen, of
the work which had been so well begun.   Instead of
this he saw the leaders of his party enter on a course
which he felt sure must lead to issues ruinous to the
cause they really had at heart.   As he and everybody
must have known, the Court religion must inevitably
prejudice the interests of the new faith, and precisely
in quarters which it was most important to win over.
And in point of fact, when the failure of the schemes
of the politicians eventually produced a crisis, it was
found that, year by year, the example of the Court
had told heavily on the numbers and zeal of the
Protestants.

Always girt for battle, Knox at once joined issue
with his politic brethren.   The very day the Act
of Council was proclaimed, the Earl of Arran produced a protest which could have come only from
the hand of Knox himself.[2]   But it was on the following Sunday that Knox found his real opportunity.
From his pulpit in the Church of St. Giles he then
spoke of the doings of the preceding week.   He has

---

[1] Knox has preserved this Act for us.—*Works*, ii. 272 *et seq.*

[2] *Ibid.* ii. 273-275.

KNOX'S PULPIT

himself recorded the purport of his discourse ; but one sentence embodies its whole aim and scope. One mass, he said, " was more fearful to him then gif ten thousand armed enemyes war landed in any pairte of the Realme of purpose to suppress the hoill religioun." [1]

The Protestant Lords would, doubtless, be among Knox's hearers ; and they must have been convinced that, if their present policy was to have a fair chance of success, he must either be silenced or gained over. Knox, it is to be remembered, was no mere pulpit declaimer, who provided entertainment for a few hours on preaching days. Both the Queen and her new counsellors were fully aware that his opposition was a serious force to be reckoned with in any scheme affecting the future of the country. In Edinburgh the body of substantial citizens were at his back ; and in the country at large he had the confidence of the barons and gentry through whose influence the late revolution had been mainly carried through. A few days before Knox delivered the above sermon, Randolph, whose sympathies at this time were all with the Lord James and Lethington, could write that Knox "ruleth the roste, and of hym all men stande in feare." [2]

To win the refractory preacher a remarkable step was taken. Apparently with the consent, and probably at the suggestion, of her advisers,[3] Mary summoned

---

[1] *Works*, ii. 276. It was probably after listening to this sermon that Randolph wrote to Cecil (7th September 1561) : " Where your Honour exorteth us to stoutnes, I assure you the voyce of one man [Knox] is able in one hour to putt more lyf in us than fyve hundreth trumpettes continually blustering in our eares."

[2] *Ibid.* vi. 129.

[3] To one familiar with Knox's style this seems implied in his own words.—*Ibid.* ii. 277.

Knox to a private interview in Holyrood. It was certainly an emphatic tribute to Knox's predominance that Mary should ever have consented to admit him to her presence. Before her return she had already recognised Knox as her natural enemy. " I understand," wrote Throgmorton to Elizabeth, "that the Queen of Scotland is thoroughly persuaded that the most dangerous man in all her realm of Scotland, both to her intent there, and the dissolving of the league between your maj : and that realm, is Knokes."[1] The few days she had been in Scotland must have convinced Mary that she had not exaggerated either Knox's hostility or his dangerous influence. The encounter between these two famous personages has a dramatic aspect which is apt to obscure its deeper historical interest. In Mary and Knox we have the perfect incarnation of two types that have divided the world since Christianity displaced the Pagan religions. In Knox we have the representative, in its extremest form, of the theological view of life which subordinates this world to the next, and insists on

---

[1] The rest of this letter, which is printed by Tytler (*Proofs and Illustrations*, vi. 467) deserves to be given. " And therefore is fully determined to use all the means she can devise to banish him thence, or else to assure them that she will never dwell in that country so long as he is there ; and to make him the more odious to your maj : and that at your hands he receive neither courage nor comfort, she mindeth to send very shortly to your maj : (if she have not already done it) to lay before you the book that he hath written against the government of women ; (which your maj : hath seen already), thinking thereby to animate your maj : against him ; but whatsoever the said queen shall insinuate your maj : of him, I take him to be as much for your maj : purpose,—and that he hath done, and doth daily, as good service for the advancement of your maj : desire in that country, and to establish a mutual benevolence and common quiet between the two realms, as any man of that nation : his doings wherein, together with his zeal well known, have sufficiently recompensed his faults in writing that book ; and therefore [he] is not to be driven out of that realm."— Throgmorton to Elizabeth, 13th July 1561.

"the one thing needful." Of "the child of nature," at home in the existing order of things, and making the most of what life has to offer, no more charming example is to be found than Mary. At the last, like so many of the type to which she belonged, she was driven by stress of fate to bow to the force that lies in the Christian teaching ; but at the period of which we are speaking she was as far from St. Teresa as any woman of Pagan antiquity.

The issue of the encounter could not be doubtful. Knox, in his panoply of an iron creed, was invulnerable to all the spells of rank and educated grace, to which the morosest man of the people has so often succumbed. Yet, doubtless, both looked forward with some confidence to the interview. In all her previous experience Mary had probably never met the man on whom her charms had not told. On his part, Knox, as we have seen, had some experience of feminine nature, and had not been unsuccessful in bringing women to his feet.

The interview took place on the 26th of August— the Lord James being the only other person present.[1] Mary's tone from the first was the reverse of concilia- tory. On the ground of various parts of his past conduct, she taxed him with being a disloyal subject. He had been a leader in the late rebellion against her mother; in his book on the Monstrous Regiment of

---

[1] Two gentlewomen, Knox tells us, " stood in the other end of the house " (*Works*, ii. 277). We have only Knox's reports of his different interviews with Mary ; but we have no reason to question their essential truth. The best evidence for their accuracy is that Mary, as reported, fully holds her own with her formidable adversary. Further, it is more than probable that the conversation was carried on in the Scottish language. Nicolas White, writing to Cecil in 1578, speaks of Mary's " pretty Scottish speech." Moreover, in certain passages, Knox appears to give the very words used by Mary.

Women he had taught treason against her own authority; in England he had been a notorious disturber of the peace; and, lastly, it was believed that he was in compact with the powers of darkness. The conversation lay mainly with Knox, who addressed himself to rebutting the above charges. But the most memorable part of his discourse is that where he denies the right of the prince to impose his religion on the people. This doctrine could hardly have been new to Mary, as it was in truth the fundamental political question of the day. Never before, however, could she have met face to face so hardy a champion of what to her was flat rebellion, nor heard the doctrine defended in such uncompromising fashion. After citing Scriptural examples with his usual fluency, and in the utterly unhistorical manner of the age, he concludes :

"And so, Madam, ye may perceave that subjectis ar not bound to the Religioun of thair Princes, albeit thei ar commanded to geve thame obedience."

"Yea," quod sche, "but none of thai men raised the sweard against thair Princes."

"Yit, Madam," quod he, "ye cane not deny but that they resisted; for these that obey nott the commandiments that ar gevin in some sort resist."

"But yit," said sche, "thei resisted not by the sweard?"

"God," said he, "Madam, had not gevin unto thame the power and the meanes."

"Think ye," quod sche, "that subjectis having power may resist thair Princes?"

"Yf thair Princes exceed thair boundis," quod he, "Madam, and do against that whairfor they should be obeyed, it is no doubt but they may be resisted, evin by

power. For thair is neather greattar honour nor greattar
obedience to be gevin to kings or princes then God
hes commanded to be gevin unto father and mother:
But so it is, Madam, that the father may be stricken
with a phrensye, in the which he wold slay his awin
childrene. Now, Madame, yf the children aryese, joyne
them selfis togetther, apprehend the father, tack the
sweard or other weaponis frome him, and finallie
bind his handis, and keape him in preasone, till that
his phrenesy be over past; think ye, Madam, that the
children do any wrang? Or, think ye, Madam, that
God wilbe offended with thame that have stayed thair
father to committ wickedness? It is even so," said
he, "Madam, with Princes that wold murther the
children of God that ar subject unto thame. Thair
blynd zeall is no thing but a verray mad phrenesie;
and, thairfor, to tack the sweard frome thame, to bynd
their handis, and to cast thame selfis in preasone till
that thei be brought to a more sober mynd, is no dis-
obedience against princes, but just obedience, becaus
that it aggreith with the will of God!"[1]

After this outburst Knox tells us that "the Quene
stood as it war amased more then the quarter of ane
hour." By this point the Lord James must have seen
that the interview was not likely to have the end
desired. But the temper of the two disputants was
now fairly up, and every word emphasised their essential antagonism. Recovering herself, Mary at length
retorted:

"Weall then I perceave that my subjectis shall
obey you, and not me."

"God forbid," was the reply, "that ever I tack
upoun me to command any to obey me, or yitt to

<hr>

[1] *Works*, ii. 281, 282.

set subjectis at libertie to do what pleaseth thame. Bot my travell is that boyth princes and subjectis obey God. And think not," said he, " Madam, that wrong is done unto you, when ye ar willed to be subject unto God : for it is he that subjects people under princes and causses obedience to be gevin unto thame ; yea, God craves of Kingis that thei be as it war foster-fatheris to his Churche, and commands to be nurrisis to his people. And this subjectioun, Madam, unto God, and unto his trubled Churche, is the greatest dignitie that fleshe can get upoun the face of the earth, for it shall cary thame to everlasting glorie."

Mary's retort was as vehement and decided as any utterance of Knox's own.

" Yea, but ye are not the kirk that I will nureiss. I will defend the Kirk of Rome, for I think it is the true Kirk of God." [1]

Instead of smoothing the way of the politicians, this interview made Knox more than ever the determined opponent of their present policy. The impression Knox had received from Mary had only deepened his distrust of her character and intentions. " Yf thair be not in hir," was his report, "a proud mynd, a crafty witt, and ane indurat hearte against God and his treuth, my judgment faileth me." [2] From his own account of Mary's words and bearing, her "craft" is certainly not very apparent. Cleverness she undoubtedly showed ; but as the object of the meeting was specially to conciliate Knox, what is specially noteworthy is rather her lack of prudence and self-control. It was enough, however, that in her quick intelligence,

----

[1] *Works*, ii. 283.

[2] *Ibid.* p. 286. In a letter to Cecil he also says : " In communication with her, I espyed such craft as I have not found in such aige."—vi. 132.

in her passionate temper, and her hostility to all that
was dearest to himself, Knox saw an ominous menace
to the cause of which he was now almost the solitary
champion.[1]

The backsliding of the Protestant Lords, especially
of the Lord James, now preoccupied all Knox's
thoughts. "My eyes," he wrote to Mrs. Locke on the
2nd of October, "have seene manie things and yitt I
feare one more terrible than all others."[2] A few days
later an incident confirmed his worst fears. In accordance with ancient custom the magistrates of Edinburgh commanded the statutes of the town to be
publicly proclaimed on the 21st of September.[3] Among
the statutes was one ordering all malefactors, with
whom "papists" were now classed, to quit the town.
A peremptory message from the Queen was the consequence, consigning the magistrates to the Tolbooth,
and enjoining the immediate election of a new muni-
cipal body. Of herself, Knox felt that Mary would
hardly have ventured on such a step, and he formed
his own conclusions as to who were at her back. "Ye
know my Lord James and Ledington," he wrote to
Cecil, "whome yf God do not otherwiese conduct, thei
ar liek to lose that which, not without travall, hath
heirtofore bien conquest : Att this verrey instant ar the
Provost of Edinburgh and Balleis thairof command to
ward in there Tolboght be reason of thare Proclamation against papists and hoormongers."[4]

[1] Randolph thus refers to Knox's first interview with Mary. "He
knocked so hastelye upon her harte that he made her weep as well you
knowe ther be of that sexe that wyll do that as well for anger as for greef."
Randolph to Cecil, 7th September 1561.—Wright, *Queen Elizabeth*,
i. 72.   [2] *Works*, vi. 130.

[3] *Ibid.* ii. 289. Keith accuses Knox of inaccuracy in asserting that
there was such a custom ; but the Council Records prove that the custom
did exist.   [4] *Works*, vi. 132. Knox to Cecil, 7th October 1561.

On the 1st of November another incident widened the breach between Knox and his former friends. The festival of All Saints, celebrated "with all myschievous solemnitie," once more raised the question of the Queen's right to set aside the existing law against the mass. At the house of the Clerk Register, James Makgill, the point was formally discussed between the ministers and the politicians. The Lord James, the Earl of Morton, the Earl Marischal, Lethington, and other leading Protestants maintained that the Queen possessed an exceptional privilege, Knox and the chief ministers holding the contrary. The abstract question it was agreed to refer to Calvin; but in effect the Lords carried their point, Knox and his friends protesting that "her [Mary's] libertie should be thair thraldome or it was long."[1]

Every day now intensified Knox's opposition to those whom he called the "reullaris of the Courte." A General Assembly of the Church in December brought into full relief the misunderstanding between the Protestant Lords and the mass of those who were of the same religion. At previous meetings of the Assembly, the lords, the lesser barons, gentlemen, and ministers had met in one place to consider the business of the Church. On this occasion the Lords refused to take part in the Assembly, and on grounds which showed the strength of Knox's position. To a deputation sent to them at Holyrood Abbey the Lords complained "that the Ministeris drew the gentilmen into secreat, and held counsallis without thair knowledge."[2] The discussion that followed revealed what was practically a schism in the Protestant party. Through their spokesman, Lethington, the Lords even denied the right of the Church to

<hr>

[1] *Works*, ii. 292.　　　　[2] *Ibid.* p. 295.

hold its assemblies without the consent of the Queen. As in most of these disputes between the Lords and the ministers, the discussion resolved itself into a duel between Lethington and Knox. In view of the existing position and prospects of the new Church Knox, might well be staggered by the above contention. "Yf the libertie of the Churche," he replied with manifest truth, "should stand upoun the Quenis allowance or dysallowance, we are assured not onlie to lack assemblies but also to lack the publict preaching of the Evangell."[1] As a compromise the Lords agreed to the continuance of the General Assemblies on condition that the Queen's interests should be represented at their meetings.[2]

The Book of Discipline was next discussed, and on this subject the ministers received less satisfaction. When they suggested that the Queen should be asked to ratify the Book, the Lords, again through Lethington, refused even to regard the matter seriously. "How many of those," they asked, "that had subscrived that Buke wald be subject unto it?" The very question proves how powerfully the mere presence of Mary in Scotland had affected the course of affairs. A few months before her arrival the large majority of those who composed her Secret Council had signed the Book of Discipline with the express pledge that they would "sett the samin fordwarte at the uttermost of oure poweris."[3] How was it that a few months had sufficed to change their minds so completely? The accepted explanation, for which Knox himself is mainly responsible, is that if the Book became law, the wealth of the old Church would simply have passed into the hands of the new, and the Protestant Lords would not have been a penny the better for all their late trouble. In

---

[1] *Works*, ii. 296.   [2] *Ibid.* p. 297.   [3] *Ibid.* p. 257.

the case of every revolution we must give due place
to the lower motives that influence even the noblest
spirits ; but the above explanation is a totally inadequate account of the political and religious situation
in which the Protestant Lords now found themselves.
As we have seen, the return of Mary was a serious
menace to Protestantism in Scotland. A false step on
the part of the Protestant leaders might revive the
late tumults, in which the country, sick of civil strife,
would almost certainly declare for the Queen. But to
ask Mary, who knew her own strength, to ratify such
a document as the Book of Discipline, would have
been to drive her to measures which would have
risked what the new religion had already gained. To
maintain their hold on Mary, to keep her from the
counsels of the Catholic party, the Protestant Lords
were forced to make concessions, and to hold out
promises, which, as practical politicians, they recognised
as a necessity of their position. Knox and his brother
ministers, therefore, might storm as they pleased ; the
Lords were resolved that the Book of Discipline should
not be forced on Mary to the ruin of all their plans.

On one point, however, the ministers, supported
by the barons and gentlemen, were determined that
something should be done ; and as the leader of this
body Knox played his usual prominent part. In spite
of all the recent legislation, he tells us that "unto that
tyme the moste parte of the Ministeris had lyved
upoun the benevolence of men."[1] Whatever they
might do with regard to the Book of Discipline, the
Lords were now told that the ministers must be
decently provided for. So threatening was the Protestant feeling throughout the country,[2] that their

----

[1] *Works*, ii. 298.   [2] *Ibid.* pp. 300-303.

demand could not be set aside. In truth, the position of the Lords grew every day more embarrassing. The Protestant congregations insisted that their ministers should receive permanent stipends from the property of the old Church to which they were the legal heirs. But to effect this end classes must be sacrificed whom it was impolitic to offend in the interests of Protestantism itself. The bulk of the Catholic clergy were still in possession of their incomes;[1] and to deprive them at this particular moment was beyond the strength of the Protestant leaders. Lay lords, both Catholic and Protestant, had become masters of much of the ecclesiastical property; and them it would have been still more impolitic to unite in a common selfish interest. An ingenious escape from their difficulty occurred to Mary's advisers. In the name of the Queen herself a certain portion of the rents of the Church should be appropriated.[2] According to Knox himself, the Crown had no shadow of a claim on the property of the Church;[3] but the old clergy would submit more readily to be robbed for the benefit of a Catholic queen than for the increase of a heretical sect. As a good Catholic Mary might have shrunk from the sacrilege of enriching herself at the expense of the Church; but, as various events of her career sufficiently prove, religious scruples did not weigh much with her when they stood in the way of her own passions of the moment.[4] At this time,

---

[1] This is implied in the Acts of the Privy Council ordaining the clergy to produce the rentals of their benefices. These Acts are given by Knox, ii. 299 *et seq.*   [2] *Ibid.* p. 307.   [3] *Ibid.* p. 312.

[4] It should be remembered that she married Bothwell, a professed Protestant, according to Reformed rites; and, what is probably as bad in the eyes of Catholic orthodoxy, cut up Church vestments to make a garment for her lover, and a counterpane for her child.—Robertson, *Stat. Eccles. Scotic.* vol. i. pp. clxxii., clxxiii.

moreover, she was in as needy a condition as the ministers themselves. She had brought back with her the luxurious habits of the French Court, and she was soon involved in expenditure which all her sources of income were inadequate to meet.[1]

With the consent of the Queen, therefore, and under the shelter of her name, her Council imposed a tax of one-third on all the ecclesiastical property in the country. Of this third a half was to go to the Queen, and the remainder was to be distributed among the ministers. When we remember the high hopes of Knox a year before, we need not wonder that this pitiful concession wounded him to the quick. In the Book of Discipline it was calmly taken for granted that the entire possessions of the old Church had passed into the hands of the new. If the old clergy were provided for, it would be purely out of charity on the part of the Reformed Church, and from no deference to their own legal claims. Now all this was reversed, and it was the ministers who were to be fed by charity, and "the priests of Baal" who were to dispense it. In the end, as will be seen, this cautious policy of the Protestant Lords led to issues which it was their main object to avert. By their apparent deference to the Queen's wishes they now gave deep offence to the great body of their fellow-Protestants, on whom, if things came to the worst, they must in the long run depend. Speaking from the pulpit, Knox gave utterance to the feeling of the Protestants in general regarding the late arrangement. "Weill, yf the end of this ordour, pretended to be tacken for sustentatioun of the Ministeris, be happy, my judgement failleth me; for I am assured that the Spirit of God is nott the

---

[1] Her dowry as widow of Francis II. was not regularly paid.

auctor of it; for, first, I see Twa partis freely gevin to the Devill, and the Thrid maun be devided betwix God and the Devill. Weill, bear witnes to me, that this day I say it, or it be long the Devill shall have Three partis of the Thrid; and judge you then what Goddis portioun shalbe." [1]

Though set aside by the Lords of the Congregation, Knox, both at home and elsewhere, was recognised as one of the forces in the country. Elizabeth's minister, Cecil, was in constant communication with him; [2] and the leaders of the Huguenots counted him an efficient ally. In the last days of 1561, De Foix, the ambassador of Catharine de' Medici, had secret meetings with him in Edinburgh with a view to common action between the Protestants of France and Scotland; [3] and we have it from Knox himself that he was in close touch with French public men. [4]

In March 1562 Knox's services were called for in an affair which for many reasons must have deepened his gloom at the prospects of his religion. Since the return of Mary, the Hamiltons had lost the importance that had naturally fallen to them during the late revolution. Their past conduct had not been such as to commend them to Mary; and for personal reasons they could not fall in with the policy of Lethington and the Lord James. Yet Knox, as we have seen, had formed such good hopes of Arran that he would gladly have seen him a person of importance, and in a position to counteract the mischievous tendencies of the

---

[1] *Works*, ii. 310.

[2] This is implied in Knox's letter to Cecil dated 6th October 1563 —*Ibid.* vi. 528, 529.

[3] Kervyn de Lettenhove, *Relations politiques des Pays-Bas et de l'Angleterre, sous le règne de Philippe II.* L'Évêque d'Aquila à Cardinal de Granville, 3rd Jan. 1561, 1562; ii. 658.   [4] *Works*, ii. 330.

Queen's present counsellors. Through the mediation of Knox, Arran and the Earl of Bothwell were induced to lay aside a long feud and apparently to become good friends. Whatever may have been his object, it was Bothwell who in the first place had sought the reconciliation. But the new association was not happy for Arran. Shortly afterwards he came to Knox with a wild story, which was doubtless, in large degree, the product of his own imagination ; but which, considering Bothwell's character, may yet have had some foundation in fact. Bothwell, he said, had suggested to him a plot to seize the Queen, to make away with her present advisers, and to place themselves at the head of affairs. Whatever may have been the truth of the story, it had taken possession of Arran's mind, and his wits, never very strong, gave way under the strain. Among the higher nobility, therefore, there was no longer one with whom Knox was in accord as to the best guidance of the country.

As things now went at Court, it was only through the general gatherings of the Church that Knox could hope to influence the direction of affairs. The presence in Edinburgh of a numerous body of Protestant barons and gentlemen was a menace to the Queen and her advisers that the danger of another war of religion was never far off. On the 29th of June 1562 the Assembly once more met to deliberate on the state of the Church, —the most notable outcome of its proceedings being an address to the Queen drawn up by Knox.[1] The burden of the address was still the old demand, now so distasteful to men like Lethington, that the Book of Discipline in all its length and breadth be made the law of the land. If this did not happen speedily,

---

[1] *Works,* ii. 337 ; *Booke of the Universall Kirke,* p. 9.

it was frankly stated, the Assembly would not be responsible for the result.[1] Couched as it was in Knox's vigorous style, this address was singularly inopportune for the Queen's advisers, and they did their best to have its terms modified before it was submitted to her. One passage especially was thought to savour of disloyalty. In plain words it had been implied that Mary had no intention of giving up her own religion, but had the full purpose of restoring the ancient Church to its former place and honour. But it was precisely the object of her advisers at once to gain Mary to the new religion, and to create the impression that sooner or later she would be induced to take this step. Through Maitland's eager efforts, therefore, the address was eventually put into his own hands to be modified as he thought best. In his haste to undo the work of Knox, however, Maitland, as sometimes happened to him, overreached himself by his own ingenuity. As the document left his hands it had so little the character of a Protestant manifesto that Mary's suspicions were naturally raised. " Here," she exclaimed, " ar many fair wordis ; I can not tell what the heartis ar."[2] It was the weakness of their present policy that the Protestant Lords had neither the confidence of the Queen nor of the congregations who were led by Knox.

The autumn of 1562 brought a succession of events which seemed to show that Mary was in reality working into the hands of her Protestant advisers. On the 11th of August she left for the north of Scotland, and did not return till the 21st of November.[3] The journey was a memorable one, and ended in results as decisive

<hr>

[1] *Works,* ii. 342. [2] *Ibid.* p. 345.
[3] Chalmers, *Life of Queen Mary,* vol. i. sect. iv.

as they were probably unforeseen. The Catholic Earl of Huntly, the mightiest noble in Scotland,[1] fell in a revolt against the Queen's authority, and his power passed to her natural brother, the Lord James. The day after Mary left for the North, Knox set out on a visitation of the churches in Ayrshire and Galloway, the great strongholds of Protestantism. In the circumstances his journey could have but one great end. The Queen's errand in the North, accompanied as she was by her chief advisers, filled him with deep misgivings. Whatever might be the issue of their doings, he could have no hope that they would be for the good of the faithful. It was to prepare for the worst, therefore, that he now undertook his visit to the West. During August and September, it would seem that he toiled to waken the chief men in Ayrshire to a sense of the danger that threatened their Church. As the result of his labours, a " Band " was subscribed at Ayr on the 4th of September by which the signatories bound themselves to mutual defence and common action against all enemies of their religion.[2] Knox had, in truth, every reason to be satisfied with his mission. The Earl of Glencairn and above a hundred barons, gentlemen, and burgesses, put their names to the Band, so that if the worst should come, in Ayrshire there was always a solid phalanx of zealous believers who would show an unshaken front.

During his visit to Ayrshire Knox had an encounter, which deserves a passing notice as a characteristic incident of the time. One of the most zealous and accomplished of the old clergy was Quintin Kennedy,

---

[1] Knox says of Huntly that "under a prince thair was not suche a one these thre hundreth yearis in this Realme produced."—*Works*, ii. 358.

[2] *Ibid.* p. 348.

fourth son of the second Earl of Cassillis, and at this time Abbot of Crossraguel, near the town of Maybole. If we may judge from his writings that have been preserved to us, Kennedy was the ablest champion the ancient Church counted in its ranks. In 1558 he had published a little book[1] in which he stated the case for the Roman communion with a persuasiveness and ability that perceptibly affected the progress of the new opinions.[2] In his zeal for the tottering Church, also, Kennedy had, a year later, challenged John Willock to a public discussion, which, however, did not take place.[3] On the appearance of Knox in Ayrshire, Kennedy at once threw down the glove to the most redoubtable of all the Protestant champions. After a testy correspondence, in which the Abbot shows little evidence of an apostolic temper, the meeting was fixed for the 28th of September, at the Provost's house in Maybole. On the day, and at the place appointed, the dispute began at eight o'clock in the morning, and lasted for three days. By previous arrangement the persons present consisted of the Earl of Cassillis, twenty friends of each disputant, the reporting notaries, and as many others as the house could conveniently hold.

The discussion was a fresh illustration of what has already been so often pointed out. Though they differed so widely in their conclusions as to the teaching

---

[1] The title of this book is " Ane Compendius Tractive, conforme to the Scripturis of Almychtie God, Reassoun, and Authoritie, declaring the nerrest and onlie way to establische the conscience of ane Christiane man in all materis (quhilk ar in debate) concernyng Faith and Religioun. Set forth in the yeir of God, 1558 yeris." 4to. It is printed in the *Wodrow Miscellany*.

[2] John Davidson, Principal of the College of Glasgow, in his reply to Kennedy's "Tractive," expressly admits this. See *Wodrow Misc.* i. 91, 186.

[3] See *Wodrow Misc.* vol. i. for correspondence between Willock and Kennedy.

of Scripture, in their fashion of handling its texts there was no essential difference between the representatives of the two faiths. Of the historic relations of individual texts Knox was as unconscious as his opponent who represented the full tradition of the ancient Church. For the modern reader their debate is as devoid of significance as any scholastic dispute ever held within the walls of the Sorbonne. In the mere trial of wits, however, Knox was more than a match for the Abbot, whose excitable temper unfitted him for oral controversy. In the very choice of his position Kennedy gave himself away to his antagonist. " I define the Messe," he said, "as concerning the substance and effect to be the sacrifice and oblation of the Lordes bodie and blude, given and offered by him in the latter Supper, and takis the Scripture to my warrand according to my artickle as it is written. And for the first confirmation of the same," he adds, "groundes me upon the sacrifice and oblation of Melchisedec." [1] By their common methods of reasoning Knox had little difficulty in putting his opponent in a strait place. It was a precarious conclusion from the bare text of Scripture that the sacrificial Mass was in "substance and effect" the original Lord's Supper; and it was a still more hazardous argument to find the chief authority for that Mass in Melchisedec's offering bread and wine to Abraham.[2]

But his duel with the Abbot of Crossraguel was for Knox a mere casual incident of his visit to the South and West. In connection with this visit he took credit for achieving results of the first importance to

---

[1] *Works*, vi. 196.

[2] Ninian Winzet, another Catholic writer, also challenged Knox to a controversy. Beyond a few remarks from the pulpit, however, Knox took no notice of this challenge.

the country. As the autumn wore on, the most conflicting rumours prevailed regarding events in the North. Now the story went that the Lord James and his friends had been cut off; and, again, that Mary and Huntly had joined arms against her late advisers.[1] The parts of the South, according to Knox, were in a state of vague uneasiness, which at any moment might grow to civil war. To avert such an issue he himself was indefatigable. In Nithsdale he held confidential communication with the Warden of the West Marches, the Master of Maxwell, whom he persuaded to bring his influence to bear on the Earl of Bothwell, at this moment living in the hope of a revolution to better his fortune. To Châtelherault, also, Knox wrote, eagerly pressing on him to give heed to his brother the Archbishop, and, as he valued the safety of his house, to have no dealings with Huntly. " By such meanis," he complacently writes, " war the South partis keapte in reassonable quyetness, during the tyme that the trubles war in brewing in the North." [2]

By November Knox was again in Edinburgh, and on the last Sunday of that month entertained a small supper-party at his house, consisting of the Duke of Châtelherault and the English resident, Randolph. By this date, it should be said, the Queen also had returned to the capital, and her future action was exercising Knox as much as ever. In view of all contingencies it was still Knox's steadfast conviction that England and Scotland must go hand in hand if religion were be saved in both countries. Moray and Lethington had once been of the same opinion; but he no longer shared their counsels, and dark rumours now went of

<hr>

[1] *Works*, ii. 351. [2] *Ibid.*

a scheme to which they had given their approval—the very thought of which must have cost him many a spiritual wrestle. Of such sympathisers as were still left to him, he had now to make the most. Châtelherault was no longer a leading force in the country, yet, if well counselled, he might be a check on the policy of the Court. On the occasion of the supper, therefore, Knox drew from him three distinct pledges as to his future conduct. He should abide a faithful Protestant and an obedient subject to his sovereign, and should do his best to maintain the amity between the two realms. "I wyll beleeve them all," wrote Randolph, "as I see them tayke effecte, but truste that yt shall never lye in his worde alone."[1]

During the last months of 1562 the prospect was not cheering for those who, like Knox, looked for the eventual triumph of Protestantism in Europe. Civil war between the two religions had broken out in France; and the Huguenots, though supported by Elizabeth, had suffered heavy reverses. The Guises were again in the ascendant, and in England and Scotland their ascendency was already influencing the relation of the two Queens. With the triumphs of Mary's relatives in France, Knox justly or unjustly associated the unusual festivity of the Court at Holyrood in December 1562; and his wrath was further moved by the stories he heard of the cruelties inflicted on the brethren in France. From the pulpit he denounced the Queen's merrymaking in terms that made her demand another interview with her untractable subject.[2] The object of the interview was doubt-

---

[1] *Works*, vi. 145. Randolph to Cecil, 30th November 1562.

[2] *Ibid.* ii. 331. This interview took place on the 15th December 1562, as we learn from a passage in a letter of Randolph to Cecil (16th December 1562). "Upon Sundaye laste he inveied sore agaynst the

less to overawe Knox, and in the case of most men
the circumstances under which he was received would
sorely have tried their steadfastness. "The Quene,"
he tells us, "was in hir bedchalmer, and with hir besydis
the ladyis and the commoun servandis, war the Lord
James, the Erle of Mortoun, Secreatarie Lethingtoun,
and some of the garde that had maid the report."[1]   In
a "long harangue or orisoun" the Queen taxed him
with exceeding his privilege as a preacher, and of
seeking to make her odious to her subjects.   But
Knox would not admit that she had been rightly informed as to the real purport of his discourse and,
nothing loath, as we may believe, he recapitulated text
and sermon as they had been actually delivered.   Even
as reported by himself, his words were not such as
have often been heard in Courts; yet Mary was
pleased to say that they were less offensive than she
had been led to believe, adding that in future he
should tell her to her face when her conduct displeased
him.   "I am called, Madam," was the unflinching
reply, "to ane publict functioun within the Kirk of
God, and am appointed by God to rebuk the synnes
and vices of all.   I am not appointed to come to
everie man in particular to schaw him his offense;
for that laubour war infinite.   Yf your Grace please
to frequent the publict sermonis, then doubt I nott
but that ye shall fullie understand boyth what I like
and myslike, als weall in your Majestie as in all otheris.
Or yf your Grace will assigne unto me a certane day

Quene's dansynge, and lyttle exercise of her self in vertue or godlines:
the report hereof beinge broughte into her cares yesterdaye, she sent for
him.   She talked longe tyme with hym, lyttle lykynge ther was betwene
them of th' one or th' other, yet dyd theie so depart as no offence or
slaunder dyd ryse ther upon."—*Works*, vi. 147.
  [1] *Ibid.*

and hour when it will please you to hear the forme
and substance of doctrin, whiche is proponed in publict
to the Churches of this Realme, I will most gladlie
await upoun your Grace's pleasur, tyme, and place.
But to waitt upoun your chalmer-doore or ellis whair,
and then to have no farther libertie but to whisper my
mynd in your Grace's eare, or to tell to you what
otheris think and speak of you, neather will my conscience nor the vocatioun whairto God hath called me
to suffer it.   For albeit at your Grace's commandiment
I am heare now, yitt can not I tell what other men
shall judge of me, that at this tyme of day am absent
from my book and wayting upoun the Courte."

This second interview, like the first, only widened
the breach between the Queen and the preacher.
With all his stern enthusiasm Knox could not sub-
jugate a mind which like Mary's revolted from the
very type to which he belonged.   To this haughty
rejoinder she curtly replied, " You will not alwayis be
at your book."   As for himself, he adds in one of the
famous passages of his History, "the said John Knox
departed with a reasonable meary countenance ; whairat
some Papistis offended said, 'He is not effrayed.' Which
heard of him, he answered, 'Why should the pleasing
face of a gentill woman effray me ?   I have looked in
the faces of many angrie men, and yitt have nott bene
effrayed above measure.' "[1]

The day following this interview Randolph wrote
a letter to Cecil in which we have an interesting glimpse
of Knox.   "Mr. Knox hathe oftayne tymes tolde me,"
he writes, "that he is to blame that he hathe not wrytten
unto your Honour of longe tyme.   Of late he required
me to convoie letters unto your Honour.   I knowe his

[1] Works, ii. 334, 335.

good zeal and affection that he beareth to our nation. I knowe also that his travaile and care is great to unite the hartes of the princes and people of these two realmes, in perpetuall love and hartie kyndnes. I knowe that he mystrustethe more in his owne Soveregnes parte then he dothe of ours, he hathe no hope (to use his owne termes) that she wyll ever come to God, or do good in the common welthe. He is so full of mystrust in all her doyngs, wordes, and sayengs, as though he wer eyther of God's privie consell, that knowe howe he had determined of her from the begynynge, or that he knewe the secretes of her harte so well, that nether she dyd or culde have for ever one good thought of God or of his trewe religion."[1] Randolph undoubtedly reports Knox's fixed conviction regarding Mary; but more even than the Queen her Protestant advisers roused his indignation. "And yitt," he bitterly exclaims, "who gydis the Quene and Court? Who but the Protestantis?"[2] These words likewise refer to the close of 1562, and we shall see that Knox was to have still further reason for deploring the declension of his former friends and allies.

A week after Knox's last interview with the Queen the General Assembly met in Edinburgh (25th December). As at every previous meeting there were loud complaints of the lack of ministers, the meagreness of stipends, and the progress of idolatry; but there seems to have been no direct collision between the Assembly and the Court. One unpleasant business, however, devolved upon Knox, which he had a grim satisfaction in discharging. Paul Methven, who had been a fervent preacher in the days when there was

---

[1] *Works*, vi. 146. Randolph to Cecil, 16th December 1562.
[2] *Ibid.* ii. 363.

real danger in publicly professing Protestantism, had been accused of adultery in the town of Jedburgh. That such a charge should hang over a minister of the Reformed Church was not to be tolerated, and Knox, along with certain Edinburgh elders, was despatched to Jedburgh to ascertain what truth lay in the scandal. On satisfactory evidence the charge was found to be true, and at a subsequent meeting of the Assembly Methven was publicly excommunicated and deprived of his ministerial functions. " For two causes," Knox concludes his curiously minute account of this affair, " we insert this horrible fact, and the ordour keapt in punishment of the same : formar, To forwairne such as travaill in that vocatioun, that, according to the admonitioun of the Apostle, ' Suche as stand, tack heed lest thei fall.' . . . The other caus is, that the world may see what difference thair is betwix light and darknes, betwix the uprychtnes of the Churche of God, and the corruptioun that ringes [reigns] in the synagoge of Sathan, the Papisticall rable." [1]

From the general tendency of affairs since Mary's arrival the Catholic clergy were naturally encouraged to form good hopes for the near future. As the law stood, they were forbidden the public exercise of their religion ; but the slackness of the government had in some degree made the law a dead letter. During the Easter of 1563 the mass was celebrated in different parts of the country in such open fashion that the Protestants resolved on stringent measures. In the West, where the new opinions were most widely spread, certain priests were placed under ward, and others were

---

[1] *Works*, ii. 366 ; *Booke of the Universall Kirke*, p. 14. See Appendix C for a slander raised in Edinburgh against Knox's own character.

warned that the punishment of idolaters would be duly meted to them, regardless alike of Queen and Council. The news of this reaching the Queen's ears, she once more sent for Knox, as the soul of all the mischief.[1] As she was then at Lochleven, Knox had the trouble of a journey all the way from Edinburgh. For two hours before supper Mary laboured with him to use his influence in keeping the peace between the Protestant gentlemen and the priests. Knox was not to be moved. It was the law of the land that mass should not be said in public, and if her Majesty would not enforce the law it lay with her subjects to see that it was enforced. "Will ye," asked Mary, "allow that that thei shall tack my sweard in thair hand?" The answer was ready. Samuel slew Agag, Elijah slew the prophets of Baal; and in either case the act was independent of royal authority. As on the previous occasions the interview came to nothing, and Mary closed the conversation with manifest displeasure.[2]

On leaving the Queen, Knox had communicated to Moray[3] the result of the meeting. It was probably at Moray's suggestion, therefore, that Mary sought another interview next morning, apparently with the purpose of parting on better terms with her trouble-some subject. The meeting took place before sunrise, to the west of Kinross, the Queen being abroad thus early on her favourite diversion of hawking. She appeared to have forgotten the misunderstanding of the previous evening, and with an air of winning candour sought and volunteered advice on certain

---

[1] This interview probably took place on the 13th of April 1563. On the 15th of that month Mary left Lochleven for Perth.

[2] *Works*, ii. 371 *et seq.*

[3] The Earldom of Moray had been conferred on the Lord James during the late expedition to the North against Huntly.

matters in which they had a common interest. Twice in the course of their talk Knox exhibited traits of character for which Mary, of a generous and high spirit herself, must in her heart have done him justice. When she blamed Lethington for procuring the admission of Lord Ruthven into her Council, the reply was, "That man is absent for this present, Madam, and thairfor I will speak nothing in that behalf." As we have seen, Knox was convinced that Lethington was the source of all the evil of the last two years, and to Mary herself Lethington was ever the object of deep-rooted suspicion. But it was the nature of Knox to be a fair and open enemy, and he disdained to lay a train even against one who had so often made a jest of his own most cherished aspirations. When Mary also warned Knox against Gordon, titular Archbishop of Athens, he again refused to listen, because Gordon was at that time on terms of intimacy with himself. Evidently bent on making herself gracious, Mary further asked Knox's good offices in a matter that concerned her own family. Her half sister, Lady Argyle, had long been on bad terms with her husband, and her conduct was giving room for public scandal. Would he use his influence to effect a better understanding between the husband and wife? And with happy art she closed the interview with a remark which had, doubtless, been her main object in seeking it. "And now," she said, "as tueching our reassonyng yisternycht, I promess to do as ye requyred; I sall caus summond all offendaris, and ye shall know that I shall minister Justice."[1]

Mary had now been nearly two years in the country, and Parliament had not been once summoned.

---

[1] *Works,* ii. 373 *et seq.*

For this there were reasons of home and foreign policy
which have been implied in what has already been said.
The governing object of Mary and her advisers was
to have her recognised as Elizabeth's successor to the
English throne ; the desire of Elizabeth was to have
the Treaty of Edinburgh formally sanctioned by the
Scottish Queen and Estates. In postponing the meeting of the Estates, therefore, lay Mary's chief hope
of forcing the hand of Elizabeth. In the state of
parties in Scotland, also, there were special reasons
why neither Mary nor the Protestant Lords should
desire the meeting of the Estates. Mary had the
natural fear that she might be forced to make concessions to Protestantism, binding her to a course of
action from which there might be no retreat. The
Protestant Lords, on the other hand, were not in a
position to carry such decided measures as in their
hearts they might think were for the good of the
country. The Queen, they knew, would never consent
to such demands as Knox and his supporters would
certainly lay before them. When the Parliament did
meet, therefore, it was with the mutual understanding
of the Queen and her Council that no great measures
should be passed that would seriously affect the existing state of affairs alike in policy and religion.

Before Parliament met, a politic step was taken by
way of conciliating the main body of zealous Protestants. In accordance with Mary's promises to Knox at
Lochleven, forty-eight persons who had defied the law
regarding the mass were tried before the Court of
Justiciary on the 19th of May.[1] As no less a person
than Archbishop Hamilton was among the accused,

---

[1] *Works*, ii. 379 ; Pitcairn, *Criminal Trials*, i. 427 ; *Diurnal of
Occurrents*, p. 75.

and as Hamilton himself and the majority of the others were committed to ward for breach of law, it seemed that the government was at last taking decided measures for the final establishment of Protestantism. In reality, neither Mary nor her Council had any such intention when they summoned the present Parliament. Yet by this apparent hard dealing with the old clergy they attained the end at which they doubtless aimed. Had the Reformed barons and burgesses swarmed to the meeting of Estates as in 1560, the result might have been serious for the public peace. But when the most zealous of the Protestants saw Catholic clergy placed under ward all over the country, they confidently hoped that their day of triumph was at last approaching. Knox was not deceived by what he knew to be a transparent artifice, and his wrath was proportionably great as he saw its success with so many on whose steadfastness he reckoned. "Sche" [Mary], he writes "obtained of the Protestantis whatsoever sche desyred ; for this was the reassone of many. We see what the Quene has done ; the lyck of this was never heard of within the Realme : we will bear with the Quene ; we doubt not but all shalbe weill."[1]

The Parliament met on the 26th of May with a splendour and ceremony which was specially distasteful to Knox, knowing as he did the real intentions of the Court ; and the popular admiration of the Queen drew from him the most splenetic outbursts against female vanity in particular. His fears were now justified to the full. Parliament would have nothing to do with the Book of Discipline or any serious measures in favour of true religion. At this moment, Knox and his friends were told, it would be impolitic to press the

[1] *Works*, ii. 380.

Queen to further action against her own faith. But
her marriage could not be long deferred; and as she
would herself have favours to ask, then would be
the time to insist on her making the necessary reforms
in the Church. It was with Moray that Knox was
specially disappointed in the crisis through which they
were passing. In spite of what he deemed the Earl's
backsliding during the previous two years, he had never
lost hope that he would yet be the Joshua who should
lead them into the Land of Promise. When Moray
now failed him, therefore, it was as keen a disappoint-
ment as life had brought to him. "The mater fell so
hote," he says, "betwix the Erle of Murray and some
otheris of the Courte, and Johne Knox, that familiarlie
after that tyme thei spack nott together more then a year
and a half; for the said Johne by his letter gave a discharge to the said Erle of all further intromissioun or cayr
with his affaires." In a letter addressed to Moray he
recalled to him their first intercourse, their now ancient
friendship, and concluded in words which must have
stung Moray none the less that they implied a misappre-
hension of the deepest motives that determined him.
"But seing that I perceave myself frustrat of my
expectatioun, which was that ye should ever have preferred God to your awin affectioun and the advancement
of his treuth to your singular commodite, I commit
you to your awin wytt, and to the conducting of those
who better please you. I praise my God, I this day
leave you victour of your enemyes, promoted to great
honouris, and in credytt and authoritie with your
Soverane. Yf so ye long continew, none within the
Realme shalbe more glad than I shalbe: but yf that after
this ye shall decay (as I fear that ye shall), then call to
mynd by what meanes God exalted you; quhilk was

neather by bearing with impietie, neather yitt by manteanyng of pestilent Papistis." [1]

By this quarrel of Moray and Knox the Protestant party received the heaviest blow that could have befallen it. They were the two most powerful men in the country, and if they had made common counsel, they might have dictated terms to Mary which she could not have refused without the risk of civil war. That Moray chose to work with Lethington rather than with Knox is the best proof that at heart he was loyal to Mary both as his sister and his Queen. For Mary, therefore, the breach between the two Protestant leaders was of the first importance; and we may readily believe what Knox tells us that her friends " ceassed nott to cast oyle in the burnyng flambe." [2]

As at every important juncture, Knox's inevitable sermon and interview with Mary followed the meeting of Parliament; " befoir the most parte of the Nobilitie " he discoursed in his most moving tones of the mercies that had attended their steps till the great victory that was sealed by the Parliament of 1560. Even the sternest of his hearers could not have heard without emotion such a passage as the following, delivered, as we know it would be, with that prophetic fervour which was Knox's special gift as a preacher. " From the begyning of Goddis mychty wirking within this Realme, I have bein with you in your most desperat tentationis. Ask your awin consciences, and lett thame answer you befoir God, yf that I (not I, but Goddis Spirite by me) in your greatest extremitie willed you nott ever to depend upoun your God, and in his name promissed unto you victorye and preservatioun from your enemyes, so that ye wold only depend upoun

<hr>

[1] *Works,* ii. 382, 383.   [2] *Ibid.* p. 383.

his protection and preferr his glory to your awin lyves and worldlie commoditie. In your most extreame dangearis I have bein with you : Sanct Johnestoun, Cowper Mure, and the Craiggis of Edinburgh, ar yitt recent in my heart ; yea, that dark and dolorouse nyght whairin all ye, my Lordis, with schame and feare left this toune, is yitt in my mynd ; and God forbid that ever I forgett it."[1]

In the circumstances in which the sermon was delivered the Queen could not escape the preacher's animadversion. It was the plea of the Protestant Lords that deference to Mary as their Queen stayed their hands from completing the work of the Reformation. The plea met short quarter from one who could not understand how a woman, even though a Queen, should stand in the way of realising the work of God. "The Quene, say ye," he burst forth, "will not agree with us. Ask ye of hir that which by Goddis word ye may justlie requyre, and yf she will not agree with you in God, ye ar not bound to agree with hir in the Devill : Lett hir plainelie understand so far of your myndis, and steall not from your formar stoutness in God, and he shall prosper you in your interpryses."[2] But the part of the sermon which gave special offence to Mary, was where the preacher took upon him to censure the rumoured project of her marriage. What these rumours were we shall afterwards see.[3] For Mary it was enough that Knox had dared to question her right to bestow her hand where she might choose ;

---

[1] *Works*, ii. 384. The "dark and dolorouse nyght" to which Knox refers was that of 6th November 1559, when the Lords of the Congregation were forced to leave Edinburgh. See p. 59 above.

[2] *Ibid.* p. 385.

[3] At this time Knox had reason to believe that Moray and Lethington were in favour of a marriage between Mary and Don Carlos of Spain.

and for the fourth and last time she summoned him to her presence.

Accompanied by a troop of his friends, Knox made his way to the Abbey; but with the exception of Erskine of Dun none were allowed to attend him to the Queen's presence. On this occasion Mary made no attempt to disguise her real feelings. In "a vehement fume" she broke into reproaches against the immitigable preacher. But the whole passage in which Knox has described the interview is so memorable that it must be quoted in full. As mere literature, these pages may be considered as exhibiting Knox's highest qualities in the dramatic presentment of the materials of his History. What is more to our purpose, we here see the character of the two speakers in a moment of intensity, when the depths of human nature are revealed unconsciously.

"The Quene, in a vehement fume, began to cry out, that never Prince was handled as she was. 'I have,' said sche, 'borne with you in all your rigorouse maner of speaking, bayth against myself and against my Uncles; yea, I have sought your favouris by all possible meanes. I offerred unto you presence and audience whensoever it pleassed you to admonishe me; and yitt I can nott be quyte of you. I avow to God I shalbe anes revenged,' and with these wordis, skarslie could Marnock,[1] hir secreat chalmerboy, gett neapkynes to hold hyr eyes drye for the tearis; and the owling, besydes womanlie weaping, stayed hir speiche.[2]

<hr>

[1] "Evidently," says David Laing, "the same person with Marna, whose name occurs among the 'gentilhomes servans' in the 'Menu de la Maison de la Royne, faict par Mons. de Pinguillon,' 1562."—Knox, *Works*, ii. 387, *note*.

[2] It was Mary's habitual practice to burst into hysterical tears, whenever she was crossed in conversation.

"The said Johne did patientlie abyde all the first fume, and att opportunitie answered, 'Trew it is, Madam, your Grace and I have bein att diverse controversies, into the which I never perceaved your Grace to be offended at me. Butt when it shall please God to deliver you fra that bondage of darknes and errour in the which ye have been nurisshed for the lack of trew doctrin, your Majestie will fynd the libertie of my toung nothing offensive. Without the preaching place, Madam, I think few have occasioun to be offendit at me; and thair, Madam, I am nott maister of myself, but man obey Him who commandis me to speik plane, and to flatter no flesche upoun the face of the earth.'

"'But what have ye to do,' said sche, 'with my marriage?'

"'Yf it pleise your Majestie,' said he, 'patientlie to hear me, I shall schaw the treuth in plane wordis. I grant your Grace offered unto me more than ever I requyred; but my answer was then, as it is now, that God hath not sent me to await upoun the courtes of Princesses, nor upoun the chamberis of Ladyes; but I am send to preache the Evangell of Jesus Christ to such as please to hear it; and it hath two partes, Repentance and Fayth. And now, Madam, in preaching reapentance, of necessitie it is that the synnes of men be so noted, that thei may know whairin thei offend; but so it is, that the most parte of your Nobilitie ar so addicted to your affectionis that neather God his word nor yitt thair Commonwealth ar rychtlie regarded. And, thairfoir, it becomes me so to speak that thei may know thair dewitie.'

"'What have ye to do,' said sche, 'with my mariage? Or what ar ye within this Commounwealth?'"

"' A subject borne within the same,' said he, 'Madam; and, albeit, I neather be Erle, Lord, nor Barroun within it, yitt hes God maid me (how abject that ever I be in your eyis) a profitable member within the same; yea, Madam, to me it apperteanes no lesse to foirwarne of suche thingis as may hurte it, yf I foirsee thame, then it does to any of the Nobilitie; for boyth my vocatioun and conscience craves playness of me.   And, thairfor, Madam, to your self I say that whiche I speak in publict place; Whensoever that the Nobilitie of this Realme shall consent that ye be subject to ane unfaythfull husband, thei do as muche as in thame lyeth to renunce Christ, to banish his treuth from thame, to betray the fredome of this Realme, and perchance shall in the end do small conforte to your self.'

"At these words owling[1] was heard, and tearis mycht have bene sein in greattar abundance than the mater requyred.   Johne Erskine of Dun, a man of meek and gentill spreit stood besyd, and entreated what he could to mitigat hir anger, and gave unto hir many pleasing wordis of hir beautie, of hir excellence, and how that all the princes of Europe wold be glaid to seik hir favouris.   But all that was to cast oyle in the flaming fyre.   The said Johne stood still without any alteratioun of countenance for a long seasson, whill that the Quene gave place to her inordinat passioun; and in the end he said, 'Madam, in Goddis presence I speak: I never delyted in the weaping of any of Goddis creaturis; yea, I can skarslie weill abyd the tearis of my awin boyes whome my awin hand correctis, much less can I rejoise

---

[1] As used by Knox, this word had not the coarse suggestion it has at present.—Cf. *Macbeth*, Act iv. Scene iii.:

Each new morn
New widows *howl*, new orphans cry, new sorrows
Strike heaven on the face.

in your Majesties weaping.   But seing that I have
offered unto you no just occasioun to be offended, but
have spocken the treuth, as my vocatioun craves of me,
I maun sustean (albeit unwillinglie) your Majesties
tearis, rather then I dar hurte my conscience, or betray
my Commounwealth through my silence.'[1]

" Heirwith was the Quene more offended, and commanded the said Johne to pass furth of the cabinet,
and to abyd farther of hir pleasur in the chalmer.
The Laird of Dun taryed, and Lord Johne of Colding-
hame com into the cabinet, and so thei boyth remaned
with hyr neyr the space of ane houre.   The said
Johne stood in the chalmer, as one whom men had
never sein (so war all effrayed) except that the Lord
Ochiltrie bayre him companye : and thairfor began he
to forge talking of the ladyes who war thair, sitting in
all thair gorgiouse apparell ; whiche espyed, he mearlie
said, ‘O fayre Ladyes, how pleasing war this lyeff of
youris, yf it should ever abyd, and then in the end that
we myght passe to heavin with all this gay gear.
But fye upoun that knave Death, that will come
whitther we will or not ! And when he hes laid on his
areist, the foull wormes wilbe busye with this flesche, be
it never so fayr and so tender ; and the seally sowll, I
fear, shalbe so feable that it can neather cary with it gold,
garnassing, targatting, pearle, nor pretious stanes.’"

What impression do these various interviews of
Knox and Mary leave as to the respective traits of
their mind and temper ? From the foregoing narrative
it will have appeared that one current opinion has little
to support it. Considering the actual relations of the
two parties, it is absurd to speak of Knox as a coarse
man of the people bullying a defenceless queen.   The

____

[1] *Works,* ii. 387 *et seq.*

truth is, that if there was any attempt at browbeating it was on Mary's part, and not on that of Knox. When she summoned him to her presence, it was with the express purpose of imposing silence on him by force of her own will and the opinion of the Court. As she arranged their interviews, Knox had nothing to fall back upon but his native force of character, and the intensity of his conviction. It was amid the frowns and sneers of Catholic and Protestant alike that he held his own with the mistress whom they were all equally disposed to humour even at the cost of their convictions. In truth, the most pertinent question regarding these interviews is, Why did they take place at all? One meeting, at least, might have satisfied Mary that Knox was not the man to be browbeaten from what he believed to be his plain duty. As she could make no concessions that would conciliate him, it would have been the part of prudence to avoid scenes that could only compromise her dignity, and result in increased irritation. In seeking these repeated interviews, therefore, we believe that Mary gave but another proof of that lack of self-control and self-respect which was her most serious defect as a woman and a Queen. In reading Knox's report of his own speech and bearing, it is to be remembered that to judge him fairly we must apply the standard of his own age. Forgetting this, we might easily infer that Mary herself, from certain of her reported speeches, was essentially a coarse-minded woman. As we now think, Knox might have said what he had to say in more courtly fashion; yet in the essentials of all his dealings with Mary he but acted as practical men have found it necessary to act in all ages of the world. It would be difficult to name two men more curiously unlike than Knox and Lamartine; yet Lamartine, poet and sentimentalist, is here at one with the austere Reformer of the sixteenth century. When the Duchess of Orleans put herself in the way of a policy he believed to be in the interests of the country, with all the sternness of Knox, he hardened his heart against her tears and her misfortunes.[1]

In the autumn of 1563 Knox took a step that seemed likely to put him at last in the Queen's power, and seriously to weaken his authority in the country. During the summer Mary had made a progress in the West, and, carrying the mass into this stronghold of the reformed religion, "had dejected the hearts of many." When the report of this reached Knox, he was so moved that he composed a special prayer which he thenceforth regularly used in his household.[2] Under his own eyes, also, the rites of the old religion were celebrated more publicly than ever they had been before. As the arrangements between the two religions stood, it was only in the Queen's presence that mass could be said within the bounds of Scotland. During the Queen's absence, however, this understanding had been systematically disregarded by the Catholics in Holyrood. As this was not to be borne, certain of the

---

[1] Lamartine, *History of the French Revolution of 1848* (Bohn's translation), pp. 116-118. George Herbert, also, a spirit as far removed from Lamartine as from Knox, describing his "Constant Man," says of him that he is one

> Who, when he is to treat
> With sick folks, women, those whom passions sway,
> Allows for that, and keeps his constant way.

[2] The significant clause in this prayer was as follows : "Continew us in quyetnesse and concord amangis our selfis, yf thy good pleasur be, O Lord, for a seassone." When asked his reason for this conditional petition his answer was, "that he durst nott pray but in fayth ; and faith in Goddis word assured him that constant quietness could not continew in that Realme, whair Idolatrie had bene suppressed, and then was permitted to be erected agane."—*Works*, ii. 391.

leading Protestant burghers were deputed to present themselves in the chapel and ascertain the names of those who appeared at the service. The sight of the idolatrous exhibition was too much for the zeal of the visitors, and one of them, Patrick Cranston, protested aloud against the manifest breach of the law. According to Knox's account this was the end of the matter as far as the deputies of the Congregation were concerned. However this may be, the affair was duly reported to the Queen, who immediately took steps to have the offenders brought to punishment. Two of the most active of the Protestant deputies, Patrick Cranston and Andrew Armstrong, were cited "to underlie the law" on the 24th October on the charge of violently invading the Queen's palace.

But if these two brethren should suffer for their zeal, Knox felt that the cause of Protestantism was lost. With the consent of the faithful in Edinburgh, therefore, though probably on his own initiative, he addressed a circular letter to the Protestants throughout the country, urging them for the safety of their religion to appear in Edinburgh at the date of the approaching trial. Knox was fully aware of the boldness of this step; but, as we shall see, he had carefully reckoned the chances of its success. The letter falling into the hands of Mary, however, she was quick to conclude that she had at last caught her adversary in a net. In thus summoning her lieges on his own responsibility she held that he had been guilty of treason, and should be made to abide the law. The Privy Council found the charge relevant, and decided that Knox should be called to answer for his action. But, as Knox doubtless foresaw, the majority of the Council found themselves in an embarrassing dilemma, from which there was, in truth, but one way of escape. Before the day of trial both Moray and Maitland made a strenuous effort to wring from him an admission of guilt. But there was a double reason why Knox should abide by his action. By admitting a breach of law he would have compromised the claim of the Church to assemble its members independent of the State. Knowing also the real mind of the Council, he could with some confidence reckon on an issue of the trial, which might result in a triumph for the cause which he represented.[1]

The trial took place on the 21st of December, between six and seven at night. A crowd of Knox's supporters waited eagerly without to learn the fate of their great leader. The members of the Council having taken their places, the Queen entered " with no littill warldlie pomp," and took her place between Maitland and the Master of Maxwell. " But," adds Knox, in his account of the scene; " hir pomp lackit one principall point, to wit, womanlie gravitie ; for when sche saw John Knox standing at the uther end of the tabill bair-heided, sche first smyleit, and efter gaif ane gawf lauchter. Quhairat quhen hir placeboes gaif thair *plaudite*, affirming with lyke countenance, ' This is ane gude begyning,' sche said, ' But wat ye whairat I lauch ? Yon man gart me greit, and grat never teir him self : I will see gif I can gar him greit.' "[2]

Called on to read the incriminating letter, Knox acknowledged himself to be its sole author. Two main charges were based on its contents. As a summons to the Queen's lieges, it implied a treasonable act on the part of the writer; and in one of its ex-

<hr>

[1] *Works*, ii. 393 *et seq.*   [2] *Ibid.* p. 404.

pressions, the Queen urged, she was herself accused of personal cruelty. On the first charge, Knox could have little difficulty in setting himself right with the majority of the Council. In calling the Congregation together for self-defence, he had only followed their own example in the days before the coming of the Queen. Maitland might urge that then was then, and now was now, but the Council well knew that if Knox were judged guilty, a precedent would be set which might one day be turned against themselves. On the other charge, Knox could equally count on the interests and private convictions of the judges. The Queen accused him of charging her with personal cruelty; but the expression implied only that Papists naturally sought the harm of Protestants.[1] When he appealed to his audience as to whether this was true, the majority, in view of their professed opinions, could give but one answer. By the unanimous vote of the Council, therefore, Knox was acquitted of both charges, and, to the mortification of Mary, was dismissed without a rebuke. It had been her hope, on the ground of a purely secular offence, to compass Knox's fall by the help of the men who held his own creed; but with real dexterity Knox had turned his trial into a question between the two religions, and carried his lukewarm friends along with him. Four days later, it may be added, Knox received the full approval of the General Assembly for his conduct in issuing the offending letter.[2]

Another proceeding of Knox, according to Randolph, seems to have specially exasperated Mary. On Palm-

---

[1] The sentence is as follows : "Thir feirfull summondis is direct aganis thame (to wit, the bretherin foirsaid), to make, no doubt, preparatioun upoun ane few that ane dore may be opened till execute creweltie upoun ane grytter multitude."—*Works*, ii. 407.

[2] *Ibid.* p. 415.

Sunday of 1564 Knox was married to Margaret
Stewart, daughter of Andrew, Lord Stewart of Ochiltree, and thus distantly connected with the royal house.
As a matter of fact, Ochiltree was a person of little
standing or consequence;[1] and in public estimation
there was no disparity between an inconsiderable Scottish baron and the great religious leader who spoke on
equal terms with the first men in the country. What
is singular is that Knox should have married as he did,
and married at all. He was a widower with two
young children; but his mother-in-law was now under
his roof, and does not seem to have been too old to
take, in some measure, the place of her daughter.
What accentuated the freak was that Knox was now
in his fifty-ninth year, and the wife he chose was not
over sixteen.[2] The whole business of marrying and
giving in marriage was then carried out in a fashion
that is apt to revolt the better feeling of the present day.
In the case of certain of the finest spirits of the sixteenth century we experience a shock at what seems the
brutality of their relations to their wives. Sir Thomas
More, the most delicate nature of his time, married his
second wife within a month of the death of his first.[3]
From the histories of the leading Reformers we learn
that the choice of a partner in life was as often as not
entrusted to a judicious circle of friends, who did at
once the part of the lawyer and the lover in bringing
about the desired arrangement. "It is the will of
God," exclaimed Melanchthon, when the good office

---

[1] As we learn from Knox's last will and testament, Lord Ochiltree
had to borrow money from his son-in-law.

[2] It is Randolph's statement that she was "not above xvi yearis of
age."—Randolph to Cecil, xxii Januarie 1563. The delay of the
marriage for a year may have been due to this fact.

[3] This appears from a letter published by Mr. Gairdner in the
English Historical Review for October 1892.

was done for himself, "I must give up my studies which made my happiness." This general attitude towards marriage should doubtless be before us in judging this singular step of Knox's old age ; but, as it happens, we have the judgment of Calvin himself on a similar marriage made by his friend and brother-reformer, William Farel. Farel, it should be said, more than any other of the great Protestant leaders, reminds us of Knox, both by his personal character and the nature of the work he performed in Geneva. At the age of sixty-nine, ten years older than Knox, therefore, Farel married a girl under sixteen ; and his brother ministers at Neuchâtel consulted Calvin as to what steps should be taken to put the Church right in the eyes of the world. How Calvin regarded the conduct of Farel may be gathered from the opening sentences of his reply. " Dearest brethren," he writes, " I am in such perplexity that I know not where to make a beginning. Certain it is that our poor brother, Master William, has for once been so ill-advised that we must all needs be in shame and confusion on his account."[1]

Each General Assembly, as has appeared, only intensified the antagonism between the Protestant Lords and the Congregation. At the June gathering of 1564, however, the misunderstanding reached its height. On the first day of meeting, the " Courtiers " deliberately remained at home,—their evident purpose being to effect a division among the ministers themselves. On a representation being made by the Assembly, the Lords made their appearance the next day, but, as on the former occasion, retired to a separate room, whence they sent a request that the

----

[1] *Corpus Reformatorum*, xlv. 335, 351.

superintendents and certain of the leading ministers would meet them in conference. The Assembly perfectly understood the drift of the message, but offered to send representatives on the condition that all matters discussed should be eventually referred to the Assembly itself. This condition being accepted, ten of the leading ministers appeared before the Lords, Knox, by special request, being added as the eleventh.

The conflict really lay between the Court and Knox, as the soul of his party; and on this occasion as usual the discussion seems to have been left almost entirely in the hands of Maitland and Knox. The subjects on which their controversy ran are sufficiently familiar to us from the preceding pages, yet the meeting itself, so curiously characteristic of the age, deserves a passing mention. On the one hand a few Protestant ministers, on the other all the leading men in the Queen's Council, solemnly discussed a clause in the prayer of a popular preacher as a question on which the destinies of the nation might depend. Of late Knox had all but abandoned his originally faint hope of Mary's eventual salvation, and in his public prayer for her welfare restricted himself to the equivocal petition,—" Illuminat hir hairt, gif thy gude plesour be." [1] In the view of Maitland and those for whom he spoke, such a form of prayer conveyed an impression that the Queen's salvation was past praying for. But, as we have seen, Mary's conversion was precisely the issue which the Protestant Lords desired, and which by their present policy they hoped one day to ensure. It was at once as a statesman and a theologian, therefore, that Maitland so keenly discussed

[1] *Works*, ii. 428.

with Knox the scriptural authority for such conditional prayers for the salvation of any fellow-creature. Two other charges brought against Knox prolonged the debate till Maitland was fain to plead fatigue in this encounter of wits with his unweariable opponent. Did the Bible justify such language as Knox used of the Queen's personal character, and did it inculcate such principles as he laid down as to the relations of ruler and subject? In thirty-six pages of his History Knox reports the conversation that took place on these points ; and it is certain that neither Moray nor Maitland would have thought that he exaggerated its importance.

Meanwhile the policy of the Protestant Lords was steadily tending towards the result that Knox had so confidently predicted. It was now nearly three years since Mary's return, and Elizabeth, in spite of threats and promises, had not yet agreed to name her as her successor to the English throne. In their straits Moray and Maitland took a line of conduct which could only have been diplomatic play, but which filled Knox with inconceivable alarm. To bring Elizabeth to reason they made overtures to Philip II. for a marriage between his son Don Carlos and Mary.[1] For England this marriage would have been the most disastrous event that could happen in the position in

---

[1] These negotiations were carried on during the spring and summer of 1563. In a mission to England and France Maitland secretly pressed them. The secretary of De Quadra even came to Scotland and had a secret interview with Moray and Maitland on the same business (Mignet, *Marie Stuart*, ii. Appendix C). But it is hardly possible that Maitland, and still less Moray, could have seriously contemplated such an alliance. In a letter of Kirkcaldy of Grange to Randolph, there is a sentence which almost certainly explains the real intentions of both. "Morower, the Quene Mother hathe writtin to our Quene that Lid [dington] said to hir, that all that was spoken of the mariage with Spaine, was done to caus England grant to our desyris." This letter is printed in Laing's *Knox*, vi. 539, 540.

which she now found herself; and the very thought of it was sufficient to make Elizabeth and her ministers reconsider all their political relations. At length, in March 1564, the exigencies of her position drove Elizabeth to take one step towards satisfying the Scottish Queen and her advisers. By her order Randolph suggested Lord Robert Dudley as a suitable match for Mary.[1] As a safe arrangement both for England and Scotland this marriage had much to recommend it. Dudley was a Protestant, and would have been acceptable to the parties both of Moray and Knox.[2] The match would thus have strengthened the hands of Protestants in Scotland; and the Catholics of England, who were a standing menace to the existing government, would have been deprived of all incentives to active measures. Yet whether from her own weakness for Dudley, or from her nervous dread of designating a successor,[3] Elizabeth made no serious effort to bring the union about.

Seeing no fruit of their action, Mary grew impatient of her Protestant advisers, and in the year 1564 she passed under new influences which eventually involved her ruin. Acting on other counsels than those of Moray and Maitland, she turned her thoughts to her cousin Darnley as the most suitable helpmate for all the ends she had at heart. As to what these ends were there can be no uncertainty: to unite the two crowns, to restore the old religion, to be in her realms what the French and Spanish monarchs were in theirs —were objects which by temper and upbringing she

---

[1] Keith, ii. 224.

[2] Knox was a correspondent of Dudley.—Cf. *Works*, vi. 530.

[3] Even the Spanish ambassador De Quadra admitted that Elizabeth had reason to fear the result of publicly recognising Mary as her successor.—Philippson, ii. 154.

naturally desired to compass. To everybody it was apparent that her union with Darnley was admirably fitted to further these ends. After herself he had the best claim to the English crown, and as of her own religion he had the support of all the English Catholics. In Scotland his religion was a disadvantage; but, as events showed, not so serious as might have been anticipated. As Elizabeth still put her off, Mary had good reasons for taking a line of her own. First, the Earl of Lennox, and, a few months later (February 1565), Darnley, were brought to Scotland and reinstated in the family honours which had been forfeited twenty years before. Between Mary and her brother, the Earl of Moray, there ensued an open breach, and Maitland was quietly set aside for other advisers. Chief among these was David Rizzio, whose sinister influence over the young Queen grew every day till his presence became intolerable. Under these new counsels, and borne along by her own passion and ambition, Mary publicly[1] celebrated her marriage with Darnley on the 29th of July 1565. For Moray this marriage implied the end of all his striving since the day when he threw in his lot with the Congregation. It foreclosed the English alliance, since Elizabeth was both indignant and alarmed at a union which had been carried out in her despite, and whose significance she saw every day more clearly. There was also an end to all hope of completing that reform in religion which at one time it had seemed as if Mary herself would be constrained to accept in her own interest and that of the country. To share her government, as she was

---

[1] She had already been privately married to Darnley in Rizzio's chamber between the 7th and 10th of April (Philippson, ii. 337, 338) —a singular proof of the headstrong impulsiveness of her nature.

now disposed, had for Moray become impossible. Even had he acquiesced in the new policy, his life would not have been safe a day with Rizzio and Darnley in the position they had attained.[1] In his extremity there were but two sources where he was likely to find the support he needed,—the English Court and the Protestant barons and gentlemen who were devoted to Knox. But it was now brought home to him that his policy of the last four years had been built on sand. So precarious was Elizabeth's own position that she could give him no open countenance while he was only a rebel against his sovereign. As for the most earnest section of the Protestants, he had done so little to conciliate them, that they felt no confidence that his restoration to authority would greatly benefit their cause. When he now appealed to them in the interest of their religion, there was no such response as in the days of Mary of Lorraine. In less than three months after her marriage Mary had beaten him at all points, and triumphantly driven him and his associates across the border to be further humiliated by a chilling reception at the English Court.

In this ruin of the Protestant politicians Knox must have had the grim satisfaction of seeing the fulfilment of his endless prophesying. These youths, who had first sat at his feet and then scorned his

---

[1] "How long the kindness will stand between my Lord of Moray and Lord of Lenox, your Honour may judge of by this, that my Lord of Lenox hath join'd himself with those whom my Lord of Moray thinketh worst of in Scotland; what opinion the young Lord hath conceived of him, that lately talking with Lord Robert [Stewart], who shewed him in the Scottish map what lands my Lord of Moray had, and in what bounds, the Lord Darnly said that it was too much. This came to my Lord of Moray's ears, and so to the Queen, who advised my Lord Darnly to excuse himself to my Lord of Moray."—Randolph to Cecil, 20th March 1565; Keith, ii. 274, 275.

counsels, had been taught who was the true interpreter of God's ways with His people. But if this feeling touched him, it was lost in the gloom of the new situation. As far as eye could see, the cause of true religion seemed at length to be fatally wrecked. Its most powerful friends were in exile, two papist sovereigns sat on the throne, and papists ruled all their councils. Knox, who knew everything, was well aware of Mary's correspondence with Rome,[1] though she openly professed the most friendly disposition towards his own party. One notable opportunity came to him of bearing his testimony in this new and terrible probation. The Protestants were still too strong a body to be set at naught, and the two sovereigns were constrained to make a show of goodwill which was not likely to blind such a man as Knox. As a part of this policy, Darnley, though known to be a Catholic, appeared at a service in the Church of St. Giles on Sunday the 19th of August. His experience did not encourage him to repeat the visit. The service lasted more than an hour longer than he had bargained for; and Knox in his sermon made references to Ahab and Jezebel, the point of which could not easily be missed. The king, we are told, "was so moved at this Sermon, that he would not dine; and being troubled, with great fury he past in the afternoon to the hawking."[2] But Knox, on his part, learned that times were now changed. That

---

[1] See Labanoff, *Lettres de Marie Stuart*, i. pp. 177, 179, 355, 369. In these letters Knox has his complete justification in maintaining against Moray and Maitland that, since her return, Mary had never ceased to work for the restoration of the old religion in Scotland.

[2] *Works*, ii. 497. The following reference to this affair occurs in the *Diurnal of Occurrents*. "Upoun the xix day of August the King came to Sanctgellis Kirk, and Johne Knox preachit; quhairat he was crabbit, and causit discharge the said Johne of his preitching."

very evening he was summoned from his bed by the Privy Council to defend the words which had made Darnley so uncomfortable. Knox was attended by a large following of prominent citizens; but the Council was no longer what it had been when he last appeared before it; and he was summarily ordered to abstain from preaching so long as the King and Queen should remain in the town. The Town Council strongly protested against the silencing of their minister,[1] but apparently without success.

Though the outlook was thus so desperate, Knox bated not a jot of hope that all would yet be well. No one saw more clearly that for the moment all the advantage was with the enemy. In his sermon before Darnley he declared that "he that seeth not a fier begonne, that shal burne more than we loke for, unlesse God of his mercie quenche it, is more than blinde."[2] But, as was his unfailing habit, he closed with words of hope for the "little and despised flocke." For our own negligence, he told his hearers, "God gave us over in the handis of other than suche as rule in his feare, that yet he let us not forget his mercy, and that glorious Name that hath bene proclaymed amongst us; but that we may loke throughout the dolorous storme of his present displeasure, and see aswell what punishment he hath appointed for the cruell tirants, as what reward he hath laid in store for such as continue in his feare to the ende."[3]

---

[1] *Council Register*, 23rd August 1565.

[2] *Works*, vi. 245.

[3] *Ibid.* pp. 272, 273. This is the only sermon of Knox that was ever printed by his own authority. In a short introduction giving his reasons for its publication, there occurs perhaps the most extraordinary passage in all his writings. "Wonder not, Christian reader, that of al my studye and travayle within the Scriptures of God these twentye yeares, I have set forth nothing in exponing anye portion of Scripture, except this onelye

The cause of Knox, as we shall see, did in the end prevail, though after a succession of events which terribly revealed the division of heart and mind which the breach with its ancient religion had wrought in the Scottish people.

rude and indigest Sermon preached by me in the publicke audience of the Churche of Edinbrough, the day and yeare above mencioned. That I did not in writ communicat my judgement upon the Scriptures, I have ever thought and yet thinke my selfe to have most just reason. For considering my selfe rather cald of my God to instruct the ignorant, comfort the sorrowfull, confirme the weake, and rebuke the proud, by tong and livelye voyce in these most corrupt dayes, then to compose bokes for the age to come, seeing that so much is written (and that by men of most singular condition), and yet so little well observed ; I decreed to containe my selfe within the bondes of that vocation, wherunto I found my selfe especially called. I dare not denie (lest in so doing I should be injurious to the giver), but that God hath revealed unto me secretes unknowne to the worlde ; and also that he made my tong a trumpet to forwarne realmes and nations, yea, certaine great personages, of translations and chaunges," etc.

CHAPTER II

BESIDES his strivings with the Queen and the temporising Protestants, Knox had all these years been engaged in a task the importance of which can hardly be exaggerated in any estimate of his life and work. It will be remembered that at the instance of the Lords of the Congregation he had undertaken to set forth their doings from the commencement of their contest with Mary of Lorraine till the return of her daughter in August 1561. As originally conceived, the work was simply to be a defence and justification of the actors in that revolution. But the work had grown upon his hands, and before he had done with it, it had attained a scope that fully justifies the title by which it is known—The History of the Reformation in Scotland.

Had Knox not written this book, it may be safely said that he would not have been the figure he is in Scottish history. For our impression of him we should have been confined to the notices of contemporary historians and the casual references in a few State Papers. But the Scottish writers contemporary with him had no adequate sense of the great events in which they were spectators or actors. Even to those on his own side, Knox was but an

eloquent preacher, who along with his fellow-ministers
had done good service in lending his hands to the
overthrow of the strongholds of Satan.   In Buchanan's
History his name occurs only four times, the reference
in each case being of the most casual kind.   Sir James
Melville, also a Protestant, evidently considered himself a much more important person than any preacher
in the country.   To the Catholic bishop, Leslie,
Knox was a pestilent fellow, risen from the dregs of
the people to be a plague to society and all good
Christians.[1]   By Beza, indeed, Knox was emphatically
stamped as the great apostle of his country;[2] but
even the authority of Beza could not have created
the image of Knox familiar to the mind of every
Scotsman.   It is in his History of the Reformation
alone that is to be found, in all its scope and dis-
tinctiveness, the essential spirit of Knox and his work.
In his bare narration of the part he played we have
sufficient proof of the national importance of his
achievement; but it is in the character he has stamped
upon this narrative that we have the fullest testimony
to the commanding force of a personality such as
appears but once or twice in the history of any
people.   It was thus the rare fortune of Knox, among
religious leaders, to set forth a complete presentment
of his own character and aims as he would have them
judged at the bar of posterity.

The bibliographical history of the book has an
interest of its own, and it may be considered a lucky

---

[1] In one passage Leslie speaks of Knox as follows: "Homo nec
humanitate nec artium cognitione, nec aliis vel naturae vel ingenii
dotibus (nisi effrenatam audaciam, ac virulentae linguae volubilitatem,
stulte sine artis praescripto fluentem, dotes appellare volueris) ornatus."
—*De Reb. Gest. Scot.* lib. x. p. 537.

[2] Beza, *Icones.*

chance that it has survived in such form as we now possess it. What is noteworthy is that Knox was unwilling that it should be published during his own lifetime. To a correspondent who had apparently been pressing him to give it to the world, he writes as follows : " My purpose, beloved in the Lord, concerning that which oft and now last ye crave, I wrote to you before, frome which I can not be moved, and, therefore, of my friends I will ask pardon, howbeit in that one head I play the churle, reteaning to myself that which will rather hurt me than profit them, during my dayes, which I hope in God sall not be long ; and then it sall be in the opinion of others, whether it sall be suppressed or come to light." [1]   As we have seen, there were reasons why Knox might well desire that he should be in his grave before many things he had written should see the light. Immediately after his death, however, steps were taken to put his manuscripts in a shape suitable for publication. His secretary, Richard Bannatyne, brought the matter specially before the following General Assembly. The History, Bannatyne wrote, was in completed form as far as the year 1564, but after that date his master's papers were in such confusion that considerable pains would be required to set them in order. If the Assembly would grant him a " reasonable pension," he would undertake to put the whole work in a shape fit to be given to the world.[2] The request was granted,[3] yet there was no immediate fruit of Bannatyne's labour. Possibly those who saw the book may have thought that its publication would be ill-timed in the interests of

[1] *Works,* vi. 558.

[2] Bannatyne's letter to the General Assembly is given in the edition of Knox's History, published at Edinburgh in 1732, p. xliv.

[3] Peterkin, *Booke of the Universall Kirk of Scotland,* p. 135.

the very cause to which Knox had given his life. At length, in 1586, a manuscript of the History was placed in the hands of the printer, Thomas Vautrollier, with a view to its immediate publication. But the book seemed doomed to misadventure. Having taken the manuscript with him to London, Vautrollier had printed 1200 copies when he received an order staying their publication.[1] In 1644 the book was at last given to the world, though still under auspices that testified to an evil fate. In passing through the hands of the censor in London it suffered mutilation against which Milton in his *Areopagitica* vehemently protested, as an injury done to liberty of thought and the memory of a great man.[2] What was still more unfortunate, its editor, David Buchanan, did his work with so easy a conscience that for nearly a century the authenticity of the book was seriously called in question. By his tampering with the text, and his arbitrary omissions and interpolations,[3] difficulties were presented which

[1] In Calderwood's larger MS. History occurs the following passage: "Vautrollier the printer took with him a copy of Mr. Knox's History to England, and printed twelve hundred of them ; the Stationers, at the Archbishop's command, seized them the 18 of February [1587]; it was thought that he would get leave to proceed again, because the Council perceived that it would bring the Queen of Scots in detestation." Copies of Vautrollier's unfinished edition found their way into the hands of the public. They are now very scarce.

[2] *Areopagitica, A Speech of Mr. John Milton for the Liberty of Unlicens'd Printing*, addressed to the Parliament of England. London, 1644, p. 22. As expressing Milton's opinion of Knox, the following passage is interesting. "Nay, which is more lamentable, if the work of any deceased author, though never so famous in his lifetime, and even to this day, come to their hands for licence to be Printed or Reprinted, if there be found in his book one sentence of a ventrous edge, utter'd in the height of zeal, and who knows whether it might not be the dictat of a divine Spirit, yet not suiting with every low decrepit humor of their own, though it were *Knox* himself, the Reformer of a Kingdom, that shake it, they will not pardoun him their dash," etc.

[3] Specimens of Buchanan's alterations are given in a letter of Robert Wodrow, Librarian of the University of Glasgow, to Bishop Nicolson,

were hardly consistent with the assumption that Knox was its author. An edition published in 1732 set this question at rest. Based on a manuscript in the possession of the University of Glasgow, this edition was produced with a pious care that left nothing to be desired,[1] and it was only the discovery of an earlier manuscript that enabled Laing to print what may be considered the definitive text of the History as it came from the hands of Knox.[2]

It is in October 1559 that we first hear of Knox's intention to write his book.[3] By reports spread at home and abroad the cause of the Congregation was being seriously compromised, and its progress hindered. Before Knox's return in May 1559 the Protestant leaders had issued a manifesto in Latin,[4] in which they sought to justify their proceedings in the eyes of all Christian princes. It was still more important, however, that they should set themselves right in the public opinion of England and Scotland. With this object they called on Knox to compose a history of their past and present doings which should set forth their true aims, and materially advance their cause. In the preface to the second book, Knox has in set terms

printed in part in Nicolson's *Scottish Historical Library*, Appendix VI., and in full in the edition of Knox's History, 1732. Laing has printed a fuller list, Knox, *Works*, ii. 569 *et seq.*

[1] *The Historie of the Reformatioun of Religioun within the Realm of Scotland. . . .* taken from the Original Manuscript in the University Library of Glasgow, and compared with other ancient Copies. Edinburgh, 1732. The editor was the Rev. Matthew Crawfurd.

[2] Knox, *Works*, i. xxx. *et seq.*

[3] "The authoritie of the Frenche King and Quen is yet receaved, and wilbe in wourd till thei deny our most just requeastes, which ye shall, God willing, schortlie hereafter understand, togetther with our hole proceadings from the begynninge of this matter, which we now ar to sett furth in maner of Historie."—Knox to Gregory Raylton, 23rd October 1559, *Works*, vi. 87.

[4] See above, ii. 53.

declared the motive and object of his work. "Least that Sathan," he says, "by our long silence shall tak occasioun to blaspheym, and to sklander us the Protestantis of the Realme of Scotland, as that our fact tendit rather to seditioun and rebellioun then to reformatioun of maners and abuses in Religioun, we have thocht expedient, so trewlie and brievlie as we can, to committ to writting the causes moving us (us, we say, ane great parte of the Nobilitie and Baronis of the Realme) to tak the sweard of just defence against those that most injustlie seak our destructioun."[1] The main lines of his work were thus clearly laid down ; yet even had no charge been laid upon him, Knox was not the man to write a history which should hold the balance straight when his own deepest convictions were in question. That such a history could be written even by a zealous believer, was proved later in the century (1581) by the History of France, of the Huguenot La Popelinière. "I have put in practice," says that writer, "a new method of representing the designs and actions of contending parties, remaining neutral and dispassionate as a historian ought to be." So little was this self-effacement appreciated in the sixteenth century, that the unfortunate historian was handled as roughly by his fellow-Huguenots as by the Catholics.[2]

As originally conceived, the narrative was to be confined to events between 1558 and the arrival of Mary in Scotland—the ground actually covered by the second and third books of the History as we now possess it. On second thoughts, however, an introduc-

---

[1] *Works*, i. 297, 298.
[2] *Histoire Universelle par Agrippa D'Aubigné, Édition publiée pour la Société de l'Histoire de France*, par le Baron Alphonse de Ruble, i. 371-376.

tory book was added by way of leading up to the special work of the Congregation.[1] The fourth book may be considered in inspiration, conception, and treatment, as, beyond all its companions, the specific expression of Knox's own individuality. From this book, as we shall see, is in large measure derived that image of Knox which has passed into the minds of his country-men. The fifth and last book bears in no degree the characteristics of Knox, and at best must be regarded as the orderly presentment of the "Scrolls" found among his papers after his death.

Of all the four books, the first is that which best exhibits Knox's gifts as a historian. The succeeding three are so largely made up of documents and conver-sations that he has no opportunity of rising to a full and flowing narrative. In his first book, however, he had ample scope for every gift of the historian ; for his subject was the origin and development of a movement that resulted in the awakening of the national conscious-ness. Of the success with which he performed his task there is one irrefragable proof. The story, as he has told it, has gone into the popular mind as effectively as the chant of an epic poet. The Lollards of Kyle, the martyrdom of Patrick Hamilton, the rout of Solway Moss, the mission and death of Wishart, the slaughter of Cardinal Beaton, the siege of the Castle of St. Andrews—it is mainly through the pages of Knox that these scenes and persons stand forth with such vivid-ness in Scottish history and tradition. Nor can the story, as he has told it, be impugned as a close and accurate presentment of the facts he professed to record. In treating the period which this first book covers, succeeding Church historians have in large

[1] *Works*, i. 4.

degree only reproduced with their own idiosyncrasies the materials supplied by Knox.

The second and third books, as has been said, comprise the whole work as it was originally conceived. Practically they were written from day to day as events happened which the writer deemed worthy of record.[1] Intended in the first place as a justification of the Protestant party, these books bear on their face a character distinct from the others. The writer speaks throughout in the name and with the authority of the nobles and barons at whose request the work was undertaken. Though their avowed object might thus seem to discredit them as trustworthy history, these books are, in truth, the most valuable portion of the work. To carry conviction of the truth of his representations, Knox was led to choose the method which it is the boast of the present age to have rigorously applied to historical study. Fully three-fourths of these two books consist of original documents, from which the reader is enabled to form his own judgment on the points at issue between the contending parties. In the actual narrative we have convincing proof alike of the writer's good faith, and of his perception of the conditions of historic truth. What he relates is either based on what he has himself seen, or on the authority of those on whose testimony he had every reason to place his faith. In spite of his unconcealed bias, therefore, we have in this part of Knox's work an exposition of the most momentous epoch of Scottish history which can hardly be overestimated. He has preserved many documents which but for his labours could in all prob-

---

[1] This appears from the narrative itself. For the early period treated in these books, notes and materials must have been supplied to Knox, as he did not return to Scotland till May 1559. The Preface to the second book seems to have been written before the Treaty of Edinburgh.

ability never have been recovered.[1]   In this part of his work the later Church historians, Calderwood, Spottiswoode, and Keith, have for the most part only drawn their materials from the pages of Knox.   In his conception of his task, also, Knox shows a full understanding of the scope of the revolution in which he was the most distinguished actor.   From the account of that revolution which has been given in the present work it appears how largely that account was necessarily based on Knox's own reports of the events and personages that make up its history.   Without accepting his opinions as to these events and personages, we find in his presentment of facts the adequate explanation of the breach which the Scottish people then made with its past.   The causes—economic, political, moral, and spiritual—which produced the Scottish Reformation are set forth in these pages with a precision and emphasis which cannot be misapprehended.   It is thus, perhaps, the unique distinction of Knox to have been at once the maker and the writer of history on a scale that may be safely described as of national and even European importance.

If the second and third books have the highest value as history, it is in the fourth that we must look for the manifestation of Knox's spirit.   Composed mainly in the year 1566,[2] it is evidently based on full

---

[1] In a letter of Randolph to Cecil (23rd September 1560) we have an interesting testimony to the pains which Knox took with his work. " I have tawlked at large with Mr. Knox concerning his Hystorie.   As mykle as ys written thereof shall be sent to your Honour, at the comynge of the Lords Embassadours by Mr. John Woode.   He hath wrytten only one Booke.   If yow lyke that, he shall continue the same, or adde onie more.   He sayethe that he must have further helpe then is to be had in thys countrie, for more assured knowledge of thyngs passed than he hath hymself, or can come bye here : yt is a work not to be neglected, and greatly wyshed that yt sholde be well handled."—Knox, *Works*, vi. 121.   [2] *Works*, ii. 265.

and careful notes which had been made with a view to
the continuous narrative in which it took final shape.
In the period which it records—the first three years of
the reign of Mary[1]—Knox had a theme after his own
heart, which could hardly fail to draw forth all the
strength and weakness of his character and intelligence.
When he addressed himself to his task, be it said, he
was in the mood of the prophet rather than of the
historian. As he looked around him, he saw the apparent ruin of all his hopes for his country and his
religion. The Book of Discipline was farther than
ever from being accepted as the law and testimony of
the nation, and the enemies of the truth were rearing
their heads in triumph. What embittered the situation
was that it had been brought about, as it seemed to
him, by the lukewarmness of friends rather than the
strength of opponents. With these feelings in his
heart, Knox sat down to write the story of the years
since the ill-omened return of the Queen. In this
portion of his work he could no longer speak as the
representative of the whole body of the Congregation.
Though he does not make use of the first person, it is
himself and his own words and deeds that are the
central theme of his narrative. The Protestant nobles
having taken a course of their own, he was virtually
the sole champion of the cause which these nobles
seemed to be giving away. In the preface to the
fourth book he frankly announces the line he is about
to take. True religion, he says, had come to its present
pass "becaus that suddandlie the most parte of us
declyned from the puritie of Goddis word, and began
to follow the warld ; and so agane to schaik handis

---

[1] It would seem that Knox had no intention of carrying his History
beyond this date.—*Works*, ii. 422. But see above p. 216.

with the Devill, and with idolatrie, as in this Fourte Booke we will hear."[1] How he performed his task has sufficiently appeared from a preceding chapter. There we have seen how his sermons in St. Giles's, his conversations with the Queen, his wrangles with Lethington, his alienation from Moray — form the staple of his narrative of these years of backsliding and shame. It was little wonder that he should wish his eyes closed before a narrative appeared which the Protestant nobles, and Moray in special, might justly regard as a perversion of their real aims and motives. More than any of their enemies, Knox is responsible for opinions regarding these nobles which ignore the difficulties of their position and the policy that under- lay their relations to the Queen. According to his representation, they played into the hands of Mary for their own selfish interests, and betrayed the Church to which they had professed their devotion. How far this was from the whole truth we have already seen ; and in his later years Knox may himself have come to see that in his haste he had done gross injustice to certain men whom in his heart he regarded with affec- tion and esteem.

Of the fifth book of the History little need be said. In passing to it from the others we descend to a lower plane of intelligence and feeling. In its flaccid and monotonous narrative we are the width of heaven from Knox's outpouring of spirit and passionate delivery of his subject. How it assumed the form in which it now stands it seems impossible to explain.[2] It has been ascribed to David Buchanan, who edited the History

---

[1] *Works*, ii. 265.

[2] We have no definite information as to whether Richard Bannatyne carried out the task of editing Knox's papers, as he proposed.

in 1644; but from internal evidence this seems unlikely. If we may judge from Buchanan's authentic work, he was somewhat wrongheaded, but not without a certain force and ingenuity of mind. In his mode of expression he was disposed to elaboration, and at times he verges on the euphuism of Sir Thomas Urquhart.[1] But the style of this fifth book is as devoid of literary preoccupation as any style could be. On the subject of religion, also, Buchanan had fervid convictions, which must have left their stamp even in his serving-up of another's materials. But though the compiler, whoever he may have been, shows unmistakable Protestant sympathies, he was evidently incapable of the energy of feeling of which Buchanan has given such emphatic proof. What seems the most probable conjecture is that Richard Bannatyne may actually have completed the work he undertook, and have wrought Knox's papers into a consecutive narrative. In point of execution the narrative seems the appropriate work of a secretary trained to method and order, but of no great culture or force of mind; and such we know Richard Bannatyne to have been.

For various reasons it will be seen that Knox's History of the Reformation holds a unique place in English literature. As the work of one who both made and wrote history on a scale of such importance, it has an antecedent and special interest of its own. But in itself it possesses qualities which compel us to recognise it as a notable product of character and genius. It is when we compare it with the contemporary vernacular narratives of Bishop Leslie and

---

[1] In the long Preface on the history of the Scottish nation with which he introduces his edition of Knox's History we have a characteristic example of Buchanan's style.

Sir James Melville that we realise all the superiority of Knox. Preoccupied with petty details, and incapable of philosophical and spiritual insight, these writers had no conception of the momentous issues that hung on the events which they record. Among the historians of the century, indeed, there is but one who by the quality of his talent may be fitly compared to Knox— the Huguenot, Agrippa D'Aubigné. By the identity and intensity of their convictions they naturally suggest a parallel, and the literary characteristics of the one are largely those of the other. Yet, vivid and dramatic as is the work of D'Aubigné, it cannot be put beside that of Knox as the expression of the awakened consciousness of a people.

For the biographer of Knox, however, his History is mainly interesting for the light it throws on the mind and heart of the man. In his other works, with the exception of a few letters, it is as the politician or the theologian or the preacher that he exclusively presents himself. In his History there is a play of mind and feeling from which we may draw some image of the man with his innate aptitudes and affinities. The dominant characteristic of the book cannot be missed by the most casual reader—the abounding vitality that quickens it from the first page to the last. On the face of it, it is the production of one whose function it was to speak and not to write, whose habit was to emphasise with tone and gesture every sentence that rose to his lips. The intensity of the writer's likes and dislikes would of itself save the book from dulness ; but his energy of feeling is manifest in the smallest details with which he concerns himself. The notion of Knox as a one-eyed fanatic, groaning under the burden of his mission, is certainly not borne out by

these two volumes of his History.   On every page the
fact is thrust upon us that he was the keenest of
observers, and that he had a specially wide knowledge
of the practical aspects of life.   When he describes a
battle, as he more than once has done, it is with the
gusto of one whose immediate ancestors had died
under the banner of their feudal superior.   From the
" meary bourds"[1] with which he enlivens his narrative,
we may infer that his daily conversation was not always
of justification and predestination ; but that he could
tell his story and exchange his jest as time and place
were fitting.   What distinguishes him from men like
Calvin or Savonarola is precisely that sense of a humorous side of things, which made him at once a great
writer and a great leader of men.   Of the value of this
quality in the conduct of human affairs he was himself
perfectly conscious, and deliberately employed it both
in his writings and in his dealings with his fellows.
" Melancholius ressouns," he said in one of his debates
with Lethington, "wald haif sum myrth intermixed."[2]
Studied anticlimax, grim irony, humorous exaggeration, are as distinctively his characteristics as they
·are those of Carlyle, in whom also they are relieving
qualities to narrow intensity and an overbearing
temper.   With humour is usually found pity and the
power of pathos ; and in Knox, more than once, his
harsh austerity softens into a mood the more impressive
that it comes so seldom.   As he has told it, the story
of the mission and death of George Wishart is a
masterpiece of that stern pathos which is not common
in literature, for those to whom it is natural do not
usually become men of letters.   In the passage where
he describes the arrest of Wishart there is a brief

----

[1] Lively jests.   [2] *Works*, ii. 450.

intensity which will not be easily matched in English literature. "After suppar he [Wishart] held comfortable purpose[1] of the death of Goddis chosen childrin, and mearely said, ' Methink that I desyre earnestlye to sleep;' and thairwith he said, ' Will we sing a Psalme?' And so he appointed the 51st Psalme, which was put in Scotishe meter, and begane thus :—

> Have mercy on me now, good Lord,
> After thy great mercy, etc.,

which being ended, he past to chalmer, and sonar then his commoun dyet was, past to bed with these wourdis, ' God grant qwyet rest.' Befoir mydnycht the place was besett about that none could eschape to mack advertisement."[2]

---

[1] Conversation.

[2] *Works*, i. 139-140. There is an interesting paper on Knox's History in the *Miscellaneous Essays and Addresses* of Sir William Stirling-Maxwell. As will afterwards be seen, the composition of his History occupied Knox to the very close of his life. Cf. *Works*, vi. 611 ; and Richard Bannatyne's *Memoriales, passim*. From his long residence in England and his subsequent intercourse with Englishmen on the Continent, it was natural that Knox should express himself in a kind of Anglicised Scots. Accordingly, Ninian Winzet could say to him : "Gif ze, throw curiositie of nouationis, hes forzet our auld plane Scottis quhilk zour mother lerit zou, in tymes cuming I sall wryte to zou my mynd in Latin, for I am nocht acquyntit with zour Southeroun."
—*Certain Tractates*, etc. i. 138 (Scot. Text Soc.).

CHAPTER III

IN the overthrow of Moray and his associates Knox could not but see the temporary ruin of all his hopes for true religion. Not since "that dark and dolorous night" of November, when the Lords of the Congregation were driven from Edinburgh, had the prospect been so gloomy as now. Mary was triumphant on all hands, and, secure in her victory, gave Rizzio precedence in her counsels over the first of her Catholic nobles. As early as the 3rd of June Randolph had written to Cecil: "David now worketh all, and is only governor to the King and his family; great is his pride, and his words intollerable;" and every day since, the Italian's power had gone on increasing. But as the known agent of the Pope, Rizzio's predominance could lead to but one issue, which, as things now went, could not be far off. The last few months had already wrought disaster in the ranks of the ministers. Even during the ascendency of Moray, their means of subsistence had been meagre and precarious; but for the whole year following Moray's breach with the Queen, not a penny of their allotted stipends was forthcoming.[1]

---

[1] This appears from a letter of Mary entitled "Assignation for the Ministerie by the Queen," 20th December 1566. See *Booke of the Universall Kirk of Scotland*, pp. 95, 96.

Some of them, it was said, died in the streets for hunger and cold.[1] It is not wonderful, therefore, that certain were drawing back from an office so ungrateful, while others, to the scandal of religion, sought to conjoin secular pursuits with their sacred functions. From its troubles within and without it was evident that if another revolution did not come soon, the new Church would be in no better case than in the days of its controversy with Mary of Lorraine.

All that Knox could do in this time of eclipse he appears to have done with his usual vigour. The ban on his preaching applied only during the residence of the King and Queen in Edinburgh,[2] and the autumn of 1565 saw him as active as ever in his function of prophet and censor. The burden of his preaching now was the evil state of a country when its best citizens were banished and God's servants oppressed. His words were reported to the Queen, and seemed likely to bring him into trouble ; but on this occasion he found an unexpected champion. Lethington, now set aside for Rizzio, and therefore not on the best of terms with the Court, testified that he had heard the incriminating sermons, and that in none of them had a word been said "whereat any man need to be offended."[3]

On December 25th the Church held its half-yearly Assembly, and raised its usual protest against the policy of the Court. In the absence of its most influential members, however, it was no longer the formidable body it had been during the last few years.

---

[1] Letter of the Commendators of Arbroath, Kilwinning, etc.—*Booke of the Universall Kirk of Scotland*, p. 62.

[2] For a time his preaching must have ceased, as Craig, his colleague, desired assistance at this time "in respect he was alone."—Calderwood, ii. 340.　　　　　　　[3] *Works*, ii. 514.

In view of their unhappy estate, the Assembly determined that a public Fast should be held for the national
sins, which had brought the displeasure of Heaven on
Church and State alike.   No such means of grace had
been counselled before, because it had seemed to be a
concession to the idle practices of the Pope's religion.
To justify this new departure, and to make the Fast
a harmless and profitable exercise, was a matter that
demanded circumspection.   As beyond suspicion of
any compromise with superstition, Knox was entrusted
with the task of placing in its true light the meaning
and efficacy of public and private fasts.   In discharging his task he took the opportunity of producing a
manifesto, in which he reviewed at length the condition and prospects of the Church.   On their own
zeal and devotion, he told his readers, must they
depend for the advance of godliness in the nation.
Any hope they had of the Queen's eyes being opened,
they must now resolutely set aside.   In plain words
she had publicly told them that she would never
abandon the religion in which she had been reared.[1]
Three reasons for the public Fast are specially adduced
—the abounding sin "in all estates," "the great
hunger, famine, and oppressioun of the poure," and
the state of the afflicted brethren "in France, Flanders,
and other parts."[2]   Besides this "Order of the General
Fast," Knox, also in the name of the Assembly, wrote
a special "exhortation" to all classes of Protestants, in
which he besought their support in that crisis of their

---

[1] In a letter to the Assembly Mary had said that "she neither may
nor will leave the religion wherein she has been nourished and up-
brought."—*Booke of the Universall Kirk*, p. 34.   Mary's letter was
written after her triumph over Moray.

[2] *Works*, vi. 428.—Tytler is mistaken in associating this Fast
with the murder of Rizzio.   The Fast, and the reasons for it, were
settled in the December of the year preceding Rizzio's death.

faith. Soon no minister would be left to announce to them the truth they professed to cherish. Appealing as usual to Scriptural examples, he puts to them the following question : " Did a man feede an hundered servauntes of the Lorde, and in that tyme when things were most scant, and yet both the King and the Queene sought the subversion of true religion and the destruction of all God's true servants, and shal not a thousand of us and moe that have professed the Lord Jesus in this Realme, upon our charges, sustaine two or three hundereth of such as have travailed, and yet travaile to advance the kingdome of Jesus Christ amongst us ? " [1]

With his best friends in exile, and the Court now guided as it was, Knox could hardly be safe in Edinburgh, if he went on as he had been doing. A request came from St. Andrews that he would take charge of the congregation in that town, but the Assembly refused to consider it.[2] Possibly to put him out of harm's way Knox was charged, during the ensuing months, to make a preaching tour in the south, and to remain " so long as occasioun might suffer."[3]

During these months a train was laid in which Knox had probably no part; but which would doubtless have had his hearty approval. An upstart foreigner at the head of affairs could not long be borne by a body of men like the nobles of Scotland. That Mary, in the policy she had at heart, should have given her confidence to Rizzio is easily intelligible ; but that she should have flaunted him before the world, as she did, was imprudence that approached imbecility. By the

[1] *Works*, vi. 435.
[2] Keith, iii. 127. He was wanted at St. Andrews to fill the place of his friend Goodman, who had just gone to England.
[3] Calderwood, ii. 306.

obtrusive favours she heaped upon him, she alienated her husband, and turned him, weak as he was, into a dangerous tool in the hands of a disaffected party. So wholly did the future seem to be in the hands of Rizzio, that this party saw no hope as long as he was at the ear of their Queen. In these circumstances they took the counsel which nine-tenths of the public men in Europe would have winked at or approved as a satisfactory means of removing a political enemy.[1] Less than a century before, the Scottish nobles had summarily hanged the Court favourite Cochrane for reasons which had the approval of the country. With this precedent before them, Morton, Lindsay, Ruthven, and other Protestants of inferior rank exchanged oaths with Darnley and his father Lennox, to cut off the offending foreigner before his evil action should be beyond repair. At the next meeting of Parliament (4th March 1566) the designs of Rizzio were to take effect in measures which would be disastrous to the future of Protestantism. Among these measures were to be enactments in favour of the old religion, and the forfeiture of those who had taken part in the late rebellion.[2] Before these measures should pass it was decided that the enemy should be cut off as Cochrane had been cut off at Lauder Bridge.

In the atrocious deed of the 9th of March Knox in all probability had neither art nor part. Morton

---

[1] The Council of Henry VIII. approved the plot for the murder of Cardinal Beaton. Similarly on the 7th June 1571 Philip II.'s Council of State deliberated on a scheme for the assassination of Elizabeth.—Mignet, ii. 161.

[2] "The spirituall estate being placed therein [that is, in the Parliament] in the ancient maner, tending to have done some good anent restoring the auld religion, and to have proceeded against our rebels according to their demerits."—Mary to Archbishop of Glasgow, 2nd April 1566; Labanoff, i. 343.

affirmed this, and it was but simple worldly policy on the part of the conspirators that no breath of suspicion should attach to the chief minister of their religion. Of the manner in which the deed was done we may be certain that Knox would disapprove as vehemently as any of his contemporaries. From gratuitous bloodshed he shrank with a keenness of feeling which assuredly was not common in his age and country. When Kirkcaldy of Grange asked him if it were permissible to escape from prison by slaying his gaoler, Knox's answer was a stern negative.[1] On the other hand, of the original plan of removing Rizzio by summary trial and execution[2] he would have unconditionally approved. In his eyes, Rizzio had broken the highest law in the land in abetting the mass, and labouring to bring back the Pope. Any trial of him, therefore, could be only to give the wretched man the opportunity of possible repentance. In any event, the greatest crime would have been to permit him to live, and imperil the spiritual welfare of a people. In this sense only we must understand the following words in which he expressly applauds the act of the Protestant leaders : "And to lett the world understand in plane termes what we meane, that great abusar of this commoun wealth, that pultron and vyle knave Davie, was justlie punished, the nynt of Merch, in the year of God, J^m V^c three-score fyve, for abusing of the Commoun wealth, and for his other villany, which we list nott to express, by the

---

[1] *Works*, i. 229.

[2] The Protestant nobles who took part in the deed wished to have the form of a trial ; but Darnley would not listen to this suggestion.— Narrative of Morton and Ruthven, Keith, iii. 264 ; Bedford and Randolph to the English Council, 27th March 1566. Robertson, *Hist. of Scotland*, iii. 317 (edit. 1812) ; Spottiswoode, ii. 37 (Spottiswoode Society) ; Knox, *Works*, ii. 521 ; Hume, *History of the House of Douglas and Angus*, pp. 289-290 (1644).

counsall and handis of James Douglas, Erle of Morton, Patrik Lord Lyndesay, and the Lord Ruthven, with otheris assistaris in thare company, who all, for thare just act, and most worthy of all praise, ar now unworthely left of thare brethrein, and suffer the bitterness of banishement and exyle." [1]

The removal of Rizzio had not the immediate results that had been intended. On the night following his death, Moray and the exiled lords made their entrance into Edinburgh ; and, had Darnley kept his pledge, the Protestant party would have regained its ascendency. Detaching Darnley from his fellow-conspirators, however, Mary carried him to Dunbar, whence she returned to the capital in the course of a week (18th March). With Darnley, Bothwell, and the Catholic Lords on her side, she was at least stronger than she had been during the first four years of her reign, and in a securer position than during the unnatural ascendency of Rizzio. Three months after Rizzio's murder Moray told the English resident Killigrew that he had less power in the country than after his breach with Mary regarding the Darnley marriage.[2]

After the death of her favourite, Mary was in no temper to endure the scoldings of preachers ; and as Moray was not in a position to protect him, Knox, so closely connected with the party that had so mercilessly disregarded her feelings, deemed it prudent to quit the capital.[3]   In Kyle, in Ayrshire, the most

---

[1] See Appendix D, *Knox and the Rizzio Murder.*

[2] Philippson, iii. 223.

[3] *Works*, ii. 526.   *The Diurnal of Occurrents* contains the following entry for 17th March 1566 : "John Knox, minister of Edinburgh, is in likewyse depairtit of the said burgh at twa hours efternone, with ane greit murnyng of the godlie of religioun."

strenuously Protestant district in the country, he seems to have found a home till the ensuing autumn, though even here Mary made efforts to reach him.[1] Knox regarded his severance from his congregation as exile, but he was not without his consolations. One event especially must have brought him some cheer in the general gloom of the situation. The district of Carrick, in Ayrshire, had hitherto been as notable a stronghold of the old religion as Kyle had been of the new. During Knox's sojourn in the west, however, Carrick also was gained for Protestantism in unexpected fashion. The lord of the district, the redoubtable Earl of Cassillis,[2] married a Protestant wife, the sister of Lord Glammis, "by whose persuasion," we are told, he embraced the new faith, and set himself with vigour to bring all his neighbourhood to his own way of thinking.[3]

It was during this period, as has been said, that Knox may have wrought up his notes for the fourth book of his History of the Reformation. The preface to that book, at least, was certainly written at this time; and one passage shows us precisely what thoughts were passing through his mind during these months of exile and discomfiture. "But from whence (allace) cumeth this miserable dispersioun of Goddis people within this Realme, this day, Anno 1566, in Maij? And what is the cause that now the just is compelled to keap silence? good men ar banished, murtheraris, and such as ar knowin un-

---

[1] Archbishop Grindal to Bullinger, 17th August 1566 (Strype's *Grindal*, p. 492 (1821).

[2] This was the Earl of Cassillis who is reported to have "roasted" the Commendator of Crossraguel in order to secure the temporalities of the Abbey. The story, it appears, has been greatly exaggerated.— *Charters of the Abbey of Crossraguel*, p. 1 (50).

[3] *Works*, ii. 533.

worthie of the commoun societie (yf just lawis war put in deu executioun), bear the hoill regiment and swynge within this Realme? We answere, Becaus that suddandlie the most parte of us declyned from the puritie of Goddis word, and began to follow the warld; and so agane to schaik handis with the Devill, and with idolatrie, as in this Fourte Booke we will hear."[1]

As the year 1566 wore on, signs were visible that a fresh upturning was imminent in public affairs. Of Catholic and Protestant, neither was strong enough effectually to keep down the other, and so long as they were so nearly equal in strength, a stable government was an impossibility. The royal authority had always been weak in Scotland, but in Mary's hands it hardly counted in the strife of the contending factions. The "beastly liberty" of the Scottish nobles (to use the phrase of Sir Ralph Sadler) was only kept in check by the fear of the decisive triumph of their enemies, which inevitably led to confiscation and exile. To these constitutional evils were added the uncertainties arising from the humours of a feminine ruler. Mary's relation to Darnley had now settled into its final phase. She had passionately given herself away to him at their first acquaintance; but between two such lovers, both equally incapable of continuity of feeling, the transition to jealousy and antipathy was as rapid as their loves. In his miserable rage Darnley had cut off Rizzio, in whom he saw not a public enemy, as was the case of his fellow-conspirators, but a rival in the affections of his wife, and the obstacle in the way of his boyish ambition. For a woman who gave her affections so adventurously as Mary, the crime was unpardonable, and shortly after Rizzio's

[1] *Works*, ii. 265.

death the relations of the royal couple became the scandal of Europe. Mary belonged to the type of woman whose heart and mind must be given to the keeping of another. Her new lover and adviser was, in his way, as strange a figure as Rizzio himself. Among the Scottish nobles Bothwell has an individuality all his own. He professed to be a Protestant, but had consistently acted in the interests of the other party. Both to Mary and her mother he had given proofs that he could be of real service when it pleased him; but his whole career proves that he was a born outlaw and incendiary. With many of the Scottish nobles, both Protestant and Catholic, patriotism and religion were real motives, for which they ventured both life and fortune. To Bothwell such motives could not present themselves; and in the career of piratical desperado to which he took in the wreck of his fortunes, we have the revelation of the essential nature of the man. Through the summer and autumn his influence with Mary had steadily increased; and by the date we have reached he was as powerful in the country as any one man could be in the existing state of affairs.[1]

But the general situation was still further complicated by the state of the Protestant party. By the flight of Morton, Ruthven, Lindsay, and others, from the vengeance of the Queen, the party had lost for a time the majority of its most powerful supporters. But a more serious, because more permanent, source of weakness was the fact that in their extremity they could not count on the support of Elizabeth as they had confidently supposed. In their late contest with Mary, Elizabeth had not only refused her support to

[1] Cf. Mignet, i. 266, *note*.

the rebel lords, but had put a public affront on their
leader Moray.[1]   It had been their hope that if things
came to the worst they would have such help from Elizabeth as had formerly made united action possible to the
Protestant leaders.   Now that it was seen that Elizabeth used them only to her own purposes, this union
was at an end, and thenceforward there was a division
in their ranks which was never permanently closed
during the remaining years of Knox.   Moray and
Morton still continued to believe that Elizabeth really
meant them well, and held consistently by their former
policy.   On the other hand Argyle,[2] Ruthven, Boyd
—to name only the chief men—are found more often
than not in open hostility to their ancient associates.
Such was the state of affairs in the autumn of 1566 :
the situation had in fact become impossible ; constitutional means of setting it right did not exist, and in
Scotland there was a traditional method of cutting the
knot in cases of peculiar emergency.

As affairs stood towards the close of the year, the
way was once more open for Knox's return to Edinburgh.   Bothwell was the most powerful man at Court,
and Bothwell was a Protestant, and had been the feudal
superior of Knox's family.   From Mary, therefore,
Knox had no longer anything to fear.   In the beginning of September he appears to have been in St.
Andrews, as his name is attached to a letter in which the
Scottish ministers expressed their approval of a Confession of Faith which had been sent to them by Beza;[3]

---

[1] This is implied even in Knox's reference to the interview between
Elizabeth and Moray.—*Works*, ii. 513.

[2] Argyle was specially indignant at Elizabeth's treatment of the
Scottish Protestants.—Philippson, iii. 199, 200.

[3] *Works*, vi. 544-550.   He apparently was in Edinburgh in September.—*Town Council Records*, 25th September 1566.

and in December we find him in Edinburgh, taking part in an Assembly which met under circumstances that must have taxed its collective wisdom.

What now exercised Knox and his brethren was the equivocal attitude of the Queen towards the two religions. At three successive meetings of the Privy Council decrees had been passed in the highest degree favourable to the ministers.[1] In consideration of their pressing need special bounties, in the shape of money and victuals, had been assigned to them. But it was the fundamental doctrine of the Scottish Reformers that each congregation should support its own minister. The Assembly, therefore, looked on the gifts with suspicion, but, apparently after some hesitation, agreed to accept them in view of the existing state of the country.[2] Coming from the source it did, the bounty was in itself suspicious ; but another act of the Queen proved how little encouragement was to be drawn from it. On the 23rd of December the Archbishop of St. Andrews was restored to full consistorial jurisdiction, contrary alike to the Acts of 1560 and to the Queen's own express pledge on her return from France. This was the most daring step that Mary had yet taken in favour of her own Church, and it filled Knox with consternation and dismay. What the step meant became apparent a few months later ;[3] but it now seemed to threaten the return of the whole monstrous brood that had been swept from the country six years before. To Knox the Assembly entrusted

---

[1] These Acts of the Privy Council will be found in Peterkin's *Booke of the Universall Kirk*, pp. 93-96.

[2] *Ibid.* pp. 46, 47.

[3] The only act of the Archbishop after his reinstatement was " to confirm the sentence of nullity of marriage between Bothwell and his Countess."—Bellesheim, *Catholic Church in Scotland*, iii. 109, Translator's note.

the task of waking the Protestant nobles to a sense of the terrible danger that menaced them. Knox not only did what he was asked, but added an epistle general of his own in which he addressed the whole Protestant community on the alarming nature of the situation. As a veteran pamphleteer he puts in a glaring light the equivocal action of Mary. "And yet," he exclaims, "we have heard that a certaine summe of money and victuals should be assigned by the Queen's Majestie for sustentation of our Ministrie. But how that any such assignation, or any promise made thereof, can stand in any stable assurance, when that Roman Antichrist (by just laws once banished from this Realme) shall be intrused above us, we can no wise understand."[1]

Possibly at his own suggestion the Assembly further imposed on Knox what must have been a congenial duty. In England men whom he may have known in Geneva were now being deprived of their ecclesiastical functions, for objecting to the use of "surplice, corner-cap, and tippet." As ardently sharing these antipathies, Knox must have heard with some indignation of the treatment these men were receiving. At the bidding of the Assembly, therefore, he addressed a letter to the pastors and bishops of England, in which in the name of the Reformed Scottish Church he besought them to deal tenderly with the consciences of their brethren.[2] What gave this matter an additional interest for Knox was the fact that at this time he had resolved to visit England in person. His two sons, now respectively nine and ten years of age, were with their mother's relatives in the North of

---

[1] *Works*, ii. 542.
[2] *Booke of the Universall Kirk*, p. 49.

England. Mainly to see them, but doubtless, also, to renew old intimacies in Berwick and elsewhere, he demanded permission of the Assembly for leave of absence from his duties in Edinburgh. Permission was cordially granted, but on the strict understanding that he should be again at his post in June of the following year, the date of the next meeting of Assembly. In accordance with custom he was supplied with an eloquent testimonial to his talents and services from the superintendents, commissioners, and ministers of the kirk.[1]

What parts of England he visited during his sojourn is not recorded; but we can hardly be wrong in supposing that the greater part of the time was spent at Berwick-on-Tweed. There probably was the residence of his children, and to that town of all England he was bound by the strongest ties of ancient friendship. In Berwick, it would seem, the seed he had sown sixteen years before must have borne abundant fruit, to which his labours on this occasion may have given still greater increase. Eighteen years later, the diarist, James Melville, bore emphatic testimony to the godly dispositions of the town. "Trewlie," he says, "I fand sic fectfull professioun of trew Christianitie in Bervik, as I haid never sein the lyke in Scotland."[2] At Dieppe we have seen that the preaching of Knox for a few months influenced the history of Protestantism in France. In Berwick he had also been the first to preach the new doctrines; and, as it would seem, with such effect that he gave a permanent direction to the religious feeling of the town.

[1] *Booke of the Universall Kirk*, p. 48.
[2] James Melville, *Diary*, p. 119 (Ban. Club).

While Knox was in England, events were happening in his own country which were to restore his former importance in public affairs, and were to end in the definitive establishment of Protestantism and the final overthrow of the ancient religion. During these months Darnley was murdered (10th February); Mary was married to Bothwell (15th May); and a section of the nobles, Catholic and Protestant, took up arms against the royal pair, and imprisoned Mary in Lochleven Castle on the 16th of June. For Knox and Protestantism the significance of these events was their influence on the intelligent opinion of the country. At the point to which Scotland had now come, its destinies were no longer in the hands of a few powerful nobles.[1] Whether consciously or unconsciously, the Protestant preachers had spent their labours in the very direction which was to lead to the triumph of their cause. From the beginning it had been the special aim of Knox to gain the great towns to the new opinions, and by the date at which we have arrived his endeavours had been largely crowned with success. Edinburgh, Perth, Dundee, St. Andrews, Glasgow, and Ayr, all were decidedly Protestant in their sympathies. By the sensational events of the last few months the labours of the ministers had been powerfully seconded. The belief was almost universal that Mary had a share in the murder of her husband; and her marriage with Bothwell, who was certainly known to have been a ringleader in the deed, shocked even the coarsest feelings of that coarse age. Many quiet citizens who had hesitated between religion and

---

[1] The words of Killigrew, the English resident in Scotland, may be again quoted. Writing to Burleigh, 11th November 1572, he says: "Methinks I see the noblemen's credit decay in this country; and the barons, burrows, and such-like take more upon them."

loyalty must now once for all have had their course made clear to them. At a later date, as we shall see, the misfortunes of Mary wrought a certain revulsion of feeling, which, working with other causes, prolonged the struggle with the new order. The majority of the nobles, Catholic and Protestant, combined in her interests ; yet, strenuous as were the efforts they made, they had to do battle with a force as elusive as it was irresistible. The few lords who stood by the Protestant cause, by the mere support of intelligent public sympathy, eventually carried Scotland with them in the revolution which had been imperfectly achieved by the Treaty of Edinburgh.

In the new turn of affairs the meeting of the General Assembly on 25th June was an event of prime importance. Mary was in prison, and Edinburgh was in the hands of a few Protestant nobles, of whom, as Moray was abroad, the Earl of Morton was the leading spirit. Though Morton and his party seemed to have gained an easy victory, their position was in the highest degree precarious. The large majority of the Protestant leaders, Châtelherault,[1] Argyle, and Huntly, among the rest, stood out for the Queen, and only waited an opportunity for striking a blow in her favour. What was to be done with Mary was a further question which could hardly fail to create a fresh division in the ranks of her enemies. For a few Protestant Lords to call a meeting of Estates was out of the question, and as the next best shift they had recourse to the General Assembly, on whose support they could securely count. At such a crisis Knox was not likely to be wanting, and he duly made his appearance in Edinburgh for the Assembly of 25th June.

[1] He was at this time in France.

From the split in the ranks of the Protestants, the Assembly[1] was necessarily a meagre one, and its chief business was to decide that another meeting should be held on the 26th of July following.[2] As the ministers were aware, the very existence of their Church depended on the success of the friendly lords: to win over the other Protestant chiefs, therefore, was an object for which they were bound to strain every nerve. By order of the Assembly a letter was addressed to these lords, and signed by Knox and five others, in which every argument was used that might work on the interest and sympathy of any honest supporter of the reformed religion. That no means should be untried, the same six signatories were charged to confer in person with their refractory brethren—Knox being entrusted to deal with those in the parts of the West.[3]

Four days before the meeting of the Assembly Knox returned to Edinburgh. From the circumstances in which it met and the affairs with which it had to deal, this was the most important Assembly of the Church that had yet been called. Hitherto, at each critical juncture, as in 1560 and 1563, it had been overshadowed by the simultaneous meeting of the Estates. On this occasion there could be no meeting of the Estates, and the Assembly must be the sole exponent of the desires and aims of the party that for the time was in the ascendent. The matter on which it had to decide was no less than the fate of the hereditary sovereign of the country, and the settlement of the future government of the nation. So fraught with dangerous consequences did this Assembly threaten

---

[1] George Buchanan was its Moderator.

[2] *Booke of the Universall Kirk*, p. 55.

[3] Throgmorton to Elizabeth, 14th July 1567.—Stevenson, *Illustrations of the Reign of Queen Mary*, p. 208.

to be, that by the express order of his mistress, Throgmorton, the English agent in Scotland, did his utmost to stay its meeting.[1] On Knox's arrival in Edinburgh, Throgmorton at once sought an interview in the hope of gaining him over. Throgmorton was an old acquaintance of Knox,[2] and formerly at least had a good opinion of him. At this juncture, however, there could be no common understanding between them. Elizabeth had every reason to fear and dislike Mary, but that subjects should dethrone and judge their sovereign was sacrilege which left her no course but to become the champion of the Scottish Queen—as far as prudence would allow. To carry out this policy was now Throgmorton's chief mission in Scotland; but to Knox his arguments seemed the mere promptings of that worldly wisdom of which he had seen such evil fruits during all the years since Mary's return.

Never, indeed, had Knox's course been clearer to him than now. At length, the woman who had been the sole obstacle in the way of national salvation had been delivered into their hands. By the people's will, he held, the true religion had been established in the country, and surrounded with every legal sanction. From the moment of her return Mary had set herself to undo this work, and to restore an idolatrous system which involved the eternal ruin of all who bowed the knee to it. To Knox, moreover, it was easy to believe, and it was, in truth, his immovable conviction, that Mary was at once the murderer of her husband and the paramour of her partner in crime. As a common criminal and the

---

[1] Throgmorton to Elizabeth, 14th July 1567.—Stevenson, p. 207.

[2] See above, p. 162.

betrayer of her people, but one judgment could be meted to her. To spare her would be a mistaken mercy which must call down the wrath of Heaven on the nation that suffered crime and idolatry to pass unpunished in its midst.

Daily from his pulpit Knox harangued the people on the burning question of the day.[1] The English alliance and the condign punishment of Mary—on these two themes he concentrated all the vehemence of his zeal, so long baffled, but now, as it seemed, at last in sight of its end. When the Assembly met, it was found that the large majority of the Protestant Lords had not responded to the appeal which had been made to them,—four earls and five lords alone representing the higher nobility.[2] As far as its influence went, however, the proceedings of the Assembly were all that Knox could wish. Mary was found to have forfeited the crown, and a temporary authority was to be set up in the name of her son. The Acts of 1560 establishing the new religion were confirmed, with the pledge on the part of the lords, that at the next meeting of the Estates the civil power should renew its assent to all the laws that had been passed in favour of the ministers and the poor.[3]

At no period since his return to Scotland had Knox been so important a person as now. In the action taken by the confederate lords it was to Protestant opinion they looked, and to Knox beyond every other man, for securing that opinion. A few days after the Assembly rose, he was called to take

[1] Throgmorton to Elizabeth, 21st July 1567.—Stevenson, p. 240.
[2] *Booke of the Universall Kirk*, pp. 68, 69.
[3] *Ibid.* pp. 65-68.

part in a proceeding which one day might endanger his head, or drive him from Scotland for the rest of his life. On the 29th of July the young prince was crowned at Stirling, and Knox, as the chief of the ministers, was appointed to preach the coronation sermon. No account of the sermon has been preserved; but George Buchanan, who may have been among the audience, describes it as an "excellent discourse."[1] One part of the ceremonial—the act of anointing—did not meet his approval as being a weak concession to popish frivolity.[2] Nevertheless, in that day's proceedings he must have seen the fair beginnings of a work, which, if it should prosper, would by ways the most unexpected realise all the prayers of himself and his brethren.

To maintain the new government was now the work to which Knox addressed himself with all his might. In Edinburgh he found a ready response, as there the prince's coronation was signalised by "dauncynges and acclamacyouns."[3] But a large part of the Protestant nobility still stood aloof, and without their co-operation the country could look only for new distractions of which it was impossible to predict the end. By Knox, therefore, the return of Moray,[4] and his appointment as Regent on the 22nd of August, was welcomed as the happiest event that

---

[1] "Mr. Knox preached, and tooke a place of the Scripture forthe of the bookes of the Kinges, where Joas was crowned verye yonge, to treate on." Throgmorton to Elizabeth, 31st July 1567.—Stevenson, p. 257.

[2] "Mr. Knox and other preachers repyned at the ceremonie of anointing, yitt was he anointed" (Calderwood, ii. 384). As representative of the Church, Knox was empowered to ask "acts" and "instruments" in connection with the coronation.—Keith, ii. 723.

[3] Stevenson, p. 258.

[4] Moray arrived in Edinburgh on the 11th of August.—Stevenson, p. 272.

could befall the country. The temporary breach between them had been healed before Moray's flight to England, and thenceforward they worked into each other's hands with undivided aims. With Mary no longer to distract him, Moray addressed himself to the work of government in the very spirit of Knox. He sought, says Throgmorton, " to imytate rather some which have led the people of Israell than anye capytayne of our age." [1]

The result of their united labours was seen in the Parliament which met on the 15th of December. So strong had Moray then become that the chief earls and barons, Catholic as well as Protestant, deemed it prudent in their own interest to put in an appearance. Knox preached the opening sermon, and in the proceedings that followed, all that he had laboured for received the imprimatur of the Estates. In accordance with the pledge made to the Assembly of July, the Acts of 1560 were confirmed, and commissioners (Knox being one of them) were appointed to ascertain with precision " the jurisdictioun, privilege, and authoritie of the said Kirke." [2] In these circumstances the Assembly that met a few days later (25th December) had no great duties to perform. If things only went as they were going, all would be well. Meanwhile the present duty of the Church was to rouse a spirit in the country that would ensure the continuance of the existing government; and, doubtless with this in view, Knox was deputed to visit the various congregations between Stirling and Berwick,[3] and afterwards to proceed to Ayrshire.

---

[1] Stevenson, p. 282.
[2] The Act will be found in Keith, iii. 185, *note*.
[3] Calderwood, ii. 394.

With the same purpose the Assembly wrote to John Willock, then in England, to request his speedy return to help in the good work. "Our enemeis, praised be God," they wrote, "are dashed; religioun established; sufficient provisioun made for ministers; order takin, and penaltie appointed for all sort of transgressioun and transgressers; and above all, a godlie magistrat, whom God, of his eternall and heavenlie providence, hath reserved to this age, to putt in executioun whatsoever He by his law commandeth."[1]

The victory was by no means so assured as the Assembly gave out, and in the midst of his ceaseless labours Knox longed for the quiet of his old home in Geneva.[2] Between foreign and domestic enemies the danger was imminent that Moray would not be long able to hold his own. In itself the act of dethroning a lawful monarch was a defiance to every ruler in Europe, and on this point, France, Spain, and England were agreed.[3] The hope of Moray was that the old jealousies and fears would still be strong enough to prevent the common action of these countries in Mary's favour, and in this, as the event proved, he was not deceived. Strangely enough his most formidable enemy for the moment was the Queen of England, who, in her wrath against those whom she considered mere rebels, openly countenanced the supporters of Mary.

---

[1] Calderwood, ii. 399.

[2] Knox to John Wood, 14th February 1568.—*Works*, vi. 559.

[3] Thus, Catharine de' Medici, writing to Elizabeth (26th May 1568), says that they ought to assist the Queen of Scots against her rebel subjects: "D'autan que cecy nous touche à tous, et que nous debuions ambrasser le faict et protection de cette royne désolée et affligée, pour la remectre en sa liberté et en l'auctorité que Dieu luy a donné, et laquelle de droict et équité luy appartient, et non à autre."—Anderson, *Collections*, vol. iv. part i. p. 45.

As he knew Cecil to be his friend, however, Moray
believed that Elizabeth must in the end be convinced
that the deposition of Mary was the most fortunate event
that could have happened for England. At home, the
whole Hamilton faction detested the Regent as the
supplanter of the head of their house, and a permanent
enemy to the claims of their family. By the attitude
of Elizabeth, also, the disaffected Protestant chiefs
were more convinced than ever that the Regent was
engaged in a hopeless battle which, sooner or later,
could end only in one way.

In the course of the following year (1568) the
dangers that threatened Moray came to an unexpected
head. On the 2nd of May the Queen escaped from
Lochleven, and within a few days was surrounded by
three-fourths of her nobility. In their consternation
the ministers at once decreed a public fast ; and in his
own name Knox addressed a general letter to all the
faithful in the country.[1] This, he wrote, was the result
of misplaced mercy in sparing a woman who by
God's law should have died the death of murderers
and adulterers. In the horrors that would now be let
loose on the land they would suffer just retribution for
the sinful remissness of their lukewarm faith. The
worst fears of Knox were not realised. Within a
fortnight after her escape from Lochleven the forces of
Mary were beaten at Langside, and she herself was a
fugitive seeking the tender mercies of Elizabeth. For
the moment the triumph of Moray was complete, but his
enemies were too many and too powerful to leave him
long at peace. From a letter of Knox, dated the 10th

---

[1] Though this letter appeared in the name of Spottiswoode, Superintendent of Lothian, Calderwood is certainly right in assigning it to
Knox (ii. 481).

LETTER OF KNOX TO SIR WILLIAM DOUGLAS OF LOCHLEVEN

of September, we have an interesting glimpse into his own state of mind in relation to public affairs. " We looke dailie for the arrivall of the Duke[1] and his Frenchemen, sent to restore Satan to his kingdome, in the persone of his deerest lieutenant, sent, I say, to represse religioun, not from the King of France, but from the Cardinall of Lorane in favour of his deerest neice. Lett England take heed, for assuredlie their nighbours houses are on fire. I would, deere Brother, that ye sould travell with zealous men that they may consider our estate. What I would say yee may easilie conjecture. Without support we are not able to resist the force of the domesticall enemies (unlesse God worke meraculouslie), muche lesse are we able to stand against the puissance of France, the substance of the Pope, and the malice of the house of Gwise, unless we be conforted be others than by ourselves. Yee know our estate, and therefore I will not insist to deplore our povertie. The whole comfort of the enemies is this, that be treasoun or other meanes they may cutt off the Regent, and then cutt the throat of the innocent King. How narrowlie hathe the Regent escaped once, I suppose yee have heard. As their malice is not quenched, so ceasseth not the practice of the wicked to put in execution the crueltie devised. I live as a man alreadie deid from all affairs civill, and therefore I praise my God; for so I have some quietnesse in spirit, and time to meditat upon death and upon the troubles I have long feared and foresee."[2]

The uncertainty of the future may partly explain this tone of despondency, but the truth seems to be that his old energy was rapidly failing, and that he was

---

[1] Châtelherault, who was at this time in France.
[2] Knox to John Wood, 10th September 1568.—*Works*, vi. 561.

no longer equal to the calls that were made upon him. Henceforward his duties as minister of his congregation appear to have taxed all the force that still remained to him. It was with an effort that he even kept up correspondence with friends whose attachment he specially valued. In another letter that has been preserved, we have the expression of an utter weariness, of those "hopes all flat," which are apt to come in old age to men of his type. "Yit," he writes, "have I negligentlie pretermitted all office of humanitie toward you, wherinto I acknowledge my offense. For albeit I have beene tossed with manie stormes, all the time before expressed, yit might I have gratified you and others faithfull, with some remembrance of my estate, if that this my churlish nature, for the moste part oppressed with melancholie, had not stayed tongue and penne from doing of their duetie. Yea, even now, when I wold somwhat satisfie your desire, I find within myself no small repugnance. For this I find objected to my wretched heart: ' Foolish man! what seekes thou in writting of missives in this corruptible age! Hath thou not a full satietie of all the vanities under the sunne! Hath not thy eldest and stoutest acquaintance buried thee in present oblivion, and are not thou in that estate by age that nature itself calleth thee from the pleasures of things temporall? Is it not then more than foolishnesse unto thee to hunt for acquaintance on the earth, of what estate or condition so ever the persons be ? ' "[1]

The severest trial of Knox's life came to him in these years of weariness and depression. The Regent Moray, on whose life humanly speaking the future of the Reformed Church seemed to depend, was assassin-

[1] Knox to a Friend in England, 19th August 1569.—*Works*, vi. 566.

ated on the 23rd of January 1570. For Knox, alike on public and private grounds, the loss of Moray was irreparable. By the strongest ties that bind men to each other — ancient friendship, a common faith, common aims, and common fears — Knox was bound to Moray. By Knox, it would seem, Moray had first been led to adopt the religious beliefs to which he had remained consistently faithful to the last. In the relation of teacher and disciple they had lived, with the exception of one memorable breach, for the space of eighteen years,[1] and for a great part of that time they had been in daily intercourse, interchanging the deepest thoughts on the highest matters that concern human life. Their mutual respect and affection is, in truth, an interesting testimony to the character and fundamental aims of each. Knox's eulogy of Moray only bears out what his career leaves us no room to doubt. Like Admiral Coligny, du Plessis-Mornay, and William of Orange, Moray is one of the great public characters fashioned by the Calvinism of the sixteenth century. In all of them there is discernible the same moderation and breadth of view, the same practical statesmanship, penetrated by profound religious feeling. In their judgment on the essential trend of the life and actions of public men the people do not go astray ; and it was from a sure instinct of his even justice, his consistent aims, and his capacity as a ruler, that men spoke of Moray with affection and reverence as " the Good Regent."

The news of Moray's death reached Knox on a Saturday, and at the close of his sermon on the following day, he gave vent to his feelings in a

[1] They probably first came together in London in 1552.—Cf. *Works*, ii. 382.

prayer, which, in its strange blending of passionate
grief, piercing regret, and fervour of anathema, is
singular even among the utterances of Knox.[1]   Three
weeks later (14th February), the Regent's body was
borne from Holyrood to St. Giles's Church, and before
the burial Knox preached a sermon from the text:
" Blessed are these that dee in the Lord."   The sermon
has not come down to us, but Calderwood has preserved the tradition of the preacher's eloquence:
" He moved three thowsand persons to shed teares for
the losse of suche a good and godlie governour."[2]

[1] *Works*, vi. 568-570.   [2] Calderwood, ii. 525, 526.

CHAPTER IV

Knox lived for nearly two years after the death of
Moray, but during these years, to take him at his own
word, he was a "dead man."[1] This, however, was
only his vivid mode of expression ; and the simple
truth is that to the end he was a centre of force in
the country. The weary consent to circumstance that
sooner or later comes to most men, never came to
Knox : his sinews might wax feeble, but the attitude
of Heaven's champion he could abandon only with
his life.

As he now looked around him, Knox might well
wish his mortal journey were done. Of all the lamentable periods of Scottish history these years are the
most lamentable. Even with Moray at its head, the
King's party had with difficulty held its own ; but
with no leader to fill his place its prospect was so
unpromising that men who had anything to lose made
haste to join the other side. Not only the Catholic
nobles were ranged on the side of Mary : the leading
Protestants were even more strenuous in their en-

---

[1] Last Will and Testament. Bannatyne, *Memoriales* (Ban. Club),
p. 370.

deavours to effect her restoration. The Hamiltons with the Duke as their nominal head, Argyle, Huntly, Crawford, Lords Boyd, Herries, Ogilvy, and Sir James Balfour,[1] all professedly Protestant, upheld the Queen's authority in their respective parts of the country. Above all, the Queen had the services of Lethington, who, now that Moray was gone, had only the formidable Morton for an equal adversary. Every day also the opinion gained ground that Elizabeth would eventually make some arrangement which would enable her to restore the Scottish Queen with safety to herself.[2] Against this powerful confederacy stood a few Protestant nobles, backed by the intelligent opinion of the country. In the end, these nobles believed that in her own interest Elizabeth must take their side, since from past experience she must know that by no form of treaty could Mary be reinstated in her kingdom without permanent risk to England. The event proved that they had reckoned aright ; but, meanwhile, in their own strength they had to maintain a government in the face of an enemy more powerful than themselves.

In the coming struggle between the two factions, Edinburgh was the chief centre ; and in Edinburgh Knox made his abode till May of the following year. The majority of the well-to-do citizens were staunchly Protestant ; and, with an admiring congregation hanging upon his words, his position had its alleviations. But to be happy, as things were around him, was not in Knox's nature. Moray had hardly been in his grave, when a pasquinade appeared which stung Knox to the quick.[3] In the form of an imaginary conversation the

<hr>

[1] Bannatyne, *Memoriales* (Ban. Club), p. 39.   [2] *Ibid.* p. 70.
[3] The author was Thomas Maitland, a younger brother of Secretary

writer represented six of Moray's friends, Knox being one of them, as offering him counsel. The object of the writer was to discredit Moray, and to caricature the distinctive traits of the different interlocutors. So cleverly was the thing done that it passed as the report of an actual conversation. Like all men with a mission, Knox keenly resented any ridicule directed against himself; but the ascription of unworthy motives to Moray awoke in him all the wrath of which he was capable. In his next sermon he drew attention to the unhallowed production, and solemnly declared that its author could only have been the father of lies. He even ventured on a prediction as to the end of the human instrument who had put himself to such evil uses : he would die in a strange land, and with not a friend by him to hold up his head. The story adds that the prediction had its fulfilment, since the unhappy man "departed out of this life in Italie, while he was going to Rome."[1]

From the date of Moray's death the centre of all Knox's thoughts, as it was the centre of all Scottish interests, was the Castle of Edinburgh. On Moray's appointment as Regent he had entrusted the Castle to Kirkcaldy of Grange, as at once an experienced soldier and devoted to the Protestant cause. Mainly, as was supposed, under the influence of Lethington, Grange had gone over to Mary, and now openly held the Castle in her interest. For the next two years, therefore, that stronghold was the resort of all her friends, and a constant check on the action of the party of the King. As we have seen, Grange was among the

Maitland, who appears in Buchanan's dialogue *De Jure Regni.* The pasquinade will be found with slightly different readings in Calderwood, ii. 513, and in Bannatyne's *Memoriales*, p. 5.

[1] Calderwood, ii. 525.

oldest associates of Knox. They had been together in the Castle of St. Andrews during the siege that followed the murder of Cardinal Beaton; both had been prisoners in France; they had continued their intimacy in England; and in Scotland they had been friends and fellow-workers till Grange's equivocal action during the later days of Moray's regency. That a place so important should be in the hands of the enemy was itself a matter of the gravest concern; but that this should be the doing of his ancient co-worker and disciple was gall and wormwood to Knox. What Mary and Holyrood had been for Knox in the past, Grange and the Castle were to be in the future—the embodiment of all the powers that fought against righteousness and truth.

Of the outer and inner life of Knox from the opening of the year 1570, we have the faithful record in the Memoriales of Richard Bannatyne.[1] From the date of his return to Scotland, we have seen, Knox had made notes of the chief events that happened in the country. In the fourth book of his History we have these notes wrought up by his own hand, and in the fifth we have them re-cast by some unknown editor. At the date to which we have now come, Knox still continued his Diary; and from the Memoriales of Bannatyne we ascertain the manner in which he kept it. The book associated with the name of Bannatyne contains passages partly written by Knox; and is in its entirety the veritable expression of his spirit. As the book has come down to us, we find in it entries by Knox's own hand, passing expressions of his opinions, and various ejaculations, which he threw upon paper as they came direct from his heart. Even in the first

---

[1] Edited by Robert Pitcairn for the Bannatyne Club in 1836.

part of his work we trace the hand of Bannatyne in a feebleness of phrase which strikingly contrasts with the style of Knox, but in the latter half it is wholly the work of the secretary, though writing under the direct inspiration of his master. A simple fact proves that the work is to be regarded as essentially the production of Knox : after his account of his master's death, Bannatyne subjoins a few documents, and brings the work to a conclusion.

In the pages of this Diary there is a vividness and consecution which give them an interest fully equal to the finished History. It is the Castle and its inmates, we see, that are ever before the writer's eyes. As he thinks how the cause of religion is retarded by those who had once professed to be its best friends, his self-communings reveal all the bitterness and mortification of his spirit. Noting the influx into Edinburgh of the leaders of the Queen's party, he concludes the entry with the exclamation, " Lord, disclose treassonabill hypocrisie." [1] On the last day of the disastrous year 1570[2] he cries, " Lord, yit oppone thy power to thair pryde! And thus I end this yeir, with a dolorus hart, the 24 of Marche 1569. Lord, give thy spreit in abundance to sic as it sall pleis the to appoynte to write efter me these thingis which I but ruidlie twiche." [3]

As yet the two parties had not come to actual blows, but it was every day more evident that only the sword could settle their quarrel. The appointment of the Earl of Lennox to the Regency gave the occasion for the friends of the Queen to assert her claims by

---

[1] Bannatyne, *Memoriales*, p. 19.
[2] The year then ended on the 24th March.
[3] Bannatyne, p. 22.

arms; and for three years, with some intervals of truce, the struggle went on with a ferocity only surpassed in the contemporary civil wars of France. From other sources we know that the following picture of the time is within the limits of truth.   "You should have seen," writes Spottiswoode, "fathers against their sons, sons against their fathers, brother fighting against brother, nigh kinsmen and others allied together as enemies seeking one the destruction of the other.   Every man, as his affection led him, joined to the one or other party; one professing to be the King's men, another the Queen's.   The very young ones scarce taught to speak had these words in their mouths, and were sometimes observed to divide and have their childish conflicts in that quarrel.   But the condition of Edinburgh was of all parts of the country most distressed, they that were of a quiet disposition and greatest substance being forced to forsake their houses; which were partly by the soldiers, partly by other necessitous people (who made their profit of the present calamities), rifled and abused."[1]   As he saw the wild passions let loose around him, did the suspicion ever come to Knox that his life might have been a mistake and his gospel after all be a delusion? Of such a suspicion Knox was constitutionally incapable.   To Luther there came moments when he looked back half sadly to the Church he had left; but such moments, as far as we know, never came to Knox.   As it appeared to him, the internecine strife raging around him was simply a struggle between God and Antichrist, permitted in Providence for the trial and eventual salvation of his people.

[1] Spottiswoode, *Hist. of the Church of Scotland* (Spottiswoode Soc.), ii. 158.

In the autumn Knox received a warning that as far as he was concerned the fight was nearing its end. A stroke of apoplexy affected for a few days "the perfect use of his tongue."[1] The strange rumours that went about regarding his illness are sufficient testimony to his continued influence in the country. Both in Scotland and England it was told with exultation "that he was become the most deformed creature that ever was seine; that his face was turned into his necke; that he was dead; that he wold never preich nor yet speike."[2] But Knox had still two years before him, and a few more battles to fight before his account should be closed with his adversaries. In a few days he was able to resume his preaching, though thenceforward his ministrations were confined to Sundays.[3]

In the end of the year Knox was led into a controversy which proved that his illness had neither mollified his spirit nor weakened his powers of denunciation. For a year past the doings of Kirkcaldy of Grange had taxed all his powers of forbearance; but hitherto for old friendship's sake he had abstained from denouncing him in public. On the night of the 21st of December, however, Grange performed an action which passed the limit of Knox's endurance. With some of his own followers from the Castle, aided by the men in the street, he broke into the Tolbooth, and carried off a servant of his own imprisoned for his share in a riot which had resulted in manslaughter. This open defiance of the constituted authority, and by one who had been among the foremost supporters of the good cause, gave Knox the occasion for which he must long have wished—of openly denouncing

---

[1] Bannatyne, p. 62.   [2] *Ibid.*   [3] *Ibid.*

Grange for his lamentable apostasy. On the Sunday following he declared from the pulpit "that in his dayes he never sawe so slanderous, so malepairte, so fearfull, and so tyrannous a fact." A report of the sermon, that lost none of its offensiveness in the carrying, was duly poured into the ears of Grange. As the words were reported to him, he was accused of being "a murderer and a throatcutter." Even from his minister and spiritual father this was not to be borne, and Grange despatched a testy note to Knox's colleague, calling on him to give the charge a public contradiction at the afternoon sermon. Craig, whose other actions prove him to have been a prudent person, declined to meddle in the dispute. Not to be put off, Grange laid the case before the kirk-session, and demanded that an apology should be made as publicly as the charge. The result was a series of recriminations, leading to nothing, and notable only for the fact that on Knox's side the controversy was carried on in as warlike a tone as that of the fiery captain of the Castle. In the end rumour even went that Grange was about to employ the arm of flesh, since his appeal to spiritual authorities had failed. In this belief Knox's friends in the West, who always regarded him as their special charge, wrote a letter to Grange, so interesting in itself that it deserves to be given in full.

"Sir, After hartlie commendatioune in the Lord; Forsameikle as into this our Assemblie at Ayre, the secund of Januare, we have hard be report of some, that not only ye have conceived ane offence against our brother Johne Knoxe, but also that ye are purposet to injure him be sum way of deid (a thing hard to believed of us); For albeit in materis of civile regiment ye doe not fullie agrie with us, yit in the actione of religione, God hes heirtofoire sa far used your labouris to the furtherance thairof, that ye have not bene a simple professore only, but also a chiefe defendar thairof, with the hasard of your lyfe, landis, and guidis: And, thairfoir, hard it is to persuade us that ye shuld be movit to doe ony harme to him, in whose protectione and lyfe (to our judgment) standis the prosperitie and incres of Godis kirke and religione; and so, be the injureing of him, to cast doun that worke which with so grit labouris and manifold dangeris ye have helpit to build. Yit, nochttheles, the grit cair that we have of the personage of that man, whome God hes made both the first planter, and also the cheif waterer of his kirk amonges us, and moves us to write these few lynis unto you; protesting, that the death and lyfe of that our said brother is to us so pretious and deer, as is our owin lyves and deathis. Desyring to have a plaine declaratioune of your mynd in this matter with this beirar, whom we have directed unto you with further credite. And this nocht trubling yow with farder wryting, we committ yow to the regiment of the Spreit of God. From Ayre, the 3 of Januare, 1571." [1]

To discredit Knox was, in truth, a matter of high importance to the Queen's party in the Castle. As we have seen, the majority of the citizens of Edinburgh were steadfast supporters of Knox, and in the present position of affairs the attitude of the capital was of special consequence to either party. With the other ministers, Lethington wrote to Mary, something might be done, but Knox was inflexible. [2] To weaken Knox's influence, therefore, a clever device was tried.

---

[1] Bannatyne, pp. 80-82.   [2] *Works*, vi. 567.

On the subject of the Queen and her deservings
certain of his brethren were not disposed to take up
the extreme position of Knox ; and by emphasising
this difference his enemies now sought to effect their
end.   During the Assembly that met in March
four " libels," all anonymous, were directed against
Knox, one of them being thrown into the place of
meeting, the other three affixed to the outer door.
In the first three he was charged with defaming the
Queen from the pulpit, and of neglecting to pray for
her.   The fourth threw in his teeth his " Regiment of
Women," and accused him of inconsistency in not only
recognising Elizabeth as a lawful queen, but in seeking her support in the affairs of his own country.   In
a certain measure these attacks were attended with
success, as they revealed the weakness or the moderation of the Assembly.   On the subject of Knox's
speeches regarding the Queen, they declared that they
would share his responsibility, but refused to pass an
act formally approving them.[1]

In spite of this fainthearted support, Knox still
denounced Mary as the root of all the ills that afflicted
the country.   But in Edinburgh, at least, his de-
nunciations were now to be effectually silenced.   To
recover the Castle became at this time the urgent
object of the Regent Lennox ; and in self-defence
Grange began preparations to meet the approaching
siege.   As the friends of Mary swarmed into the
capital, the situation of Knox became every day more
precarious.   A shot fired into his house one night
missed its mark only because he had accidentally left
his usual seat ;[2] and on the night of the 19th of April
his friends deemed it necessary to place a guard round

<hr>

[1] Bannatyne, pp. 94, 95.   [2] Calderwood, iii. 242.

his house.[1] At last the necessities of his position forced Grange to a decided step. If a siege was before him, it would be well that the town should not be the stronghold of his enemies. On the 30th of April he issued a proclamation, commanding all such to quit the town within the space of six hours. To none could this proclamation have been more directly applicable than to Knox; nevertheless he would fain have lingered at the post where in any case the term of his labours could not be far distant. This, however, his friends could not allow. Grange himself would have been loath to see any harm come to the man whom in his heart he held in honour and affection; but in the present state of Edinburgh he would not be responsible for any man's life. Knox, he let it be known, must either quit the town or take up his abode in the Castle, where he would at least be safe from injury. When such were the alternatives presented to him, Knox could have little difficulty in coming to a decision. On the 5th of May, at the urgent treaty of his friends, he left Edinburgh, and on the 8th of the same month crossed the Firth of Forth to Abbotshall, near Kirkcaldy, where he found a temporary residence with the laird of the place.

Immediately before his departure Knox made one of a deputation, which had been sent to the Castle on a sufficiently hopeless errand. As the last occasion on which he met Grange and crossed swords with Lethington, the interview deserves a passing mention. It is from Knox's own hand that we have the account of it, and though something of the old vigour is gone, it bears the unmistakable stamp of his

---

[1] Bannatyne, p. 111.

manner.[1] The interview had been sought by the leaders in the Castle, though with what purpose Knox's narrative leaves us in the dark. The deputies who accompanied Knox were his colleague Craig, and Wynram, the Superintendent of Fife; and they were met by Lethington, Grange, Sir James Balfour, and Châtelherault. The meeting took place in the bedroom of Lethington, who, though a much younger man, was as feeble in body as Knox himself. Throughout the interview Lethington sat on a chair by his bedside, with a little dog on his knee. This easy fashion in which the three ministers were received hardly betokened any serious purpose on the part of those who had invited them. As invariably happened when Knox and Lethington found themselves in each other's presence, the conversation was mainly left in their hands. The natural thought of Knox was that terms would be offered which might open the way to a reconciliation. All the men before him had at one time stood side by side in a common cause. The expectation, therefore, was not unreasonable; but Lethington soon undeceived him. The men from whom he came, Knox was told, had no lawful authority; and their fitting course was to accept such terms as their rightful sovereign might impose upon them. Coming from Lethington, who had taken a

---

[1] There can be no doubt that the " Mr. John " who figures in this interview is Knox himself. As the conversation appears in Bannatyne, there is some discrepancy in dates, but in this part of the book there is a general confusion, which may account for the difficulty. From the report of the interview it appears that it took place after the 30th of April, when Grange issued his ultimatum. As Châtelherault figures in the scene, this further fixes the date as after the 4th of May, the day when he entered Edinburgh (Bannatyne, p. 117). The interview, therefore probably took place between the 4th and 8th of May, as it is unlikely that Knox would recross the Forth on what he must have known to be a sufficiently idle errand.

prominent part in setting up the Regency, these words moved Knox to a lively protest against the speaker's inconsistency. The erection of the King, Lethington retorted, was " but ane fetche or shift to save us from grit inconvenientis."—" Bot one thing weill I wot," was Knox's reply, " honest men of simple conscience and upricht dealing meanit nothing of thir your shiftis and fetches." In spite of this keen play, however, there was no loss of temper, and with a parting thrust of Knox at Lethington, the whole company " began to mow, and as it were, every ane to lauch upoun ane uther, and so raise."[1]

[1] Bannatyne, pp. 125-132.

CHAPTER V

IT was in the beginning of July that Knox, accompanied by his family, settled in St. Andrews.[1] If he had escaped personal danger by leaving Edinburgh, he did not find repose. Like every other part of the country, St. Andrews was divided in its allegiance, though the most influential persons in the town favoured the party of the Queen. The minister, Robert Hamilton, who had succeeded Knox's old friend Goodman in 1566, took sides with his clan, and regarded Knox as an intruder. Of the three colleges that composed the University, St. Leonard's, of which George Buchanan had lately been principal, alone was friendly to the Regent.[2] Thus surrounded by adversaries, it was here once more Knox's function to lift up his voice against the defection of those who had once professed such zeal for the truth.

Of his doings in St. Andrews certain notes have been preserved which bring him vividly before us as he appeared in these last months of his life. James Melville, to whom we owe this account, was then a

---

[1] Bannatyne, p. 255. James Melville (*Diary*, p. 26) mentions the fact that Knox had his family with him. It was in the Novum Hospitium of the Priory that Knox and his family lived during his stay in St. Andrews.

[2] Bannatyne, pp. 258 *et seq.*

student in St. Leonard's College, disposed alike by family tradition and personal predilection to sit at the feet of the mighty preacher with whose name Scotland had rung all the days he could remember.[1] In his *Diary*, one of the most delightful books of its kind in the language, Melville has recorded his impression of Knox in a passage as striking as that in which he records his visit to George Buchanan.

" Bot of all the benefites I haid that yeir was the coming of that maist notable profet and apostle of our nation, Mr. Jhone Knox to St. Andros, wha, be the faction of the Quein occupeing the castell and town of Edinbruche, was compellit to remove therefra with a number of the best, and chusit to com to St. Andros. I hard him teatche ther the prophecie of Daniel that simmer and the wintar following. I haid my pen and my litle book, and tuk away sic things as I could comprehend. In the opening upe of his text he was moderat the space of an halff houre ; bot when he enterit to application, he maid me sa to grew[2] and tremble, that I could nocht hald a pen to wryt. . . . Mr. Knox wald sum tyme com in and repose him in our colleage yeard, and call us schollars unto him and bless us, and exhort us to knaw God and his wark in our contrey, and stand be the guid cause, to use our tyme weill, and lern the guid instructiones, and follow the guid exemple of our maisters. . . . I saw him everie day of his doctrine go hulie and fear,[3] with a furring of martriks about his neck, a staff in the an hand, and guid godly Richart Ballanden his servand, haldin upe the uther oxter,[4]

---

[1] Melville was born in 1556, though his uncle Andrew, he tells us, would have it that the year was 1557. The Records of the University of St. Andrews show that he matriculated in 1569, a date different from that which is assigned in his *Diary*.

[2] Thrill.   [3] Slowly and warily.   [4] Arm-pit.

from the Abbay to the paroche kirk, and be the said
Richart and another servant, lifted upe to the pulpit,
whar he behovit to lean at his first entrie, bot or he
haid done with his sermont he was sa active and vigorus,
that he was lyk to ding that pulpit in blads[1] and flie
out of it."[2]

Though he was constantly affirming that his work
on earth was done, the tasks which Knox still undertook
were enough to fill the days of an ordinary man. On his
Sunday sermon he spent much care and meditation, and
apparently had it written out in full or in copious notes.[3]
Though he could not, as he tells us, write two lines
with his own hand,[4] he never lost touch with civil and
ecclesiastical affairs.   One proof of his still indomitable
spirit should hardly be omitted.   In the Assembly that
met in August the authors of the libels against him
offered to make good their charges.   Three days before
the Assembly met Knox wrote a letter, in which he
reminds his brethren of the pledge of his enemies, and
prays that his case may have a patient hearing.   For
himself he was assured that he had neither "offendit

---

[1] Break the pulpit in pieces.

[2] Melville, *Diary*, pp. 20-26.   Melville also tells that Knox was
present at "a play at the mariage of Mr. Jhon Colvin," in which "the
castell of Edinburche was besiged, takin, and the captan, with an or twa
with him, hangit in effigie" (*Diary*, p. 22).   Melville also records the
punishment of a witch in St. Andrews "against the quhilk Mr. Knox
delt from the pulpit, sche being set upe at a pillar befor him" (*ibid.* p.
46).   In this connection may also be quoted a singular passage from
Bannatyne, relating to Knox's stay in St. Andrews : "About this tyme,
to wit, the 5 or 6 of Januar, Johne Law, the post of Sanct Androis,
being in Edinburgh, and also in the castle, ane demandit, Gif Johne
Knox was baneist Sanct Androis, and gif that his servant Richard was
deid ?   Who knowing no sic thing confessit the treuth.   But the ladie
Home and utheris wold neidis thraip in his face that he was banist the
said toun, becaus that in the yaird he had raiset some sanctis, amonges
whom thair come up the devill with hornis ; which when his servant
Richard saw, ran woude and so died."—P. 216.

[3] *Ibid.* p. 26.   [4] *Works*, vi. 602.

God, nor yet good men" in anything that had been laid to his charge.[1] From letters addressed to him we learn that he was still engaged on his History, and as assiduous as ever in the collection of original documents.[2] In foreign affairs as bearing on the future of parties in Scotland he continued to take the same interest as ever. "As I gett knowledge farder in forane materis," writes a correspondent to him in December 1571, "ye sall, God willing, be made participant."[3]

With the opening of the year 1572 began a new phase in the history of the Reformed Church in Scotland. The full significance of this phase Knox did not live to see; but, as it happened, he had to bear his special testimony in the individual case which initiated the new departure. The leading spirit of the King's party was now the Earl of Morton, though the nominal representative of the young King was the Regent Mar. Morally far inferior to Moray, Morton had steadily pursued the policy in which both saw the true interests of Scotland—union with England, and, what that union necessarily implied, the establishment of Protestantism as the religion of the country. But at no time did the success of his policy seem more uncertain than now. The struggle between the two parties still went on, and the end seemed as far off as ever. With the great majority of the nobles against them, and the chief stronghold of the country in the hands of the enemy, the only hope of the King's party was that Elizabeth would come to their rescue. But many considerations, bearing on her own immediate interests, deterred Elizabeth from taking such a step,

---

[1] *Works*, vi. 606-608.

[2] *Ibid.* pp. 606-612.   [3] *Ibid.* p. 610.

and another year elapsed before she actually despatched a force to assist in the siege of the Castle. Meanwhile, the pressing need of the Regent was for money to enable him to keep the field against the supporters of the Queen, who in addition to their own resources received occasional subsidies from France. Long ago Cecil had told the Lords of the Congregation what course they ought to pursue if they were to succeed in effectually putting down the old religion. By possessing themselves of the wealth of the Church they would at once strengthen their own hands and weaken those of the enemy.[1] Now that the ancient Church had been formally abolished by the King's parliament, the large possessions still retained by its surviving clergy might be appropriated to the state in a fashion as unobtrusive as it was effectual. As the old bishops died off, Protestant bishops should be put in their places, but on conditions that would make them the mere salaried officials of the Crown. Other reasons also moved Morton to this step, which were bound to have their own weight with a statesman in his position. The experience of the last few years had taught him that if Knox and his brother ministers had their way, the new church would dominate the State as imperiously as the church it had displaced. To bestow on the Protestant ministers all the wealth that had belonged to the Roman clergy would have given them an influence incompatible with an executive able to do justice to all the interests of the country. Moreover, if the two kingdoms, as Morton hoped, were one day to be united under the rule of Mary's son, the fusion would be more complete if the English and Scottish Churches were made one as well in polity as in

---

[1] *Works*, vi. 53.

doctrine.[1]   For these various reasons, therefore, Morton now set himself with characteristic determination and lack of scruple to force on the Protestants a form of church government regarded by the large majority of them as at once unscriptural and inexpedient.

The forces of the Regent Mar were now encamped at Leith; and in this town on the 12th of January a convention[2] of the Church was brought together to consider the proposals of Morton.   To have quarrelled with the person on whom the very existence of the Church seemed to depend would hardly have been the action of sane men, and apparently without a dissentient voice they agreed that the order of bishops should be recognised in the Church.   Armed with this warrant, Morton lost no time in putting his policy in action. By his sole direction John Douglas, Rector of the University, was nominated Archbishop of St. Andrews, in place of Hamilton, who had been hanged nearly a year before.   Well knowing that there was one man in St. Andrews whom even his iron will could not daunt, Morton crossed from Leith to see that his orders were duly carried out.   As he doubtless anticipated, Knox protested against the innovation with all the force that was left in him.   For Douglas himself Knox had a personal affection, and expressed his regret that such a burden should be laid on an old man's back.   What alarmed Knox was the high-handed action of Morton, and its threatened consequences to the liberty of the Church.   The polity of the Church, he maintained, had been settled by assemblies and parliaments, and could not be changed

---

[1] Melville, pp. 47, 48.   The motives above attributed to Morton are all implied in the words of Melville.

[2] Melville, p. 25.

by the will of one man.[1]   When he was asked to
inaugurate the new bishop, therefore, he refused to
have any hand in the business.   On the day of the
ceremony Knox preached in the presence of Morton ;
but Wynram, the Superintendent of Fife, had to follow,
and go through with the work which Morton prescribed for him.   Doubtless, it was with this incident
among others in his mind that a few months later
Morton uttered his memorable sentence at the grave
of the man who had thus defied him.

This was not the only unpleasant business that
signalised Knox's sojourn in St. Andrews.   Here, on
a narrower stage, was strikingly illustrated the division
that had rent the Protestant ranks on the dethronement
of Mary.   Of the three colleges, as has been said, only
St. Leonard's had gone with Knox and Moray, the
other two standing fast for the Hamiltons.   Between St.
Leonard's and its neighbours, therefore, arose all the
bitterness that distinguishes the quarrels of co-religion-
ists.   In their zeal the students of St. Leonard's complained to the Assembly that their minister, Robert
Hamilton, refused to pray for the Regent, and manifested
a general lukewarmness.   Another complaint which
they lodged gave rise to fierce recriminations in which
Knox came to bear a prominent part.   One, William
Ramsay, second in office in the College of St. Salvator,
had originally been a hearty supporter of the Regent
Moray.   To the indignation of St. Leonard's, however,
he was gained over by the Hamiltons, and began to
speak ill of his former friends.   In their ardour for his
recovery, the students brought his case before the Assembly ; but by an unhappy coincidence Ramsay died
immediately after he had thus been pilloried.   The

[1] Bannatyne, pp. 256, 257.

occasion was not to be lost, and it was affirmed that St.
Leonard's had as certainly murdered Ramsay as Both-
wellhaugh had murdered the Regent Moray. As in
St. Leonard's Knox had found his main support in St.
Andrews, he could not suffer his friends to be defamed
for what he deemed their godly zeal; and as soon as
the scandal reached him, he determined to carry it to
the pulpit on the following Sunday. Fearing that
Knox would take this step, Rutherford, the Provost of
St. Salvator's, wrote a peremptory letter, desiring him
to let the matter alone—the most effectual means of
defeating his own object. The next Sunday Knox
read Rutherford's letter from the pulpit, though without naming its author, and defended St. Leonard's
from the charge that had been brought against it.
But the blood of everybody was now up, and words
were flung about which were not likely to heal the
Church's divisions. Hamilton, the minister, plainly
told Richard Bannatyne that his master had little cause
to cry out against the Hamiltons as murderers, as he
himself had subscribed the bond for the murder of
Darnley. A letter from Knox, however, recalled
Hamilton to his senses, and with as ill a grace as he
could he withdrew his charge. One other enemy Knox
made in St. Andrews, who was afterwards to pursue
his memory with a deadly hate. This was Archibald Hamilton, a professed Protestant, but attached
to the fortunes of his own clan. As the favourite
theme of Knox was denunciation of that family as
the chief ill-doers in the country, Hamilton naturally refused to appear in church when Knox was the
preacher. But such a dereliction involved the censure
of the Church, and both the Superintendent and the
new Archbishop reasoned with Hamilton on his delin-

quency. Hamilton, however, was not to be convinced
that he was bound to hear a preacher who availed
himself of his function to denounce those who differed
from him; and, as he had the support of the most
influential persons in the town, the matter dropped
with a fruitless protest on the part of Knox and himself. Some years later Hamilton joined the Church
of Rome, and wrote a book in which he denounces the
Church he had left, and Knox in particular, with a
malignant ferocity which could have issued only from
a mean intelligence and a bad heart.[1]

Even amid the vexations of St. Andrews, the Castle
of Edinburgh and its inmates were never out of
Knox's thoughts. In his letters he unfailingly recurs
to the subject with a bitterness that increased as the
days went on. " Lying in Sanct Androis, half deid,"
he thus writes to a correspondent in May 1572 : " This
is that which God reveillis to me, that the actione that
is defendit against thea traytouris and murthereris of
the Castle of Edinburghe is just, and in the end sall
prevaille against Sathan, and all thame that mainteanis
that wickit society."[2] Two months later he again
writes : " Frome the Castell of Edinburgh have sprung
all the murthers first and last committed in this realme ;
yea, and all the troubles and treasons contrived in
England."[3]

For a moment in the spring of this year Knox
turned aside to another adversary already spreading
dismay in the ranks of Protestantism, but whose
eventual developments were as yet only partially

---

[1] Hamilton's book is entitled, *De Confusione Calvinianæ Sectæ
apud Scotos Ecclesiæ nomen ridicule usurpantis, Dialogus.* Parisiis,
1577. For the slanders of Hamilton and others regarding Knox, see
Appendix E.

[2] *Works*, vi. 615.   [3] *Ibid.* p. 618.

divined. At the close of 1566, on Knox's return to Edinburgh after the murder of Rizzio, a letter was put into his hands which appears to have given him some uneasiness.[1] It was the production of one James Tyrie, a young Scotsman of ability and learning, who had lately joined the Society of Jesus, and was addressed to his brother with the intention of winning him over to Rome. Knox was fully aware that the Jesuits were already no contemptible enemy, and that the decrees of the Council of Trent,[2] which had alarmed every Protestant, were largely their work. Immediately on reading this letter, therefore, he sat down, and in a few days produced a detailed reply to Tyrie.[3] For reasons which he does not fully explain,[4] the letter was not published at the time it was written. The aggressive activity of the Jesuits, however, now determined him to give it to the world, and sometime during the first half of the year 1572 it was printed by Lekprevik, who had come to St. Andrews at the same time as himself.[5] Of the controversy itself it is unnecessary to speak at length. The novelty of Protestantism and the multiplicity of its sects, as contrasted with the antiquity and unity of the Church of Rome—these are the points on which Tyrie mainly insists and which Knox seeks to rebut. But to the reply were added an introduction and an appendix, which Knox himself evidently considered the most important portions of his pamphlet, and which to us are certainly the most interesting. The introduction consists of an epistle

---

[1] *Works*, vi. 481.

[2] There are frequent references to the Council of Trent in Knox's writings. Cf. specially *Works*, vi. 402 *et seq.*

[3] *Works*, vi. 481.

[4] He simply says, "I repented of my laubour, and purposed fullie to have suppressed it."—*Ibid.*   [5] James Melville, *Diary*, p. 26.

to the Faithful, and a prayer which he used before his
congregation previous to his flight after the murder
of Rizzio. From this singular prayer we gather, what
other evidence proves, that with his physical decay
there was a progressive exaltation of feeling, which
was effectually kept in check by the absorbing pursuit
of practical ends. In such an exclamation as the following we must see the expression of emotion perilously
near the line that divides the morbid fanatic from
the great religious leader : " For being drowned in
ignorance, thow hes gevin to me knawledge above
the commoun sort of my brethren ; my toung hes
thow usit to set furth thy glorie, to oppung idolatrie,
errouris, and fals doctrine." [1]

Even more singular than the introduction is the
appendix which Knox saw fit to add to his letter.
Among the many things said of him by evil tongues
was a slander regarding his relations to his mother-in-
law, Mrs. Bowes, who had lately died. To let the
world know what these relations precisely were, he
now published a long letter which he had addressed
to her so long ago as July 1554 ; and a more effective
justification he could not have produced. Religious
hypochondria, as we have seen, absorbed the days
and nights of Mrs. Bowes, and in this letter we have
Knox in the capacity of ghostly adviser, dealing with
her hallucinations in a spirit of tender sympathy
that sufficiently explains his magnetism for women.
Accompanying this letter is another addressed to the
Faithful Reader, in which he explains his reasons for
now bringing Mrs. Bowes before the world. It was
partly, he says, to explain his own relations to Mrs.
Bowes, but partly, also, that others might profit by

<hr>

[1] *Works*, vi. 483.

her painful experience. "The letter in the end," he says elsewhere, "if it serve not for this estate of Scotland, yitt it will serve a troubled conscience, so long as the Kirk of God remaineth in either realme."[1] Some explanation was certainly needed for obtruding so purely personal a matter on the public, yet he might have justified his proceeding without such a sentence as the following : "Her company to me was comfortable (yea, honorable and profitable, for she was to me and myne a mother); but yet it was not without some croce : for besides trouble and fasherie of body susteyned for her, my mynde was seldome quyet, for doing somewhat for the comfort of her troubled conscience."[2] Indelicate as this may seem, it is right to remember that in the same century Sir Thomas More, the most refined of spirits, said and did things to his own wife at once less excusable and far more repugnant to modern feeling.[3]

With one other matter Knox's sojourn in St. Andrews came to a close. In the beginning of August the General Assembly met at Perth under circumstances that made its meeting of special importance. As he was no longer able to take part in its proceedings, Knox sent a letter in which he offered his counsel on late events affecting the interests of the Church. In the forefront of his letter he uttered a warning which his own recent experiences sufficiently explain. In St. Andrews we have seen that the majority in the University had steadily set themselves against Knox and his preaching. With this painful memory before him, he writes as follows : "Above all things preserve the Kirk from the bondage of the Universities.

[1] *Works*, vi. 617.   [2] *Ibid.* p. 514.
[3] Cf. Roper, *Life of Sir Thomas More*, pp. 67-169 (edit. 1817).

Persuade them to rule peaceably, and order thair schools in Christ; but subject never the pulpit to their Judgment, neither yet exempt them from your Juris-diction."[1]   But the warning was hardly needed: the meagre scale of the Scottish Universities has effectually prevented their dominating religious and political thought like those of the sister country.

Along with this letter Knox sent a series of suggestions, all of which were received with approval by the Assembly.   On one subject his expressions are specially interesting, in view of the later developments of the Scottish Church.   The proceedings of Morton in making bishops on his own account had raised a panic among the ministers which reflection had only increased.   In the present Assembly it was now unanimously concluded that the articles adopted by the convention of Leith should be received only as an interim.   The names—archbishop, dean, arch-deacon, chancellor, and chapter—were found to be " sclanderous and offensive to the eares of manie of the brethren, appeirand to sound to Papistrie."[2]   To the name *bishop*, on the other hand, no objection was taken. As we have seen, Knox had never held the opinion that bishops were an unscriptural institution,[3] and from the communications he now sent to the Assembly it does not appear that he had changed his mind.   That he had seriously considered the question is proved by the fact that either by himself or at his suggestion Beza had been informed of the proceedings at Leith. In a letter to Knox, dated 12th April 1572, Beza had expressed himself in this emphatic fashion: " But of this, also, my Knox, which is now almost patent to our

---

[1] *Works*, vi. 619.   [2] *Booke of the Universall Kirk*, p. 133.
[3] See above, vol. i. pp. 92, 93.

very eyes, I would remind yourself and the other
brethren, that as Bishops brought forth the Papacy, so
will false Bishops (the relicts of Popery) bring in
Epicurism into the world. Let those who devise the
safety of the Church avoid this pestilence, and when
in process of time you shall have subdued that plague
in Scotland, do not, I pray you, ever admit it again,
however it may flatter by the pretence of preserving
unity."[1] With this opinion before him, Knox raises no
objection to the office of bishop in itself. Its existence, indeed, he takes for granted, and his only concern is that fitting persons should be made bishops,
and that the Church should have its rightful part in
their appointment.[2] Had he lived a few years longer,
it may safely be said that his attitude would have been
very different. In the struggle that was to follow
between Presbytery and Episcopacy, Andrew Melville
was the true continuator of the work of Knox.

---

[1] *Works*, vi. 614. The translation is Laing's.
[2] Bannatyne, pp. 250 *et seq.*

CHAPTER VI

ON the 31st of July, through the good offices of France
and England, a truce was concluded between the two
Scottish factions. It was to begin on the 1st of August,
and to conclude at the end of September; but was
subsequently extended beyond the date of Knox's
death. The citizens, who had been forced to leave
Edinburgh, were thus restored to their homes; and
their earliest thought was to provide for their spiritual
edification. At this moment, indeed, their case was
specially unfortunate; their senior minister, Knox, was
in St. Andrews, and his colleague, John Craig, had
shown such leanings to the party of the Castle that
they determined to dispense with his services. On
the 4th of August two Commissioners were despatched
to Knox with a letter signed by the members of his
congregation in Edinburgh. In the most affectionate
terms they besought him to return to his old place in
their midst. Aware of the state of his health, however,
they left it with himself to decide whether he could
come with safety or not. Amid his uncongenial sur-
roundings in St. Andrews, Knox had doubtless longed
for the sympathetic audiences of St. Giles's, and

he readily agreed to return to Edinburgh. One condition he made to prevent such misunderstandings as had occurred in the past. He must have perfect liberty to speak his mind regarding those persons in the Castle whose doings were bringing destruction on the country. The reply was that he might " speike his conscience, as he had done afoir tymes." [1]

On the 17th of August Knox left St. Andrews, and landed at Leith on the 23rd. After a few days spent in Leith, he proceeded to Edinburgh, and preached in St. Giles's on the last Sunday of the month. In his best days his voice had not reached the vast crowd which had assembled in that church ; but in his present broken health he was totally unequal to his former exertions. For the short time he was still to preach, therefore, he addressed his audiences in a portion of the church known as the Tolbooth. [2]

The appointment of a colleague and successor at once demanded Knox's most earnest consideration. His own labours, he felt, were fast approaching their term ; Craig, once his stout and faithful ally, had gone over to the enemy ; and men of learning and zeal were not so abundant as to make the choice easy. The man on whom he fixed was James Lawson, sub-principal of the University of Aberdeen. Knowing that any day might now be his last, Knox at once wrote to Lawson, praying him to come to Edinburgh, that they might " conferre together of heavenlie thingis," adding the urgent postscript—" Haist, leist ye come to late." Within a fortnight Lawson appeared, and the

---

[1] Bannatyne, p. 255.
[2] *Ibid.* p. 263. The part of the church in which Knox preached was probably the south-west corner of the nave. For an account of the various " Tolbuiths " in Edinburgh, see Appendix to *Our Journall into Scotland,* by C. Lowther (Edinburgh, 1894).

impression he made was as favourable as had been hoped. In the stormy times that were to come, Lawson showed a courage and steadfastness not unworthy of Knox himself, and finally sealed his devotion by dying in exile for the trust he had received.[1]

This duty settled, Knox could turn with an easier mind to public affairs, which had never been more absorbing than now. With his foot in the grave he was still the old power in the country. Just at this moment the news of the Massacre of St. Bartholomew had reached Scotland, and had stirred the nation to its depths. For the cause of the King nothing could have been more opportune ; and with all the vigour that was left to him, Knox drove home the terrible lesson to the hearts of his countrymen. Mainly by his action, the Regent's Council took up the matter, and issued a proclamation summoning the leading Protestants to meet in Edinburgh on the 20th of October. From the pulpit he denounced the French king in terms which led Du Croc, the French resident in Edinburgh, to lodge a complaint with the Council. But in rousing the popular mind against France, Knox was doing effectual service to the cause which the Council upheld ; and Du Croc was coolly told that the lords could not even stop the preachers from denouncing themselves.[2] On the 20th of October the Convention of Protestants met ; but with a few exceptions it consisted wholly of ministers—a convincing proof that the party of the King had its chief support in popular feeling. Such as it was, however, the Convention drew up a series of articles, which, if not actually penned by Knox, must have been directly inspired by him. Public

---

[1] Bannatyne, p. 264 ; Melville, *Diary*, p. 146.
[2] Bannatyne, p. 273.

humiliation for the national sins, pains and penalties for those who preached the old religion—such were the recommendations of the first two articles. But it is in the suggestion of the third and last article that we see the direct result of St. Bartholomew. In self-defence against all Papists an alliance was to be formed with England and other Protestant countries, while at home a bond was to be drawn up pledging the subscribers " to be readie at all occasiounes for resisting the enemies forsaid." [1]

Wielding the power he still did, Knox could not be ignored by public men in any scheme affecting the country at large ; and at this period a matter was in hand which concerned not only the future of Scotland but of Europe. As the leaders of the King's party had always hoped, Elizabeth had at length discovered that no arrangement was possible with Mary which could consist with the safety of England. Even as a close prisoner the Scottish Queen was a standing menace which only her death could remove. To effect this end in the safest way for England was now the special object of Elizabeth's minister Cecil ; and the plan that met his approval was to send Mary to Scotland, there to be put through the form of a trial and publicly or privately executed. [2] On certain conditions, which should at once assure the triumph of the King's party and the independence of Scotland, Morton and the Regent Mar accepted Cecil's proposal. Knox, to whom the scheme was likewise communicated, could have no hesitation in the matter. It had been his

---

[1] Bannatyne, pp. 276-279.

[2] Murdin, *State Papers*, pp. 224, 225. The question as to how Mary was to be removed, whether in public or secretly, is beside our present purpose. As far as Knox was concerned, he would have preferred the deed to be done in the broadest light of day.

constant contention that had Mary suffered her merited punishment after her surrender at Carberry the country would have been saved all the disasters of recent years. For him the death of Mary was no measure of political expediency as it was for Morton and Cecil. It was an act of absolute justice that the murderer of her husband, the betrayer of her country and its religion, should die the death appointed alike by human and divine law to the perpetrator of such crimes. When Killigrew, the English agent, approached Knox, therefore, he found a ready response to his proposals. " I trust to satisfy Morton," he writes to Cecil, " and for John Knox, that thing, ye may se by my dyspatch to Mr. Secretary, is don and doing dayly ;" and he concludes with a description of Knox's bodily state and disposition of mind as he appeared rather more than a month before the end : " John Knox is now so feble as scarce can he stand alone, or speak to be hard of any audience ; yet dothe he every Sonday cause himselfe to be caried to a place, where a certayn nombre do here him, and precheth with the same vehemence and zeale that ever he did. He dothe reverence your Lordship myche, and willed me once agayn to send you worde, that he thanked God he had obtained at His hands, that the gospel of Jesus Christ is truely and simply preached throwout Scotland, whiche dothe so comfort him as he now desireth to be out of this miserable lyffe. He said further, that it was not long of your Lordship that he was not a great bischope in England ; but that effect growen in Scotland, he being an instrument, dothe myche more satisfy him. He desired me to make his last commendations most humbly to your Lordship, and withall, that he prayed God to increase His strong spirit in you, saying, there was never more nead. And quoth he to me, ' Take heed how you believe them of the Castle, for sure theye will deceave you ; and trust me, I know they seake nothing more than the ruyne of your Mistress, which they have been about of long tyme.' "[1]

Killigrew's letter was written on the 6th of October, and about a month later (9th November) Knox performed his last public duty on earth. This was the induction of his successor Lawson in the great church of St. Giles. So feeble had he now become that only a few could distinguish the words that fell from him. Leaning on his staff and attended by almost the entire congregation, he made his way home to his house at the Netherbow Port.[2] Of the fortnight he had still to live the faithful Bannatyne has left a record which leaves nothing to be desired in its minute fidelity and simple pathos.[3]

On Sunday the 11th he was stricken with a convulsive cough, followed by a difficulty in breathing, which gradually wore away his strength. By Thursday he was so weak that he had to desist from his ordinary reading of the Bible ; and, feeling the end was near, desired his wife to pay the servants their wages. The next day, under the belief that it was Sunday, he made an effort to rise at an earlier hour ; but was so reduced that it was with difficulty he could even keep a sitting posture. On Saturday two friends, John Durie and Archibald Stewart, called about midday,

---

[1] Killigrew to Cecil, 6th October 1572. Knox, *Works*, vi. 633.

[2] See Appendix F, " Knox's Places of Residence in Edinburgh."

[3] Bannatyne is our chief authority regarding Knox's last days ; but a few details are also supplied by Thomas Smeton in his reply to Archibald Hamilton. Smeton's work is entitled, *Ad virulentum Archibaldi Hamiltonii apostatæ Dialogum, De Confusione Calvinianæ sectæ apud Scotos, impie conscriptum, orthodoxa responsio.* Cf. Knox, *Works*, vi. 645 *et seq.* Calderwood in his account of Knox's death takes his facts from Bannatyne.

apparently unaware that he was not in a state to receive them. To show his good feeling he exerted
himself to sit at table, and ordered a hogshead of wine
to be broached in their honour. As long as the wine
lasted, he told them, they must continue to send for it,
as he himself "wald never tarie untill it wer drunkin."
On Monday the 17th the office-bearers of St. Giles's
came at his express desire that he might say the last
words they should hear from him. For himself, he
said, he had taught nothing but true and sound doctrine. If he had ever spoken harshly of any man, it
was from no ill feeling against his person, but for the
evil that abode in him. Never had he made merchandise out of the gospel it had been his privilege to
preach. On the great question of the day his last
counsel was that no truce should be made with those
in the Castle, so long as they persisted in their present
purposes. A few days before Lethington had complained to the kirk-session that Knox had in public
and private slandered him as "an enemy to all religion."
In the state in which he was, Knox had been unable
to answer the complaint; but he now appealed to
those who heard him if the allegation were not borne
out by Lethington's own actions. For Kirkcaldy of
Grange all his old affection awoke, and he made one
last effort to persuade him of his errors. Lawson and
David Lindsay, the minister of Leith, conveyed this
last message, which at the time was slightingly received by Grange, but less than a year later was
recalled in circumstances that were a terrible commentary on Knox's dying counsel.[1]

---

[1] On the capture of the Castle of Edinburgh the following year,
Grange was taken prisoner and publicly executed. In his last hours he
was attended by David Lindsay, who had conveyed Knox's dying mes-

Two days later Morton, Boyd, and the laird of Drumlanrig came and held talk with him on matters that were never divulged.[1] Other nobles and barons —Lindsay, Ruthven, and Glencairn among the rest— also came to offer their services and to spend a few moments by his bedside. To a certain lady of rank who was praising his services to the Church he showed a flash of his old spirit in his stern rebuke of her ill-timed flattery. "Ladie! ladie!" he exclaimed, "the blake ox hes never tramplit yet upoun your foote." On Friday the 21st he directed Bannatyne to give orders for his coffin; but he had still three days to live. On Sunday during the time of sermon he thought the end had come, and called on the standers-by to "sie the worke of God." The last night of his life he passed in a spiritual wrestle such as he had never known before: Satan, he declared, had tried him with a new form of temptation—the plea that his own merits were sufficient in the sight of God; but by special grace he had gained his final victory.

The last day came at length—the 24th of November. About nine or ten in the morning he insisted on rising, and sat in his chair for half an hour. All through his illness favourite chapters had been read to him from the Bible—specially the 53rd of Isaiah and the 17th of the Gospel of John, "in which he had first cast anchor"; and on this last day he was still able to listen to certain passages which comforted him. At five in the afternoon he requested his wife to read once more the chapter in John, and though he seemed

sage to him. Melville in his *Diary* (pp. 28, 29) gives an account of the last moments of Grange, which would satisfy the taste of the most exacting realist of the present day.

[1] In his famous *Confession* Morton professed to give the purport of his last interview with Knox.—Calderwood, iii. 569.

to sleep he signified that he had heard every word. About half-past ten the usual household worship was held, and he followed the service with a joyful fervour which he expressed to all who were present. Towards eleven there came from him "a long sigh and sob," and with the exclamation, "Now it is come," he entered on the last struggle. Asked to give a parting sign that he was at peace, he lifted his hand, and apparently without pain passed quietly away. On the same day, adds the faithful chronicler, the Earl of Morton was proclaimed Regent of Scotland.

On the Wednesday the 26th Knox was buried in the graveyard which then lay to the south of the church of St. Giles, the funeral being attended by all the nobility who chanced to be in the town. As he stood by the grave, the Regent Morton, with that sententiousness of speech for which he was noted,[1] pronounced the memorable eulogy on the dead—"Here lies one who neither flattered nor feared any flesh."[2] The burial-ground where Knox was laid has long since disappeared,[3] but immediately behind the church, and, by a curious freak of circumstance, under the very shadow of an equestrian statue of Charles II., a flat stone now marks the spot to which tradition points as the resting-place of Knox.

---

[1] "He [Morton] keipit the sam countenance, gestour, and *schort sententius form of language* upon the skaffalde, quhilk he usit in his princlie government."—Melville, *Diary*, p. 84.

[2] As reported by Calderwood (iii. 242), Morton's words were as follow : "Here lyeth a man who, in his life never feared the face of man : who hath beene often threatned with dag and dager, but yitt hath ended his dayes in peace and honour. For he had God's providence watching over him in a speciall maner, when his verie life was sought." The speech given in the text is from Melville's *Diary* (p. 47), and seems more in accordance with the occasion and with Morton's laconic habit.

[3] In 1633, when the Parliament House and other buildings were erected on the site it occupied.

By his first wife, Marjory Bowes, Knox had two sons, Nathanael and Eleazer, born in Geneva in 1557 and 1558. Eight days after their father's death they matriculated at the University of Cambridge.[1] Both became fellows of St. John's College, and the second son Eleazer was subsequently vicar of Clacton Magna in the Archdeaconry of Colchester.[2] Nathanael died in 1580 in his twenty-third year, and his brother survived him till 1591. By his second wife, Margaret Stewart, Knox had three daughters, Martha, Margaret, and Elizabeth, all of whom were married. Of other relatives Knox mentions only his brother William, and his son Paul. As far as has been ascertained, no lineal descendant of Knox exists.[3]

At the time of his death the whole substance of Knox, more than half of which consisted of moneys due to him, amounted to £1526 : 19 : 6, Scottish money. To fix the relative value of money for this period is perhaps impossible ; but whatever this sum may indicate, the fact is that the wife and daughters of Knox were left in poverty. So true were the words of his will, " Nane I haif corrupted, nane I haif defraudit ; merchandise haif I not maid."[4] On the very day of his burial, however, the Regent Morton wrote a letter to the General Assembly in which he " effectuously required " that Knox's stipend should be paid to his widow for the year following his death. The Assembly

---

[1] There is no ground for the common statement that it was by Knox's wish that they entered the English Church.

[2] For an interesting account of Knox's sons see an article in the *Scots Magazine* for December 1894, by the Rev. Dr. Leishman.

[3] Laing has collected all the information that seems to exist regarding Knox's family.—Knox, *Works*, vi. pp. lxi. *et seq.* Knox's second daughter, Margaret, married Zachary Pont, the brother of Timothy Pont, the geographer ; and his third daughter, Elizabeth, Mr. John Welsh, one of the most notable Presbyterian ministers of his time.

[4] Knox, Last Will and Testament ; Bannatyne, Appendix, p. 370.

did not meet till March of the next year; but it then readily responded to Morton's request, as remembering the "long and faithfull travells" of the leader whom they had lost.[1]

In a letter to Beza, of which an account is given elsewhere,[2] Peter Young, best known as Buchanan's assistant in the education of James VI., thus describes the personal appearance of Knox before he was shattered by his last illness: "In stature he was slightly under the middle height, of well-knit and graceful figure, with shoulders somewhat broad, longish fingers, head of moderate size, hair black, complexion somewhat dark, and general appearance not unpleasing. In his stern and severe countenance there was a natural dignity and majesty not without a certain grace, and in anger there was an air of command on his brow. Under a somewhat narrow forehead his brows stood out in a slight ridge over his ruddy and slightly swelling cheeks, so that his eyes seemed to retreat into his head. The colour of his eyes was bluish-gray, their glance keen and animated. His face was rather long; his nose of more than ordinary length; the mouth large; the lips full, the upper a little thicker than the lower; his beard black mingled with gray, a span and a half long and moderately thick."

Judged by the scale and significance of his work, Knox may fairly be called a figure of European importance. More than any other man he has a right to be called the founder of Puritanism in England. By his five years' labour in that country he left a per-

---

[1] *Works*, vi. pp. lxvi. lxvii.
[2] See Appendix G, "The Portrait and Personal Appearance of John Knox."

manent stamp at once on ritual and doctrine; and in Frankfort and Geneva, where Puritanism first gained a clear consciousness of itself, he continued this influence with still more direct and more abiding results. Among the English exiles in both of these towns he held the first place—being, as we have seen, their minister and teacher and chosen champion; while in the work these men afterwards did in their own country they perpetuated the spirit they had imbibed during the four years they listened to Knox in Geneva. By the victory of Knox in Scotland he gave still another impulse to Puritanism in England, which it may be difficult to appraise, but which was none the less operative and real. In France, also, he has a part in the development of religion, which earned for him the malediction of French Catholic historians. Through his preaching more than that of any other, Dieppe became the " La Rochelle of the North"; and thus materially affected the course of the reformed religion in France.

But it is by his achievement in his own country that his relative place must be assigned among the great characters of history. However the tendency of that achievement may be regarded, of its far-reaching issues no doubt can exist. Had Mary on her return to Scotland found her people united in their allegiance to Rome and their predilection for France, the course of British history must have been different from what it has actually been. With three-fourths of her subjects Catholic, Elizabeth could not have held her own against a sovereign in Mary's position, backed by the dominant opinion of Europe. But to Knox more than to any other single person was due that revolution in policy and religion which put it out of Mary's power to realise the destiny which seemed to await her. In the revolution of 1567, which completed the work of 1560, the influence of Knox is less apparent only because his own pen has not described it. In reality, the part he bore in the settlement that followed the dethronement of Mary was as conspicuous and as significant as in the overthrow of her mother. In the following century it lay again with Scotland to determine at a critical period the course of events in the two countries; for in the quarrel of the English Parliament with Charles I., it was the action of Presbyterian Scotland that decided the issue between them.

But the revolution of 1560 was not the mere substitution of one religion for another: it was the highest consciousness of the nation deliberately choosing between the old and the new order, between authority on the one hand and individualism on the other. In its violent breach with the past the Scottish character and genius were for the first time revealed in their essential aptitudes and affinities. As realised in Scotland the Reformation has a character all its own; and the best proof that it was no outcome of mere temporary circumstance is the persistence of its spirit and teaching among the people that adopted it. Broadly viewed, the true worth of Knox was that in a measure beyond any other of his countrymen he revealed the heart and mind of the nation to itself, and thus made clear its precise vocation among the peoples. Among the great personages of the past it would be difficult to name one who in the same degree has vitalised and dominated the collective energies of his countrymen.

What is true of all leaders of men is specially true

of Knox — to understand him we must distinguish between the man and his function. By the conditions under which his work was done, it is in his function as prophet and revolutionary that he stands before the world in rigid and immitigable traits. Except for a few years in Geneva, Knox, during every part of his career, found himself in deadly battle with the prevailing powers around him. His whole public life was thus absorbed by the mere struggle to hold the ground he had won, or to push his advantage over the enemy. In the six volumes that make up his writings there is hardly a passage that directly or indirectly does not bear on the work to which he gave his life. With the men who stood by his side and their immediate successors the conditions were the same. Hence alike in his own writings and in the contemporary and traditional notices of him, it is the traits of the apostle that are almost exclusively reported. Of the man in his home, in his friendships, in the unconscious action that discovers the temper and the will, we have for the most part only those casual suggestions which have been emphasised in the preceding pages.

What has been said of all religion when it takes full possession of man's nature is eminently true of the religion of Knox: it was something "savage and bare, but infinitely strong." It was the religion of St. Columba, who rushed knee-deep into the sea after a sacrilegious robber, pursuing him with curses;[1] of St. Bernard, who believed that the slaying of an infidel was a service to God; of a religious leader of our own time, who said that a heresiarch should meet with no mercy, "as if he were embodied evil."[2] Among the

[1] Adamnan's *Life of Columba* (Historians of Scotland), p. 166.
[2] Cardinal Newman. Newman, it should be said, carefully dis-

men who led the great schism from Rome there is no one who by his character and work may be fitly compared with Knox. In the circumstances under which Luther carried through his labours, there was no call for the peculiar qualities that were needed in Scotland. From the first Luther found a prince able and willing to protect him, and to the end he was never subjected to the constant pressure of immediate hostility which is apt to beget a narrow and truculent intensity. In Calvin we have the systematic thinker and practical organiser—functions which Knox was never privileged to exercise even if he had been fitted to discharge them. As the leader of a religious revolt Savonarola offers an obvious parallel to the Scottish reformer, which in its points of likeness and contrast emphasises the distinctive qualities of each. In both we have the same absolute religion, the same blasting denunciation, the same gift of infectious enthusiasm. By his picturesque environment, his poetical eloquence, his tragic end, Savonarola is the more attractive figure for the imagination. On the other hand, in the practical sense of Knox combined with unflagging zeal, we have precisely what distinguishes the great religious leader from the mere religious visionary. To the shrewd and homely Scottish preacher the "burning of the vanities," the ecstatic visions and spiritual antics of the last years of Savonarola, would

tinguished between his natural human feeling, and the sentiments that became him as an orthodox son of his Church. In his *History of the Arian Heresy* he had said : "The latter [the heresiarch] should meet with no mercy : he assumes the office of the Tempter ; and, so far forth as his error goes, must be dealt with by the competent authority, as if he were embodied evil." Commenting on this passage in his *Apologia pro vita sua*, p. 47 (1873), he says, that "not even when I was fiercest could I have even cut off a Puritan's ears, and I think the sight of a Spanish *auto-da-fé* would have been the death of me."

have seemed the mere tricks of Satan in mimicry of the kingdom of heaven.

Besides being a great historical figure, Knox is emphatically a typical man of his own people. In the four great personalities whom Scotland has produced—Knox, Buchanan, Burns, and Carlyle—there are distinctive features which mark them off from a similar succession in any other country. The great characters of England are men of another order from these four Scotsmen, in all of whom there is a substantial likeness that cannot be missed. Between Buchanan and Burns as between Knox and Carlyle, there is a family resemblance that is evident on the surface: what is common to all four is a primitive force of passion, an inborn unrest, which constitutes their individuality as men of action and genius. As the exaggerated type of his own countrymen, Knox, like Voltaire and Dr. Johnson, necessarily repels men of other nations; while his own people, even those who differ most widely from his religious and political teaching, regard even his asperities with the kindly allowance that is made for family idiosyncrasies.[1]

By the conditions of his work, as has been said, the social side of Knox's nature has been hardly touched either by himself or those who have spoken of him. That this social side had its own place in the life of himself and his co-workers there is excellent evidence to prove. Touches there are, indeed, which indicate that, points of doctrine apart, Luther himself

---

[1] Thus, Sir William Stirling-Maxwell, a conservative by instinct and conviction, speaks in the warmest terms of Knox. Of Knox's services to his country Sir William says: " No man in England or Scotland who values liberty, national, civil, or religious, can speak of Knox without reverence and gratitude."—*Miscellaneous Essays and Addresses* (1891), pp. 298, 299.

would not have found Knox an uncongenial spirit. It was customary, it would seem, to transact religious business at a friendly feast;[1] and we are told of a certain godly minister who objected to the "lang denners and suppers at General Assemblies."[2] Of Andrew Melville, a more uncompromising spirit than Knox himself, we read that he "warranted" his opinion for "a pint of wine," his opponent, also a minister, offering to make it a quart.[3] At table his nephew tells us that it was Melville's usual custom to "interlace mirrie interludes," and to drink to the health of his various guests.[4] That Knox would not be a marfeast at such entertainments the humorous strokes in his History sufficiently assure us; and with his varied experience of life from king's courts to the galleys, his ready wit and effective speech, he could hardly fail to be the soul of every company into which he was thrown. But besides mere responsive geniality, there was indubitably in Knox a soul of yearning that made human affection a necessity of his nature.[5] *Rien n'est tendre comme l'homme austère;* and the essential tenderness of Knox is vouched by the love of women, by abiding friendships, by the idolatrous regard of those who, like Richard Bannatyne, went in and out with him in intimate contact of mind with mind and soul with soul.

In estimating great historical figures at such a distance from us as Knox we must take account, on the one hand, of the opinions of individual thinkers, and, on the other, of the deposited impression of collective bodies of men. In the case of Knox both testimonies have been forthcoming with unmistakable clearness

---

[1] Melville, *Diary,* p. 87. [2] *Ibid.* p. 58.
[3] *Ibid.* p. 50. [4] *Ibid.* p. 103.
[5] His own expression may be recalled here: " I have rather need of all then that any hath need of me."

and emphasis. To men of strong theological convictions, but doctrinally opposed to his own, he has always seemed a wild heresiarch, permitted by an inscrutable providence to work strange havoc in the Christian Church. To artists and men of letters of a certain type he has appeared as a mere "scourge of God," who is properly ranked with apparitions like Attila or Timour. On the other hand, thinkers as wide as the poles apart from him in their views of human life and destiny, have seen in Knox one of the great emancipators of humanity, whose work left undone would irremediably have injured the highest interests not only of his own country but of the community of civilised nations.[1] In every Christian country, also, there have been men of the same temper as himself, who have regarded Knox as the exponent of a religion which by its absolute acceptance of the facts of life, its unflinching distinction between good and evil, between the natural man and the man of the spirit, is the truest expression of the mind of the Founder of Christianity.

But in the case of all men who have distinguished themselves beyond their fellows, the definitive judgment must rest with the people from whom they spring, and to whom the heritage of their labours

---

[1] The opinions of two very different thinkers regarding the work of Knox may be quoted. Renan (*Hist. du Peuple d'Israël*, iii. 155) has the following passage: "Il nous est bien permis au XIX⁰ siècle d'être pour Marie Stuart contre Knox ; mais au XVI⁰ siècle le protestantisme fanatique servait mieux la cause de progrès que le Catholicisme, même relâché." More sympathetically Pfleiderer (*Gifford Lectures*, i. 4) says : "But as regards Knox's activity, in what else did it consist but in the establishment or restoration of *Natural Christianity?* His object was to free Christianity from the deformation and disguises which it had suffered in the dogmas, worship, and hierarchy of the Roman Church, and to bring its genuine, original, or natural truth in faith and morals again to recognition."

is a permanent and vital question of the balance of good or ill. In this final court of appeal the judgment is undeniably for Knox and against all his cavillers. For the mass of his countrymen—those who have shaped the nation's destinies in the past as they must shape them in the future—Knox is the greatest person their country has produced, and the man to whom in all that makes a people great they owe the deepest and most abiding debt. "What I have been to my country," he himself said when within sight of the end he looked back on the long travail of his life, "what I have been to my country, albeit this unthankful age will not know, yet the ages to come will be compelled to bear witness to the truth;"[1] and the consenting testimony of three centuries is the evidence and pledge that his assurance was not in vain.

[1] *Works*, vi. 596.

KNOX'S BURIAL-PLACE

APPENDIX A (vol. i. p. 166)

CONDITIONS OF THE GRANT OF THE CHURCH OF THE WHITE LADIES IN FRANKFORT

I AM indebted to the Rev. Professor Mitchell of St. Andrews for the following extract, which states precisely the exact conditions on which the use of the Church of the White Ladies was permitted to the English exiles :—

"Nun war bey Ankunft der Engelländer eine Kirche in Frankfurt, die einigen französischen Protestanten zum Gebrauch eingeräumt war, welche nun auch zum Behuf der Engelländer in Vorschlag gebracht, und am 14 Julii ihnen wirklich angewiesen wurde. Doch machte der Rath gewisse Ordnungen, und suchte die Sache also einzurichten, das allerlei Disputen, die etwa entstehen mögten, der Weg verlaget wurde. Die vornehmsten waren diese : (*a*) dass die Engelländer und Franzosen einerley Lehre und Ceremonien führen sollten ; Daher sollten jene (*b*) der Franzosen Glaubensbekäntniss, das diese N.B. dem Rath überreichet hatten, unterschreiben. (*c*) Liessen sich die Engelländer gefallen, dass das Volk bey dem gemeinen Gebet das Amen nicht mehr laut sagen sollte, wie sonst in der Kirche von Engelland üblich ist. (*d*) Dass die Prediger das weisse Chorhemde, nebst vielen andern in Engelland eingeführten Ceremonien abschaffen sollten, als welche den Einwohnern, die solcher Dinge ungewohnt wären, einstossig seyn könnten. Und was der gleichen Umstände mehr waren, welche die Engelländer, um desto eher zum Stande zu kommen, freiwillig eingiengen."

J. Hildebrand Withof, "Vertheidigung der . . . Nachricht wie es mit V. Pollane erstem Reformirten Prediger zu Frankfurt-am-Mayn . . . zugegangen," 1753, folio.

MÉMOIRE des affaires d'escosse pour d'iceulx estre escript a nr̄e S pere le pape de la part du Roy daulphin et Royne daulphine soubz le bon plaisir et Intencion du Roy.

PREMIEREMENT

Comme depuis quatre ans en ca la dicte dame et la Royne Regente du dict Royaulme sa mère ont fait continuellement entendre a sa s^teté Tant par le Reverendissime cardinal sermonette protecteur du dict Royaulme, Que autres ses parens amys et alliez la necessité qu'avoit la Republicque d'icelles d'ung bon ferme et perpetuel establissement de justice pour contenir ses subgects en devoir et obeissance spirituelle et temporelle ensemble le besoing qu'avoient les gens d'eglise du dict Royaulme d'une grande et severe Refformacion avecques Reiglement tant de la faulte qu'ilz faisoient d'instruire le peuple en la parolle de Dieu Que a cause de la depravation et corruption de leurs meurs et façons de vivre, dont les seculiers estoient tellement scandalisez qu'ilz entroient en contempnement et mespris de la Religion [1] et de l'eglise Romaine.

Comme aus dictes necessitez n'estoit possible a la dicte dame bonnement pourvevir sans l'ayde et faveur de la dicte saincteté. Ayant icelle dame la guerre sur les bras contre les Anglois et peu de Revenu a sa couronne, de la quelle ses predecesseurs ont distrait meilleure part du patrimoyne, pour doner et enrichir les eglises du dict Royaulme.

Pour lesquelles causes et autres plus au long déclairees par les memoires cy-devant envoyez la dicte dame auroit fait tres humblement supplier la dicte saincteté de luy vouloir ayder et subvenir en cas si urgents et Raisonnables, et a ceste fin luy taxer et assigner une bonne somme de deniers en Rente et Revenu annuel sur le patrimonie des eglises de son dict Royaulme pour l'establissement

---

[1] Regilion, MS.

de la dicte justice.   Suyvant pareil octroy qui auparavant auroit esté fait tant a ses predecesseurs.   Et pour la Reformacion et Reiglement de l'eglise deleguer et envoyer es partyes du dict Royaulme quelsques bons saints et notables personnaiges instruicts de toutes choses requises et necessaires, Comme en semblable auroit este fait auparavant par de bonne memoire pape Paule troiz^me.   Lequel de son temps par deux diverses fois envoya le patriarche d'Aquilée, Grimain, et l'evesque de Veronne, Lypomain, avec bonnes et grosses sommes de deniers pour parcille Refformacion et le soustenement et deffence de l'eglise Romaine contre les nouvelles sectes qui commancerent lors a seslever au dict Royaulme par le moyen de leurs voisins suivant l'eglise changee en Angleterre.

A laquelle supplicacion la dicte s^tete occupee comme il est croyable a autres affaires et pour quelque bonne occasion n'auroit peu vacquer et auroit tousjours différé faire response resolutive.   Et cependant et que la dicte dame a esté empeschee en la dicte guerre contre ses voisins est advenu que par la negligence des prelatz ceste doctrine nouvelle qu'ilz appellent evangelicque a esté secretement et soubz main semee et enseignee par plusieurs partyes du dict Royaume au desceu de la dicte dame et de la dicte dame Regente sa mere. Laquelle ayant esté finablement advertye que en lune des villes d'icelluy Royaulme s'estoit eslevé ung predicant.   Instruisant et enseignant le peuple publicquement soubz la faveur des cytoiens dicelle ville a la forme de l'eglise de Geneve auroit fait toute dilligence d'admonester les prélatz d'assembler Incontinant le clergé pour deliberer et trouver quelque bon expedient premierement pour reformer leur maniere de vivre et apres pour reprimer ceste dicte doctrine Promectant la dicte dame Regente toute concurrance de sa part.

Et neantmoings ne voullant icelle dame pretermetre dailleurs tous moyens de obvyer a ung si grand scandalle auroit assemblé les principaulx des estatz du dict Royaulme pensant avoir quelque bon conseil et ayded'eulx a ceste fin Avecques lesquelz tant s'en fault qu'elle ait trouvé le secours qu'elle esperoit en cest affaire.   Que la plus part des seigneurs temporelz luy proposoient a part et hors du conseil certains articles touchans l'exemption de la jurisdiction et charge des gens d'eglise et l'establissement en partie de la nouvelle Relligion.   Ce que la dicte dame Royne Regente leur reffusa tout a plus les advertissant comme son devoir le requeroit et pareillement les gens d'eglise de faire prompte et exacte Refformacion en leur clerge par concille provincial.

Lequel concille a esté veritablement tenu touttefois sans ce qu'il en soit reussy aulcun fruict ains plus tost scandalle.   Qui a esté cause que le peuple s'est esmeu et esleué a faire prescher publicquement leurs prédicans en meilleures parties et endroitz du dict Royaulme.   Et mesmement en certaines villes d'icelluy.

A quoy voulant la dicte dame obvyer par tous moyens a elle possibles. Selon les forces qu'elle a peu mectre ensemble, se sont enfin descouvertz et desclairez ouvertement plusieurs des contes, lordz et seigneurs du dict pays soubz la bannyère et auctorite desquelz s'est faite et formée une congregacion qu'ilz disent estre pour l'advancement de la gloire de Dieu. Laquelle avec main armee de ceste heure s'est mise a abbatre les ymages, ruyner aultelz et tabernacles de la plus part des eglises du dict Royaulme, prohiber la messe et changer les seremonyes accoustumées en Icelluy Royaulme, Rager les chartreurs, l'abbaye de Scun, six couvents de Cordeliers et aultant de Jacobins. Sans avoir pardonné aux arbres fruictiers des jardins d'iceulx.

Et dujourd'huy sont en Intencion de parachevers (*sic*) leurs entreprinses et Ruyner et desmolir le surplus des monasteres et couvents qui restent. Et d'avantage s'efforsent contraindre la dicte dame a l'establissement de leur dicte religion. A quoy ne voullant icelle dame obtemperer mais resister a son povoir, S'est actendant secours retiree en une place forte du dict Royaulme. Pour n'avoir de present forces suffisantes pour reprimer le rage de ceste congregacion avec laquelle la noblesse les villes et la pluspart du populaire concours [1] apperteinent. Et le surplus connyve de telle sorte que la dicte dame n'en a ayde ne faveur aulcune. Comme aussy n'a elle des prelatz et gens de l'estat du dict clergé. Lesquelz se sont absentz de sa court et retirez ou bon leur a semblé. Ne scait la dicte dame si c'est par intelligence ou par craincte.

Et pour ce que le peril est eminant, et le feu si allumé que s'il n'y est pourveu d'heur et en toute dilligence et extremité. Il y a dangier que l'on ne puisse jamays voir l'eglise Romaine Restaurée au dict pais, Que avec effusion de sang universel les dicts s^r et dame n'ont voullu faillir de faire advertir la dicte saincteté. A laquelle comme chef de l'eglise chrestienne. La tuicion et deffence de ceste cause appartient et supplient tres humblement icelle de vouloir contribuer avec leurs ma^{tes} a les ayder d'argent pour reprimer cest attemptat fait en la dicte eglise. Et faire pugnition de ceulx qui seront trouvez faulteurs. Et neantmoings deleguer et envoyer au dict Royaulme aucuns discrets grands et capables personnaiges pour in pugner et extirper ceste faulce doctrine. En quoy faisant ne feront les dicts seigneur et dame faulte aleur devoir tellement qu'ilz esperent que en brief la gloire et honneur de Dieu sera congneue comme auparavant et l'eglise remise en sa pristine liberté.

---

[1] Concuroe, MS.

SLANDER AGAINST KNOX

THE following minute from the Records of the Town Council of Edinburgh will explain itself:—

"18*mo Junii* 1563.—The samyn day, in presence of the baillies and counsale, comperit Jhone Gray, scribe to the kirk, and presented the supplicatione following, in name of the haill kirk, hering that it was laitlie cummen to thair knawledge bi the report of faythfull bretherins, that within this few dayis Eufame Dundas, in the presence of ane multitude, had spokin divers injurious and sclandarous wordis baith of the doctrine and ministeris. And in especiall of Jhonne Knox, minister, sayand, that within few dayis past, the said Jhonne Knox was apprehendit and tane furth of ane killogye with ane commoun hure; and that he had bene ane commone harlot all his dayis. Quhairfore it was maist humblie desyrit that the said Eufame myt be callit and examinit upone the said supplicatione, and gif the wordis above written, spoken bi hir, myt be knawin or tryit to be of veritie, that the said Jhonne Knox myt be punist with all rigour without favour: otherwyse to tak sic ordour with hir as myt stand with the glory of God, and that sclander myt be takin from the kirk. As at mair length is contenit in the said supplication. Quhilk beand red to the said Eufame personallie present in judgment, scho denyit the samyn and Fryday the 25th day of Junii instant assignit to hir to here and see witness producit for preving of the allegiance above expremit, and scho is warnit apud acta."

The only further notice of the case is in a minute of the 25th June, from which it appears that Knox's procurator produced proof that the woman had actually uttered the words as reported. As she denied the charge, however, the case seems to have been dropped, and no more is heard of it. It was partly out of this affair, doubtless, that the Catholic slanders regarding Knox arose, which are noticed below (p. 311).

KNOX AND THE RIZZIO MURDER

In the seventh volume of his *History of Scotland*[1] Fraser Tytler has directly charged Knox with complicity in the Rizzio murder. As has been said in the text, the death of Rizzio was for Knox a necessary act of justice, demanded alike by the laws of God and man. If the sovereign would not put her hand to the righteous deed, it was in perfect accordance with Knox's teaching that the subjects who stood nearest to the throne should take the responsibility of ridding the country of a dangerous enemy.[2] Nevertheless, it is intrinsically improbable that Knox would ever have consented to the manner in which the deed was done.

In the fifth book of his History the following account of the murder is given: "They [the conspirators] first purposed to have hanged him [Rizzio], and had provided cords for the same purpose; but the great haste which they had, moved them to despatch him with whingers or daggers, wherewith they gave him three and fifty strokes."[3] Even if we go with Tytler, it does not follow that Knox deliberately approved of the deed described in the latter half of this sentence.

The main proof on which Tytler bases his charge against Knox is contained in a document which he found in the State Paper Office; and in support of what he considers this direct proof he adduces certain presumptions which appear to him to strengthen his conclusion. The murder of Rizzio, he says, was in keeping with Knox's principles, and was fitted to advance the cause he had at heart; it was natural that the leading conspirators, most of whom

---

[1] Pp. 427-438.

[2] John Major held similar views. Discussing, in his Commentary on Matthew, the slaughter of Eglon, he remarks: "It is for the chiefs of the State to consider the matter. Eglon was a public enemy of Israel and a foreigner who disturbed Israel, and Ehud was a public person at the head of the State, but even if he had been a private person it would have been lawful for him to remove Eglon."

[3] Knox, *Works*, ii. 521. Cf. p. 231, and *note* above.

were Protestants, should take him into their confidence ; on Mary's approach to Edinburgh from Dunbar " he [Knox] fled precipitately and in extreme agony of spirit to Kyle," and he did not return to Edinburgh till after the murder of Darnley.[1]

To three of these presumptions no importance can be fairly attached. It is more natural to suppose that Knox should have been deliberately kept ignorant of the conspiracy than that he should have been made privy to it. From its very nature Knox could have been of no practical service in carrying it into execution, and it was mere worldly wisdom that the chief Protestant minister should be above suspicion of being party to such a deed. That Knox fled from Edinburgh in "extreme agony of spirit" is both a misleading statement and a rhetorical turn which betrays the forensic character of Tytler's reasoning. It is true that Knox fled from Edinburgh on Mary's approach, but there was ample reason for his flight apart from the circumstances of Rizzio's murder. That Mary had so long abstained from laying hands on him was due to the fact that he had hitherto had powerful friends at his back. On her return to Edinburgh, however, she was for the moment all-powerful, and not even Moray was in a position to ensure his safety.[2] For Knox's state of mind during his flight and exile the most precise authority is the passage in the preface to the fourth book of his History[3] and in that passage there is certainly no suggestion that conscious guilt was the cause of his troubled thoughts. In one sentence he has told us the root of that "agony of spirit" which Tytler attributes to him. "And what is the cause that now the just is compelled to keap silence? good men ar banished, murtheraris, and such as ar knowin unworthie of the commoun societie (yf just lawis war put in deu executioun), bear the hoill regiment and swynge within this Realme?"[4] It is

---

[1] In the body of his History (vii. 26, 33, 34) Tytler affirms that the General Fast and the directions for the prayers and sermons that should accompany it were specially planned and prepared in view of Rizzio's murder, which, he says, the Edinburgh ministers knew to be imminent. The truth is that all the arrangements for the Fast were made by the General Assembly in the December of the previous year. For the special reasons of the Fast see above, p. 228.

[2] Cf. pp. 229, 232 above.

[3] ii. 265. When Tytler says that Knox left Edinburgh in "extreme agony of spirit," he means the reader to infer that this feeling arose from conscious guilt and the dread of punishment. In support of this implication Tytler refers to a prayer composed by Knox on the third day after Rizzio's murder. As a matter of fact, this prayer proves that Knox was specially well pleased with himself and all his doings.— See the passage quoted above, p. 276.

[4] *Works*, ii. 265.

a further error to say that Knox did not return to Edinburgh till after the murder of Darnley, since in December of 1566 he was taking an active part in the General Assembly held in that town.[1] It is doubtless true that it was in keeping with Knox's teaching that the chief nobility should put Rizzio to death if Mary would not otherwise dispose of him ; but that Knox was bound to approve the deed as it actually happened, is an implication which further proves that Tytler unduly strained his case.

As regards the incriminating document itself, it has been justly maintained[2] that Tytler assigns to it an importance which is justified neither by its contents nor by its authority. The document in question is a slip of paper pinned to a letter of Randolph to Cecil, relating to the Rizzio murder. As printed by Tytler, the paper appears as follows :—

Martii, 1565.

Names of such as were consenting to the death of David.[3]

The Earl Morton	Lochleven
The L. Ruthven	Elphinston
The L. Lindsay	Patrick Murray
The Secretary	Patrick Ballantyne
The Mr. of Ruthven	George Douglas
Lairds	Andrew Car of Fawdonsyde
Ormiston	John Knox } Preachers
Brunston	John Craig }
Haughton	

All these were at the death of Davy and privy thereunto, and are now in displeasure with the Q. and their houses taken and spoiled.

To understand the precise significance of this list, certain facts have to be borne in mind. On his flight from Edinburgh, Lord Ruthven, one of the Rizzio murderers, made for Berwick-on-Tweed, where the Earl of Bedford, the governor of the town, and the well-known Randolph were at that time resident.[4] On the 21st[5] of March both Bedford and Randolph wrote to Cecil in reference to the late doings in Edinburgh, their information being directly gained from Ruthven. In Bedford's letter the only passage with which we are concerned is as follows : "For that Mr. Randolph writeth also

---

[1] See above, pp. 236-239.

[2] Specially by the Rev. Thomas M'Crie (son of the biographer of Knox) in his *Sketches of Scottish Church History* (1841), Note A, " Mr. Tytler's Charge against John Knox." Cf. also Dr. Crichton's edition of M'Crie's *Knox* (Belfast, 1874), pp. 455 *et seq.*

[3] According to Tytler, this endorsement is in the hand of Cecil's clerk.

[4] Tytler, vii. 428, 429.   [5] *Ibid.*

more at large of the names of such as now be gone abroad [that is, of those who had fled after Rizzio's murder], I shall not trouble you therewith."   Turning to Randolph's letter, we find the information to which Bedford refers.   First come the names of "the lords of the last attemptate," which exactly correspond to those in the list pinned to Randolph's letter.   In the case of the subordinate conspirators there is a slight discrepancy between the documents. While Randolph gives only eight, the pinned list gives nine, and two names appear in each which do not appear in the other.   The most significant difference, however, is that the pinned list concludes with the names of Knox and his colleague Craig.   With the exception of these discrepancies, the names given in both lists are the same.   The question, therefore, is, What authority should be attached to the list pinned to Randolph's letter?   According to Tytler, the list is in the hand of a clerk who was at that time in the employment of Bedford.   If this be a fact, and as such we may accept it, it is evident that it at once stamps the document with a certain claim to consideration.   Yet this being granted, there are difficulties connected with its contents which deprive it of definitive authority. If the list were really sent as a supplement to that of Randolph, we should naturally expect it to be a document at once exact and complete.   In point of fact, it is less precise than the communication made by Randolph.   Speaking of the nobility who conspired against Rizzio, Randolph calls them "the lords of the last attemptate"; and he introduces the minor agents in the plot with the phrase, "Besides these that were the principal takers in hand of this matter."   In these expressions we have the words of one who has a definite meaning in his mind.   To the pinned list, on the other hand, we have a confused and blundering note, which seems to prove that its author had no clear notion of what he was writing. "All these were at the death of Davy and privy thereunto, and are now in displeasure with the Q. and their houses taken and spoiled."   On this note Tytler comments as follows : "It is certain that this cannot mean that all whose names are to be found in this list were personally present at the act of the murder ; it should be understood to mean that 'all those were at the murder of Davy *or* privy thereto.'"   A more natural commentary on the note is that its author, whoever he was, wrote in a loose way of facts which he had imperfectly ascertained.   What proves his ignorance, indeed, is that Craig did not leave Edinburgh, and that there is no evidence that either the house of Craig or Knox was "taken and spoiled."   On the strength of such a document, and it is the only direct evidence that has yet been adduced, it seems hardly historical justice to make a charge so definite as Tytler has seen fit to make against Knox.

In support of Knox's innocence Tytler quotes two authorities, both of which, however, he sets aside in favour of the pinned list. Besides his letter referred to above, Randolph sent another communication on the same subject, dated the 27th of March. This second communication bears the following title: "The names of such as were doers, and of council, in the late attempt for the killing of the secretary David at Edinburgh, 9th March 1566, as contained in the account sent to the Council of England, by the Earl of Bedford, Lieutenant of the North, and Sir Thomas Randolph, ambassador from England to Scotland at the time dated Berwick, 27th March 1566."[1] In this second list the names of neither Knox nor Craig appear, but for two reasons Tytler will not allow the same authority to this list as to the pinned one. In the first place, as written to the Council and not directly to Cecil, it has less claim to be considered an honest statement of facts. To this objection it seems a sufficient reply that in Randolph's first letter, which was specially addressed to Cecil, the names of Knox and Craig do not appear, and that it remains to be proved that Randolph was the author of the pinned list. Tytler's second objection is based on a supposition which may be easily turned against himself. The conspirators, he says, had failed, and Mary had escaped their hands. Baffled in their enterprise, it was the interest of the fugitive lords, and of Bedford and Randolph who abetted them, to keep the world ignorant that any Protestant minister had his hand in such an ugly business. The second communication of Randolph and Bedford, therefore, was deliberately concocted to serve this purpose; and to prove that the fugitive lords were interested in this artifice, Tytler quotes the following passage from a letter addressed to Bedford by Ruthven and Morton: "It is come to our knowledge that some Papists have bruited that these our proceedings have been at the instigation of the ministers of Scotland. We assure your lordship, upon our honour, that there were none of them art nor part of that deed, nor were participate thereof." The obvious criticism on this part of Tytler's argument is that it bears the character of legal pleading rather than of historical reasoning. Whether they won or not, it was surely the policy of Rizzio's murderers to conceal the fact that their ministers had the most distant connection with a deed that must have discredited the whole Reformed Church. If there be one point in the argument to which serious weight should be attached, it is the affirmation of Ruthven and Morton that the ministers were neither "art nor part" in the deed. Whatever might be the event of Rizzio's removal, it was the interest of the Protestant leaders that their ministers, whose influence on public opinion was their chief hope for the future, should

---

[1] This letter is printed by Ellis, *Original Letters*, ii. 207. The number of conspirators given in this letter is thirty-one.

have their hands clean in proclaiming to the world the righteousness of their cause.[1] Yet, with a perverse subtlety, Tytler discredits the express averment of Ruthven and Morton. Both of these nobles, as we have seen, pledge their words for the truth of their statement, yet so eager is Tytler to make good his case that he puts Ruthven aside, and deals with the statement as if Morton alone were its sponsor. Fourteen years later, on the eve of his execution, Morton made a distinction which, according to Tytler, puts him out of court in the case before us. Accused of being concerned in the Darnley murder, Morton made use of these words among others: "And howbeit they have condemned me of art and part, foreknowledge and concealing of the king's murder, yet, as I shall answer to God, I never had yet art or part, red or counsel, in that matter. I foreknew, indeed, and concealed it, because I durst not reveal it to any creature for my life." On this passage Tytler comments as follows: "It is perfectly clear, therefore, that Morton's declaration that none of the ministers of Scotland were art and part of Riccio's murder, does not necessarily imply any declaration that Knox had not a foreknowledge of the murder; on the contrary, it is quite consistent with his having known it, and, according to the term used by one of his brethren to James, allowed of it." The only answer to such reasoning is that, by its ingenuity and perversity, it is conceived in the spirit of an advocate and not of a historian. For the most part a just and careful writer, the discovery of his interesting list seems to have warped Tytler's mind by a temporary exuberance of feeling.

There is still another list, however,—one to which Tytler does not refer, but which is of higher authority than any of those which he has produced. The day after Mary's return to Edinburgh from Dunbar, she held a meeting of her Privy Council,[2] which took up the affair of Rizzio's murder. As the result of its meeting, there

---

[1] A parallel case may be found in the plan for assassinating Elizabeth projected by the leaders of the Catholic party in 1583. Thus on 2nd May, the papal nuncio wrote from Paris to the Cardinal of Como :— "The Duke of Guise and the Duke of Mayenne have told me that they have a plan for killing the Queen of England by the hand of a Catholic. . . . The Duke asks for no assistance from our Lord [the Pope] for this affair. . . . As to putting to death that wicked woman I said to him that I will not write about it to our Lord the Pope (nor do I), nor tell your most illustrious Lordship to inform him of it ; because though I believe our Lord the Pope would be glad that God should punish in any way whatever that enemy of His, still it would be unfitting that His vicar should procure it by these means."—*Letters and Memorials of Card. Allen,* p. xlvi.

[2] Keith, iii. 279-281. In Keith the 10th of March is erroneously given as the date of its meeting. It should probably be the 19th, the day after Mary's return to Edinburgh.

was issued a " Charge on the Persons delatit of the Slaughter of David
Riccio," in which appear the names of seventy-one lords, barons,
knights, and servants.   In this long and minute list the names neither
of Knox nor of Craig appear, yet if Knox could have been pointed
at, this was the moment for Mary to have her revenge on her ancient
adversary.   She was furious and triumphant, and Knox had not a
friend strong enough to raise an effective hand in his defence.   That
he is not mentioned in this specific charge against those even
remotely responsible for the death of her favourite, is strong evidence that there existed no ground for his incrimination.[1]

To sum up the foregoing discussion : valid evidence there is
none that Knox had any knowledge of a plot to assassinate Rizzio,
or that he approved of the deed as it was actually carried out.
But apart from the question of detailed evidence is the larger
historical question of Knox's attitude towards the general spirit
of the Rizzio conspiracy.   The aim of Morton and his associates
was to remove Rizzio in some such fashion as Cochrane had been
removed in the preceding century, and thus to restore the Protestant
ascendency in the country.   Of both of these acts Knox, beyond a
doubt, would energetically have approved.   That he had any col-
lusion whatever in the actual execution of the first is not proved
by any evidence that is yet to hand.

---

[1] After the baptism of her son, Mary issued a pardon for such as
had had any hand in Rizzio's murder, George Douglas and Ker of
Fawdonside being expressly excluded.   In this list seventy-nine persons
are mentioned, but the names of Knox and Craig are not among
them.

CATHOLIC LEGENDS REGARDING KNOX

No notice has been taken in the text of the extraordinary legends circulated respecting Knox by his Catholic adversaries. As a curious page from the sixteenth century, however, a few of these may be quoted here. In truth, our notions of that century are incomplete till we realise that men of position and education could write in the strain of the passages that follow. In our estimate of men like Knox it should not be forgotten that it was in an atmosphere such as these performances so vividly suggest that they lived and did their work. In much of his own six volumes Knox transgresses what we now consider the limits of fairness and good taste towards opponents. Compared with his revilers, however, he appears as a delicate and impartial controversialist.

To attempt any refutation of these calumnies would, of course, be absurd. Essentially, indeed, they belong rather to folklore than to documentary history. In the case of all the great leaders of the Protestant movement—Luther, Calvin, Buchanan, Knox, and others —the same stories are told of monstrous offences against all the laws of God and man. That Knox had once been a priest, that he proved one of the most formidable enemies of the religion he left, that he married twice, and that women flocked to him as a spiritual teacher and consoler—in these facts, and possibly the story referred to in a preceding page,[1] we have doubtless the origin of the mountain of iniquity that was laid at his door. Of the three traducers, who supplied the materials for succeeding imitators, it is sufficient to say that one of them, Archibald Hamilton, had once been a Protestant, and was the personal enemy of Knox ; and that the other two, Nicol Burne and James Laing, were Knox's fellow-countrymen, and detested him as the apostate priest who had done more than any other man to ruin their Church and bring low their Queen. On the whole question of Knox and his maligners the last word was long ago said by Bayle : "C'est

---

[1] Appendix C.

rendre sans doute quelque service à la mémoire de Jean Knox, que de faire voir les extravagances de ceux qui ont dechiré sa reputation."

It has been related above how Hamilton quarrelled with Knox at St. Andrews,[1] and how he afterwards took his revenge on his great adversary. As a specimen of Hamilton's manner we take this passage from his *De Confusione Calvinianae Sectae*, in which he describes the circumstances of Knox's death:[2] "The opening of his mouth was drawn out to such a length of deformity, that his face resembled that of a dog, as his voice also did the barking of that animal. The voice failed from that tongue which had been the cause of so much mischief, and his death, most grateful to his country, soon followed. In his last sickness, he was occupied not so much in meditating upon death, as in thinking upon civil and worldly affairs. When a number of his friends, who held him in the greatest veneration, were assembled in his chamber, and anxious to hear from him something tending to the confirmation of his former doctrine, and to their comfort, he perceiving that his death approached, and that he could gain no more advantage by the pretext of religion, disclosed to them the mysteries of that Savoyan art (*Sabaudicae disciplinae*, magic) which he had hitherto kept secret; confessed the injustice of that authority which was then defended by arms against the exiled Queen; and declared many things concerning her return and the restoration of religion after his death. One of the company, who had taken the pen to record his dying sayings, thinking that he was in a delirium, desisted from writing, upon which Knox, with a stern countenance and great asperity of language, began to upbraid him! 'Thou good-for-nothing man! why dost thou leave off writing what my presaging mind foresees is about to happen in this kingdom? Dost thou distrust me? Dost thou not believe that all which I say shall most certainly happen? But that I may attest to thee and others how undoubted the things which I have just spoken are, go out all of you from me, and I will in a moment confirm them by a new and unheard-of proof.' They withdrew at length, though reluctantly, leaving only the lighted candles in the chamber, and soon returned, expecting to witness some prodigy, when they found the lights extinguished, and his dead body lying prostrate on the ground."[3]

From Hamilton's reply to Smeton[4] we take another passage, which is better left in the original: "Pueritiam prematura venere

---

[1] See above, pp. 273, 274.

[2] The translation is that of Dr. M'Crie.—*Life of John Knox* (1855), p. 405.

[3] *De Confusione Calvin. Sectae apud Scotos*, p. 66.

[4] See above, p. 285, *note*.

et polluto insuper patris thoro infamem notavi. Inde adolescentiam perpetuis assuetam adulteriis designavi." And again : "Itane vero in maledictis ducitis, quae impurus homuncio non uno aut paucis, sed multis, et fere dicam omnibus attestantibus, designavit—patris thorum infami incestu pollutum, et tot commissa adulteria, quot in aedibus, intra quas admittebatur? Relicta vestigia etiamnum recitant Laudonienses omnes, juxta et ignobiles." [1]

From James Laing, a doctor of the Sorbonne, in a book published in 1581, we have something to the same effect as these passages from Hamilton. "Statim," he says, "ab initio suae pueritiae omni genere turpissimi facinoris infectus fuit. Vix excesserat jam ex ephebis, cum patris sui uxorem violarat, suam novercam vitiarat, et cum ea, cui reverentia potissimum adhibenda fuerat, nefarium stuprum fecerat." And again : "Continuo cum tribus meretricibus, quae videbantur posse sufficere uni sacerdoti, in Scotia convolat. . . . Ceterum hic lascivus caper, quem assidue sequebatur lasciva capella, partim perpetuis crapulis, partim vino, lustrisque ita confectus fuit, ut quotiescunq. conscenderet suggestum ad maledicendum, velim precandum suis, opus erat illi duobus aut tribus viris, a quibus elevandus atq. sustentandus erat." [2]

The following lively passage referring to Knox's second marriage has often been quoted from Nicol Burne : [3] "Heaving laid asyd al feir of the panis of hel, and regarding na thing the honestie of the warld, as ane bund sklave of the Devil, being kendillit with ane inquenshible lust and ambition, he durst be sua bauld to enterpryse the sute of Marriage with the maist honorabil ladie, my ladie Fleming, my lord duke's eldest dochter, to the end that his seid, being of the blude Royal, and gydit be their fatheris spirit, might have aspyrit to the croun. And because he receavit ane refusal, it is notoriouslie knawin how deadlie he haited the hail house of the Hamiltonis, albeit being deceavit be him traittorouslie it was the cheif upsetter and protector of his hæresie. And this maist honest refusal would nather stench his lust nor ambition ; bot a lytil eftir he did perseu to have allyance with the honorabil house of Ochiltrie of the Kingis M. awin blude ; Rydand thair with ane gret court, on ane trim gelding, nocht lyke ane prophet or ane auld decrepit preist, as he was, bot lyk as he had bene ane of the blude Royal, with his bendis of taffetie feschnit with Goldin ringis, and precious stanes : And as

---

[1] *Calvinianae Confusionis Demonstratio,* etc. (Paris, 1581), p. 253.

[2] *De Vita et Moribus atque Rebus Gestis Haereticorum nostri temporis,* etc. p. 113 *et seq.* In his last days, it will be remembered, Knox was actually helped into the pulpit by Richard Bannatyne and another servant. See above, pp. 267, 268.

[3] *Disputation concerning the Controversit Headdis of Religion,* etc., pp. 143, 144.

is planelie reportit in the contrey, be sorcerie and witchcraft did sua allure that puir gentil woman, that scho could not leve without him ; whilk appeiris of great probabilitie, scho being ane Damosel of nobil blud, and he ane auld decrepit creatur of maist bais degrie of onie that could be found in the cuntrey : Sua that sik ane nobil hous could not have degenerat sua far, except Johann kmnox had interposed the powar of his maister the Devil, quha as he transfiguris him self sumtymes in ane Angel of licht ; sua he causit Johanne kmnox appeir ane of the maist nobil and lustie men that could be found in the warld."

KNOX'S PLACES OF RESIDENCE IN EDINBURGH

ACCORDING to the information we possess, it was in the autumn of 1555 that Knox first made a temporary residence in Edinburgh. Doubtless at an earlier period he must more than once have visited the capital, lying as it does only some sixteen miles from his home; but to such visits no reference has been discovered. During his sojourn in Scotland in 1555-1556 he made his quarters in Edinburgh chiefly at the beginning and end of his stay. In connection with these visits only one house is specified as his temporary home—that of James Syme, a citizen burgess of Edinburgh.[1] Where this house stood has not been ascertained. Immediately before his return to Geneva it is further mentioned that he preached during ten successive days in the "great lodging" of the Bishop of Dunkeld,[2] the site of which also has not been determined.

On his final return to Scotland in May 1559, Knox spent two nights in Edinburgh (where he does not specify) before proceeding to Dundee and Perth.[3] During the succeeding year he paid flying visits to the capital; but it was not till April of 1560 that he definitely made it his home.[4] Thenceforward, till his death in 1572, it is Edinburgh that is the chief scene of his labours, though duty or the pressure of circumstances often drove him elsewhere for longer or shorter periods. What is noteworthy regarding Knox's house-keeping is his constant change of residence during these twelve years. It would seem, indeed, that he never possessed a home that could really be called his own. From the entries in the Town Council Records referring to his domestic arrangements we may infer that a furnished house was provided for him, and that his own possessions consisted chiefly of his books.[5] From the same source we gather

---

[1] *Works*, i. 246.   [2] *Ibid.* p. 251.   [3] *Ibid.* p. 318.
[4] Records of the Burgh of Edinburgh, 8th May 1560.
[5] In his last Will and Testament Knox's books, " alsweill upoune the Scriptures as uther prophane authoris," are valued at £130 Scots; while "in utensile and domicile the airschip being deducit," his effects

that his rent was not regularly paid,[1] and that more than once there was some difficulty in raising his stipend.[2]

On his coming to Edinburgh in April 1560, Knox occupied for fifteen days the house of David Forrest—possibly the same person who entertained John Willock in Haddington, twice held the office of General of the Mint, and was an ardent supporter of the Reformed Church.[3] For the next few months Knox has a new landlord, John Cairns, whose name occurs twice in the Records as the recipient of the minister's rent. The site of neither of these houses has been ascertained.

In an entry for 4th September 1560 we read of another arrangement for Knox's accommodation. A tailor, named John Durie, has been removed from "the ludgeing occupyit be the Abbot of Drumfermeling" to give place to the minister.[4] The Council, it would appear, had a sense that they had acted with a high hand, as, after ordering that Durie should receive full indemnity, they undertake that he will be restored "how sone thai may provide the said minister ane uther ludgeing." Such a lodging, however, does not seem to have been readily obtainable, since for the next four years Knox continued to reside in Durie's house—a longer space than he remained in any one home from the day when he broke with the ancient Church. This new house had for its owner one Robert Mowbray, and stood on the north side of the High Street, on the west side of Trunk Close,[5] well down towards the Nor' Loch.[6] As described in a contemporary document, it was a "great mansion and building, with a garden and waste land" attached,[7] and was therefore a residence of some pretensions. Here with his household, consisting of his wife, mother-in-law, and two children, Knox passed the eventful years during which he strove with Moray and Maitland in their policy of

---

are said to be worth only £30. In this connection it may be mentioned that a few weeks before his death Rizzio received from Mary and Darnley £200, "for the reparatiounis of his chalmer."

[1] Burgh Records, 25th September 1566.

[2] T. C. Records, 11th June 1563; 24th April, 1564.

[3] D. Laing gives an account of Forrest or Forrester.—Knox, *Works*, i. 563, *note*. The Forrest meant, however, may be a bailie of that name who acceded to his office in 1561.

[4] T. C. Records, 4th September 1560.

[5] Also known as Turing's, Old Provost's, and Knox's Close.

[6] *Proceedings of the Society of Antiquaries of Scotland*, xxv. 144-146. Article by Mr. Peter Miller, F.S.A. A reply to Mr. Miller's paper by Mr. C. J. Guthrie, advocate, will be found in the same volume.

[7] This description is from a Sasine of date 8th April 1563. Mowbray's house is there referred to in these words: "Magnam suam mansionem et edificium una cum horto et cauda ejusdem nunc inhabitatam per Joannem Knox ministrum."—*Ibid.* p. 144 *note*.

concession to the Queen; here in November of 1562 he entertained Châtelherault and Randolph to supper on Sunday evening after sermon; and hence he made his way down the Canongate to his memorable interviews with Mary.

In 1565 Knox has once again changed his residence, and is being dunned for rent in his new tenancy. Through one John Davidson, a writer, he informs the Town Council that he "wes craiffit, at the leist sutit, for his Mertymes termes maill, in the yeir of God jᵐ vᶜ and lxv be Robert Scottis spous."[1] The date of this entry is 25th September 1566, and seems to prove that Knox must have crossed from St. Andrews to Edinburgh during that month.[2] In what house he and his family were then living no entry informs us. For himself, during the whole of 1566, he was more out of Edinburgh than in it. In the first months of that year he had gone on a preaching tour by the express order of the General Assembly, and after the murder of Rizzio he was again absent till September. At the end of 1566 or the beginning of 1567 he set out on his journey to England, and did not return till June of that year.[3] From this date, with brief intervals, he remained in Edinburgh till May 1571. For the whole of this period only two notices indicate his places of residence.[4] In both entries John Adamson is mentioned as his landlord, and in both it is implied that he was at odds with his tenant regarding necessary repairs. From contemporary documents we gather that Adamson's house was near the foot and on the east side of Trunk Close[5]—in the same quarter, therefore, as Knox's previous home in the house of Robert Mowbray.

The last entry referring to Knox's places of residence in Edinburgh is dated 4th March 1569.[6] Where did he live during those two years and eight months that yet remained to him? It is here that we find a place for the tradition that points to the tenement at the Netherbow, now known as Knox's house, and exhibited to the world as such. In Knox's day the proprietor of this house was one James Mosman, a goldsmith and burgess of Edinburgh. Whether Mosman occupied the house or not, there is no authority to show; but from his own character and antecedents there is a strong presumption that for a certain period Mosman's house may have been open to receive a tenant before Knox's death in November 1572. By family tradition, as apparently by conviction, Mosman was

---

[1] T. C. Records, 25th September 1566.

[2] See above, pp. 236, 237.   [3] See above, p. 239.

[4] 19th November 1568; 4th March 1569. There is a third indirect reference for 20th February 1568.

[5] *Proc. of Soc. of Antiq. of Scot.* xxvii. 409.

[6] No records of the Council exist between 1st May 1571 and 13th November 1573.

attached to Mary and the old religion. His father had made the crown which was placed on the head of Mary of Lorraine ;[1] and he himself in February 1570 married as his second wife the daughter of Alexander King, "a malicious papist."[2]   But this was the month following the murder of the Regent Moray, and when we remember the state of Edinburgh in the times that followed,[3] the presumption is that Mosman must have found it prudent to take refuge with Grange in the Castle. In the town itself, it is to be remembered, the majority of the well-to-do citizens were strongly opposed to Mary ; and Mosman must in many ways have been made to feel that he was a traitor and a vile papist in their midst. Sooner or later he did enter the Castle, for, when in 1573 it fell into the hands of Morton, he was one of those considered sufficiently important to suffer public execution along with Kirkcaldy of Grange.[4]

Between March 1569 and November 1572, therefore, the probability is that Mosman's house was open to receive Knox. On his return from St. Andrews in August 1572 it may well have been that this house was assigned to him as probably the last it must be his lot to occupy. Morton, though not yet Regent, was supreme in the town, and Knox's friends would naturally do their best to make the closing days of their minister as comfortable as lay in their power. From the state of health in which he now came among them, it could at the most be only a few months that they would profit by his counsels. In Mosman's house, apparently one of the most commodious residences in the town, he would have the comfort that his age and health demanded ; and it was, moreover, within easy distance of the church where he ministered. As for the removal of any goods that belonged to him, a few books, as has been said, probably made the bulk of his possessions.

To Mosman's house, at all events, tradition points as the residence of Knox ; and if we attach any weight to the tradition, that house would in all probability be the one in which his last days were spent. Considering at once the prominent position of the house . itself, and the unparalleled place which Knox has ever held in the minds of his countrymen, the wonder would certainly be that tradition should either be silent or should by any chance have gone astray. The circumstances under which Knox's last days were spent were in themselves fitted to associate his name inseparably with the house where he died. To this house, wherever it was, his congregation attended him after his last public appearance at the induction of his successor Lawson ; here, as he lay dying, were daily seen coming

---

[1] *Proc. of Soc. of Antiq. of Scot.* xxv. 161 (Paper by Sir Daniel Wilson).

[2] *Ibid.* xxvii. 410.   [3] See above, pp. 235 *et seq.*

[4] *Proc. of Soc. of Antiq. of Scot.* xxv. 161, 162.

and going many of the first personages in the country ; and to that house during his last fortnight's illness all men's minds were turned with such hopes and fears as their sympathies prompted in connection with the man whose life and death meant so much for his country. That this house should be remembered in tradition, therefore, is precisely what we should expect. As far as is ascertained, the tradition is first mentioned by Stark in his *Picture of Edinburgh*, published in 1806 ;[1] but this late reference need throw no suspicion on its validity. Before the present century the modern guide-book had not been invented. In such histories of Edinburgh as those of Arnot and Maitland it was beyond the writer's scope to specify the private residences of all the notable characters to whom they made reference. That Stark correctly reported the tradition is proved by the fact that it was accepted by such an accurate writer as M'Crie,[2] whose *Life of Knox* appeared in 1811.

The evidence in favour of the tenement at present known as Knox's house may be thus briefly summed up. As far as James Mosman is concerned, the presumption is that he entered the Castle of Edinburgh at some date previous to Knox's death. Against the tradition that points to Mosman's house as a residence of Knox no satisfactory evidence has been adduced. In regard to the tradition itself, it was natural, under all the circumstances, that it should be at once precise and continuous. Before this tradition is rejected, therefore, it seems reasonable to ask for facts which it directly contradicts.

---

[1] Stark describes the house as follows : "Among the antiquities of Edinburgh may be mentioned the house of the great Scottish Reformer, John Knox. It stands on the north side, at the foot of the High Street, and projecting into the street, reduces it nearly one half of its width." In Galt's *Annals of the Parish* (1821) there is the following reference to Knox's house. Mr. Balwhidder is speaking of his visit to Edinburgh in 1779. "In short, everybody in Edinburgh were in a manner wearisome kind, and we could scarcely find time to see the Castle and the palace of Holyrood-house, and that more sanctified place, where that Maccabeus of the Kirk of Scotland, John Knox, was wont to live."

[2] M'Crie, *Life of Knox*, p. 270, *note* (edit. 1855).

THE PORTRAIT AND PERSONAL APPEARANCE OF JOHN KNOX

ABOUT the year 1875 there was some talk of a national memorial to John Knox. The proposal raised an unexpected question—Does an authentic portrait of Knox exist? Among others who took part in the discussion was Carlyle, who in a paper contributed to *Fraser's Magazine* (April 1875)[2] impugned the authenticity of all the accredited portraits of Knox. Refusing to accept any of these as a possible likeness of a man with the character and history of Knox, he brought forward another portrait, with the confident assertion that if it was not John Knox, the Scottish hero and evangelist, he could not conjecture who or what it was. This portrait, the property of Lord Somerville, had been first published in 1836 by the Society for the Diffusion of Useful Knowledge, and was reproduced in 1849 by Charles Knight in his *Pictorial History of England*. It was in Knight's History that Carlyle first saw it, and so struck was he by the type of features it represented, that he readily accepted it for what it was given out to be—an authentic portrait of the Scottish Reformer. Further inquiries into the antecedents of the Somerville portrait strengthened his conviction that of all the representations of Knox we possess, this has the best claim to be considered a trustworthy likeness.

In reply to Carlyle, Mr. James Drummond, Curator of the National Portrait Gallery of Scotland, read a paper to the Society of Antiquaries the month following the appearance of the article in *Fraser's Magazine*. Mr. Drummond had no difficulty in showing that there was no evidence whatever for the authenticity of the Somerville portrait. Before 1766, the year when it is supposed to have come into the possession of the Somerville family, the portrait has no record, and it cannot be established that even at that date it was accepted as a portrait of Knox. But one fact seemed to dispose

---

[1] The bulk of this paper originally appeared in the *Scotsman* of 20th May 1893.

[2] Afterwards reprinted along with his *Early Kings of Norway*.

of Carlyle's contention. In 1797 Sir William Musgrave applied to the Lord Somerville of that day for a list of the portraits in the possession of his family. The list was supplied; but it contained no hint of any portrait of Knox. The truth is, as Mr. Drummond showed, that Carlyle's sole argument was his individual impression that the Somerville portrait more adequately than any other embodied the conception he had formed of Knox's character and genius. As will presently be seen, Carlyle was as far astray in his physiognomic as in his historical conjectures.

In his claim for the Somerville portrait Carlyle had no solid ground to go upon: in impugning the authenticity of the accepted portraits, however, he had reasons which could not be conclusively refuted. Of all these portraits it is agreed that the original exemplar is that in Beza's *Icones*, the first edition of which appeared in 1580. Besides that of Beza the only two portraits that deserve serious consideration are the Torphichen portrait and that engraved by Hondius for Verheiden's *Imagines* in 1602. The Torphichen portrait, which is given in M'Crie's *Life of Knox*, is manifestly a mere modification of that of Beza. The engraving of Hondius fully deserves Sir David Wilkie's praise; but it also is indubitably based on the portrait in Beza's *Icones*. The question whether we possess a trustworthy likeness of Knox, therefore, turned on the authenticity of this Beza portrait, and, as Carlyle was able to show, the evidence for its authenticity could not be considered conclusive. The following entry in the Treasurer's accounts for June 1581 was, in truth, the only evidence forthcoming to prove that Beza had applied to Scotland for an original likeness of Knox :—

"Itim [*sic*] to Adriane [*sic*] Vaensoun, Fleming painter, for twa pictures painted be him, and send [*sic*] to Theodorus Besa, conform to ane precept as the samin producit upon compt beris. 8li. 10s."

These "twa pictures," it was argued, could only have been the portraits of James VI. and John Knox that appear in the *Icones*. But the date of the above entry is 1581, and Beza's book appeared in 1580. To Carlyle, prepossessed in favour of the Somerville portrait, the inference appeared wholly unjustifiable. Again, it was maintained in support of the Beza portrait that Beza must have seen Knox in Geneva, and would not permit an impossible presentment of him to appear in his book. But Beza's letters to Knox do not imply personal acquaintance, and there is no other evidence to prove that the two had ever come face to face. What seemed to complete Carlyle's triumph over the Beza portrait was the curious circumstance that in a French translation of the *Icones* published in 1581 by Simon Goulart, a colleague of Beza's in Geneva, a totally different portrait of Knox appeared in place of the one in the original book. In explanation of this blunder it was asserted that it was due to the printer and not to the translator. Yet the fact that such blunders

could happen was not fitted to increase our faith in books of this class.
For sceptical critics, therefore, there was still room to question the
authenticity of the original of all the accredited portraits of Knox—
more especially as no detailed description of his personal appearance was known to exist.

During a visit to the Continent in search of traces of Knox the
following document came into my hands. As will be seen, it
definitely settles the difficulty regarding the portraits of Knox, and
supplies details regarding his personal appearance of greater interest
than even the portrait itself. That this document has come to light
is due to the labours of two Genevan scholars, M. Aubert and M.
le Pasteur Eugène Choisy. In the course of preparing an edition
of the letters of Beza, these gentlemen had occasion to examine
certain manuscripts belonging to the Ducal Library at Gotha.
Among these was the following letter of Peter Young to Beza, to
which M. Aubert drew my attention, and which he courteously placed
at my disposal. Peter (afterwards Sir Peter) Young, it may be said, was
assistant to George Buchanan in the education of James VI., now in
his fourteenth year. Knox had been dead seven years when the letter
was written, and Buchanan had reached the age of seventy-three.

After this letter there can be no reasonable doubt that the
portrait of Knox sent by Young to Beza is the original of that which
appears in the *Icones*.[1] Tested by its fidelity to Young's description
of the personal appearance of Knox, the Beza portrait must be
regarded as an admirable likeness, though the engraving of Hondius
in Verheiden's *Imagines* is even a more striking presentment. On
the other hand, the Somerville portrait, so confidently put forward
by Carlyle, does not even remotely suggest the features and expression delineated in the letter of Young.

(INSCR. HERZOGLICHE BIBLIOTHEK GOTHA, CODEX CHARTACEUS
A. 405, fol. 341 : orig. autogr.)

Redditae mihi sunt v.[ir] c.[larissime] mense superiori a
Servino vestro humanissimae tuae literae, quum paulo ante a nostrate
quodam alias accepissem, sed ante sesquiannum in Serrani gratiam
a te scriptas. Ego utrisque tuis literis pro virili satisfacere conatus
sum. Nam Serrani Platonem, hoc est eius in Platone illustrando
industriam, verbis apud Regiam Maiestatem ornavi quantum potui,
necnon huius Servini labores in suo genere non contemnendos, ac
pro meo instituto ipsas tuas literas ad verbum eius Maiestati perlegi,
quibus ille certe magnopere afficitur. Amat enim mirum in modum

---

[1] In his statue of Knox in the quadrangle of the Free Church College,
Edinburgh, Mr. John Hutchison, R.S.A., has admirably rendered the
resultant impression from Beza's portrait and Young's description.

doctos omnes ac pios, ac te imprimis, vestramque adeo hierapolin, quam ut piorum omnium ac doctorum asylum et portum deperit, quod literis quoque suis ad S.[enatum] P.[opulum] Q.[ue] G.[enevensem] publice scriptis testatum voluit.

D. Buchananus, quem tuo nomine salutavi, te officiosissime resalutat, mittitque ad te Baptistam suum, una cum Dialogo de jure regni.—Is, tuo maxime hortatu, quamvis morbis ac senio confectus, recudere Psalmos suos statuit, cumprimum Tremellianam interpretationem nactus fuerit.

Quod petis, ut ad te illustrium virorum qui in promovenda Dei gloria apud nos desudarunt, praesertim D. Cnoxi, imagines mittam, sic habeto eam semper fuisse nostrae gentis incuriam, ne quid gravius dicam, ut nihil unquam huic studio tribuerit. Quo fit ut ne Cnoxi quidem, viri sempiterna memoria dignissimi, effigies ulla extet. Adii tamen pictores nostros, qui si modo pollicitis steterint, una cum hisce imaginem eius accipies. Interim ego hic tibi eius vultum ac habitum meo penicillo, quantum vel ipse meminisse, vel ex ipsius familiariss.-[imorum] dum vixit relatu (quos in consilium super hac re adhibui), consequi potui, utcumque describam. Coeterum eius integram historiam a D. Lausonio expectabis.

Fuit itaque statura corporis paulo iusta minor, apta et eleganti membrorum compositione, humeris latioribus, digitis longiusculis, caput modicum, capillus niger, facies subnigricans, nec aspectu ingrata. In vultu gravi et severo inerat, non sine gratia quadam, dignitas et maiestas naturalis, nec aberat in ira supercilio auctoritas. Sub fronte angustiore modice assurgebat superciliorum vallum, malis etiam subrubris ac leviter tumentibus, quo fiebat ut oculi retrocedere et cavi viderentur. Color eis erat in fusco caeruleus, aspectus acer et vividus, facies longiuscula, nasus longior, ore amplo, labris magnis ac superiore paulo crassiore, barba nigra, variantibus eam canis, sesquipalmum longa ac modice densa.—Decessit undesexagesimo aetatis anno.[1] Coetera Lausonius.

D. Buchanani patris mei observandissimi elogium ad te mitto, una cum ipsius effigie ad vivum expressa. Plura mitterem, ni temporis angustiis excluderer. Sed haec alias.

Gaudeo consobrinae meae dignum maioribus utriusque virum contigisse, atque utinam faustum utrique ac felix sit hoc coniugium.

Quid Groslotius agat, tum ex ipsius literis, tum ex hoc poteris ntelligere. Mihi certe ac merito cura erit. Vicissim ego tibi T.

---

[1] This would make Knox's birth-year 1513 instead of 1505, the date usually assigned. Curiously enough, in his account of Knox in the *Icones*, Beza assigns 24th December 1572 as the day of his death. It is usual to speak of Knox and Buchanan as having been born in the same year: there seems at least to have been only a few months between them.

Lindeseium, nobilem adolescentem nostratem qui apud vos agit, commendo.

Unum adhuc addam, quod mihi modo venit in mentem. Locus est in Epist. Pauli ad Cor. priore, cap. XI°, v. 10 : διὰ τοὺς ἀγγέλους, in quem annotasti [1] quid illud sit, nondum tibi liquere. Ego, quum diu me torsissem, tandem probabili coniectura ductus, quamvis reclamantibus omnibus exemplaribus quae mihi videre contigit, ac interpretibus ipsis, τοὺς ἀνθρώπους, postulante id sententia, necnon scripturae ac literarum affinitate, reponendum censui. Atque ita scriptum fuisse ab Apostolo existimo : ἀνοὺς vel sic ἀγοὺς, quod librarii, compendio scribendi decepti, ἀγΤοὺς vel ἀνΤοὺς, hoc est ἀγγέλους legerunt, nullo sensu. Tu iudica ac vale, v.[ir] clarissime. D. Jesus te Ecclesiae suae quamdiutissime servet incolumem.

Dat.[um] Edinburgi XIII° Novembr. 1579.

TUUS JUNIUS

Quum hasce obsignarem, commodum advenit pictor qui mihi una pyxide Buchananum et Cnoxum simul expressos attulit.

---

[1] See Novum Testamentum, Textus graecus cum duabus interpretationibus, et annotationibus Th. Bezae [Genevae], 1565, fol. p. 271, 272.